Challenger Park

Challenger Park

STEPHEN
HARRIGAN

ALFRED A. KNOPF
NEW YORK
2006

THIS IS A BORZOI BOOK
PUBLISHED BY ALFRED A. KNOPF

www.aaknopf.com

Knopf, Borzoi Books, and the colophon are
registered trademarks of Random House, Inc.

Library of Congress Cataloging-in-Publication Data
Harrigan, Stephen, [date]
Challenger Park / Stephen Harrigan.— 1st ed.
p. cm.
ISBN 0-375-41205-0
1. Astronauts—Family relationships—Fiction.   2. Women astronauts—Fiction.
3. Marital conflict—Fiction.   4. Space shuttles—Fiction.   I. Title.
PS3558.A626C47 2006
813'.54—dc22   2005049403

Manufactured in the United States of America
First Edition

For Maggie, Sissy, and Robbie

Note to Readers

The shuttle mission upon which the action of this book hinges, STS-108, is the designation of an actual spaceflight that occurred in December 2001. I hope those who flew and worked that untroubled mission will forgive my elaborate fictional distortions, which include imaginary crew members and grave emergencies.

At the time in which this novel takes place, the loss of the space shuttle *Columbia* has not yet occurred. That tragedy, with its shattering personal and institutional toll, is still several years in the future.

Challenger Park

Chapter One

She thought she had a chance to make the light at the intersection of NASA Road One and Space Center Boulevard, but the driver in front of her maddeningly decelerated as he answered his cell phone, and now he had come to a full stop while the turn arrow was still yellow. Well aware of her own vulnerability to panicky frustration, Lucy Kincheloe made a point to remind herself there was no real hurry. The light was two minutes long at most, the familiar voice on the phone had been calm, and Lucy herself had already made this trip four times this year. She had trained for enough emergencies to know that beneath almost every sort of raging anxiety there was a calm pocket, a perfect little vacuum in which both thoughts and actions were crisp and clear. She could find that place if she needed to, but for now she just lightened her grip on the steering wheel, then stared in contemplation at the recessed Chrysler logo at its center, as if it were some sort of ancient mandala-like emblem.

The man in front of her swung his head back and forth as he talked on his cell phone. He wore a baseball cap and sunglasses, and on the back of his Range Rover there was a bumper sticker that read, "When a Man Is Tired of Lubbock He Is Tired of Life." Very funny. Lucy looked away and gazed out across the lake. The morning haze had burned off, and in the noon light the brackish water appeared deceptively lovely, its surface undisturbed except for a single Jet Ski carving a white wake whose exhausted wavelets lapped at the riprap at the side of the road. On the distant Kemah bridge, where the lake merged into Galveston Bay, a procession of cars glinted in the sun, and a smallish flock of pink spoonbills meandered in from the opposite shore, heading past the Hilton toward the marshy channels and bayous beyond Bay Area Boulevard.

It all made for a lilting tableau, even in her agitated state, even if she knew that beneath its present blue sheen this particular body of water was a mudhole. It had always galled her that these boosterish Texans could get away with calling it Clear Lake. Reared in the honest precincts of New England, she could not get used to Texas place-names that advertised mountains that were barely more than hummocks or supposedly mighty lakes that would not have qualified as a pond back home. Even the storied Rio Grande, which she and Brian had seen on a disagreeable weekend trip several years ago to Matamoros, was hardly more than a drainage ditch.

The light had still not changed. The driver ahead of her was still yammering on his phone. When the sense of alarm she had been holding so coolly at bay suddenly broke through, she made a lightning assessment of the oncoming traffic and with a breathtaking lack of deliberation jerked her steering wheel to the left and whipped past the Range Rover as she made a left turn against the light. She offered a cringing wave of apology to a flabbergasted driver from the opposite corner whose own impending turn she had not taken into consideration. In her rearview mirror she could see the guy in the Range Rover glaring at her through his polarized sunglasses and switching his cell phone to the opposite hand so he could give her the finger, but she didn't dwell on his opinion of her for more than a moment.

As she drove down Space Center Boulevard, the tires of her minivan teased the grooves of the newly resurfaced street, producing a wavering banshee tone that matched the cloudy dread that had suddenly entered her mind. The road curved along the back side of the Johnson Space Center, an expanse of empty ground bordered by leafless winter trees, where deer patrolled the fence line and joggers wended in and out of sight, following the exercise trail through a thin screen of forest. "Go Atlantis!" read a banner attached to the chain-link fence, cheering on the space shuttle that was currently on orbit.

The lights were with her the rest of the way, and it took her only seven or eight minutes more to reach the school. At this hour the circular drive in front was empty of buses and carpooling Suburbans, so she was able to lurch to a stop just steps away from the front door. She left the car in one fluid motion, not even pausing to push the locking button on her security key, and entered the school and walked urgently down the hall, past the display of photographs of "Astronaut Moms and Dads" grinning in their orange pressure suits as they held up models of the space shuttle. When she opened the door to the office, the first thing she saw was Davis sitting all by himself in a chair, staring vacantly at a Black History Month poster of Sojourner Truth on the opposite wall.

"Are you feeling tight, sweetie?" Lucy asked her son as she knelt down in front of him and reflexively stroked his cheek.

"A little," he said.

"Scale of one to ten?"

"It was seven but now it's five."

"You're sure?"

He nodded, though Lucy could still hear a more-than-faint wheeze in his breathing. His skin was pale, he was trembling, and though he was seven years old he seemed to his distraught mother as vulnerable as a newborn—the whorls of his ears almost translucent, his eyes wondrously blank. Still, she knew he was not in any acute danger. There was no justification at all for the way she had allowed herself to surrender to blind fear. What if she had caused a wreck? What if she had broadsided a child in a car seat? At the very least, if the vindictive man in the Range Rover had had the presence of mind to write down her license plate number, she might still hear from the police.

"His peak's a little better," Lorelei Tran said as she entered the room with Davis's inhaler. "I gave him two puffs right before I called you. We're up to two-ninety now, but he's still pretty constricted."

"I don't think two puffs is going to do it."

"I wanted to wait till you got here to give him another dose. That's a lot of albuterol. Do you want the machine?"

"No, let's just do the inhaler."

Lorelei attached the spacer and handed it over to her as Davis compliantly opened his mouth. Lucy administered a single sustained dose. She had gotten to the point where the sound of her son taking in this vaporous bronchial-dilating cocktail troubled her as much as it comforted her. She knew that every relief-bringing puff of albuterol brought with it an unrelenting jitteriness that was as painful for her to watch as it was for Davis to endure. Sometimes, after an intense bout with the nebulizing machine, his hand shook so much that he could not even write his name. And the other medications for asthma often demanded a more powerful reckoning, cruel side effects like weight gain or stunted growth or humped back that could conceivably one day be visited upon the innocent perfection of her little boy's body.

"He told Mrs. Ortiz right away he wasn't feeling well," Lorelei said as she put the inhaler and spacer back into a drawer. "You're a smart kid, aren't you? You don't fool around when you know something's not right."

Davis gave a sideways smile, trying not to show the pleasure he took in this validation of his character from the school nurse, whose wispy sexiness, Lucy suspected, was a factor in the prompt reporting of his symptoms. Lorelei was wearing a cobalt blue polo shirt whose banded sleeves emphasized her slender arms and whose collar rose to meet the feathery edge of her chic haircut. The youngest of seven hyperachieving children of a Vietnamese shrimper in Kemah, she had been born in exile on the South China Sea, her mother going into frightened labor shortly after their refugee boat was boarded by pirates. But not a trace of her family's epic dislocation had Lucy ever seen in Lorelei's demeanor, which was as buoyantly American as a strip shopping mall. The school nurse was Lucy's crucial advocate, never needing to be convinced of the seriousness of Davis's asthma, confident enough in her own judgment to intervene at the moment he needed it, rather than allowing him to suffer while she tried to find Lucy or fretfully sought out approval from some higher medical authority.

Lucy could hear her son's breath returning. In a few minutes Lorelei brought out the peak flow meter, and when Davis blew into it he was back nearly to his normal reading of 380. She thought his trembling lip was just the albuterol delivering its systemic jolt, but then she noticed that tears were pooling in the bottom of his eyes.

"What's the matter, honey?" she asked, at which point his stoic forbearance gave way. He started to blubber loudly enough for a pair of fourth-grade girls who had just walked by the open door of the office brandishing their hall passes to come back and gawk. Lorelei shooed them away, and Davis, preoccupied with his emotional earthquake, mercifully didn't see them.

"He's all right," Lorelei said. "He's just a little discombobulated."

Just a little terrified, Lucy thought as she held her quaking son. She had no firsthand knowledge of what it was like to feel your breath being squeezed off, to live in a world whose very atmosphere was a constant taunt, whose bountiful oxygen was as capriciously out of reach as a rainbow. The closest she could come was a memory of snorkeling, trying to draw in air from a plastic tube clogged with seaweed. He had asked her once, during a bad stretch six months ago, when he was being treated regularly with formidable steroids, if he was going to die. With a maternal ferocity stronger than any she could recall, she had swooped down upon that tremulous thought and crushed it, almost bellowing her reassurance that he was safe and always would be as long as he let her or his father or Mrs. Ortiz or Ms. Tran know when he was having trouble breathing. But the inchoate survival fear was still there. How could it not be? And on top of it was the more graspable everyday bewilderment of a sick child: the humiliation of being suddenly removed from class, the disappointment of missing a trip to the IMAX theater or to the rain-forest exhibit at Moody Gardens, the growing awareness of a defining and isolating vulnerability.

"Am I going back to school?" he asked when he grew calm again. As he spoke, a little bubble formed from the tears and mucus saturating his upper lip.

"I'll take his peak again after lunch," Lorelei volunteered. "You can go back to work."

"I think I'll keep an eye on him for an hour or so." She looked at her watch and turned to Davis. "Want to have lunch with your mother?"

The McDonald's on NASA Road One, just down the street from the Saturn Lane gate of the Johnson Space Center, featured a giant fiberglass astronaut floating out from the roof in the posture of one of the old Gemini spacewalkers, holding an order of fries in his outstretched left hand. Davis and his sister, Bethie, had been entranced since infancy by this figure, by its bulbous, ghostly white space suit, its forever-unseen face behind the glistening visor of its helmet, its suggestion that perhaps within the interior of the McDonald's there existed some secret gravity-free realm.

The astronaut's mysterious totemic power had ebbed a bit for Davis, but Lucy noticed that he still looked up at it appraisingly as they walked across the parking lot. Inside she ordered him a Happy Meal with no mustard or ketchup on the hamburger—he had a distaste, amounting almost to a horror, of condiments. For herself, she ordered a dispiriting salad and a Coke—a real Coke just this once, not Diet. While Davis took off his shoes and set them in the plastic shoe racks at the base of the giant coiling hamster maze that commanded the front of the restaurant, Lucy sat down beneath a signed poster of the crew of STS-95—an ancient John Glenn among them—and dialed the number of Dr. Trimble's office from memory.

"You definitely want to keep an eye on him," said Margaret, the more up-to-speed of Trimble's two nurses, when Lucy described the details of Davis's latest attack. "And you better neb him every four hours just to be on the safe side, and bring him in tomorrow if he's not feeling better."

Great. Another round of the pitiless nebulizing machine, another night of waking Davis up every four hours so that the hose attached to the shoebox-sized device could deliver the misty medication that would restore his breath but rattle his fragile body. By the time it was over she'd be jumping out of her skin too, sleepless and ragged with worry and no good for work.

As soon as she pressed the End button on her cell phone it rang again. The caller ID displayed a JSC extension number, but not hers. When she answered, the connection was exquisitely clear, with just the faintest suggestion of a voice lag.

"So I was floating through the Node when I saw the green light on the IP phone and I thought I'd just—"

"Brian?"

It was her husband, calling from space.

"Pretty amazing, huh? Just pick up the phone and call. Did you watch the docking on the feed?"

"It looked smooth."

"Smoother than any sim they threw at us, that's for sure. And then we ripped through the transfer like you wouldn't believe. So where are you if you're not in your office? I left you a message there, by the way."

"I'm at McDonald's."

"Going on a junk-food binge while I'm gone?"

"I was hoping you'd never find out."

"I'm the eye in the sky, don't forget. I see your every move. Kids okay?"

"They're fine. I took Davis out of school for lunch. He had a little attack this morning."

"Not serious?"

"No, he's okay. Do you want to talk to him?"

"Davis? Sure I want to talk to him. . . . I've only got a minute, though. They need me in the Lab."

"All right, hold on," she said. She could see Davis in the top tier of the playscape, moving along in its transparent coils like something being digested. Before she called him down she remembered to put the phone to her ear again and say "I love you" to her husband as he floated in the International Space Station 240 miles above the earth. "Love you too," he said cheerfully. "See you in four—" and then the connection linking their voices suddenly disappeared.

She knew enough about the vagaries of satellite uplinks not to be rationally concerned, but even when a call was dropped on earth it never failed to give her an ominous twinge, as if some dark power had been listening in and had decided for abrupt reasons of its own not to allow these two people to talk any further.

"Guess who called on the phone just now?" Lucy said when Davis had emerged from the playscape and his special-order Happy Meal was finally ready.

"Who?"

"Your father. He was calling from space just to talk to you, but then we lost the signal. He told me to tell you and Bethie how much he loves you and how he can't wait to see you. He's coming home Friday, you know."

"How come we can't go to the Cape and watch him land?"

"Because you have school."

"If we went to the Cape we could go to Disney World. That's what Joseph got to do."

"Yes, but Joseph's dad's mission was in the summer."

He seemed to accept this explanation as just, for once not barraging her with a series of aggrieved arguments. She watched him as he chewed his dry hamburger and studied his Happy Meal toy, a plastic figure of Dumbo, the latest in a series promoting the hundredth anniversary of Walt Disney's birth. McDonald's and Disney: an imperial alliance of shoddy nutrition and manufactured nostalgia. Still, it tugged at her, the idea of the shuttle landing safely at the Cape, Brian arriving at crew quarters to swoop his children into his arms, and the four of them heading off to Disney World with all the danger of the mission past—with

Brian exhilarated and satisfied for once, and Lucy's own ambitions quietly on hold, and nothing for either of them to achieve now but the happiness of their children.

Davis swung his legs as he ate, an echo of that metronomic contentment he had possessed when he was a baby, always waving his arms, making clacking noises with his tongue against the roof of his mouth, eager to announce in any way he could his pleasure at his own existence. Her children were still so young—Bethie was only three—and yet Lucy already had a nostalgia for the radiant days of their infancy, a nostalgia that was so strong that sometimes she felt it would crush her. Had she dwelled in that time more fully, she wondered, had she not fretted so much about what might be happening in the office while she was on leave, would she miss it so deeply? What should have been languid mother-baby afternoons, hours richly spent in studying every feature of her sleeping children, of lying back on the bed while she nursed them and then succumbing to a logy maternal sleep herself, had been in fact days of fretful alertness. That was her nature, she supposed, to always live with the knowledge—with the threat, really—of some hovering unspecific, untended business. And those had not been happy years particularly, with Brian training so much of the time, and sometimes miserable and constrained when he was at home, and her own nascent career threatening to skitter out from under her. But there had been rapturous moments. She knew there had been, because the pang of missing them was so sharp.

What she wanted most right now was to keep Davis out of school, to take the rest of the afternoon off and go home and do nothing. She wanted to sit in the leather armchair with Davis snuggled up against her as they ate potato chips and watched *Oprah,* with its unfathomably abstract adult dilemmas that Davis found so hypnotizing, or one of the hyperactive, blackhearted cartoons that were now in style. He was still young enough to go happily along with such an abrupt notion, still young enough to crave being with his mother. In another few years that would all change. But Colleen would be picking up Bethie in an hour or so anyway and bringing her home, and Lucy herself had a meeting at three with six overscheduled participants who had managed to set a time and place only after weeks of furious e-mailing.

"You know what we should do?" she heard herself saying.

"What?"

"We should buy you a toy."

"Really?"

The poor child was almost dumbfounded, so great was the breach she had opened in his everyday reality. She had always fought hard to maintain her parental leverage, and the capricious bestowal of a toy on a day that was not Christmas or his birthday was, she knew, the most powerful weapon in her arsenal. Was she granting it now out of guilt? Of course she was. But not entirely. She was a mother, and he was her little boy, and what was wrong with going out of bounds just this once to try to make him happy?

The traffic on Bay Area Boulevard was heavy for this time of day, and it took them almost half an hour to reach the mall on the other side of the freeway. Though Lucy had lived in Clear Lake City for almost a decade, she had managed to develop only a grudging tolerance of its all-pervasive car culture. They were supposedly finally starting work on a commuter rail system in Houston, but the center of Houston was twenty miles away, and it would be a generation, she figured, before it reached Clear Lake, which was in her mind the embodiment of an exurban nowhere place, a "city" with no perceptible center. It was merely a grid of clogged streets lined with semi-permanent retail strips, where there was nothing of visual interest but the excruciating faux architecture of the theme restaurants: the artfully peeling stucco of ersatz Mexican cantinas, the salt-stained Gulf Coast "fish houses," the Tuscan villas featuring all-you-can-eat breadsticks and aria-singing waiters. And on top of it all, a climate so hot and sodden that even if there were any place to walk to the thought of doing so would never arise.

Brian, who had grown up outside Dallas in an even more colorless suburb, thought Clear Lake was positively exotic because of the mere fact that it was close to the water, that its baking asphalt and rows of fast-food franchises stood on the brink of a mysterious world of marshes and twisting bayous and interconnected bays that led finally to the ocean. Brian loved Clear Lake, he loved the comforting blandness of it, and he loved the way it stood as a portal to other realms, not just to the tempestuous expanse of the Gulf of Mexico but to the infinity of space. And though her Yankee heart would not quite let her admit the fact, Lucy supposed she loved it too, because it was the world her children had been born into and was thus dearly familiar to them.

At Toys R Us, Lucy followed as Davis raced through the towering maze-like aisles, past the shelves of board games and infant toys, past the girls' section with its Special Edition Barbie dolls and prancing plastic horses with silky manes. She knew exactly where he was going—to the two aisles given over to action figures in their endless seasonal variations. The hobbits and elves and skeletal orcs from *Lord of the Rings* claimed most of the shelf space at the moment, though there were still leftover toys from the *Planet of the Apes* boomlet and a perennial supply of *Star Wars* figures. Davis ignored them all, heading instead for the shrinking display space allotted to *Atlantis: The Lost Empire,* a relatively unheralded Disney movie that for some reason had claimed his imagination, even before he learned that *Atlantis* would be the name of the vessel in the shuttle fleet that would carry his father into space. Lucy had seen *Atlantis* only on video, watching it with Davis and Bethie in snatches after bath time over the course of a week. Though she had a firm no-TV-at-night rule, she had suspended it so that she could see this movie that had so infatuated her son, so that she could watch it with him. Lucy knew she was trying to claim for herself a moment that was fundamentally irrecoverable, the moment she had missed when she had been at the Cape on business and Colleen had taken Davis to a matinee on an idle summer afternoon. There, in the fiercely air-conditioned multiplex, some sort of primary wonderment had visited her son, a near-ecstatic awareness of the possibility of life beneath the sea, of worlds unseen. When Lucy returned, Colleen had told her, laughing, about Davis's enraptured appreciation of this forgettable cartoon. Colleen was a kind and levelheaded nanny, a finance major at the University of Houston at Clear Lake who could be counted on for anything. But her casual chatter about Davis's epiphany had left Lucy unaccountably irritated. She knew, by the rapt silence with which her son played with his *Atlantis* action figures, that he now possessed some inexpressible imaginative secret, a secret whose origin she would have witnessed if she had been there with him in that darkened theater.

"Don't you already have all of those?" she said now to Davis, as he studied the rectangular packaging of a "collectible figure gift set."

"I don't have Milo Thatch anymore. He got lost in the sandbox, remember? And these are collectible. Joseph says if you get collectible ones and don't ever take them out of the box, when you grow up you'll be a millionaire."

He studied the figures in their windowpane displays and then gravely turned his attention to something called the Ulysses Battle Vessel. Lucy knew from experience that this was going to take forever. He could be a maddeningly deliberative child, always gauging every option, always instinctively retreating from the precipice of decision. She knew it was pointless to rush him, and so as he weighed the future investment value of the collectible figures against the more immediate pleasures of the battle vessel, Lucy drifted aimlessly up and down the aisle, noting the eclectic range of culture heroes available in action figure form. Not just the predictable figures from children's movies, but hockey players and wrestlers, and—in the aftermath of September 11—an "American Heroes Collection" featuring police and firefighters and even New York Port Authority personnel. There were characters from the cast of *Saturday Night Live,* and weirdly accurate figures of everyone from Jerry Garcia to Frank Sinatra. Among this strange mix of plastic effigies Lucy spotted a familiar blue NASA flight suit. The doll that was wearing it had molded curly hair and a wide, almost manic smile, and the top of the package read, "Legends of American Space Flight. Christa McAuliffe: Teacher in Space."

Lucy stared at the figure's perky expression for a long moment. She felt momentarily hollow. She had been in her early twenties when *Challenger* blew up, living back in her parents' house while she finished graduate school, beset by loneliness and low prospects, feeling for the first time in her life a sense of stasis and flagging conviction. Her father, only a few years into what should have been his vigorous fifties, was recovering from a heart bypass that the surgeon had glowingly termed a "beautiful success" but that had left in the patient's mind a crushing sense of despair. Her father had said nothing as they watched the accident on television—the erratic, splitting contrails in the blue sky, the look of hopeful confusion on the faces of Christa McAuliffe's parents as they gazed upward from the viewing stand—but Lucy could sense the gloom gaining that much more purchase on his soul.

"Okay," Davis said, holding up the Ulysses Battle Vessel. "I made up my mind. But can I get another Milo Thatch?"

The battle vessel was an unexpected bargain at $9.98, so she let him buy a replacement Milo—the last one on the shelf, and maybe the last they would ever make unless this forgettable movie had a startling revival. She bought Bethie something as well—a Fisher-Price Beach House on sale for $7.99, featuring a "fully articulated poseable family"—and then drove Davis back to school. He was quiet on the way, sitting in his booster seat as he glided his slug-shaped battle vessel through an imaginary ocean. In the unexpected silence Lucy thought about the glossy, grinning replica of the Teacher in Space sealed in its transparent display package. She remembered an article she had read in the newspaper shortly after the *Challenger* disaster. A reporter had visited the McAuliffe home and spoken to the shell-shocked husband and mentioned a reverberant detail that had seared itself into Lucy's mind: a refrigerator door, crowded with magnets holding up children's artwork and reminders of soccer practices and orthodontist appointments that this devoted but now vanished mother would never keep. Christa McAuliffe's children had been nine and six. She had taken her son's stuffed frog into space.

Lucy parked in front of the school again and escorted Davis back to class. He was past the age where he would thoughtlessly take his mother's hand, but he still walked close enough beside her that his arm brushed against the seam of her cotton slacks, and he did not seem to mind the light but proprietary touch of her hand on the back of his neck. When they reached his classroom, Mrs. Ortiz waved him in through the open door and gave him a hug before he returned to his seat. Lucy lingered for just a moment, to see if Davis would turn back to her for a parting glance, but he was too busy basking in the attention of his curious classmates to think further about his mother. That was as it should be, Lucy decided. She slipped away down the hall, checking her voice mail on her cell phone as she went. When she walked past the "Astronaut Moms and Dads" photos, she glanced briefly at her own face, almost repelled by the bright, untroubled smile she saw there.

Chapter Two

Walt Womack made a point of eating dinner at Luby's Cafeteria no more than twice a week. Although he was not yet fifty, he could easily see himself falling into a solitary old man's routine: standing in the serving line with his folded newspaper under his arm, gazing up at the menu board with its unvarying selections in white plastic letters, along with its abrupt declaration of a physiological verity—"Possibility of bone in any fish."

Luby's, he knew, suited him perhaps too well. The cafeteria's clientele was reliably anonymous, mostly families with young children and elderly couples who pushed their trays along the rails with quavering concentration. He was not likely to encounter any of the members of his team here, most of whom were still single and in their early thirties and had too much attitude to be caught dead in the blandest eating establishment on earth. Walt was not notably vain, but a team lead needed a touch of gravitas, and he had the feeling that as a habitual solo diner he radiated an air of lonely defeat. It was not resignation that brought him to Luby's, though. It was, God help him, the food. The LuAnn Platter—entrée, two vegetables, cloverleaf roll, $4.89—was rich in the sameness he seemed to be craving at this point in his life, while at the same time it served as a perfect little paradigm of nutritional variety and order.

"Baked fish tonight?" asked the smiling, hairnetted woman on the other side of the translucent sneeze guard. Was it comforting or frightening that she knew him so well that she could guess what he was planning to order?

"Yes, thanks, Carmen."

"Just a little bit of tartar sauce? *Un poquito?*"

"*Sí, un poquito.*"

She smiled again. At some point they had embarked upon a frisky little badinage in Spanish, though Walt could not remember when or why. He watched as Carmen, wielding her spatula, cut a rectangle of pallid fish in half, to conform to the LuAnn Platter's policy of "reduced-portion" entrées. Since he was making an effort to become an abstemious eater, Walt didn't mind. He had always been lucky in his metabolism, but in the last year or so it had started to fail him, so that now a simple bowl of red beans and rice at PeTe's could be neutralized only by a four-mile run along the JSC jogging path. It did feel subtly wrong, however, to reject the bounty of nearby Galveston Bay—still teeming, despite generations of degradation, with shrimp and crabs and oysters and supernal redfish—for this flavorless square of thawed Icelandic cod.

He received the bill for his outlander fish, after another bouncy exchange with the cashier, and then took his tray to an empty table by the window. He unfolded the *Houston Chronicle* he had not found time to read that morning, glanced at it just long enough to survey the day's global calamities, then set it aside and looked out the picture window, across the parking lot and NASA Road One to the sprawling acreage of the Johnson Space Center. In many ways the JSC complex was the most familiar locale of his life, but for just a moment it looked alarmingly alien, as if its acres of graceless institutional buildings had only just now appeared on the marshy nothingness he still recalled from his boyhood. From his table Walt could see the great Saturn V rocket that had once heaved men to the moon, lying on its side by the main entrance. It was nothing but a mammoth keepsake now, a relic of an age that in Walt's conflated memory still seemed immediate, but that in the eyes of the onrushing world was already hauntingly distant.

A poignant awareness of time was natural to a man his age, he supposed, and certainly to be expected in someone still tossing about in the backwash of bereavement. But there was something about his profession that kept the fleetingness of life in particularly sharp perspective. As a team lead he was responsible for the training of shuttle crews, so he was subject to the emotional hazards of all teachers everywhere, most acutely the creeping realization that not just individual classes but whole generations were vaulting into the future without him. On his best days, Walt thought of himself as a crucial standard of measurement and achievement, a reliable static point in a universe of swirling change. In other moments—like this out-of-nowhere low point in Luby's—he just felt sort of left behind.

But he knew from long experience that his mood tended to drop between missions, when all those months of intense training were over and the crew was launched and on their own and a new one had not yet been assigned to take their place. It was not an idle time. Getting the hall decorated for the return of the crew was almost a full-time task in itself, and since STS-106 would be landing in only four days they would soon be into the training debrief. But he was probably another month away from the next crew pickup, unless there was some sudden change in the manifest or unanticipated acceleration of the flight rate. So it would be a while before they were back to the time he craved, the twelve-hour days in the simulator when it was just him and his team and the crew eating cold pizza and waiting for the inevitable late-night breakthrough on some thorny Prox-Ops problem. He knew he was past the age where this sort of crunch management was common, or even appropriate. Most team leads did the job for a few years and then went on to become simulation supervisors—SimSups—or to work somewhere in administration or take some corporate job in the outside world. He had meant to take that route himself, but he kept putting it off for reasons that never became clear to him until after Rachel died, when a bedrock loneliness in his life was suddenly exposed and he saw the familial intensity of training for what it had always been—a crucial emotional tether.

The job was changing, though. Gone now were the days when Walt would rent a van with his own money and the whole team would drive down to the Cape to watch the launch. Nowadays, in the heightened security after September 11, training teams couldn't even get onto the site without some sort of elaborate justification. They couldn't even get car passes to watch the launch from the causeway. In the old days—not so long ago, just three missions past—it would have been unthinkable for the team not to be there at the Ops and Control building for the crew walk-out. The crew *needed* to see them there, they needed the consolation of familiar faces as they walked past the news crews and anonymous well-wishers to the Astro Van that would take them to the pad, where they would be put atop a bomb holding 1.6 million pounds of explosive fuel. It was serious business, this ritual photo op. Men and women were *leaving the earth*. Their departure, in its shuddering violence, had always seemed to Walt a fundamentally transgressive act against the nurturing atmosphere. The tranquil air of the Florida marshlands would shatter like glass, shorebirds would flap away in panic as the flames and smoke and concussive shock waves spread out to engulf them. The men and women sitting at the top of the stack, riding this pinnacle of fire as it burned through the sky, were courting perils that, even after *Challenger,* had still to be encountered and cataloged. More than one astronaut, Walt knew, had practiced his walk-out grin and his wave in front of the mirror, desperate not to let the blank terror show.

This time, Walt had just stayed at the center and watched the walk-out on the feed. There had been hardly anyone for the crew to wave at as they entered the van, just a NASA photographer and a fully outfitted SWAT team and sharpshooters up on the roof of the O&C building. The launch itself had been flawless, and so far the mission was nominal all the way. It was a tight crew. Bill Kokernot, as had been evident from the first day of training, was up to the job of commander. Elise Trube's mother had died ten days before the launch, but Elise had flown herself to Michigan for the funeral in a T-38 and was back for quarantine with her emotions heroically in poise. If she performed as well as pilot on this mission as Walt expected her to, she'd be commanding her next flight. Lori Primus had no discernible personality, but she was inoffensive and companionable and had the best feel for the robot arm of any mission specialist Walt had ever known. And Brian Kincheloe was, well, Brian Kincheloe. He'd been solid throughout training, however, with only one minor flare-up that, in retrospect, was totally justified. Walt appreciated how hard he'd worked to keep his famous grievances to himself, and how from time to time he'd even managed to slide forth a witticism about his own star-crossed career. By the time of the last simulation run, Walt was convinced that Brian was far more of a team player, and had more of a sense of humor, than his reputation allowed. After this mission, there was no reason his ill-fated tenure on *Mir* should continue to define his whole career.

During the four or five minutes he had been in the cafeteria line, Walt reflected, *Atlantis,* coasting on orbit at 17,500 miles per hour, had covered a few thousand miles of the earth's surface. It was not unlikely that it had even passed almost directly above him. If so, it was already beyond the curve of the earth, over New Orleans perhaps. Walt looked out the window again, at the still-bright evening sky, trying to imagine the blackness that lay beyond it like the backing of a mirror. He had been training crews for almost twenty years, but he still had no real idea what it would be like to look down upon the earth from the orbiter's flight-deck windows, to see the continents silently coasting by, to watch from above as lightning twitched and throbbed within vast storm fronts, to grow ecstatically accustomed to weightlessness, until you sensed those distant clouds as being more tangible, more crudely material, than your own body.

He'd always had a keen curiosity about the sensations of space-flight, but no desperate longing of his own to experience them. He didn't see how weightlessness could be more satisfying than the heavy lifting required to achieve it. The uncountable components of each mission were as intricate, as infinite really, as the invisible protein spirals that somehow made up the flesh and bones of a human organism. But a mission was not an unknowable manifestation of nature, it was a deliberate enterprise, an orchestration of vast systems of machinery and thought whose crescendo was no less awesome to those on the ground than to the astronauts rattling up into space. Walt liked it that his job culminated at liftoff, with him remaining resolutely on earth. Professionally and personally, he was fond of gravity.

As he finished his meal, he was disappointed to notice that it was not yet even six o'clock. Eating dinner too early was, he knew, a symptom of impending geezerhood. But he had the excuse tonight of being responsible for a program at church, and if he didn't eat early he would be light-headed by the time the program was over.

Our Lady Queen of the Heavens was only a mile or so away from Luby's, at the edge of a subdivision off El Camino Real. Walt drove past the once-"modern" sculpture out in front—a queasy, swirling amalgam of rocket thrust and scattered stars and outstretched divine hands—and through the empty parking lot to the rectory. When he knocked on the door he was greeted by Susan, a slender, silver-haired woman in her sixties who was Father Mondragon's happily beleaguered clerical assistant.

"Oh, there you are," she said. "Slides or PowerPoint? I can do both, but I need to know in advance."

"I think she said slides."

"Well, if she changes her mind let me know as soon as you can. I'll be over in the hall setting up the chairs. Father's upstairs."

Walt wandered familiarly up to the second floor, where he found Louis Mondragon sitting at the desk in his private office drinking a Dr Pepper and listening to the *O Brother, Where Art Thou* sound track.

"So who'd you get for me?" Louis said.

"Sorry, your top picks weren't available. Eileen Collins has got another must-do in L.A. And Shannon Lucid's on vacation."

"So who?"

"Lucy Kincheloe."

"Who's that?"

"She's okay."

"She even flown?"

"She will one of these days."

"Jesus. So much for star power."

"You've gotten into the habit of taking the Lord's name in vain, Louis," Walt said as he opened the little dorm-sized refrigerator in the office and helped himself to his own Dr Pepper. "And by the way, don't even bother to thank me for finding you a speaker in the first place."

He sat down on the couch and put his feet up on a coffee table covered not just with various Catholic magazines like *First Things* and *Commonweal* but with back issues of *Premiere* and *Film Comment*. The snide back-and-forth was nothing personal. He and Louis had perfected a wiseacre conversational style in the fifth grade, and neither of them had ever seen fit to grow beyond it.

"What time is she coming?" Louis asked.

"I told her six thirty."

"She doing PowerPoint?"

"Slides. I already told Susan."

Louis took this in with a faintly dismissive nod. He had always been something of a techno-geek at heart, but Walt assumed you could take such interests only so far in the priesthood. Louis's computer, for instance, was an embarrassingly out-of-date Macintosh Performa with an even more embarrassing Stations of the Cross screen saver that some member of the altar society had given him for Christmas and that therefore had to be conspicuously displayed. Above the computer was a big corkboard crowded with pictures of his nieces, and next to it a poster of *The Hudsucker Proxy,* Louis's favorite Coen brothers movie, and next to that one of those old-fashioned plastic 3-D portraits of Jesus with his sacred heart winking in and out of view in his chest, a bit of subversive kitsch that Louis had held on to throughout the decades.

"You know that Dr Pepper Museum in Waco?" Louis said, pondering his soda can. "Susan used to be a docent there."

"They have docents at the Dr Pepper Museum?"

"You'll find docents wherever there is culture. Wait, here it is."

He turned up the volume on the stereo as Alison Krauss, Emmylou Harris, and Gillian Welch began to sing "Down to the River to Pray."

It was a nice song, but Walt wasn't in the mood to sit there in attentive silence until it was over, a hostage to Louis's enthusiasm. So he reached into his pocket and handed him the bio on Lucy Kincheloe that he had printed off one of the many NASA Web sites.

"I highlighted the parts you'd probably want to use in the introduction."

Louis nodded, joined the girls on the chorus in his surprisingly evocative tenor voice—"Who shall wear the starry crown? / Good Lord show me the way"—and read the bio as the song continued to wash through the room. Father Mondragon chewed his lip as he read, then took a distracted sip from his Dr Pepper, his priestly countenance enhanced by his deepening concentration. From his father, a Mexican oil geologist, he had inherited a grave, fleshy face and a full head of tuxedo-black hair that was only just now starting to sprout a few metallic coils of gray.

"I don't suppose she's Catholic?" Louis said innocently when he looked up.

"Oh, so I was supposed to find you a *Catholic* woman space hero?"

"It's my job to wonder."

"I wouldn't ask her a question like that. I hardly know her."

"It's not like asking her if she's gay, Walt. Not everybody's as secretive about their religion as you are."

Walt let this pass without comment, though in truth it was an unfair assault upon the fortress of banter they had spent a lifetime erecting. Those defenses had remained proudly in place even after Rachel's death, when Father Mondragon had undertaken to console Walt not through plain speech but through elaborate layers of coded witticisms. But you didn't have to say everything outright to care about people. Walt and

Rachel had had their own code, their own conversational bank shots and sly evasions and perturbed glances loaded with ironic freight. Now that she was dead, he had a whole repertoire of sparring impulses that were suddenly useless and vestigial.

They lingered in Louis's office long enough to hear Ralph Stanley sing "O Death" and then walked over to the parish hall, where Susan was setting up the slide projector and only about a third of the thirty or so folding chairs were occupied. Walt had tried to tell Louis that in Clear Lake City, the world headquarters of human spaceflight, an appearance by an astronaut, particularly an astronaut who had not even flown in space, was hardly going to be a major draw. But Louis had pressed him anyway, insisting that a woman astronaut would be an inspiration to the listless young mallrats of his parish. None of those girls were here, though. In fact, there was no one in the audience under the age of forty except for a three-year-old child who had squirmed out of his mother's lap and was now overturning Susan's artfully arranged cookie tray. Walt, who was grudgingly in charge of finding the speaker for the church's monthly "Careers in the Community" program, had drawn better crowds for everyone from local TV weathermen to commercial deep-sea divers.

It was almost seven. Walt didn't know Lucy Kincheloe well and had never really worked with her except for a few low-fidelity sims during her astronaut candidate training. But because he was team lead for her husband's latest mission, he had chatted with her from time to time at various informal get-togethers and at the cake cutting after the launch of STS-105 when Brian and his crew were moved up to the primary mission slot. His impression was of someone who had spent a lifetime taking on too much, and as a consequence was always sharply aware of time and forever checking herself against some merciless gauge of achievement. Since she was the sort of person who would gladly surrender her life rather than be late for a commitment, even an inconsequential must-do like this one, Walt was not surprised to see her entering the parish hall, breathless with apologies, at five minutes to seven.

"I hope you didn't think I'd forgotten," she told him, as he took the slide tray from her and handed it to Susan.

"There was a problem with my son at school, and when I got back to the office I had a meeting that lasted all afternoon and all these backed-up messages to return, and by the time I was able to stop by the Appearances Office to get the slides nobody was—"

"It's really not a problem," Walt told her. "You're five minutes early. Relax."

He introduced her to Louis, who greeted her with such a display of pastorly charm—seizing her hand in both of his and staring warmly into her eyes and thanking her effusively for carving time out of her schedule—that Walt barely recognized his snarky friend. Even though Louis had been a priest for over twenty years, there was still the possibility he was just pretending.

"I'm afraid we've failed to provide as big a turnout as you deserve," Louis said.

"Oh, don't worry about that. I'm always flattered when *anybody* shows up."

She smiled at Louis with apparent sincerity, turning her head to include Walt. He'd never really noticed how tall she was, and how imposingly physical. A lot of women astronauts tended to be slight, but Lucy had real mass, with broad shoulders and long arms and an unfashionable stolidity in her hips. With that sort of strength and reach, she'd be a natural choice for a spacewalk slot when she finally got assigned to a mission.

Louis told her he wanted to wait a few more minutes before introducing her—there were always latecomers—and so the three of them stood there chatting about her husband's mission, the flawless lift-off, Bill Kokernot's expert rendezvous-and-docking, the surreal call Lucy had received from Brian while she was sitting in, of all places, McDonald's.

"Well, I guess it's showtime," Louis said at five minutes after seven, when it was painfully obvious there would be no latecomers. He introduced her to the audience with impressive casualness, as if he knew the particulars of her life through long acquaintance and was not reading them from the highlighted bio that Walt had provided him.

"Our speaker tonight was born in Newton, Massachusetts. She is a graduate of North High School and of Amherst College, where she received a bachelor of science degree in geology. Having made a thorough study of terra firma, she moved offshore, so to speak, and received a Ph.D. in oceanography from the University of Rhode Island. And I suppose it's no wonder that, after becoming an expert on both earth and water, she would set her sights on space. As you can see, we are dealing with a very *elemental* woman here."

Louis endured a good-natured groan from the audience and plunged ahead, mentioning Lucy's two young children and her orbiting husband, and stealing her anecdote about the outer-space phone call in McDonald's.

When the introduction was over and Lucy got up to speak, Walt was surprised. He had assumed her A-student earnestness would translate into a robotic public presence. He had known in his career maybe a dozen astronauts who were naturally comfortable in front of an audience, and a few of those had been alarmingly that way, so galvanized by themselves that they had gone on to careers as motivational speakers. But the general run of astronauts tended to be people who kept their thoughts to themselves and a tight focus on their tasks, and in standing behind a lectern they often had the alarmed look of an animal pulled from its burrow. They clicked the slides forward in the carousel, they recounted their adventures in training or on orbit with a deadpan studiousness and an occasional canned quip about the space potty, but there was a reason these occasions were known as "must-dos."

Lucy Kincheloe was different. Standing in front of this sparse audience seemed not to ratchet up her anxiety, as Walt had expected, but to almost release her from it. He had never had occasion to notice her voice before, but it was soft and confiding, strikingly so in the harsh space of this parish hall, with its gray folding chairs and retractable room dividers and paneled walls adorned with dreary posterboard effusions— "Alleluia!" "For God So Loved the World," "Behold I Am with You Always."

Maybe he was just rooting for her because he did not want her to fail. He knew that a striver like herself would lie awake at night afterward, obsessively replaying every moment of her talk, torturing herself with the memory of misfired jokes or the look of crushing indifference on the faces of the audience. But Walt could see from the pleased look on Louis's face, and from the relaxed attention of the other people in the room, that she was making a genuine connection of some sort.

She had started off with a sly comment or two about life in a two-astronaut family—the children's refusal to be impressed by their parents' glamorous occupation, the leaky toilet that neither spouse, despite all the splendid technical training, had the remotest idea how to fix;

the envy and resentment she couldn't help feeling while her husband was circling the earth in the shuttle and she was driving through the streets of Clear Lake in her minivan at two in the morning looking for an all-night pharmacy to refill a prescription for her daughter's ear infection.

Now she was moving briskly through slides of astronaut candidate training, the Neutral Buoyancy Lab, the simulator, and finally the views of the earth from the shuttle and the International Space Station, views that she admitted she herself had never seen firsthand.

"But one of these days," she said, "it'll be my turn. One of these days I'm going to toss Brian the keys to the minivan, remind him to take out the trash on Wednesdays, kiss the kids good-bye, and take that ride into space that I've been dreaming of all my life."

It was the sort of observation that called for bouncy élan, but she spoke instead in an honest near-monotone, flattering somehow to her listeners, as if she were revealing to them a truth she had meant to keep to herself. She smiled and set down the remote control for the slide tray and stood up a little straighter and asked confidently for questions.

Louis, as he always did, put up his hand first, prefacing his question with a cringe-worthy little homily about the questing spirit of the human species. Walt understood it was Louis's duty to gently nudge the discussion in a transcendental direction, but it hardly seemed possible that his childhood friend, a young man who had escaped from the seminary one night to catch a midnight showing of *Faster, Pussycat! Kill! Kill!*, could be uttering such platitudinous mush.

"So I guess what I'm asking," he finally concluded, "is what you think the origin of *your* questing spirit might be?"

It was obvious what he was fishing for, an acknowledgment from her that space exploration might be an expression of the atavistic longing to know God. But her answer was bracingly secular. She traced her own spirit back to her parents. Her late father, an economics professor at Boston University, had taught her with never an overt word of instruction about clarity, thoroughness, unhurried deliberation. From her mother, who had almost died in a terrible car wreck at the age of sixty and then gone on to start her own business in the middle of an economic downturn, she had learned about ambition and fearlessness.

"And I suppose in everybody there's a kind of inborn curiosity about what's out there, what's *up* there. I mean, we wouldn't be human if we didn't feel it, if we didn't want to take a look. It's just lucky for me that I landed in a business where we actually get to *do* that."

Louis smiled his approval, though he had clearly hoped for more, the beginning of one of those splendidly airy theological tussles that Walt had decades ago stopped indulging him in.

Walt watched her. He was only half listening as she answered other questions about what it was like to train for weightlessness in the Vomit Comet, about whether she thought we would make it to Mars in her lifetime, and whether women might have an advantage over men in the prolonged period of weightlessness that such a voyage would require.

She wore a lavender cotton sweater, whose sleeves she had pushed up during the course of her talk, and crisp khaki slacks with a braided belt. Her hair, not quite to her shoulders and gathered casually in back with a barrette, had a distinct auburn cast. Walt, who had sometimes pondered the "before and after" pictures of makeover cases in Rachel's copies of *Redbook,* thought she might be better served by a more severe haircut, since her features were so cleanly delineated and her brown eyes so commanding. In general, though, he was a "before" guy, attracted to the enticing plainness those women seemed to possess before they were sent off for reconditioning. Lucy Kincheloe, he realized, had that sort of look. Not a "look" in the sense that the women's magazines used the term, not some tried-for effect, but a permanent natural bearing, a comfortable, purposeful, maybe even beautiful demeanor. But if she was beautiful, wouldn't he have noticed long before now?

There had been two or three moments in Walt's life when a woman's appearance had suddenly awakened in him a quaky sense of destiny. He remembered a trip through the Jemez Mountains of New Mexico when he was nineteen or twenty, where he encountered a girl at an improbable roadside smoothie stand. She had been intoxicatingly slim, swaying a little in the breeze to some blissful orchestration playing inside her head, thick strands of hair tumbling out of her bandanna onto her brow, her eyes as pale as tap water. She seemed as authentic an expression of her environment as the buoyant mountain air or the precise, glorious light. He was in her presence for maybe five minutes while she made his smoothie in a blender on top of a card table, grinning at him, pointedly without speaking, as if words between these two knowing souls would be ludicrous. It still troubled him a little—just a little—that when she handed him the smoothie and whispered, "It's on the house" he had not had the wit to understand that it was an invitation and not just some impulsive harmonic gesture. He'd thought about her all through the long fourteen-hour drive back to humid Texas, and all through the rest of his life. She had been no different, he supposed, than any of the other hippie sirens who had roamed the earth in those days, and if something had actually happened between them, if he had lingered in her presence instead of obtusely leaving, she might almost be forgotten by now. As it was, she had a phantom's hold on his memory.

Many years later, on his first trip to Moscow, where he was to help with the impossible task of coordinating Soviet-American training protocols, Walt had seen a woman of such mournful beauty leaving a bus that the words "It's her!" actually formed in his mind and almost escaped from his mouth. Had he not been newly married to Rachel, had he not been in a crowd of American space contractors and Soviet escorts and interpreters, he might have raced off after her, trying to explain to her their mystical connection with his hard-won vocabulary of perhaps three dozen Russian words. Even though, over the course of the next few days, it had become comically obvious to him that mournful beauty was a national characteristic of Russian women, the pang of a missed destiny did not recede. It was, even today, obstinately alive.

Something similar was happening to him tonight, a slow accrual of cosmic contentment. He allowed himself just a moment to bask in it, though he was old enough to have the plain sense to know that these seeming soul convergences were illusory. Just because you felt your scalp prickle as you sat reading the newspaper did not mean there was a ghost floating around in your house. Just because you were focused and inquisitive enough to become an astronaut did not mean, despite Louis's theorizing, that God had you in his tractor beam.

Walt knew what real destiny felt like. Destiny had been Rachel, his life's companion whom he had met without any thunderclap of recognition, just a casual introduction among friends one night at Frenchie's, another chance meeting at a softball game, a dinner out, a movie a week later, a congruent sense of what was funny and what was weighty, the almost undetectable sensation of two lives growing together.

Anyway, Lucy Kincheloe was a married woman, with two young children. He had just finished nine months of training with her husband and would probably be training her for her own mission one of these days. It would not do, it would not be appropriate, for any such reverie to gain purchase. But he liked the idea that it could, that at an age when he knew better he could still be blindsided by a forlorn longing.

He had set his pager on Silent, but when it went off it began to vibrate against the metal chair he was seated in, creating an intrusive thrumming that Lucy, in the middle of answering her last question, nervously registered. Walt knew her eyes were on him as he stealthily excused himself and slipped out the door into the parking lot to call in on his cell phone. He heard the applause starting as he dialed. She was hastily wrapping up. She may not have known that Walt was on real time mission support this week, and thus certain to be called if there was a significant problem involving *Atlantis*. But her husband was on orbit, a member of the shuttle crew that had gone up last week to deliver part of a new module to the space station. Since Walt was the team lead who had trained the mission, any page he got was bound to get her attention.

"Better call out the posse and come on down here to the Action Center," Lance Briscoe, the flight manager, told him when he came on the line. "I'll fill you in when you get here. Might want to bring your toothbrush."

Walt could tell from the tense and even accusatory tone in Lance's voice that it was bad. He was weighing whether to just get in his car and leave or go back in to make his apologies the best he could when the door opened and Lucy Kincheloe strode out of the parish hall and planted her feet in front of him.

"You're on RTS?" she said.

Walt nodded.

"Did anything happen? Are they okay?"

"Some sort of mal. I'm sure the crew's fine. I won't know exactly till I get to the Action Center. You want me to call you when I find out?"

"No. I'll go down there too."

"Could be a zoo."

But her mind was made up, and she didn't argue further. When Louis came out of the hall he had to pursue her across the parking lot just to hand her the slide carousel she had forgotten. He thanked her again for coming and gave her the usual speaker's honorarium, a lapel pin version of the hideous space sculpture in front of the church. When she smiled back at him and told him how flattered she was to have been asked to speak and how sorry she was to have to rush off, her voice had the calm, overenunciating timbre of someone trying to find her mental footing in a crisis. Walt noticed, as he left the parking lot behind her and followed her down El Camino Real, that her driving was elaborately steady as well. For all she knew, her husband's lifeless body could at that moment be circling the earth in silence 240 miles above her, but she drove close to the speed limit. Maybe she was thinking that if she stayed on the nominal, everything else would too.

Chapter Three

The first four speed-dial positions on Walt's cell phone were reserved for the members of his team. In the seven or eight minutes it took him to reach the center, he had managed to contact them all. Sylvia Molina was down in Galveston, at a party celebrating her brother's finally passing the CPA exam. She could be here in an hour. Mickey Flato and his wife were pulling out of the parking lot at Taco Cabana. Kyle Olson was at home reading. Because Gary Upchurch was in a theater watching a Vin Diesel movie it took him a while to answer the page, but fortunately the theater was the one in the mall on the other side of I-45, just ten minutes away.

Walt followed Lucy's car through the main gate and pulled up beside her in the parking lot in front of Building 30. She had already gotten out and was standing there waiting for him.

"Let's make a deal, okay?" she said. "I know you're probably going to have a lot of work to do in there and my job is to stay out of everybody's way. But I need somebody to tell me what's going on. I need somebody to be honest with me, to talk to me as a *colleague* and not just, you know, as Brian's wife."

"All right," Walt said. "I'll do that. It may take me a few minutes to get back to you."

"I understand that. I just want to make sure there's somebody in the room who will talk to me straight."

Her eyes were level with his. He had already agreed to her request, but she wanted something more binding than his casual affirmation. She wanted a vow. So he nodded, wordless and grave, and she said, "Thank you," and they walked together into Building 30 to the first-floor conference room known as the Action Center.

Thirty or forty people were already there, scattered about in impromptu working groups, a half dozen of them talking animatedly to Lance at the same time. When Lance spotted Walt and Lucy, he threw his hands together in a time-out gesture, left the group to argue among themselves, and walked over to the door.

"She was giving a talk at my church when you paged me," Walt said, since Lance was approaching Lucy with a why-are-you-here look. "I asked her to come along."

"Okay, fine," Lance said. Walt was long accustomed to, and somewhat forgiving of, Lance's officious side. In his place he would have been more than a little annoyed as well.

"As long as you're here," Lance said to Lucy, "you should know two things. The first thing is that the crew is not in danger. It's just a software problem. The second thing is that we're probably going to be here quite a while, so you can hang around if you want, but there's not going to be anything for you to do and you might as well go home and get some sleep."

"I think I'll just go out here in the hallway and make a phone call and play it by ear," Lucy said, not in the least intimidated by Lance's peevish advice. Had she believed Lance's aside about the crew not being in danger? A "software problem," Lucy had to know, was not necessarily a negligible thing. Nevertheless, Lucy abided by her part of their bargain and walked out into the corridor and leaned against the wall, keeping an eye on the activity in the Action Center through the open door. Walt noticed a few covert glances in her direction, but most people seemed to be focused on avoiding Lucy's presence. Not a good sign. It meant it was likely that the screwup was her husband's, a supposition that Lance confirmed as soon as she was out of their hearing.

"That's all we need," Lance whispered to Walt as he led him into the center of the room. "To have *her* in here looking over our shoulders. Thanks a lot for bringing her, by the way."

"So what did he do?"

"He overstepped. He slipped up and let his fucking ego off its leash. Sound familiar? The guy is a mission specialist, Walt. He is *not* the fucking commander of this mission! Didn't you ever mention that to him in training?"

"Cut it out, Lance. Just tell me the problem."

He was an unlikely-looking Lance: a cave-chested ectomorph with colorless, thinning hair, a pair of Wal-Mart reading glasses hanging around his neck by a silver chain. But his inconsequential physical presence supported a temperament of real authority. There was a trace of sarcastic belligerence in his personality as well, and Walt was determined not to put up with it just now.

"The problem," Lance said, after taking a patient breath, "is that your friend Brian Kincheloe may have corrupted the flight software. At this point we don't even know if we can do a goddamn de-orbit burn. Your guys on the way?"

"They're on the way."

"Good. Because the Mission Management Team is already meeting, and I want to get them some kind of solution on this before midnight. I do *not* want to find myself in the position of ordering a shitload of breakfast tacos."

For the second time that day Lucy was trying to coax herself into her imaginary haven of calm. But it was hard work to keep her anxiety from achieving terminal velocity, especially given the way everybody in the Action Center seemed intent on not noticing her. She could tell, more or less, that this was not yet a life-and-death emergency. There was a brisk, problem-solving energy in the room, and the expressions on people's faces were more vexed than alarmed. So why weren't they looking at her? Why were they treating her like a tourist who had wandered in off the tram from the Space Center Houston tour? A sickening, familiar knowledge began to announce itself, settling into her like the first intimations of a fever: Brian.

She called home. She had been on the phone all day with either Lorelei or Colleen ever since she had dropped Davis back off at school. He'd passed the rest of the afternoon without trouble, and Colleen reported that when she'd picked him up he was running wildly and confidently in an impromptu game of chase with some of the other boys in front of the school. When she left the house after dinner to drive to the church and give her talk he was already in his pajamas and playing calmly with his new toy, his breathing blessedly smooth and inaudible.

"He's doing fine," Colleen reassured her now when she answered the phone. "He's in his room reading. He told me you said he could watch *America's Funniest Home Videos*. I hope that wasn't true, because I didn't let him."

"Good instincts. What about Bethie?"

"Sound asleep since about seven thirty."

"Any chance you could hang around tonight?"

"Like all night?"

"I don't know yet. Can you stay till at least eleven? I've got to come home then anyway to give Davis the machine."

"Well, if it's an emergency or something, sure. But if it's not, remember I've got that test in the morning?"

"I remember. I'll try to line somebody else up, okay? Let me call you back."

Colleen had told her that she was counting on three solid hours of study tonight after she got home, and Lucy hated the thought of pressing her to stay, both because it was unfair to Colleen and because such a favor would be a significant drawdown from the goodwill account she needed to maintain with this indispensable ally.

Maggie, the sixteen-year-old down the street, might be able to relieve Colleen until Lucy got home. If Maggie was still at ballet, maybe her younger sister Sissy could babysit, or even her brother Robbie. Lucy was in the middle of dialing the number when she remembered the whole family was gone for three months while a mold-abatement team tore their house apart. Maggie had a friend, though, who had sat for Lucy once or twice and whose name she recalled entering in the address book of her phone. But now the girl's name wouldn't come to mind, and Lucy found herself impatiently scrolling through the many names on her list, hoping to trigger her memory.

She was still scrolling when she looked up and saw Walt Womack leaving the conference room to join her in the hallway.

"You want to take a walk?" he said, almost in a whisper. "I told my team to meet me over in Building Five."

She fell into step beside him without saying anything. The door to the Action Center was still open behind them, and people were hurrying down the hallway on their way to or from the Flight Control Room or the various Multipurpose Support Rooms, so anything they said was likely to be overheard.

He stopped at a bank of vending machines near the building's entrance.

"You want something to drink?"

"All right."

"So here's the deal," he said, taking a wrinkled dollar bill from his wallet. "What Lance told you was true. Nobody's in any danger."

She watched as he began to smooth out the dollar bill and feed it into the soft drink machine. He did this in an unhurried way, as if in this rampant emergency he had deliberately decided to set his own pace.

"So are you going to tell me what Brian did?"

He glanced around to make sure that he wouldn't be overheard.

"Brian was awake in the cockpit. Everybody else was asleep. The alarm goes off, the master caution light comes on. What do you want? Everything's out but Coke and Mr. Pibb."

"Coke," she said.

He pressed a button, the can tumbled out, and he handed it to her. It was cold to the touch and her fear had made her unexpectedly thirsty. Her second full-blown Coke of the day. Even in her wild alarm she couldn't stop herself from mentally toting up the extra 140 calories.

"So he calls down to Ground," Walt continued, as he took the change out of the coin return and fed it back into the slot to get his own drink. "He reports the master alarm. He tells them there's a freon light showing on the caution and warning matrix. The freon cooling loop seems to have lost flow. Ground thinks ice crystals have probably formed in there, so they want to turn on one of the freeze-dried General Purpose Computers to dump some heat into the loop to melt it. So far, so good. But then Brian doesn't wake up Bill—"

"Oh, shit," Lucy said.

"For some reason he doesn't wake up Bill." Walt held the door open for her, and they walked out of the building and along the sidewalk toward Building 5. "He turns on the GPC himself, instead of notifying the commander and having him do it. He apparently doesn't remember that when you move the switch from Halt to Run you have to wait at Standby for ten seconds to initialize the flight software. Of course nothing looked wrong at first, and it took a while to get the data from the GPC data dump. So now nobody knows if the software is any good or not. It might be corrupted. It might not work for the de-orbit burn. We might need to engage the Back-up Flight Software, but we won't even know *that* until we go through a recovery procedure that nobody's ever even tried on orbit before."

Lucy took a long sip of her Coke. It tasted repulsively sweet and acrid. "Has anybody talked to him about it?"

"To Brian? I don't know."

"There might be some kind of explanation."

"There might be. Sure."

As they approached Building 5, where the simulator was located, Lucy could see several members of Walt's team waiting for him in front. Another car was pulling into the parking lot. Walt touched her arm, and the two of them slowed to a stop fifty yards away.

"Look," he said, "we're going to go in there and solve this. Probably the software's fine and we won't even have to engage the BFS. It's just going to take us some time to find out. In the meantime, the crew is safe. As far as Brian goes, you can stay here all night and torture yourself, but we're probably not going to really learn anything until the debrief."

She had already come to the same conclusion herself. Brian was in enough trouble already. It would not help his cause for his wife to be lurking about while half of JSC was frantically working to correct the problem he had created.

"You want me to call you when we've got things worked out?" he offered.

"Would you? I don't care how late it is. I'm not going to be asleep."

"Well, maybe you'll surprise yourself," he said. The sympathy in his voice, Lucy thought, was more than casual. Brian was, after all, their mutual problem.

"By the way," he said, "you did great tonight at the church. Everybody liked you."

"I doubt that. I sort of ran out on them."

"No, they liked you. I could tell."

Walt Womack smiled at her briefly, promised again to call her, and then walked toward Building 5 with that same calm stride she had noticed before.

Chapter Four

The Kincheloes lived on a shallow cul-de-sac in Bay Forest, in a low-slung three-bedroom house that had originally impressed Lucy with its unabashed functional plainness. Lately, however, she had begun to lose respect for it, realizing too late that the roomy front porch, with its arched columns, was nothing more than a fainthearted evocation of Mission architecture, and that its all-brick exterior disguised a number of shoddy construction shortcuts. But she was still fond of the house on Purple Plum Court, fond of its suburban anonymity, its Little Tikes plastic vehicles gathered up for the evening on the porch, the tall pine canopy in the backyard forming a feathery buffer against the raw night sky.

It was nine thirty when she got home. Davis and Bethie were asleep and Colleen was soon gratefully out the door, driving off in her semi-dependable 1988 Volvo. Colleen's duties did not include housekeeping, but since she was a young woman who prided herself on her squared-away life, she had done the dishes and seen to it that all the toys were neatly put away, a final touch that Lucy, on her own, would not have bothered to require.

She went in to check on the kids. Though Bethie had her own bed-room, she always left it sometime during the night, afraid to be alone in all that yawning space. She preferred to sleep in her brother's room, where she was comforted by the Day-Glo stars on the ceiling and unintimidated by the scowling faces of some of Davis's villainous action figures.

Lucy sat down on the edge of Davis's bed and listened to his breathing: stable and clear. She hated to wake him up in an hour or so to give him the nebulizing machine, but she knew from wrenching experience that he would need a decisive dose of medication to get over this latest attack.

Bethie was asleep on the futon they had set up for her on the other side of the room. She lay on her back, her curved right hand moving back and forth loosely at the wrist as if she were making a blasé gesture to accompany some conversation she was having in her dreams. Bethie didn't have asthma, but Lucy found herself listening to her breathing with the same keen concern. She was more than a little suspicious that this dank and tropical region of Texas, rich with humidity and allergens, home to instant new buildings constructed with the latest off-gassing materials, might be the sort of witch's cauldron in which this particular disease could be effectively brewed.

Bethie herself was alert to her brother's respiratory health in ways that transcended simple childish concern. There was not a breath that Davis took in Bethie's presence that she did not monitor and gauge on her own primitive scale of well-being. It had occurred to Lucy that a large part of the reason Bethie insisted on sleeping in Davis's room was because she imagined herself to be his guardian, a loving spirit who, even as she slept, would keep watch over her brother's breathing.

An hour crawled by while she made herself a cup of decaffeinated green tea and channel surfed among the various cable news shows, where the hectoring hosts and sputtering guests were, as usual, locked in overheated intellectual combat. Lucy had a secret addiction to these nightly gabfests. The furious, self-righteous voices had a lulling effect on her, and sometimes she would listen to them for fifteen or twenty minutes without bothering to even notice what subject they were talking about. It was the rhetorical clamor that attracted her, the choreographed arguments that were in their way as counterfeit as the moves in professional wrestling.

She gave herself some credit for watching *Hardball* rather than reruns of *Little House on the Prairie,* but even so she knew she was flirting with something—mindless television viewing—that she had grown up believing was a cardinal sin. Her family had owned the same antiquated television throughout her entire childhood, and it had sat high on a bookshelf, ignored and even despised until some epochal event like the *Challenger* explosion required its use. It was a thing to be consulted in dire emergencies, a lifeline of last resort. In normal times an orderly calm prevailed—the dishes quietly and efficiently done, Lucy and her sister studying at either end of the long dining room table as their father sat in his austere rocking chair, reading each page of the *New York Times* with unnerving absorption before taking out his mechanical pencil to dispatch the crossword puzzle. Sometimes, on Mondays and Tuesdays when the puzzle was easiest, he would complete the whole thing without even resorting to the vertical clues, just filling in the blanks from left to right as swiftly as if he were writing a letter.

From birth, Lucy had been instilled with the habits of a concentrated mind, but she had to admit to herself that this was a gift she was beginning to squander. Fifteen minutes at the end of a long day of work and child care to listen to some cable news blowhard was perhaps not so much of an indulgence, particularly when she practiced her secret vice with an avionics manual in her lap, but she was growing disappointed in herself. She was losing the glorious rigor of that high school girl at the dining room table, her posture straight, her thoughts crisp. There was so much static assaulting her concentration these days that the background chatter of television worked on her like an antidote.

But she would not surrender to it, even tonight, when the last thing she could bear was to turn her thoughts to the crisis facing Brian on orbit—the crisis *he* had created. It was unthinkable that he didn't know that he should have awakened the commander before he turned on the GPC switch. What *was* thinkable was that he didn't care, that he considered such obvious hierarchical courtesies as part of an overbearing protocol. That, more and more, was Brian's prevailing attitude: what proof can you offer that you're not out to sabotage me?

Ten thirty. It was naive of her to hope that Walt Womack would call this early and tell her that the problem had not been as bad as they suspected, that there had been a simple test to verify the software after all and it had taken only a few minutes to determine there had been no corruption and it was safe to go for the de-orbit burn. She probably wouldn't hear from him until three or four in the morning, and then only if he remembered his promise to call.

But she thought he would remember. Walt Womack had a reputation at the center as somebody you could put your trust in. He was old for a team lead—almost fifty, probably—and in another person that might have been a sign of anemic contentment, when what was valued in his corner of the space program was upward enterprise. But he did not seem stalled or stymied; he seemed content. It was necessary for Lucy to remind herself from time to time that not everyone went through life like she did, as straight ahead as a solid-fuel rocket, with a propellant of ambition always burning away at her core. Certainly Walt had had his share of frustrations and turmoil—in fact, she remembered, his wife had died suddenly only a year or so ago—but she had the impression such things were deep, slow currents in an otherwise calm sea. His routine achievements as a team lead—involving as they did the subtle transfer of knowledge and confidence to the crew—were practically invisible, but almost everyone knew that five years ago he had been selected to hang the plaque for a famously flawless mission in the Flight Control Room, an honor that rarely went to trainers, and almost never to an individual.

It pleased her that she had seemed to exceed his expectations tonight at the church. No doubt she had been way down on the list of women he had had in mind for that talk. She had probably not even been on the list. And the truth was she hadn't really bothered to prepare, other than to double-check the order of the slides and review the notes she used for all such occasions. But sometimes, standing in front of a group, you just felt comfortable and authentic for no particular reason, and this had been one of those nights. The priest had put her at her ease, which had surprised her since she was not a Catholic and not particularly religious and had always considered the medieval patriarchy of the Church— with its celibate priests and obedient nuns—to be an affront to her idea of what the present world was all about. But this priest—Father Mondragon—had been sharper and more complicated than she had expected, and he had listened to her talk with a sly, appreciative grin, especially during the question-and-answer period when she had evaded his attempts to pin her professional motivations on a search for God. And something about Walt Womack's demeanor as he sat in the audience had emboldened and encouraged her. It just now occurred to her, as she rinsed out her teacup and put it in the dishwasher, that she had been performing for him, in a way. What was that all about? A man in a sport shirt and brown pleated Dockers, an inch or two over six feet, neither slight nor stocky, with grayish sandy hair, an eye color that she hadn't bothered to notice, a Cross pen-and-pencil set—monogrammed, no doubt—in his pocket. Half the men at JSC looked and dressed like that. But they didn't carry themselves quite the way he did, with that same assurance or conviction or whatever it was that separated the people you wanted to take you seriously from those whose awareness of you didn't really matter.

At eleven she got out the nebulizing machine and gave Davis his medicine. He fought her at first as she pulled him out of his sleep, but when he was conscious enough to recognize what was going on he accepted the mouthpiece without complaint, and afterward she lay beside him and stroked his trembling back until he managed to find his way back into sleep.

After that, Lucy wanted to take a shower to try to relax, but she worried that she might not hear the phone above the noise of the running water. So she brushed her teeth and went straight to bed, where she knew she would remain rigidly awake until she heard news that was good enough, or at least neutral enough, to justify her going to sleep. What would she do with herself all night? She had never developed any workable strategies for relaxation. Her father would have passed this tense night by doing his crossword puzzles, and her mother by reading some thick, punishing novel chosen by the sober women with advanced degrees who made up the membership of her book club. But Lucy had never liked word games, and though she had been a diligent student of literature, the habit of achievement—the "A" on the multiple-choice test, the "Excellent Analysis" scribbled in the margins of the essay—had long ago made the idea of reading for pleasure seem like a game without a goal. All she had were the cable news talk show hosts, but the thought of actually watching them all night long filled her with such a keen sense of wasted hours that it felt like despair.

So she set the alarm for six on the slight chance she would actually sleep, turned off the light, and then just lay there, staring upward with her head propped on an extra pillow. There was enough illumination leaking in through the windows, and from the Miss Piggy night-light plugged into a hallway socket, for Lucy to make out the swirling contours of the plaster overhead, and to imagine her ceiling as the topography of a dead planet, a colorless wilderness of canyons and craters and shadowy ridges.

She had not yet flown in space, but she lived, had always lived, for the day when her rational, achieving mind would earn her a mystical departure from the earth. It was interesting, though, after years of training, how her fantasies had shifted from escaping the constraints of gravity to fulfilling the demands of teamwork. She daydreamed more these days about the satisfactions of performing the likely tasks of her mission—reconfiguring the cockpit, manipulating the robot arm—than she did about what weightlessness would feel like, or how the earth would look through the orbiter windows. She imagined the other members of the crew as she ate dinner or pored over checklists with them or exchanged wisecracks as they inventoried the items in the supply module with a bar-code reader. She thought about people, her fellow voyagers, and about what it would be like to work with them on a common task in a place of unutterable danger and strangeness. But, of course, space was not a *place*. Space was nothing. That was a realization that had been creeping up on her, and that had caused her to refocus her longing on dreams of human connection and shared purpose. She had a mother's instinct for gathering and drawing close, and a mother's visceral fear of limitlessness, of intergalactic distances that had once been mind-warpingly enticing but now seemed faintly obscene, of desolate moonscapes such as she saw now on her ceiling, all those infinite, unknowable realms where nothing could live or be nurtured.

She turned her head away from the ceiling and saw Bethie standing at the side of her bed. The little girl was not looking at her or saying anything, just silently standing there and staring dumbly at the opposite wall.

"Bethie?" Lucy said. "Sweetie? Is something wrong?"

At the sound of her mother's voice, Bethie grew sluggishly aware, turning her head in halting movements as if she had heard a bird chirping on a branch and was now trying to locate it.

"Are you sleepwalking again?"

"I don't know," Bethie said.

"I think you are. Come here."

Lucy drew her up onto the bed and under the covers. The girl burrowed against her, the warmth of her mother's body almost instantly calling her back into alpha sleep.

Davis was a reasonably uncomplicated child. If sometimes he seemed to invest his imagination a little too deeply in the silent scenarios of his action figures, for the most part he was enthrallingly normal: mad for video games and eager to play active sports, a good enough student but with a boy's wholesome disdain for the whole female dominion of school. Bethie was a far more interior child, ruled by secret thoughts she could not or would not share and, Lucy feared, by secret horrors as well.

Once, several weeks before Brian's launch, Davis had asked his mother about the *Challenger* disaster while she was driving him to school. Lucy explained about how the O-rings in one of the solid rocket boosters had failed, emphasizing that it was a problem that had been fixed and would never happen again. The space shuttle, she told him, was exciting and noisy, but not nearly as dangerous as people sometimes said, and he did not have to worry in the least about his father going up.

"What about you?" he had said. "Are you going up?"

"Someday," she had answered, and continued in a tone of carefree enthusiasm, though to her ears it sounded more like delirium. "And you know what? I can't wait!"

Her manufactured breeziness had been convincing enough for Davis, but Lucy still worried about how she would answer Bethie's fears when the time came. Bethie would not be fooled so easily, having come into the world alert to disaster, her unformed mind already aware that there were forces working against her harmony and safety, and that if her mother left her sight for an instant these forces would break through the fragile shield protecting her. Bethie's radar had been working when Brian went into quarantine for his launch, and it was working now that he was on orbit: a constant thrum of disquiet, manifested at night by sleepwalking and during the day by an all-purpose balkiness, a reluctance to go along with the fiction that all was well even when Daddy was circling above them in the lonely blackness of space.

Even so, Lucy and Brian had worked hard at that fiction, talking about the launch to their children as casually as if they were talking about a shopping trip to the mall, betraying no fears and no emotions other than excitement. Lucy had decided not to take Davis and Bethie along with her to the Cape for the launch, and she was glad that she hadn't, because it had been delayed and lost its launch window twice, once to weather and once to a flock of migrating birds that had some-how made an anomalous pattern on the radar. When *Atlantis* had finally lifted off, in a fiery nighttime ascent, Lucy—despite her training, despite her witnessing of half a dozen other such events—had herself mistaken the normal violence of the launch for a catastrophic eruption. It took a moment or two for her cogent mind to override her alarm, for her scalp to stop prickling and her heart to beat again. If her children had been with her, they would have seen it. They would have known, despite Lucy's careful and constant downplaying of their fears, how close to annihilation their parents actually stood.

When Brian had first flown in space, four years earlier, Davis had been only three and Bethie not yet born. Lucy had been four months pregnant at the launch, relieved in a way to be temporarily sidetracked from the pressures of competing in the program, proud that her husband had been chosen to spend five months on *Mir* in the company of two Russian cosmonauts. It should have been a time of adventurous fulfillment. Brian's first mission was a high-profile international event, and Lucy had found such an unexpected completeness in motherhood that the ferocity of her own ambition sometimes seemed no longer relevant, like some outgrown adolescent emotion. She knew, however, that that ambition would resume, that in a year or so she would return to the active astronaut roster, and that the odds were strong that she would be assigned her own mission by the time she was thirty-six or thirty-seven.

But what should have been a bright time for her and Brian was not. It was not just the anxiety of the launch, or the prospect of five months of loneliness and impossible distance. It was that almost everything about the mission had been sour from the beginning. *Mir* had been the prototype of the International Space Station. At the time of Brian's mission, it was already a relic, a fading reminder of Soviet grandeur still circling the earth ten years after the Berlin Wall had come down. The idea of a joint U.S. and Russian crew on *Mir* had started out as an election-year initiative to celebrate the end of the Cold War. It had lingered because of NASA's interest in exposing its astronauts to long-duration spaceflight and because of the bankrupt Russian space program's desperate need for American money. Brian had been assigned to a crew not because he was fluent in Russian or exquisitely suited to a wretched confined existence in a tumbling trailer home, but because no one else really wanted to go.

Lucy had feared from the beginning that Brian was going to be a poor fit for this mission; nowadays she charted the deterioration of their marriage from the moment when she first allowed this thought to enter her mind. Brian's strengths were clear. They had been shiningly obvious to her from the first time she met him, at a MaxQ concert at the Outpost the first year of her training. MaxQ was the official astronaut band, one step up in terms of soul from, say, the Singing Senators, but it had been cooking that night, branching out into border funk like "Hey Baby, Qué Pasó?" that brought even the most sluggish patrons off their bar stools. The exception had been Brian. Lucy, fascinated by his stillness, had watched him watching the band as he stood at the bar with a beer in his hand, resolutely impervious to the music. She supposed now that he had simply been resistant to the whole idea of moving to the music's terms and not his own, but at the time his composure had seemed so singular as to be heroic.

She discovered him to be articulate, focused, alert to humor though perhaps a bit clueless about its ultimate necessity. He had been a fighter pilot in the Gulf War and was accustomed to maintaining a seemly silence about his heroics. He ran six miles a day on the JSC track and worked out hard at the gym at least four times a week. He weighed himself every day, and if he was an ounce over his sacred 170 pounds he would refuse to eat even a piece of his own birthday cake. This iron discipline, this knightly rectitude, had excited her. She herself aspired to something similar, to an existence as purposeful and calibrated as an arrow flying toward a target. But Lucy had always known she was capable of veering off course. Brian, she thought, could only fly true.

She had been truly dazzled by him in the beginning, and it had taken her years to fully comprehend his limitations. He loved his children but accepted his fatherly role as something that had been handed to him, not something he had sought. He was a man of honor, but an honor that was always in danger of being betrayed by unworthy forces. Jealous colleagues, backstabbing bureaucrats, incompetent personnel: Lucy had encountered such people from time to time, but Brian's world was crowded with them. He was not paranoid, but he was, she had to admit, a control freak, a man of sharp definition who could not abide the natural sloppiness of human endeavor.

Such was the man NASA had chosen to join two boisterous cosmonauts for five months in a crumbling space station. American astronauts were delivered to *Mir* on the space shuttle, but the greater part of Brian's training took place in Russia. Lucy, on extended maternity leave, with Davis in her arms, went with him. They arrived at Sheremetyevo Airport in Moscow on a pallid February day. Brian by that time had already had six months of Russian-language classes, but he couldn't seem to communicate with the customs agent who showed no concern about their missing luggage, or with the chain-smoking driver of the Astro Van who showed up in a grudging humor to drive them to Star City, a long hour and a half away.

Russia was breathtakingly true to her leftover Cold War stereotypes: the grim airport, with its corrupt and indifferent personnel, its burned-out lightbulbs and exposed wires; the inhuman Soviet apartment blocks; the exhausted old women in hard black shoes carefully traversing the icy streets; the white sun glaring through winter trees as they drove past forest roads that led to clearings filled with rusting industrial equipment or stacks of leaking chemical barrels. Lucy watched Brian as he looked out from the window of the van, as he tried to quiz the driver in Russian about when their luggage might arrive, or when he surveyed the grim two-bedroom flat they had been assigned in a Star City apartment building whose horrible name was the Prophylactorium. Her own heart was sinking, but she had traveled enough to know that weary disillusionment was a temporary condition. Brian's expression took on from the first an angry determination, a combative awareness that Russia was a place he would have to overcome.

Star City, where the legends of Soviet spaceflight had once trained in glory, reminded Lucy of an abandoned World's Fair site, everything shabby and moldering, weeds growing from the cracks in the sidewalks, an eccentric-looking building in the midst of it all housing a three-hundred-ton centrifuge that resembled nothing so much as an antiquated theme-park ride. There was a Soviet spaceflight museum, and a statue of Yuri Gagarin, and apartment blocks even more severe than their own.

Except for occasional visiting teams of trainers or technicians, they were the sole Americans there for the better part of six months. The cold was intermittently savage, but because they had no thermostat in their apartment they were at the mercy of a radiator heat that was consistently suffocating. When the temperature began to warm enough for them to open the windows, clouds of mosquitoes flew in and attacked Davis in his bed.

Even so, they had been happy in Star City, at least at first. They were only thirty miles from Moscow, but the air was clean and the scent of pine was strong. A kind woman in the next apartment block adored Davis and kept him for the two hours a day that Lucy studied Russian with a private instructor. The community that to her American eyes had first seemed as desolate as the setting of a *Twilight Zone* episode turned out to be peopled with vibrant Russian families, with young mothers like herself who were patient and encouraging with her halting language skills and endlessly amused by any scrap of information she could communicate to them about her glorious capitalist culture. Best of all, Davis was well, and happy, and when on reasonably mild days she met the other mothers at the foot of the Gagarin statue to talk or to go for a stroll he would reach out to them with a child's confidence that he was not among strangers.

For Brian, however, it was a time of growing frustration. He had no one but Lucy to talk to, and when he came home each day to their dreary flat he greeted her with a catalog of the day's problems. His classes were exclusively in Russian, and trying to comprehend a two-hour lecture on orbital mechanics with his slippery grasp of the language left him in a constant state of intellectual panic. There were no handouts. There were few copying machines and paper was not to be wasted, so a global understanding of certain systems of the space station resided only in the memories of the instructors, who recited their store of knowledge like homeric bards. The gym was shoddy, the physical training shockingly quaint: for days at a time they had him jumping on a trampoline or practicing back flips from a diving board. Brian felt silly and belittled. He felt alone, since NASA seemed to have forgotten about his existence and reacted only with polite indifference when he called with suggestions about dual-language training manuals or complaints about irrelevant Soviet-era medical procedures. He understood he must do his best not to take these absurdities too much to heart, to be flexible and tolerant in the face of a radically different way of doing things. She could see how much it cost him, this effort to be lighthearted about inefficiency and bureaucratic senselessness. His forbearance was heroic, she respected him for it, and it was her respect that made it possible for them to remain in love. The better he got at anticipating the obstacles in his way, the harder he could fight to overcome them, the more satisfied with himself he grew, and the happier they were. Sometimes, on the rare occasions when Brian had a few hours off, they would gather up Davis and walk for a mile or so to a hidden forest clearing and have a picnic from their store of American food. Nowadays, Lucy remembered those idle afternoons with nostalgic sadness: the three of them in a silent forest in the middle of Russia, listening for the feathery footfalls of a lynx or a fox, watching the alien birds sweep from branch to branch, drawing closer to each other within their cocoon of American perceptions.

The training got better toward the end of their stay. The strangeness had long worn off by then, and Brian's language skills had improved. The accelerated pace of training, the realization that the mission was going to happen after all, allowed him to focus on something other than the institutional insults of Star City. By the time they finally flew back to Houston, several months before Bethie's birth, he was at his best again. His goal was in sight, and since he was launching in an American shuttle to join the *Mir* cosmonauts already in orbit, there was no Russian inefficiency or petty sabotage in his way.

But once the shuttle had docked with *Mir* and departed again for earth, leaving Brian in the company of the two cosmonauts manning the station, things turned out to be far worse than even Star City could have prepared him for. In the first place, *Mir* was a ruin. When Brian arrived, it had been orbiting in space for a decade, and various crews had left behind old experiment containers and empty water tanks and reconfigured cables that snaked from one module to the next, clogging the entrances. One module that had once been an astrophysics laboratory was now essentially a garbage dump, filled with stinking trash bags that the crew had to push out of the way, gagging, as they floated through to perform maintenance or to reach the resupply vehicle that periodically docked on the other end. The five other modules were congested as well; all the discarded gear interfered with air circulation and caused the temperatures to rise, and the multiple ethylene glycol leaks that the crew had to constantly locate and clean up gave the entire structure the smell of an overheated gas station.

Brian, Lucy knew, would have gladly lived with discomfort if there had been a purpose to it, but there was only so much absurdity and indignity he could abide. The first week of his stay on *Mir*, he watched in stupefaction as his two crewmates suited up for a spacewalk and crawled outside with a giant effigy of a soft drink can so that they could film it against the backdrop of the space station. That was how the Russian space program tried to stay in business these days, by turning its cosmonauts into pitchmen. Not that the cosmonauts had much glory left to be corrupted. They had been reduced from heroes of the Soviet people to contract laborers. The Russians paid them a paltry base salary, plus a flight bonus and additional compensation for every task spelled out in their pre-flight contracts. For a spacewalk, they would earn an extra thousand dollars, maybe a hundred or two more for participating in American space experiments. Complaining about problems like the ethylene glycol leaks was risky for them. The blame might fall in their direction and cause them to lose part of the flight bonuses they desperately needed for living expenses back on earth.

Trapped in this atmosphere of bureaucratic lassitude, Brian had almost lost his mind. The food was dreadful—jellied fish, borscht. Floating weightless in Base Block, the central module of the station, his crewmates drank vodka and watched porn movies. During the staticky five minutes of radio communication Lucy had with him once a week, she tried subtly to encourage him not to hold himself apart, not to impose his unforgiving American dynamism on such a spongy enterprise. She knew he was trying and admired him for it, but she also understood that he was temperamentally unsuited to tolerate waste and uncertainty, too much of a loner to surrender fully to the badgering gregariousness of his crewmates. Things kept getting worse. His job on the station was to monitor a series of medical experiments for NASA, but the freezer containing the samples of blood and saliva he was to test overheated and the samples died, leaving him with agonizingly long stretches of time in which he had nothing to do but mop up chemical leaks and try to organize the clutter and solve the puzzles in an acrostics book.

The ethylene glycol leaks irritated his skin. The constant sounds of *Mir* expanding and contracting, combined with the sauna atmosphere, kept him from sleeping. With each day, the mutual contempt between him and the cosmonauts grew more pronounced. His one lifeline to sanity, besides the weekly communication passes, was the treadmill. Brian needed exercise the way people need air—especially so in space, where without vigorous daily workouts an astronaut's bone density could diminish alarmingly. But the treadmill was temperamental and the harness necessary to hold him in place so he could mimic the act of running in weightlessness was poorly designed. After every session he had friction burns on his shoulders and hips. He slathered antibiotic ointment on them, covered the places in moleskin, but he could not get the sores to heal enough for him to use the treadmill more than a few times a week.

Meanwhile there was constant friction with the Russian ground controllers, who dictated an unrealistic and inflexible daily schedule for the *Mir* crew while refusing to take seriously their complaints about snowballing technical malfunctions. One day, a stressed and sleep-deprived cosmonaut accidentally disconnected the wrong cable while trying to restore pressure to a module that had been damaged by a collision with a resupply vehicle. Suddenly the gyrodynes, which kept the station stabilized, could no longer talk to each other, and so *Mir* began a wild and dangerous tumble in space that was arrested only when Brian came up with the desperate idea of using the thrusters of the Soyuz escape vehicle to stabilize the station so the gyrodynes could be restarted.

The fix worked, but the crew had come close to losing all power and hence the fragile atmosphere that kept them alive in space. The Russian ground controllers were relieved but unimpressed. The crisis having passed, there was no reason to dwell on it, or even to acknowledge that it had occurred. That attitude was what caused Brian to lose it. On his next comm pass with NASA, in a now-famous diatribe, he unleashed a torrent of pent-up grievances. Within the hearing of senior controllers, he called the joint U.S.-Russian space enterprise a "Keystone Cops operation." He bitterly accused the Russians of focusing almost entirely on the bottom line and only incidentally on the safety of the crew or the success of the mission. He charged NASA with benign complicity, with a bland bureaucratic tendency to underestimate the problems and hazards on *Mir* and to essentially join the Russians in looking the other way. It was a breathtaking and mostly justified outburst. With another astronaut, one with more experience and deep reservoirs of goodwill, it might have worked. But Brian's lecture was received not as a bold stand but as a peevish one. The controllers felt irritated and betrayed. There was open talk that he had had a nervous breakdown, and extraordinary discussions took place about whether a way should be found to bring him home early.

But he managed to calm himself down over the next couple of days, and the talk of an early return died away. Two months later another shuttle flew up on schedule and docked with *Mir*, delivering an astronaut to take Brian's place and bringing Lucy's exhausted husband home. He was determined, after his weightless months, to walk out of the orbiter, and he did, shuffling like an old man to the waiting medical van.

There were photographs in the newspapers of Brian being welcomed by the NASA administrator and various grinning colleagues, but outside of the public theater his reception was cautious and strained. His impassioned lecture from space had been widely viewed as a tantrum; in a world that valued clear and unemotional responses above almost everything else, his excitability was unforgivable. Lucy welcomed him joyfully, but he became obsessed with the failure of the mission and the seeming betrayal of NASA and could not accept the simple happiness of being home on earth. Partly this was physical. After five months on *Mir,* he found gravity to be a hostile environment. Any negligible force, such as the spray of water in the shower, or the thrusting of his body against hers when they made love, filled him with instinctive alarm, since in space the slightest such pressure would have sent him careering against the panels and cluttered cables of the module. For the first few weeks after his return, he had to tie himself to the bed with a rope before he could find the peace of mind to go to sleep.

Because of the problems with the treadmill on *Mir* he had not been able to keep up with his exercises, and now back on earth he discovered that he had lost almost 15 percent of his bone density. He set about building it back with long, slow sessions in the pool, but two weeks after his return he tripped on a sprinkler head in the front yard while getting the morning paper and broke his hip. The surgery seemed successful at the time, but after a month or two on crutches the pain was still intense. There was another operation, this time to replace the ball of the femur, which had died from a constricted blood supply, with a prosthetic. Another six months on crutches, another six months of marginal astronaut jobs suited to his flagging health and fading reputation.

Brian managed to keep his temper steady most of the time, but his mood of grim distraction seeped through the family like a poison. Gradually, though, he managed to rouse himself from self-pity and find the courage to reclaim the ground he had lost. He was still an astronaut at heart, and the thought of never flying in space again was intolerable to him. He managed to will himself back into the program, to become a flawless team player, working at any task without outward complaint and saving his grievances only for Lucy's hearing.

And Lucy listened and did her best not to dwell bitterly on all the ground *she* had lost, not just from the months of pregnancy and maternity leave but from the fact that she was married to Brian. She had been on the active roster again now for enough time to have been chosen for her first mission, even with the severe budget cutbacks for the International Space Station, which had necessarily resulted in fewer shuttle flights. Instead, her assignments had shifted from CapCom to Cape Crusader to her current dreary position evaluating contract proposals as a member of the Source Selection Board. None of this was necessarily conclusive evidence that her career was on ice: all astronauts were rotated from job to job when they weren't actively training for a particular mission. But Lucy couldn't help believing that in subtle ways she had been tainted by association. It was natural for the astronaut office to fear that she harbored the same grudges that her husband did, that she would forever be his partisan instead of a neutral team player.

What selfish thoughts to be thinking while her husband was in space! If he were not in actual mortal peril at the moment, then at least he was in agonies of self-doubt. But she thought them anyway. In her heart she knew that if there were a choice to be made between her husband's career and her chance to go into space, she would not allow Brian to hold her back. She just wouldn't. He'd had his chance. Maybe it wasn't his fault, what had happened on *Mir*, or what had just happened on the shuttle, but the rigid side of his character now led to a growing dark well of defensiveness. These traits, she knew, had a way of contributing to and inflating the problems he faced on orbit. The simple fact was that he'd flown in space twice, and in some not-so-subtle way had blown it both times.

Bethie stirred beside her and twisted away in her sleep. The sudden withdrawal of her little body's warmth made Lucy feel as if a draft had entered the room. Maybe she could forsake Brian for space if she had to, but what about her children? There was a time in her life when she could have honestly said to herself that she wanted to fly in space more than she wanted the comforts and satisfactions of normal human life. But that time was fading—it was fading by the hour. What loomed in her mind these days was Christa McAuliffe's refrigerator door, with its notes and magnets and photos, its searing reminders of a motherless home.

Despite her expectations she coasted into a shallow sleep, dreaming about nothing, but feeling herself in an endless lazy free fall. When the phone rang, that slow orbital drift changed into a plummet.

Bethie whimpered in her sleep as Lucy sat upright and grabbed the phone just after the first ring.

"It's Walt Womack," he said. "I just wanted you to know everything's okay. The Procedure Verification checked out. We're going to wake up the crew in about an hour and give them the procedure."

She looked at her watch. It was a little after five thirty.

"You've been at it a long time."

"It's a pretty slow process. We had to get a flight crew into the simulator to work the procedures. There were lots of branches, and of course all of them had to be redlined, and then we had to call the changes over to the Mission Control Center. But we got through it, and now we're all over here at IHOP congratulating ourselves and eating chocolate chip pancakes."

"I wish I were there too," she said. Why on earth had she said that?

"Come on over."

"No, I have to get my kids to school. So you think—things are all right?"

"Everything's fine with the mission. They'll be back home on schedule."

"What about Brian? Did he screw up?"

"Why don't we not get into that right now?"

She was silent for a moment, trying to deal with the colliding emotions of relief at her husband's safety and renewed concern for his status.

"You okay?" he said.

"Sure."

"Get your kids to school."

"Okay."

"And thanks again for giving the talk."

"You're welcome."

It was time to say good-bye and hang up, but she had had a long, worrisome night and the sound of his voice on the phone was a comfort she hadn't anticipated. In the background she could hear the members of his team raggedly singing "Oh, What a Beautiful Morning" at the International House of Pancakes.

"They're pretty bad," she said.

"It's all right. We're the only customers."

She wanted to be there, to be part of this early-morning IHOP rowdiness. To be a member of their team instead of Brian's.

"Hey, Lucy," he said, as if aware of her wistful thoughts, "don't worry about Brian. Maybe he has some kind of explanation. He was great all the way through training, a real team player. I'll make sure people know that."

And then, before hanging up, he said something that spoke directly to her frantic spirit.

"And don't forget—you're still going to get your chance."

Chapter Five

Walt had been sitting on a pier in Bay Area Park for half an hour, studying a sign in the water that read "Watch for Alligators," when Louis finally drove up in his RAV4 and parked near the boat slip.

"I brought us kolaches," Louis said as he got out of the car and started unfastening the bungee cords that held the canoe in place on top. They carried the canoe down the slippery concrete ramp without speaking, and then Louis went back, got the paddles, and tossed Walt a white bakery bag. The kolaches inside were still warm, and Walt knew that Louis meant them as an elliptical apology for being late.

Walt held the stern of the canoe in place as Louis stepped into the bow and took up his paddle. For a supposedly humble priest, he dressed for their Sunday afternoon canoe expeditions with rigorous outdoor chic: a white canvas hat, sunglasses secured by a lavender neoprene strap, some sort of microfiber shirt and all-terrain sandals. Walt himself was wearing a long-sleeved T-shirt and jeans and a retired pair of running shoes. Though it was February and the branches of the trees lining the shoreline were bare, the day was warm enough to leave his corduroy jacket in the car.

Walt pushed them off from the slip and stepped into the stern and took up his paddle, and he and Louis stroked across the muddy water of the bayou in thoughtless conformance. They had first paddled a canoe together in an East Texas swamp during a Boy Scout campout, and three and a half decades later their routine was still the same: Walt in the command position in the stern, industriously steering their craft with the J-stroke, whose diagram in the Boy Scout handbook was forever vivid in his mind, and Louis in front dreamily dipping his paddle in and out of the water and scanning the shoreline for whatever scenery it might afford.

One night shortly after Rachel's death Walt and Louis had gone out to dinner and had started reminiscing about Camp Caddo and the fetid, shallow waters they used to paddle through, recalling how each stroke disturbed the oozy bottom and brought methane bubbles to the surface, how their corpulent scoutmaster had screamed at them from the shoreline, admonishing them over and over to keep their goddamn elbows straight, so that even today Walt held his arm almost comically rigid as he made his J-strokes. The next day, on a nostalgic whim, the two of them had driven to the REI store in Houston and gone in together on a red fiberglass canoe.

Almost every Sunday since, after Louis had said his last Mass, they had taken the little vessel out for a couple of hours or so through the sluggish bayous and meandering sloughs that bordered Clear Lake. These were pointless excursions. Neither Walt nor Louis fished, and though there was always a pair of binoculars and a water-swollen field guide in the canoe, neither considered himself a birder. On their first few trips they had explored every intriguing inlet, but then had soon settled into a monotonous routine of simply paddling up the bayou for an hour or so and then paddling back. In essence, Walt had decided, he and Louis were just aquatic versions of the mirthless mallwalkers who plodded up and down the shopping concourses in their track suits and unsullied running shoes. Even so, these aimless hours on the bayou had become the brightest spot in his week: a chance to get out into the open air, to glide upon mysterious waters, to become casually expert in the undemanding skill of piloting a canoe through calm back channels.

"Snake," Louis said from the bow, gesturing with his paddle in the direction of a nearby island that was not much bigger than their canoe. Walt grunted in acknowledgment and watched as the snake oscillated across the surface of the water toward the safety of the tangled tree roots. It swam with its head imperiously high and its patterned body trailing liquidly behind. Walt didn't know what kind of snake it was, only that it was too slender and brightly colored to be a water moccasin.

"Did you notice the high-anecdote content of my homily today?" Louis asked. "Don't ever say I don't take your advice."

"Riveting," Walt said.

"Yeah, what was it about?"

"I didn't stay awake through all of it, but there was something about Jesus descending into hell like Harrison Ford in *Indiana Jones and the Temple of Doom*."

"That's what I mean about the high-anecdote content."

"So let me get this straight," Walt said. "Until Christ was crucified and redeemed mankind or whatever, everybody who had ever died was in hell?"

"Don't start with this shit again, Walt."

"Literally in hell?"

"No, it was some kind of holding-tank deal. There weren't flames and stuff."

"So the flames came later? *After* Christ redeemed everybody?"

"You never get tired of playing the logic game, do you? You want me to admit there are fuzzy parts? Okay, there are fuzzy parts. Besides, the idea of hell is so retro now it's like *Reefer Madness*. Here's the problem with you: you've got a case of arrested development when it comes to your spiritual journey."

"Don't start with the churchy jargon."

"It's true. Ever since Sister Aloysius told you you were going to hell for stealing that Pez dispenser, you've been stuck in vindictive adolescent mode. Get over it."

"Get on with my spiritual journey."

"Exactimundo."

As they coasted past the soccer fields in Bay Area Park, the bayou widened into a narrow lake and the still water took on just the slightest chop as a negligible breeze brushed against their faces. A venerable great blue heron that Walt and Louis had come to know stood in his accustomed place on the far bank, and a dozen brown pelicans flew in procession just above their heads, outpacing the canoeists with each casual wingbeat. The vegetation, even in winter, was dense, though individual leafless trees towered over the primeval banks of foliage and sometimes rose inexplicably out of the center of the lake, their bare branches raw and spectral. As the sign commanded, Walt watched for alligators, but in all their trips he had yet to see one.

He could tell by Louis's attentive stillness in the bow that he was hoping Walt would pick up their argument again, but Walt deliberately let it fade. It was one thing to needle Louis, it was another to let himself be lured into a religious debate that the two of them were tediously incapable of resolving. Walt went to Mass because Louis was his friend and because it was a way of holding on to the fading clarity of his everyday life with Rachel. She had been raised with an unthreatening Midwestern strain of Catholicism and had regarded the rituals and demands of the Church as benevolent suggestions rather than oppressive medieval writ. Walt himself had not been immune to the nostalgic comforts of his childhood religion, and with Rachel at his side he had even felt somewhat back in place, although he no longer believed a word of any of it except for the central notion that it was better to be good than bad, better to be kind than cruel. Rachel's death had left him further exposed to the cold weather of his own rational thought. And every once in a while, harping to Louis about some doctrinal absurdity, he would become aware that beneath his lighthearted quibbles there was a pulse of anger. Walt had accepted the loss of his wife, it seemed to him, pretty well. He had not railed against the merciless universe; he had not cursed God. But there was something galling, something almost predatory, in the way Louis kept subtly trying to use the tragedy as a way of maneuvering Walt back to a faith he had never really possessed in the first place.

The breeze had died down and the surface of the water was now hypnotically motionless, so still that Walt could discern the ripples that their paltry wake made against the exposed tree roots along the shoreline. Encouraged by the glassy water, both of them paddled faster and fell into an unaccustomed rhythm for almost an hour, neither of them speaking until they had efficiently propelled the canoe beneath the NASA Road One bridge and out into the open water of Clear Lake.

After the constricted waters in which they had been paddling, Clear Lake looked vast, big enough for sailboats and stately cabin cruisers and even a lighthouse on the distant opposite shore, which was otherwise a solid mass of condominiums and resort developments. There was a light chop on the surface of the water, driven by a fitful wind, and the canoe rocked pleasantly fore and aft as Louis took a long drink of Gatorade and handed the bottle back to Walt.

"What if one of these days," Louis said, as he watched a huge fishing boat heading in from the bay to its slip somewhere down at one of the luxury homes around Lake Nassau. "What if one of these days we paddle all the way across the lake and out into the bay?"

"That'd take us all day," Walt said.

"So? We take a day. Then what if we kept going?"

"Where?"

"Across the bay."

"Okay. Add another couple of days."

"All the way across the bay, past Bolivar and right out to the Gulf."

"And then on to Cuba?"

"Seriously."

"We get out into the ship channel," Walt said, "we'll be dodging a lot of oil tankers. There's probably a law against having a canoe out there anyway. And the point would be what?"

"To boldly go. Give me the Gatorade."

Walt handed it up and Louis drank down the remaining few inches, then sat there in the bow of the canoe studying the expanse of water before them.

"Seriously," he said again.

Walt pretended to ponder it in silence, and then he took up his paddle again and with a few backstrokes had them turned around and facing back up the bayou.

By the time they had the canoe out of the water and tied up on top of Louis's car it was five thirty. Walt followed Louis back to the church and helped him store the canoe away in the scout hut, and then they got in Walt's car and headed off for an early dinner. This was part of the Sunday ritual as well. Sometimes they ranged as far as Galveston for fried shrimp, or all the way inside the Loop in Houston for barbecue at Goode Company or Otto's, but this evening they just headed up Highway 3 toward PeTe's. PeTe's was an astronaut hangout a mile or so from the entrance to Ellington Field, where the crews went for their T-38 training and where the welcoming ceremonies were held when they came back to Houston after a mission. The restaurant was a studiously ramshackle Cajun joint whose walls were covered with spaceflight memorabilia and faded crew portraits from missions going all the way back to Young and Crippen's first shuttle flight in 1981.

It was early and there was no one in the serving line. Walt and Louis each ordered red beans and rice and pulled a Dos Equis out of a big ice chest on the far side of the cash register. There were a few tables out in front, but they took their trays into the back room, a long, dark dance hall with picnic tables lining either side.

"Maybe we'd need one of those sea kayaks," Louis said.

"What?"

"A kayak would be better out on the bay than a canoe. It wouldn't take on water. They have two-person kayaks, don't they?"

"As far as I know," Walt said. He ate his red beans and rice and made a point of not offering Louis any encouragement. His hypothetical expedition across Galveston Bay was another in a long line of fanciful projects—like visiting the Mexican cloud forests, or bicycling through Wales, or climbing the Machu Picchu trail—that he had talked up over the years and then promptly forgotten about as he sank back into the consuming reality of his pastoral work.

"I'm not just rattling my cage again," Louis said. "I'm serious. You in or not?"

"Get it out of the conception stage, come to me with a solid proposal, I'll have my people look at it."

"What's her name again?" Louis said. He was looking past Walt's shoulder.

"Who?"

"The one who gave the talk the other day."

"Lucy Kincheloe?"

"Right."

Walt turned around, following Louis's gaze. Lucy and Brian and their two kids were sitting at a table at the far end of the restaurant. Lucy was occupied with wiping the little girl's face with a napkin, at the same time nodding distractedly at the boy as he gestured expansively in the middle of some rambling anecdote. Sitting beside Lucy was Brian, staring at the label on his beer bottle. None of them had yet glanced up to see Walt or Louis.

"Let's go say hello," Louis said, springing up from the table. Walt had no option but to follow him, though he would rather have avoided seeing Brian right now. The mission in which he had performed so problematically had returned only two weeks ago, and almost immediately there had been a contentious lessons-learned briefing in which Brian had started out well enough but proved himself ultimately incapable of simply admitting he had screwed up with the GPC switch. Instead, he had grown more defensive with every question, until he had managed to portray all of his colleagues in the room as prosecutors.

Walt followed Louis as he rushed up to shake Lucy's hand, to thank her once again for speaking at his church, to ask to be introduced to her children, and to introduce himself in turn to Brian and effusively congratulate him on his mission.

"Everything go pretty smoothly up there?"

"Pretty smoothly," Brian said painfully, as Lucy happened to catch Walt's eye in a questioning glance—had he told Louis? Walt responded with a barely perceptible shake of his head. She lifted up one corner of her mouth in a faint smile of gratitude and turned her attention back to her husband and Louis. Once Brian realized that Louis had no agenda other than conversation he was affable enough, talking easily about the sensations of liftoff and the relief of returning home and how he was not surprised to hear that his wife had done such a good job speaking at the church.

Louis turned his attention to the children and kibbitzed with them for a moment while Walt made small talk with Brian and Lucy. All of them were determined to avoid the looming subject of immediate concern—Brian's future in the space program—so they set aside any discussion of the lessons-learned briefing or of the ongoing training debriefs that Walt was conducting or the post-flight report he was required to write. Instead they talked about the various trips that Brian had made for the Public Affairs Office since returning to earth—flying off to Kennedy to thank the Launch Ops and Ground Ops teams, and then to Canada to show the flag to the robot-arm guys at the Canadian Space Agency.

Brian's mood with Walt was guarded. The comradely bond they had developed through their months of training had not exactly disappeared, but there was an unmistakable tension in their relationship, now that Brian saw Walt as part of the phantom tribunal that was conspiring to determine his fate.

This attitude irritated Walt, since it was he who had managed to talk Lance Briscoe out of convening a full-scale mission review team and into organizing the less formal lessons-learned briefing instead. Brian was the sort of guy who just just didn't make it easy for you to be his ally. Walt could imagine the wariness that Lucy must have felt in trying to stay on his side as a life partner, the uncertainty of the kids in trying to deal with his persecuted moods.

"Is it me or is that guy sort of unfriendly?" Louis said as they were driving away from the restaurant.

"He's an astronaut. He's taciturn."

"Something went wrong with the mission, right? That's why you got that page that night."

"Just a glitch."

"Yeah, but he caused it. Right?"

"Can't really talk about it, Louis."

"We're both professionals. Let's trade information. You tell me what he did and I'll tell you some really cool sins I heard in the confessional."

Walt laughed. Louis didn't press him, though if he had Walt might have told him more than he should. Without Rachel, he had no one anymore to gossip with or confide in about the routine resentments and occasional grievances of his work, and it just now occurred to him that this accumulation of unexpressed detail was starting to become a burden.

"I like her, though," Louis said. "Too bad she has to be married to him."

"He's not so bad," Walt felt the need to say, not just out of professional discretion. He liked Brian, most of the time. "It's sort of a tense period for him."

After he dropped Louis off at the church, he drove a few blocks east on El Dorado until a strange leaden awareness began to creep over him. Something was wrong, and it took him a while to realize what it was: he was going home to the wrong house. He pulled into the Kroger's parking lot and remained there for a moment with the engine running until he felt composed enough to turn around and go back in the opposite direction.

He had never done that before. It had been almost a year since he had sold the house on Fairwind Drive, and it was strange to him that after so long a time he would find himself thoughtlessly gravitating back toward their old street. He assumed it was normal enough, however. The "grieving process," as everyone in those first few months had insisted on calling it, was a route beset with unanticipated detours and doublebacks. Forward movement was elusive, just as it was along the twisting bayou where he and Louis paddled their canoe. Whenever you thought you were approaching open water, you were just as likely to find yourself in a marginless slough, or in a narrow channel that had finally been choked off into nothing by the sodden overgrown vegetation on either bank.

Walt's new condominium in Nassau Bay had seemed to him, in

those searing months after Rachel's death, a place of consoling charm-lessness. It was built close to the water, and although it was a relatively new complex, the salt air kept the exterior of the building in a state of dynamic corrosion. The metal pillars that held up the carports were flaky with rust, and small chunks of textured stucco regularly calved away from the exterior walls. Inside, however, all felt solid. The water pressure was strong, there was a modern abundance of electrical outlets and even a built-in DSL connection, and the walls were substantial enough that there was rarely an unwelcome sound from any of the other units.

When he came home tonight he turned on the lights and walked inside and tossed his keys into a ceramic bowl that sat on an entryway table. After that, as usual, he was at a mild loss. It seemed to him that in his old life entering his home at the end of the day had required nothing of him. There had been no decisions to make. He mumbled hello to Rachel and everything flowed from there, a seamless sequence of uncon-sidered actions and unrehearsed conversation. Now somehow there were no routines. Everything required his deliberation. Should he sit down and read a magazine? Should he watch television? Should he walk onto the balcony and stare out at the black stretch of water that was Clear Lake at night? Was it too early, eight o'clock, to think about going to bed?

He took off his shoes and walked into the bedroom and set them neatly on the floor of the walk-in closet, a cavernous space whose hang-ing racks were mostly empty. Two suits, three sport coats, a dozen or so sport shirts, four or five pairs of pants—all of them hanging with plenty of room between them. On the floor were his gym clothes and running shoes, and in a stack of transparent acrylic storage boxes from the Container Store was his collection of shirts for the missions he had trained. The latest one, STS-106, was still on top of the dresser. Like all of them, it was a polo shirt. This one was powder blue. The patch showed *Atlantis* coasting toward the uncompleted space station against a field of stars, the names Kokernot, Trube, Kincheloe, and Primus trail-ing behind the orbiter's thrusters in an awkward attempt to convey propulsion.

Walt put the new shirt into the acrylic storage box with the rest. He took off his socks. He brushed his teeth. He turned on the television and blankly tried to navigate his way through the oppressive abundance of the cable stations, then turned it off and stared at his reflection in the sliding glass door that led out onto the balcony. The wind outside was starting to blow a little, and it produced a slight keening sound as it gusted across the deep-set balconies of the condominium building the way breath might pass over the stop holes of a flute. The running lights of a few boats were visible on the dark water, and Walt's reflected face seemed to preside over their movement in a way that made him feel even more detached.

Impulsively, he put on his shoes and socks again, gathered up his keys, and went back down to his car. He drove up NASA Road One to the freeway, thinking that if the Barnes and Noble was still open he would sit in the coffee shop there and read the Sunday *New York Times* as he sometimes did, or he might go to a late movie at the multiplex in the mall. Instead, he just kept driving, all the way south on I-45 till it crossed the causeway over the bay and dead-ended at the seawall in Galveston thirty miles later. He drove up and down Seawall Boulevard. He stopped at a Wendy's, just to provide himself with some sense of purpose or destination, and bought a Frosty, and drove out to the east end of the island to eat it as he stared out his windshield at the whitecaps coming in from the Gulf.

Aimlessness, restlessness, sadness: none of it new, none of it necessarily debilitating. In another few weeks the training cycle would begin with another crew, he would be back at his console directing sims, and moments like this, moments of confused flight, would be wild exceptions in a life that was not stalled out, just ruefully stable. But staring out at the Gulf tonight did little to reinforce that conviction. The whitecaps, churning chaotically on the edge of a black ocean, seemed ominously familiar, an image of the tumultuous futility that kept threatening to rise up in his own soul.

You beat something like that back, he knew, step by step. You ran through the procedures. There was, for example, a woman he had met in Payload Planning and Integration named Lauren Bell. She was in her early forties, divorced, the sort of pilgrim-athlete who seemed to derive transcendent joy from triathlons and hundred-mile bike rides. She was, in Walt's uncertain estimation, not just vigorous but gorgeous, with windburned skin and quiet brown eyes and the rangy build of a horsewoman—a quite different physical type from Rachel, who had been dark and small and whose idea of an outdoor adventure was gardening. Walt and Lauren were on friendly terms, and as far as he knew she was unattached. But his caution was formidable. After almost twenty years of marriage, serious domestic commitment was such a reflexive condition that it seemed to him that if he asked her out there could be no turning back. If, as he half suspected, her sense of humor was limited, if her rapturous excitement about bike rides and wilderness excursions suddenly grew tedious, he did not know if he would have the strength or the tact necessary to extract himself.

He spooned out the last of his Frosty and got out of the car and walked over to a trash can and threw it in. Then he climbed up on the jetty and walked a little ways along it, following the course of the deep-water channel known as Bolivar Roads that led from Galveston Bay into the Gulf. On the beach the waves were crashing onto the sand with a thunderousness that seemed to drown out every other sound on earth, but inside, the water was dark and slack and silent. He thought of Louis's idea of paddling a canoe through the bay and up this channel into the ocean. Standing here, staring at the menacing stillness of the water between the jetties, and at the powerful waves that would greet them once they emerged into the Gulf, Walt knew he could file this proposal away along with Louis's other unrealizable schemes. He doubted he had heard the last of it, though. It seemed to him that Louis was becoming more and more invested in these fantasies, and more and more insistent that Walt share in them. Maybe it was just some universal middle-aged apprehension that life was passing him by, but made sharper in Louis's case because he was a priest and had long since forsaken the one thing that life was most insistently about. But that was just Walt's apostate imagination at work. He had no evidence—except a certain antic peevishness in Louis's manner now and then—that his friend was not still consoled by faith as he sat in his lonely rectory room every night drinking his Dr Peppers.

At any rate, this saltwater canoe enterprise was a harebrained idea, although a canoe in the ocean was certainly no more fragile a vessel than a shuttle in the immeasurably more hostile and empty environment of space, and Walt trained people for those voyages every day.

He himself of course remained on the earth, he kept to the marshy bayous rather than the sweeping expanses of open water, and every Sunday, because he had allowed it to be expected of him, he wearily professed the leftover beliefs of his childhood. And every six months or so he added another mission shirt that he would never wear to the transparent boxes stacked on the floor of his closet.

This bleak mood was intolerable. He disapproved of it, and mentally backtracked through the day, trying to locate the moment when he had opened the door to regret and futility. But all he could discern was a steady background thrum, an emotional current that had started out as familiar loneliness but was trying to oscillate its way up to something more sinister.

Running into Brian Kincheloe at PeTe's hadn't helped. Ever since the incident on orbit and the lessons-learned briefing afterward, Walt had not been able to look at Brian without contemplating his own failings as an instructor. At the briefing, when Brian had been questioned about why he had decided to throw the GPC switch himself and not wake up the commander, he had said that when Ground had suggested dumping some heat into the freon loop they had told him "you are go for the procedure." The clear implication, he said, was that "you" was him and that he was to do it himself. Lance and the other members of the briefing committee had rolled their eyes in exasperation. Then they had all glanced, one by one, at Walt. There was no real accusation in their eyes, just a look that invited Walt to consider whether he had done a thorough job of training the crew for this mission.

Walt had known from the beginning that he would share in the blame. Even in the workaday culture of NASA, astronauts were still the celebrity players, and it was natural that their occasional failings were often shifted to the training team. That was part of the reality of things, and Walt didn't dwell on it. In fact, he should have anticipated more than he had the limits of Brian's team-playing capabilities and tried to address those limits more directly during training. And in reality, the fallout for him would be negligible. He was the most experienced team lead at JSC, he had hung the plaque in the FCR, he could retire tomorrow with his reputation as a trainer intact.

Maybe that was the problem. He could indeed retire tomorrow, or take another job. What then? His plaque would stay up in the FCR until someone inevitably took it down, his collection of mission shirts would be donated to some school or to the archives of some space buff's group, he would have the memory of a satisfying and reasonably meaningful career but also the fear of a life that did not progress much beyond the resolution of that career, that did not merge in any significant way into the life of another person or branch out into another generation.

He realized, dwelling on this last thought as he walked along the jetty back to his car, that it was not running into Brian that afternoon that had set him into this mood; it was seeing his wife. Lucy Kincheloe had been wearing jeans and a sweatshirt and a baseball cap with the logo of the New York Public Library. She had tied her hair into an abbreviated ponytail and threaded it through the half-moon space in the back of the cap above the sizing strap. As she talked she had stroked her daughter's back with the fingertips of one hand and occasionally gently restrained her squirming boy with a touch on his shoulder. And she had met Walt's eyes in a way that carried the hint of a plea, or a promise: something. Something beyond his own carefully reconstructed life.

Chapter Six

It had been Brian's idea to eat at PeTe's, and Lucy had considered it an encouraging sign. Maybe he was coming out of the grudging, isolated mood he had sunk into ever since his mission returned to earth. It had been painful for her to watch him during the formal welcome-home ceremonies at Ellington Field, the way he stared impassively off into the distance during the various perfunctory speeches. Nobody said anything, of course, and the children—excited to see their father up on the platform, being honored for his bold voyage into space—never suspected that the moment was tainted. When the ceremony was over, Brian had exchanged hugs with Bill Kokernot and the rest of the crew, and with Walt Womack and the training team, but she could see the remove in his eyes, the solitary watchfulness descending once again upon his soul.

And of course it had only gotten worse after the briefings, when Brian's suspicions that he had no allies and was once again being made a scapegoat were to his mind grimly confirmed. Lucy had listened patiently to his bitter logic, heard the satisfaction in his voice as he recounted the extent of the conspiracy against him. She had no interest anymore in trying to contradict him. She did not have the emotional energy to spare. She knew that his storm of recrimination would eventually blow itself out, and that there would be a tortured period of reflection afterward that might last for weeks, and then the best parts of his character—tenacity, resolve, reinvention—would finally show themselves.

As they had been eating dinner with the kids tonight she had hopefully imagined he was entering this productive cycle, but seeing Walt Womack and having to pretend for the sake of that Father Mondragon that the mission had been a success had strained his reserves of good humor. He was silent now as he drove back to their house. The children, catching his mood, were silent as well, Davis pretending to be absorbed by the sun-streaked clouds in the darkening sky, Bethie beside him in her car seat, aware and confused.

After a moment, Bethie said, without inflection, as if she were just trying the words out, "What's wrong?"

Lucy turned to her from the front seat and smiled.

"Nothing's wrong, sweetheart."

"Nobody's talking."

"That's because we're thinking."

"About what?"

"Well, I'm thinking about whether or not we should stop at I Can't Believe It's Yogurt."

"Can we?"

"If it's all right with your father, it's all right with me."

The yogurt place was only a block farther on. Brian pulled up to the drive-in window without comment. The simple act of trying to place an order while enduring his children's endless deliberations and amendments over sprinkles and mix-ins forced him back into their world, and for the rest of the drive home the silence in the car seemed natural and contented.

When they pulled into the driveway Lucy got out and opened the sliding panel door to let the children out. Davis had already wolfed down most of his cone, but Bethie had as usual taken meticulous care with hers, licking it almost reluctantly, less interested in consuming it than in preserving the perfect spirals that the machine had extruded.

Lucy shepherded them into the house and left the door open for Brian. She was heading to the bathroom to run the water for the kids' bath when she realized she had not heard the door close.

"Where's Daddy?" she asked Davis, as she turned off the TV he had just turned on. He was making himself comfortable in front of the screen, preparing to claim squatters' rights.

"He's still out in the car."

"Watch your sister for a minute," Lucy said, pulling the PlayStation controls out of his hands.

Outside, Brian was sitting in the driver's seat of the minivan, staring at the garage door through the windshield, holding a half-melted cup of vanilla yogurt.

"What are you doing?" she asked him.

"I'm just finishing this. I'll be there in a minute."

"Do you want to talk?"

"Not necessarily."

She got into the front seat and closed the door. The dome light stayed on for a moment, and she waited for it to switch off before she slid across the seat to him. She took his upper arm in both her hands and set the side of her face against his shoulder, wishing she felt spontaneous tenderness and not just a desire, however compassionate, to distract him from his dramatic self-absorption.

"So what's going on?" she said.

"What's going on is that they're never going to let me go into space again."

"You don't know that."

"The hell I don't, Lucy, okay? I mean, what other possible outcome is there?"

He set his unfinished yogurt down on the console and glanced in her direction. "Maybe I should try to see God tomorrow."

"About what?"

"You."

"Me? What are you talking about?"

"You know, just to make sure you don't get caught in the crossfire."

Blaine Doggett, nicknamed God Doggett for his awesome authority over the lives of almost everyone involved in spaceflight at JSC, was the director of flight crew operations. He was an inscrutable being, a slightly portly man with a distantly amused air, whose features were as bland and inexpressive as those of the man in the moon. It was he, moving in his mysterious ways, who ultimately chose the crews for each mission, and Lucy had yet to meet a veteran astronaut who could explain the process by which one fell into his favor. Falling out of his favor was not so different. You just knew when it happened, though you might not ever know why. Slowly you became aware that some sort of celestial satisfaction had been withdrawn and that you were essentially alone in the universe. God Doggett himself, of course, would never speak to you about it, and Lucy had heard of astronauts who had spent the rest of their careers fruitlessly trying to discover why it had happened. The thought of Brian trying to engage this totally unengageable entity—a man who walked down the halls to the sound of colleagues humming "How Great Thou Art" behind his back—in an impassioned argument about why his wife should not be punished for his sins filled her with panic. The social obliviousness that she had once found so attractive in Brian, that she had regarded as a sign of rigorous personal integrity, seemed more and more like an aggressive refusal to understand human nature.

"Don't do that," she said quietly.

"I just don't want you to get hurt by this. It was my fuckup. And it would be just like those bastards to punish you for it as well."

"You've got enough on your mind right now, Brian. You don't have to go in there and make a case for me. I can do that for myself."

He shifted his head toward her, and she looked up into his face. In the darkness of the closed car she saw his mouth tighten into a morbid little smile.

"You don't trust me. You think I'll make it worse for you."

"Cut it out, Brian. I just don't need you to do it. It's unnecessary. It has nothing to do with trust."

"I let you down, though. Didn't I?"

"Brian," she said, in a weary, exasperated tone. By this time she had loosened her grip on his arm and moved away from him a little. They sat there in silence for a full minute, Brian still in the driver's seat, unhappily tracing the circumference of the steering wheel with his index finger, Lucy on the passenger side staring out the window at the house. The curtain on the front window parted and she saw Bethie's worried face, and an instant later the door opened and Davis walked out holding his sister's hand. Lucy couldn't roll down the power window without asking Brian to turn on the ignition, so she opened the door and called out to her children.

"We'll be right in."

"Is something the matter?"

"No," Lucy said. "Nothing's the matter. Just go back inside and we'll be there in a second.

"We can't sit out here all night," she said to Brian when the children reluctantly retreated into the house. "We have to go back inside. They're worried."

Brian nodded, still staring ahead, not looking at her. His hair was cut short as always, but with a downy fullness at the temples. His features in profile were cleanly delineated, his nose straight, his chin classically strong. Another man with this face and this body, a man with a more confident core, might have been startlingly handsome. But it just now occurred to Lucy how essentially unremarkable her husband's physical perfection really was.

"I'm sorry, Lucy," he said after a moment. And then he was quietly weeping. She reached out to him again, though the sort of quasi-maternal solace that now overwhelmed her was the last emotion she wanted to feel toward her husband. To his credit, he didn't want her to feel it either, and as he cried he nodded his head in understanding at her attempt to comfort him even as he pulled away toward the driver's side door to let her know that her tender concern was shaming him instead.

"Go inside to the kids," he said, and she was grateful to be released. She was disappointed in herself for not taking his suffering more to heart, and in him for insisting on suffering so much. There was no emotion she could summon that seemed right to feel, and so she just went inside and went about the business of assuring the children that there was nothing wrong, that Daddy was just preoccupied with a technical problem that had arisen on his mission and was trying to figure out how to fix it for the next flight. Brian came back into the house soon enough after that, and read Bethie a story while Lucy supervised Davis's bath, and after both the children had gone to sleep he stayed up watching a show about Mayan hieroglyphs on the Discovery Channel. When he came to bed after midnight he edged up to her and drew a circle with his finger around the knob of her hipbone, one of the two or three gestures he habitually used to signify that his turbulent thoughts had quieted enough for sex. She turned to him and responded with an intensity that embarrassed her a little, since he had done nothing to earn her passion and everything to dampen it. But because he had been too distraught to make love with her in the two weeks since his return, she had built up her own store of physical yearning and was able to meet his desire tonight on something like equal terms.

As she lay wide awake next to him a half hour later, with no place just then for her thoughts to hide, the question was not whether she still loved him but whether she ever really had, whether those early years of their marriage, years of striving together toward the same goals of reaching space and of building a family, had been as rich and complete as her yearning memory insisted they had been. If she could convince herself she had loved him, she could convince herself she could still.

If an armed intruder came into the house tonight, would Brian plant himself in his way and give his life so that she and the children could escape? Of course he would, without a thought. If Davis's asthma suddenly grew terribly worse, and they needed to sell the house and all their possessions to pay for the medical bills, would Brian complain? Not for an instant. Would he ever leave her for another woman? Probably not; almost certainly not. He was a man who defined himself through his willpower, and if he could not be faithful to her out of love he would make himself be faithful to her out of obligation.

And of course she would do the same. Even at such a low moment as this, divorce was an untenable thought. It was quite enough that she and Brian were willing to hold their children's well-being hostage to the high-risk demands of their own dreams of achievement. Until she became a mother, Lucy had never been the sort to worry about whether any particular endeavor could end in catastrophe, but now she never climbed into the cockpit of a T-38 without wondering whether this was the training flight that would leave her children motherless. She would not subject them to a shattered home for the capricious reason that she had lost respect for their father.

But the question still lingered: had she loved him? Could she again?

She slipped out of bed and put on her robe and left Brian sleeping as she walked down the hallway to the darkened family room. She stealthily pulled open a deep drawer next to the television and sorted through various semi-abandoned electronic devices—disposable cameras that for some reason had been used for only one or two exposures and therefore never taken to the photo place, wires and joysticks and control pods from various outmoded computer games, the handset to a cheap cordless telephone that had come with a magazine subscription and had never been used—until she found a functioning Walkman and its much-entangled headset.

From the bookshelf she pulled down one of three vinyl cases with the Audio Scholar logo. Audio Scholar was a mail-order company that sold college lectures on cassette. This lecture, *An Introduction to Economics,* by Robert C. Thorne, Clarendon Professor of Economics,

Boston University, was twenty-eight tapes long, each tape a concise twenty-five minutes or so, with a smattering of canned applause to signify the end of each lecture. Lucy still remembered the day, probably fifteen years ago now, when her father had called her in Oklahoma, where she was doing geology fieldwork in the Arbuckle Mountains, to tell her that the Audio Scholar "scouts" had visited his classroom and asked for permission to record his introductory lecture. Though he was a man who took care to play down any expression of self-regard, and though he had harrumphed away her congratulations, claiming that his would surely be the worst-selling series of lectures in the Audio Scholar catalog, Lucy thought she had never heard such happiness and pride in her father's voice.

As it turned out, his prediction was correct, or nearly so. *An Introduction to Economics* appeared in only one issue of the catalog and then quietly went out of print. But she had it still, her father's voice, speaking methodically, patiently, with an undertone of animation that the Audio Scholar scouts had presumably noticed but that was too subtle to really register without the benefit of his physical presence.

Lucy put in a tape at random. She had listened to the whole series years ago when it had first come out, and now she only dipped into it from time to time when she was lonesome for her father and wanted to hear a male voice full of strength and certainty. He was talking about the fading of mercantilism, the rise of the Physiocrats, the argument they fostered that there was no source of wealth on earth other than ownership of the earth itself. She paid no real attention to the words, though she admired them, the judicious phrases, the clarity of his argument. She just wanted *him*. She closed her eyes. As her father went on about why these new laissez-faire economists could tolerate no tax other than a tax on land, she imagined herself in the room in which he was giving the lecture, not some recording booth but a real classroom with a venerable old chalkboard and a wooden podium and a glass of water on a stool beside it. The polite, synthetic clapping on the tape called to mind a strangely antique audience of perhaps a dozen people, the men in double-breasted suits with fedoras balanced on their knees as they leaned forward to catch every authoritative utterance, the women in hats with veils and fox stoles. They were people from another age, and yet Lucy felt at home among them, beaming with pride at their quaint appreciation of the professor standing at the podium.

The fact that this fantasy was so vivid only underscored the reality of how distant her father now seemed to her. She turned off the tape for a moment and groped for real memories, not these half-hallucinatory audio fabrications. What came to her was a time ten years earlier when she had been living briefly in San Diego, studying acoustic thermometry after receiving her doctorate in oceanography. She liked the work, skimming data gathered from marine mammal migration studies and from Navy seabed receivers to determine the temperature of the ocean by how fast sound signals traveled through the water. But a large part of her was restless and unfocused, addicted to achievement but unable to see the possibility of any resolving purpose in her life. She had had two reasonably serious boyfriends, a physicist back in Massachusetts and a show runner for a sitcom she had improbably hit it off with at a party in Los Angeles, but both relationships had dwindled inconclusively away. She had been a little bit in love with the physicist, but not enough, as it turned out, to follow him to London for his two-year fellowship. The show runner had been dynamic and driven, touchingly convinced that he was making a mark on the culture with his by-the-numbers comedy and its desperate laugh track, but when the show was canceled in mid-season he sent himself into a gloomy exile and stopped calling her, as if assuming his humiliation would be too searing for her to witness.

And maybe he was right. She could not ultimately have had much patience with a man who confused the routine failure of a sitcom with the annihilation of his soul. But it had hurt to be dismissed that way, it hurt to be alone and shaken in her confidence and judgment. And she felt, in her late twenties, that she was without definition in a crucial defining period of her existence. She had resolutely studied geology and oceanography, but she was impatient for her studying life to be over and her real life to begin and could not really see the point where that might happen. She liked acoustic thermometry, she liked going out to sea on research vessels, being part of an earnest team gathering data that might one day be useful in saving the world's oceans, but she could plainly foresee the time when this work would become tedious and maybe even empty to her, when the familiar academic surroundings in which her professional life would inevitably unfold would become an airless prison.

And on top of it all was a creeping insistence that unless she fell in love with someone worthwhile and became a mother the full scope of her destiny could never be realized in any case. The more she had pondered such concerns, the more she had felt a thrumming panic. The things she had to achieve seemed to her monumental. She not only had to discover who she was and what she should be, she had to find a way to make sure that any path she chose did not lead her away from the possibility of a meaningful, centered life with a husband and children.

That was the quietly turbulent mood she had been in when her father had flown in to San Diego one day to give a lecture at UCSD. She hadn't seen him in half a year, and when she met him at the airport she saw that he had finally started to gain back some weight. It had been five years since his heart bypass and the mysterious lingering depression that followed it. He still walked with the careful step that had replaced his once heedless and confident stride, but he was beaming as he emerged from the jetway, his hair not yet entirely gray, still haphazardly barbered in the styleless style of a liberal arts professor. He wore a blazer and khakis, and his usual workhorse wing tips had been replaced by a pair of feather-light Rockports whose thick soles added an inch to his rangy height.

There had been passing moments in Lucy's life when she had been a little afraid of her father, anxious about somehow producing the crestfallen look on his face that alerted her that in some inadvertent way she had disappointed him. But she had never disappointed him much, not even in the relatively benign way her sister had. Though by then Suzanne was firmly established in her first year of medical residency, she had let off enough steam in college to make their parents wonder out loud if she had embarked on a lifelong course of vengeful depravity just to punish them for raising her in a home where accomplishment and propriety were hallowed concepts that were enforced without discussion.

Lucy's father still held to rigorous standards, but he had softened in subtle ways—as subtle as the Rockports on his feet—in the years since his heart attack. The hug he gave her in the airport was firmer than she remembered, his manner less sharp, none of that quasi-sarcastic professor's tone that she remembered from her earliest childhood, when he had spoken to her and Suzanne the way he spoke to his university colleagues, as if they had come out of the womb sharing his opinions and professional exasperations. They had gone that night to a Mexican restaurant in Old Town and then for an evening stroll along the beach in La Jolla, her father quizzing her about her work and her future plans in his relentless parental way, until she had allowed herself to break into tears more or less just so he would get the point that she was unhappy and confused. He was respectfully silent after that, though she knew that this sort of routine unhappiness profoundly puzzled him, even after more than a quarter century as the sole male in a houseful of women. In his mind there was no problem that could not be resolved through resolution, and every obstacle was a hard and clear thing with a discernible path leading around it.

After it was dark and the steady stream of Rollerbladers and bicyclists had thinned out on the beach walk, he suddenly looked at his watch and stalked out onto the sand toward the water, turning around in circles so that he could survey every quadrant of the sky.

"What are we looking for this time, Dad?" she had said, remembering the many times throughout her childhood when he had dragged her and Suzanne out of bed on some black, cold night and hustled them out onto the lawn so that they could watch a meteor shower that never appeared as advertised.

"Just wait a minute," he replied in a somewhat testy voice. They stared up at the night sky. It was murky with light from the rising moon and from the streetlamps along the beach walk, and at just the moment when she was about to observe that any atmospherical phenomenon would be undetectable against this background of light pollution, she saw something startling. It was a brilliant streak of light, brighter than any comet or meteor she could ever have imagined, and it moved across the sky, into and out of their sight, in only moments. Its velocity was ungraspable; its direct, forward, and strangely purposeful momentum was unrelatable to her reasonably sophisticated understanding of celestial dynamics. As she watched, the streak it left behind began slowly to dissipate in the night sky.

"Impressed?" her father had asked.

"Okay," she said, "I confess to having no idea what that was."

"It was the shuttle."

"The space shuttle?"

"Coming back into the atmosphere, on its way to landing in Florida. What we saw was the ionization trail."

This bold streak of light moving swiftly across the night had left her, after all the no-show meteor showers and comets of her childhood, feeling magically disarmed. She and her father were both silent as they walked back to her Honda Civic in the parking lot. Just as she was unlocking the driver's side door, he spoke to her across the car roof.

"You could do that, you know?"

"Do what?"

"Be an astronaut."

She responded with a surprised little laugh, and that was about it. Her father said nothing more about it as Lucy drove him back to the hotel, and neither did she. But the word "astronaut" had lodged improbably in her mind. It had clarity and definition and an exalted heroic dimension that she had never before been conscious of craving. But her father, in his intuitive way, had known that what his daughter needed to be happy in life was a bolder and more distinguishing sense of self.

She had not bothered to reflect at the time on what this suggestion might have cost him. She had forgotten the gloom in his eyes a few years earlier when he was still trapped in his postsurgical depression and *Challenger* was exploding on television. But the fact was that he knew the risks, and that night on the beach in La Jolla something had made him willing to promote his daughter's happiness over her safety.

Now, as she listened to his voice commandingly sort through the history of eighteenth-century economic thought, it almost broke her heart to understand what a gift her father had given her that night. Though his career had been that of a tenured professor, he had made sure a pulse of adventure ran through the family's life. He had taken his children on recklessly expensive learning vacations to England and to Greece, he had included them in his dinner-table brainstorming about the authoritative economic textbook he had spent years writing, and when the book was never adopted he had showed them how to move with dignity from failure to new prospects. And finally, at a time in her life when Lucy had needed not just a goal but a dream, he had spoken up and supplied it.

It was not her father's fault that that dream now showed every sign of a slow, impending collapse. And the fact that he had had character himself did not mean that he had been a particularly acute judge of the character of others. Perhaps he had misread Brian in the same ways she had, thinking that his rectitude and ambition and capability were the outward manifestations of a solid core. When she brought Brian home for the first time, she searched her father's eyes, she parsed his comments, for any sense of qualification or hesitation. If he was wary, she would have seen it. But he was sick again by then, his mind cloudy from the side effects of his new medication, and maybe he lacked the spirit to question Lucy's choice of a husband at a time when it was plain to everyone she was about to lose a father.

At a word from him, she would have left Brian; just as, at a suggestion from him one April night, she had sent off to NASA for the application to become an astronaut and spent the next seven years achieving that goal with the unyielding concentration her father had taught her. Even now, though, she understood that it was a good thing that he had never put himself in the way of her marriage. All her life she had been too anxious to please her father. She needed to make her own mistakes. And she wasn't sure yet that she was ready to count her marriage to Brian as a mistake, not when it had given her Davis and Bethie.

The lecture closed with a promise that in the next tape Professor Thorne would explore in particular detail the works of David Hume and Adam Smith, and then there was the pattering sound of the canned applause, a cheerless note of approval that seemed to be coming now from some forlorn chamber in the afterlife.

Lucy took the tape out of the Walkman and put it back into its vinyl folder. She had heard the voice she wanted to hear, but its very strength made her feel more alone when she walked back into the bedroom to lie down next to Brian.

Chapter Seven

Gary Upchurch showed up at Sylvia Molina's birthday party fresh from a reenactment of the Battle of San Jacinto. He was wearing the Napoleonic-looking uniform of a Mexican soldier from 1836. He had a tufted shako on his head and was carrying a musket with an attached bayonet that was taller than he was, and that the hostess at Mucho Gusto made him surrender at the door.

"Let's pretend we don't notice," Kyle Olson said as Gary threaded his way over to their table past staring diners and waitresses carrying trays of sizzling fajitas.

They pretended they didn't notice, but Gary pretended there was no reason why they should. He squeezed out of his swallowtail tunic—he was, Walt calculated, about a hundred pounds too heavy to make a convincing Mexican soldier—draped it over a chair, kissed Sylvia confidently on the cheek, and presented her with an envelope.

"A gift certificate for one to AstroWorld," Mickey Flato said, reading the card over Sylvia's shoulder. "A very thoughtful gift for a woman on her thirty-fourth birthday."

"If she doesn't want to go alone, I'll be happy to accompany her," Gary said, as he signaled to the waitress. "And I'll even wear this."

"What?" Sylvia said. "Are you wearing something unusual?"

She held on to her deadpan expression with the precision of an actress, and as the others laughed Gary was forced to smile and raise his hands in what amounted to a "touché" gesture. Sylvia settled back in the booth and met Walt's eyes as she took a sip of her margarita. It was the barest glance. They all did it. After all their missions together, the members of his training team still habitually shifted their eyes in his direction as a way of checking up on their performance. It was possible, of course, since Sylvia was the only female member of the team, that there may have been some sort of undercurrent in her glance, but Walt did not trouble himself to really think so.

Sylvia was the systems instructor on the team. She had a sharp-featured face that would have been unattractively ferret-like were it not for her warm, inquisitive eyes. Her body was as slight as a ballerina's. She was small and limber enough to sit with her legs crossed Indian fashion on the narrow booth.

"Anyway," she said to Gary, "I hope that's not really a Mexican uniform, because your Latino cred is and always will be just about zero."

"Did she just call me a fat gringo?" he asked Walt.

"I've got to get something out of the car," Walt said.

He went out into the parking lot, got Sylvia's birthday cake out of the front seat of his car, took it back into the restaurant, and handed it to the hostess, who promised to light the candles and have it delivered to their table. Walt stood there for just a moment and, warmed by a solitary margarita, watched the members of his team as they bantered and drank and gobbled down chips and queso. He felt detached in a satisfying way, the way he assumed a parent might feel watching his children, safely grown, interacting with each other as functioning adults. It was not that he had raised these people, exactly, but he had formed his team and kept it together for six missions, fighting off various bureaucratic reshuffling initiatives and poaching attempts by other team leads. They had spent thousands of hours together in the control room in Building 5, running the scenarios used to train the astronauts in the simulator. By now, Walt's core team was a deeply coherent system, as silently efficient in action as an APU turbine wheel thruster or a multiplexer-demultiplexer. Inevitably, over time, the members of his team would be reassigned or promoted, or would move on into some private-industry job, but for now they had the inevitability of family. Walt was pretty sure he could keep them together for at least one more mission.

Gary, sitting in his flouncy white historical undershirt at the end of the table, was the instructor on Walt's team responsible for the data processing system. He was almost forty and had been something of a schmooze-boy when he first joined the team, starstruck and nervous in the presence of astronauts and a little too eager to be noticed. He had a sharp mind, however, not just for data-processing systems but for the equally intricate coding of human behavior, and Walt had seen him take on gravity over the years in subtle ways, showing unexpected warmth instead of his usual sarcastic dash and gradually morphing in his own mind from an eager squire for astronauts to an equal player in a common venture. Though Gary was pallid and overweight, he had managed to marry, at least for a time, a disconcertingly beautiful young woman who worked at the Armand Bayou nature center. But she had left him after falling in love with the author of a famous birding field guide who had visited the center one fatal day, and Gary had reverted to form and taken solace in various lonely-guy hobbies.

When Walt returned to the table, Kyle was on his third margarita and sitting back in the booth watching with glossy satisfaction as Sylvia opened the new LeAnn Rimes CD he had given her. She offered Kyle a high five to express her righteous gratitude, though if she had been less self-conscious she might have kissed him. At one point, a few missions back, there had been something going on between them, and though there had been some inscrutable moments in the control room, a few testy quips here and there, a few days when Sylvia had come to work in a state of charged silence, the affair had quickly worked its way out of the team's system.

Kyle was unattached these days as far as Walt could discern, and he probably preferred it that way. He was thirty years old, though his lean face and weary eyes made him look almost middle-aged. He was an aeronautical engineer, as many of the instructors who specialized in the control systems were, a graduate of Embry-Riddle who had found his way into space work and would no doubt stay on at JSC for the rest of his professional life. It was easy to see why things had not worked out between him and Sylvia. Kyle was inherently fastidious and cautious, tinkering in an engineering sort of way with every thought that passed through his head. In the control room, where such bloodless concentration mattered, he was indispensable, but it was clear enough to Walt that he would have made a tedious boyfriend.

When the birthday cake arrived, Kyle took the opportunity to ask the waitress for another margarita. Sylvia, in the act of gathering breath to blow out her candles, caught Walt's eye again, silently inviting him to agree with her that Kyle was on his way to becoming a real drinker. Walt answered with the slightest possible nod, but if she was looking to him to solve this incipient problem he had no idea how to go about it. Walt was pretty sure that Kyle's drinking went beyond the occasional happy hour indulgence like this one, but as far as work was concerned he was always punctual and twice as sober as he needed to be.

Walt had put only a random number of candles on the cake—maybe ten or twelve instead of thirty-four—and Sylvia dispatched them all with one breath as an impromptu chorus of waiters and waitresses gathered around and sang "Las Mañanitas," the Mexican birthday song that, even in this ragged version, was so much richer in melody and depth than its perfunctory American counterpart.

The icing on the cake was white, with luxuriant clusters of Texas bluebonnets on all four corners. Walt, noting the synthetic Crisco sheen of the icing, wished he had gone ahead and taken the trouble to order the cake from a real bakery instead of his local supermarket, but nobody seemed to mind, and nobody bothered to eat more than a few bites anyway.

"Any word on when they're finally going to make crew assignments?" Mickey asked.

"This week," Walt said.

"I need a mission," Gary said. "I need a mission for my sins."

"This week for sure?" Mickey pressed.

"Probably for sure."

"That was Martin Sheen who said that," Gary said.

"Martin Sheen who said what?" Sylvia asked with marked disinterest.

" 'I need a mission for my sins.' *Apocalypse Now.*"

"It's been almost a month," Mickey said, ignoring Gary. "I'm tired of running generic sims for ASCANS when we could be training a real crew."

"Plus the hours are shitty," Kyle said.

Walt nodded patiently. It was the standard between-assignments carping. When the team had no specific crew to train, their spirits naturally flagged. The work was far more interesting when there was something at stake, when an actual crew was going on an actual mission, and when the core team's job was to challenge them in the simulator with malfunction scenarios of increasing complexity and ingenuity. Training astronaut candidates, or unassigned astronauts who were just cycling through in the proficiency flow, meant running one canned scenario after another. And because such exercises always took a backseat in terms of scheduling to assigned missions, the team found themselves reporting for work in the control room at all sorts of inconvenient left-over hours.

They all knew which mission they would be working. STS-108 was scheduled for launch eleven months from now. Its main objective was to rendezvous with the International Space Station that was under con-struction and to transfer one of the Italian cargo modules from the pay-load bay of the shuttle to the Unity Node of the station. There would also be a spacewalk to install thermal blankets over the Beta Gimbal Assemblies at the bases of the station's solar wings, as well as a lighting stanchion or two. It was a relatively uncomplicated, straightforward mission, and Walt and the rest of his team had long since reviewed the flight requirement documents and studied the new versions of the pri-mary and backup software. All that was needed to make the mission real, to rescue their lives from aimlessness and set them on a path of coherence, was a crew.

"What do you want to bet that Surly ends up commanding it?" Mickey said.

"Surly's okay with me," Sylvia said. "They can put anybody on the crew they want except for you-know-who."

"Yeah, like Brian's ever going to fly again," Gary said.

"Let's not talk about this stuff in a restaurant," Walt said. The acoustics in the high-ceilinged, fake-cantina decor of Mucho Gusto were dreadful, but you could never be sure whether or not somebody might overhear you above the echoing din.

"What about his wife?" Kyle, who apparently hadn't heard Walt, asked. "Think Lucy'll get a shot anytime soon?"

"After the way Brian performed this time?" Gary said. "Dream on."

"It wasn't her fault," Mickey said.

"I'm not saying it was her fault. I'm just saying dream on."

"Guys," Walt admonished again, and this time they chose to hear him and the conversation veered off into more or less neutral territory. Walt half listened as at last they began to chide Gary about his uniform, and as Gary and Mickey, with Kyle abstaining, began to point out male diners in the restaurant who might be suitable prospects for Sylvia to marry before her thirty-fifth birthday.

Walt was still concerned about the goo that passed for frosting on the cake, still annoyed with himself for not taking the time to drive the extra few miles to the bakery, a gesture that Sylvia, lonely and steadfast, unquestionably deserved. He was thinking as well about Terry Bonds, inevitably nicknamed Surly after "High Flight," the inspirational poem ("Oh! I have slipped the surly bonds of earth / And danced the skies on" however-the-rest-of-it-went) that had been recited on television during Walt's youth to signal the end of the broadcasting day—back when broadcasting days had an end. He definitely wouldn't mind working another mission with Surly in command. A solid veteran like that helping to shape up the crew would make his life a lot easier.

He watched Kyle take another long sip of his margarita—almost a gulp. At what point do you take it upon yourself to stage an intervention with somebody, he wondered? Or were interventions already passé, one more bygone artifact of the therapeutic nineties, with all their chatter about healing and closure?

Mickey, Walt was glad to see, seemed to be healing in the old-fashioned way, with no fuss or blather. At twenty-six, he was the youngest member of Walt's team and except for Sylvia the most mature, happily married with a two-year-old girl, bouncing back from his recent operation for testicular cancer in better time and with better prospects than anyone had anticipated. He sat at the communications console in the control room, dependable and stoic, with an agreeable crispness of manner that he had honed in the Air Force. He had let it be known once or twice that he had thought about applying to be an astronaut himself. Walt could definitely see it, and maybe if the cancer didn't come back it would still be a possibility.

Mickey was tossing some bills onto the table, saying he had to make it home for his daughter's bath time.

"I've got it," Walt pushed the money back to him.

"You already got the cake."

"Don't worry about it," Walt said.

Mickey shrugged his thanks, gave Sylvia a birthday kiss on the cheek, and scooted out. Sylvia would leave next, Walt calculated, then Kyle, and then he would be left alone to listen to Gary's sardonic maunderings about sub-par video games or slipshod reenactors who had the disrespect to wear desert boots instead of period brogans.

"I better head out," he said.

"Are you giving somebody a bath too?" Sylvia said. She was sweeping up the various comic birthday cards that were strewn over the table. The sight of the cards and their pastel envelopes gave Walt a sudden regretful pang whose origin was a mystery to him.

"I just need to swing by the office."

He didn't need to swing by the office, he didn't need to swing by anywhere, but an insistent restlessness was part of his makeup these days. Much as he thought he craved conviviality, he had a limited tolerance for it, and he was feeling that this happy hour had run its course.

Sylvia felt that way too, apparently, because she gathered up her birthday cards and gifts and the remains of the cake and followed him out of the restaurant as Kyle and Gary settled in with an order of quesadillas and another round of drinks.

"You've got your wistful look," Sylvia said to him in the parking lot as he opened her car door for her. She was standing there holding the half-eaten cake in its clear plastic box, and on top of it the birthday cards whose festive colors still tugged at him in some obscure but disturbing way.

"I didn't know I even had a wistful look," he answered.

"It's true you're mostly sort of expressionless." She set the cake down on the passenger side of the front seat and stood back up to face him across the door he was holding open. "But every once in a while I can detect a little something."

"I'm wistful because it's your birthday and you're almost all grown up."

"In all seriousness."

"I'm okay, Sylvia. I'm just waiting for a crew assignment."

"Aren't we all?"

She kissed him on the cheek.

"I wish you'd take some of this cake home. Otherwise my dog and I are going to end up finishing it off."

"Can't help you."

Sylvia got behind the wheel and gave him a stern diagnostic look.

"All levity aside?" she said.

"All levity aside," Walt reassured her. He watched as she drove out onto NASA Road One, then as he headed toward his own car a violent surge of nausea overwhelmed him so suddenly that he kept on walking into a shallow drainage ditch beyond the edge of the parking lot and threw up onto the grass. He got down on his knees, hoping that he was out of sight beyond the rim of the ditch, and vomited again. Then he sat back on his heels to catch his breath and allow the cool prickly feeling in his forehead to subside.

A margarita. Chips and queso. A piece of disgustingly sweet birthday cake. What did he expect? He stood up, put his hands in his pockets, and walked back up to the parking lot as casually as he could, hoping that anyone who spotted him might just assume he had walked over into the drainage ditch for a closer inspection of some shorebird he had spotted there. Miraculously, no one seemed to have noticed. There were no windows on this side of the peeling stucco facade of the restaurant, and certainly no strolling pedestrians on this busy suburban byway.

It wasn't until he got home and started to empty his trash that he understood it wasn't entirely the margarita and the queso and the birthday cake that had been eating away at his well-being. It was the birthday cards he had seen splayed upon the table and in Sylvia's hands.

Because there in the trash was another one of those announcements. He had tossed this one into the wastebasket without looking at it when he had brought in the mail earlier in the day, but now that he was in a warped and punishing mood he took it out and opened it.

Sometimes the envelopes were blue. Sometimes they were pink. This one was pink, addressed to Rachel Womack. Walt had once told the mailman that Rachel Womack was deceased and asked him not to deliver any junk mail with her name on it, but his condominium complex was on a postal training route and there was a new carrier every couple of weeks, and he had better things to do with his life than to stand at the door and wait for each new mailman so that he could tell him that his wife was dead. Anyway, it had been a long time since he had gotten one of these. There had been a flurry of them a year or so ago, which would have been about a year after Rachel's final attempt to have a baby.

The announcements back then had been from infant formula companies, congratulating the presumed new mother and reminding her that although nothing could ever truly replace a mother's milk, their product offered the peace of mind that came with a satisfying and vitamin-rich substitute.

Walt didn't know how these companies had the name of his wife. But somewhere in all those dozens of doctor visits over the years, all of that blood work and testing, Rachel had entered a never-ending database, and so now at every developmental stage of their phantom baby, Walt—currently the only non-phantom in the family—received congratulations and a hearty sell for some product that would make his hectic parenting life easier.

This one was for training pants. "Our records show that Baby is now two years old!" the card announced. "Ready for the independence and confidence that comes with efficient toilet training."

Walt studied the card—regretfully, resentfully. It had a chain of infant silhouettes toddling hand in hand along the border, a photograph in the center of a triumphantly grinning baby modeling the manufacturer's training pants.

He reasoned that this would probably be the end of it, that training pants were the last items in the product line that these baby companies would bother to offer him for sale. With any luck, he would have no more cruel reminders of Rachel's desperate longing to have a baby, or of what he had thought of at the time as his patient pleadings to her to accept the fact that, after five emotionally brutal miscarriages, it was not going to happen. But he knew in his heart that his arguments had not been patient; they had been desperate in their own way, urgent attempts to lure her away from a fantasy that had begun to bewitch her, that had grown more rooted in her imagination with each new failure. It had seemed to him, at one alarming point after the last miscarriage, as she refused to listen to any comforting words, as her eyes took on a glazed ferocity, a cold willingness to challenge the odds again—and again and again after that until she finally had a baby in her arms—that she was truly deranged.

But after her death he had slowly begun to realize that it was at least partly his own exhaustion during that time that had led to this conclusion, his own impatience at her determination and his bewilderment at his own reaction to all those miscarriages. It was a reaction he would not have presumed to call grief, but each miscarriage was harrowing to him in some odd muffled way, and sapped him of the concentration and spirit he needed for his work. Walt had wanted to give up this hopeless quest to save Rachel from delusion, but also to save himself from her— from her insistence on continually staking their happiness on a dream that was defiantly not going to come true.

Walt had wanted his life back. He resented the howling emptiness that seemed suddenly to be at the core of Rachel's life, he resented everything she was willing to go through to achieve or safeguard her evanescent pregnancies: the constant ovulation tests, the frantic goal-oriented sex, the blood tests and progesterone suppositories and injections of fertility drugs that left her depressed and racked with headaches. He remembered the nights when her hormone levels had dropped and she woke up in a despairing night sweat, knowing she was losing the baby. He remembered watching with her as the prenatal heartbeat on the sonogram screen grew slower, day by day, until it disappeared. He could never possibly forget her screaming for him in the shower, the placental gore of an early miscarriage lying on the tile next to her feet.

Walt had been eager to have a child, hopeful about it, wistful when it did not seem to be happening, but he was an essentially cautious man and could not approve of Rachel's boldness or share in her obsessive focus. Her fortieth birthday had come during her last pregnancy, and every passing hour seemed to toll on the clock that kept merciless track of her disappearing fertility. She lived in constant apprehension of the signals her body would send her: the breasts that ominously ceased to be sore, the uterine cramps, the spots of blood on her underwear. In the weeks leading up to that last miscarriage, she had remained in bed desperately trying to kindle the fading life inside her, to protect it from any sudden movement, unable to wrest her mind away from the intolerable state of suspense that was her only security.

She would not even allow herself to consider adoption until they had eliminated every possibility, and to his growing despair he realized there was always another possibility, always one more experimental step involving dangerous transfusions or what seemed to him to be hopeless surgeries. When Walt told Rachel, finally, that he was through, she had reacted to the news in silence for a moment, coldly studying this former husband and ally who had turned in an instant into an antagonist. Then there had been a week or two of aggrieved sparring in which she had accused him of never actually wanting a baby in the first place, and said that beneath his outward concern he hid a cold and solitary heart. And maybe she had been right. Maybe the proof of his cold and solitary heart had been the fact that he held his ground in these bitter arguments, countering her emotional assaults with quiet logic, until he had at last been able to sense her silent capitulation. The end of the war came, as he recalled, after they had spent most of an entire Saturday in tearful argument, and afterward had driven together to Galveston to clear their heads and salvage their affection for each other. They had eaten dinner at Gaido's and then walked along the seawall, not speaking of anything, not saying a word, and it was during the course of that evening stroll that Walt understood that his arguments had prevailed and that Rachel had agreed to live with a broken heart.

Things had improved from that low point, of course. Once Rachel had allowed herself to begin seriously thinking about adoption, the grim suspense that had always accompanied her attempts to carry a baby to term began to recede, and the different challenges and more reasonable hopes of the adoption process engaged her energy in a way that struck Walt as healthy.

But something was wrong with their marriage. Certainly if she had lived and they had adopted a baby they would have moved beyond the flat and cordial tone that had come into their lives during that walk along the Galveston seawall, on the day he had withdrawn his support from her and she had, in her silent way, withdrawn her trust. But she had not lived, and so that tone had become an enduring and disquieting background feature of his life without her.

It had proved impossible for Walt to live with this echoing sense of rebuke and continue to believe he had been right. The intensity of her desire to have a baby was not something he had understood. It had frightened and annoyed him, and taken their lives to a higher pitch than he could comfortably tolerate. His noble impulse to save her from a deluded quest, he now realized, had been the most selfish act of his life.

Or at least that was the feeling she had left him with, the little trace of poison that still circulated in his memory of their life together. More than a year after Rachel's death, he was still struggling with a sense of harsh, arbitrary finality, living in an unconcluded state in which his worst self was preserved and her dearest hopes destroyed.

Now, staring at the training pants greeting card, he felt such a surge of anger at this mercenary company that he ripped the thing into confetti. Then he sprinkled the remains back into the wastebasket and emptied the wastebasket into a plastic garbage bag and sealed it tight with a twist tie as if there were some evil spirit inside whose escape he was determined to prevent. Then he carried the bag down to the Dumpster and walked out by the swimming pool, where there was a commodious bench looking out over Clear Lake. He took a seat as it began to grow dark and stared at the low-wattage beacon on the lighthouse across the lake and listened to the conversations of the people on the luxury boats as they cruised along in front of the condominium complex. The flat water amplified the strangers' voices to such a degree that he could hear every word—a wife telling her husband she'd found the binoculars after all, under the seat cushions—and felt intimately included.

Then, as if to extend the illusion, the wife caught sight of him sitting on the bench and waved genially, and called out in a reverberant voice, "Lovely evening, isn't it?"

"Lovely evening," he called back, and watched the boat glide down to its mooring somewhere deep in the narrowing margins of the lake. He saw a bird—a bittern?—prowling in the marsh grass at the edge of the lawn. The thought of that shredded greeting card lying sealed in the plastic garbage bag in the condominium Dumpster was beginning to seem satisfying to him. It was possible to be content again, if not exactly happy. All he needed was a crew.

Chapter Eight

A nd if you will refer to your packets," the woman was saying. Lucy referred to her packet. It included a glossy annual report whose charts were interleaved with the usual sumptuous nature shots and photos of smiling children of all ethnicities, and a binder with the company's logo embossed on the front.

"If you will refer to tab C in the binder, you'll actually see a slightly different configuration. You'll notice that this one allows for a few more trees, but I'd like to remind you again that trees are actually a questionable amenity when it comes to parking lots, given all the avian residue they tend to generate."

Yes, we get it, Lucy wanted to scream. Birds shit on cars. There were all sorts of astronaut jobs, various duties to keep people busy when they weren't assigned to a current mission or, as in Lucy's case, when they never had been. Most of the jobs lasted only a few months, and some were more interesting than others. Lucy had enjoyed working in crew equipment, or serving as a CapCom for the space station, and the time she had spent at Cape Canaveral as a Cape Crusader running various kinds of pre-launch interference for departing crews had been memorable and gratifying. But for the last few months she had been assigned to the Source Selection Board, locked off in a grim building on the hind end of JSC for weeks at a time as she and half a dozen other civil servants—none of whom were from the astronaut office—evaluated various proposals for government contracts on everything from garbage collection to video services.

This particular presentation—for a new staff parking lot—had been droning on for two and a half hours, and the woman who was making it was a stout and severe automaton in a red tartan jacket who seemed incapable of uttering a sentence that did not have the word "actually" in it. She was so hopelessly stuck on already antiquated business jargon that Lucy, just to keep her brain alive, had started jotting the terms down on her legal pad: "win-win," "out-of-the-box," "an exciting opportunity to extend our brand."

Rotating astronauts in and out of various jobs was officially regarded as a means of keeping skills and interests sharp and wide-ranging, but the real reason, Lucy and everyone else knew, was that there wasn't enough spaceflight to go around. There were 160 astronauts, four or five missions a year. NASA's budget had been severely reduced in the last few years, and as a consequence the space station—the only real destination for the shuttle—was manned at half strength. Fewer astronauts on orbit, fewer shuttle flights to build and service the station and rotate the crews, made Lucy's chances of getting a mission seem more and more like a receding dream. Meanwhile she found herself stuck in meetings like this one, helping decide who got contracts.

When the parking lot woman finally began to show signs of finishing her presentation, she gave them each yet another handout, this one about various water retention options for reducing the impact of impermeable cover on that portion of the Johnson Space Center's acreage that was designated for wildlife habitat. Lucy slipped the handout into the pocket of her binder, planning to study it over lunch, but the woman insisted on walking them through its obvious points one by one, a process that took another twenty tedious minutes.

It was finally over at twelve forty-five. There was another presentation in an hour and a half. Some of the board members were going to Fuddruckers for lunch, but Lucy decided to use the time for a quick workout in the astronaut gym. She dug a nutrition bar out of her purse and gnawed at it as she walked to the gym, a squatty institutional-looking building whose immediate neighbor was an imposing storage tank of liquid nitrogen.

Only a few other people were in the gym at this hour: Sam Warden, a mission specialist who had been the first in Lucy's astronaut class to get a flight assignment, was doing push-ups off an inflatable training ball. Elise Trube, the pilot on Brian's flight, smiled and waved hello to her as she hopped up and down on a balance beam. Lucy waved back but was glad Elise was in the middle of an exercise that required her concentration. It was still awkward for Lucy when she ran into the members of Brian's crew, and the last thing she wanted right now was to fall into an extended conversation that would inevitably lead to some roundabout reference to his performance on the mission.

She stepped onto the elliptical trainer and set the workout time for forty minutes. Forty minutes at her customary pace, according to the digital readout on the machine, was good for almost five hundred calories. Even allowing for the fact that the machine's projection was probably only a ballpark figure, she would still be coming out ahead, since the vile nutrition bar that had served as her lunch had only three hundred calories.

It made her angry with herself, the way she habitually ran through these dreary calculations. She was becoming as bad as Brian. But she had to stay in shape, she had to be ready for a mission if one ever came her way, and for vanity's sake she was still on her lifelong crusade to lose the seven or eight—well, maybe ten or twelve—unyielding pounds that resided in her hips and thighs. Brian, on the other hand, could probably gorge himself on barbecue and Mexican food as much as he wanted and never really gain any weight at all—an experiment that would never happen, since he took so much satisfaction in self-denial.

If she really wanted to burn calories, she knew, she should devote these forty minutes to weight lifting instead of a cardio workout, but she would do that tomorrow when she had more time. And she had grown fond of the elliptical trainer and its shuffling, cyclical motion. It was a pleasingly vapid way to work up a sweat, not having to count reps or wave hello to people on the jogging trail. Once she had rigorously listened to NPR on her Walkman as she exercised, but now she had patience only for her own randomly unspooling thoughts.

She was just settling into the lulling nowhere movements of the elliptical trainer, just starting to clear her head of the various proposed renderings of the new staff parking lot and of the officious woman in the tartan jacket when her cell phone rang.

"No, there's no reason in the world you should come in," Lorelei said, after stopping her heart with the news that Davis had had another episode at school. "He was just a little bit off his peak. All it took was one puff to straighten things out. He's back in Mrs. Ortiz's class and she's keeping an eye on him."

"You'll call me if there's any problem?"

"What do you think, Lucy?"

"And you've got Colleen's cell, if you can't reach me?"

"I've got your cell, I've got Brian's cell, I've got Colleen's cell, I've got Dr. Trimble's pager, emergency number, *home* number. I've got—"

"Okay, sorry."

"I just wanted you to know I'd given him a puff."

She checked the phone's battery and set it on the little shelf in front of the machine's readout and did her best to put Lorelei's phone call in perspective. There had, after all, been dozens of such calls in the last year and a half, and Lucy knew from experience that if Lorelei was not concerned there was no realistic cause for her to be either. But instead of the lazy, drifting thoughts she craved came the familiar focused anxiety about her son's health, a fear that stalked and shadowed every moment of her day no matter how disciplined she told herself she was being.

"How's the parking lot business?"

She had been staring at the blank wall on the opposite side of the gym and had not even noticed Shorty Boudreau standing beside her machine, mopping the sweat out of his eyes with a towel.

"The parking lot business is as challenging and satisfying as ever," she said.

"Want to stop by my office this afternoon? I've got something I want to run by you."

"Sure."

"Three thirty?"

"Fine."

"Good deal. See you then."

What was that about? Shorty Boudreau was the head of the astronaut office. He was a squinty-eyed space hero of the old school who had flown some of the earliest shuttle missions back in the eighties, and whose folksy nonchalance had turned out to conceal a strategizing institutional ambition.

There was something he wanted to run by her. Crew assignments for the next few flights were due to be announced, but she harbored no illusions about that. Half the members of her astronaut class had not yet flown, and her excruciatingly inconsequential job on the Source Selection Board had been a clear signal that she was not in line for a mission for at least a year.

It had to be about Brian, she decided. Maybe Shorty would lay out for her a summary of Brian's cloudy career, and under the guise of comradely and institutional concern ask for her help in shedding light on what might be causing his increasingly unproductive attitude. Maybe Brian was about to be outright fired, and Shorty just wanted to give Lucy a heads-up about it, and to assure her that it wouldn't have any effect on her prospects for a mission, though of course it would in ways that would be subtle but nevertheless thunderously clear. Maybe *she* was being let go. It was hardly likely, almost absurd, for NASA—after spending who knew how much money in training—to lay off an astronaut before she had even flown, but maybe a merciless new round of cuts had further reduced the staffing and construction budget of the space station, and as a consequence the number of shuttle flights per year had been, say, halved. In that case, Lucy, a rookie mission specialist with a problematic husband, would be more vulnerable than anyone else in the astronaut corps.

A half dozen disastrous scenarios were vying for credibility in her head by the time she arrived at Shorty's office. He waved her in through the open door and gestured to a chair. He was on the phone, talking in a clipped monotone to somebody at the NBL, pacing back and forth behind his desk and paying her no attention. Shorty was not short. He was five ten or eleven, with a crew cut and, in his early sixties, a buff body compromised only by a droopy underchin. His nickname had something to do with a short he had accidentally caused in an electrical buss during one of the early shuttle flights.

"Okay, just get it done," he said into the phone after a few more minutes. "I've got to go. I've got somebody here in my office."

He hung up, sat down, and scooted around to the side of his desk on his wheeled office chair.

"So, Lucy," he said, "how are things going?"

"Just fine."

"Brian holding up okay these days?"

"He's holding up pretty well, Shorty."

"Well, mistakes happen from time to time. The thing is to learn from them and move on, right?"

"Right," she said, not liking the way this was going. "But I'm not sure it's all that appropriate for us to—"

"So I just wanted you to know I had a talk with God yesterday," Shorty interrupted. "He wanted me to give you a message."

This could be even worse than she thought. Was God Doggett himself expecting her to help ease her husband out the door?

"A message?" Lucy replied in a cold, tight voice. She was preparing herself to rise out of her chair and launch into a lecture about weaselly, patronizing bureaucratic behavior, about the breathtaking male arrogance behind the assumption that they had the right to even talk to her about her husband's failings.

"He wanted me to ask you if you were ready to go up. Because we've got a slot for you on 108."

A fleeting, welcoming grin appeared on Shorty's face, and it took her a moment to catch up to its meaning, wrestling as she still was with the improbable words he had just uttered. There was a low humming in her ears, the same harbinger of unreality she had experienced when her mother had called to say her father was dead, or when the obstetrics nurse had handed Davis to her and she had settled his tiny shivering body against her warm breasts.

She took a breath and let it out carefully.

"Oh . . . Good," she said. "I mean . . . All right. Boy."

"It's a tight little mission," he said. "Unload the MPLM, bring the station crew some Doritos and ice cream. Put on those thermal blankets. Up and down in eight days."

"I know." She, like everyone else in the astronaut office, had read the descriptions of the upcoming missions and daydreamed about having a role in them.

"I haven't gotten Surly's final thoughts about who he wants to do the EVA, but my guess is you'll probably be up for a spacewalk. He's commanding. Tom Terrific's the pilot, and the other mission specialists are Buddy Santos and Patti Halapeska and Chuck Nethercott. Sound okay?"

"Sounds okay."

"When are you guys finishing up the RFP on the parking lot thing?"

"Tomorrow."

"Good. So we'll pull you off the Source Selection Board and send you right into quals. You'll get your flight assignment from Surly. We done?"

"We're done," Lucy said, rising from her chair and accepting Shorty's abrupt handshake. She left his office with the world still spinning around her and had not even reached the elevators when her cell phone rang. It was Surly Bonds, congratulating her and saying how excited he was to have her on the crew and wondering if they could all get together at the Outpost tomorrow night to celebrate and go over their assignments.

It was four o'clock. There was some paperwork she had to catch up on, some calls she had to make. But she knew how fast word about the assignment would get out. Soon she would be surrounded by other astronauts who would be eager to congratulate her, or in some envious cases just make a show of doing so. That was fine, but she wanted this perfect moment for herself.

She was going into space.

She drove to Bay Area Park, parked, and walked over to a concrete picnic table overlooking the water. The park was nearly empty at this hour, the air a bit sharp and wintry. Mesmerizing gray clouds, coasting in from the bay, were slowly sealing the sky, and their steely clarity gave even sharper definition to the pelicans loping along in the confined dome of air below them.

Lucy wanted to feel happiness, and sitting there on that picnic bench, staring out at the water and then at the carpet of fallen oak leaves at her feet, she tried hard to. But there was a moody edge to her thoughts, new anxieties slowly coming into focus. When her phone rang, and she saw that the number on the caller ID was Brian's, she didn't answer it, wanting to buy herself just a little more time. For what? By now he had probably already heard the news. He was calling to congratulate her, to tell her he loved her and was proud of her and not to worry about the kids, he would take care of everything. Those were the words he would say, but as he said them she would hear the bitter, competitive undertone, and it would not be long before he would be telling her to watch out for the treachery and indifference that were built into the whole system, about how everybody was out to save their own ass and how she had to know that and understand it if she didn't want to be sacrificed for somebody else's incompetence. He would want to advise her, to make a gift of his poisonous experience, and that sort of advice was the last thing she wanted right now.

But she had already assumed once today, when she first received Shorty's summons, that ugly developments were in the works—that her first flight was not just a long way off but was being deliberately withheld from her because of some vestigial resentment, some internecine complication, over Brian's troubled career. Now she realized that God Doggett and Shorty Boudreau and everybody else involved with the decision had chosen to do the exact opposite. They had made a point of judging her on her own merits and not on her husband's shortcomings. And those merits, she allowed in this moment of mellow candor, were pretty damn good. It was just a question of admitting her worth to herself, and remembering something that Brian seemed to have forgotten: people could be fair.

As a matter of fact, in anticipating how Brian was going to react she was allowing herself to fall into the same cynical forecasting that was his least appealing feature. It was petty of her, it was supremely damaging to whatever level of trust they still shared, not to call him back immediately.

She was about to do so when the phone rang again. That would be Brian, she thought, trying once more. But it wasn't.

"Hi. Lucy?"

The voice was familiar, but not so familiar she could recognize it at once.

"This is Walt Womack. I just wanted to call and congratulate you."

"Thank you."

"And to let you know that by the time you launch, you and the rest of the crew are going to be pretty sick of me."

He spoke up again, to fill the puzzled silence.

"Because my team's been assigned to your mission."

Chapter Nine

Don't tell the kids yet, okay?" she said to Brian over the phone as she was driving home.

"Why not? They're going to be proud. They're going to be excited. Just like I am."

"I just want to think about how to tell them."

"Fine," he said. "It's your flight. You call the shots." His tone had flattened just a bit. She could feel the effort in his voice to sound thrilled and selfless, and she appreciated that effort. She had not quite expected it.

"So how are we going to celebrate?" he asked.

"I've got a few minutes. I'll swing by Seabrook and pick up some shrimp. We can all have dinner together."

She knew that Brian would rather go out. So would she, really. Going to a restaurant, being out among other people, took some of the pressure off, made them feel less isolated than when they sat at the kitchen table at home. Even with the kids at the table to distract them, Lucy always felt that she and Brian were alone in the harsh glare of solitude, that she bore the responsibility to coax him into conversation, to subtly introduce a new topic when it began to seem that he was drifting toward resentment or regret. But it was important to her that the four of them eat together as a family in their own home—especially important tonight. She wanted Brian and the children with her tonight in a cocoon of normalcy. She didn't want to tell Davis and Bethie about the mission yet because she knew, in a way that Brian did not, that there was too fine a line between celebration and anxiety, and that this might be the last time in a long while that the kids could sit down to dinner without vague oppressive thoughts intruding upon their minds.

"Whatever you want," Brian repeated. "Been getting a lot of calls?"

"I've been beeped three times already while I've been on the phone with you."

"Well, that's because everybody wants to congratulate you. They know that nobody deserves it more than you do."

His hard-won generosity truly touched her. She opened her mouth to tell him how much it meant to her to hear him say that, but she choked on the words, and tears suddenly spilled into her eyes.

"I'm just a little bit emotional," she said. "And anyway, I better not talk while I'm driving."

"Whatever. I love you, you know."

"I know," she said. "I love you too."

She drove down NASA Road One to the highway, then turned right and looped under the bay bridge, where there was a haphazard assemblage of seafood restaurants and fish markets stretched out along shell roads. In the parking lot of Rosie's, she listened to the three messages of congratulation she had just received while talking to Brian—one from Bill Kokernot, one from Cyndi Ludlow, who had graduated in Lucy's astronaut class, and one from the awkward and evasive God Doggett himself—"Just wanted to let you know we're all wishing you a great training run and a great mission. You're in good hands with Surly and Walt and, uh, well, okay . . . good-bye."

Rosie's was an exquisitely nondescript wooden building, almost a shack, and though it was a Vietnamese-owned business situated on the Texas coast it never failed to work on Lucy's native consciousness, to trigger a Yankee nostalgia for things that were raw and weather-beaten and plain. Inside, she studied the various bins of mounded, glistening seafood and finally told the boy behind the counter she wanted three pounds of medium-sized brown shrimp. He gathered them up with a metal scoop, weighed them on a scale, and poured them into a plastic bag half filled with ice. She bought a box of shrimp boil as well, just in case, though she had more ambitious plans than mere boiling. She would peel the shrimp, sauté them in olive oil and garlic, make a nice

salad with sliced avocado and a simple dressing, along with new pota-
toes and onions drizzled with oil and baked in the oven.

She hadn't really cooked in a long time. For the kids' sake, she had
always tried to maintain a semblance of a more or less normal workday,
but the time she and Brian arrived home depended on what jobs they
were assigned to or where they were in the training flow. Nevertheless,
she had managed to have them all sitting down to some kind of meal
together on most days of the week, even if that meal was eaten in a fast-
food restaurant or was thrown together at home from remnant Lean
Cuisines or pre-bagged salads or Sara Lee desserts. Now, of course, it
was going to be worse. Before she could even begin training for the mission she had just been assigned to, she would have an intimidating three-
week series of qualification lessons in the single-system trainer, and
after the quals she and the rest of the crew would be in the full-scale simulators in Building 5 for long, unpredictable hours, running increasingly complex scenarios, and on top of that—if she was indeed doing a
spacewalk—there would be intense training for that in the Neutral
Buoyancy Lab, and when her days were not filled with sims and EVA
work there would be training in a dozen other tasks, from escape procedures to the use of the space potty.

She was glad that the core training team, the one that would take
her through ascent and entry and orbital exercises in the simulator,
would be led by Walt Womack. He had more experience than anyone
else and also seemed to have a basic alertness to the nuances of human
behavior, the kind of natural empathy that was rare enough in the
ambition-saturated terrarium of the space center. She was glad for
another reason as well, one that she thought it best not to try to define.

On the way home Lucy stopped at a bakery and bought Davis and
Bethie each a garishly decorated cupcake, and resisted the temptation to
get one for herself. There was no question of buying one for Brian. In his
guilt and depression over his disastrous mission, he had embarked upon
a familiar program of ascetic denial, casting himself into some wilderness of his own making where he could be suitably purified. This process
involved a lot of solitary running on the JSC track, a lot of solemn sitting around. Indeed, by the time Lucy got home, Colleen had already
left and Brian was sitting in front of the television with Bethie in his lap,
both of them staring at *Sesame Street* as if they were trying to decode
some puzzling message from another planetary system. Davis was on
the hardwood floor with his action figures, lying on his back and hold-

ing up Milo Thatch and squinting at the silhouette the figure made against the afternoon sunlight pouring in from the sliding glass door. All three of them were so deep in odd contemplation they didn't even notice when she entered the house.

She took the opportunity to make a quick assessment of Davis. He seemed logy and contemplative, but showed no signs of fatigue or straining for breath, so the one puff of albuterol that Lorelei had given him had clearly been enough to get him past that morning's mild irregularity in his breathing. He hadn't had a significant episode in almost a month, and Lucy was beginning to allow herself the faint hope that maybe his developing lungs were outpacing his asthma.

The sound she made when she set her keys down on the counter was enough to distract Bethie's attention from Elmo.

"Mommy!" she called, then slid out of her father's lap and ran over to grab Lucy around her knees.

"You better give me a hug too, mister," Lucy said to Davis, who was still on the floor studying some detail of Milo Thatch's molded face.

"What about Dad?" Davis said.

"Him too," Lucy said, lowering her voice and exchanging a complex look with Brian, who was just rising out of his chair.

"We all better give her a hug today," he said. "You know why?"

"Why?" Davis asked.

"Because it's a special day. A really special day for your mother."

"Brian," Lucy cautioned.

"Is it your birthday?" Bethie whispered into Lucy's ear as she lifted the child into her arms.

"No, honey, it's not my birthday."

"Well, what is it?" Davis demanded.

"I can't tell you right now. I'll tell you tomorrow."

"Why can't you tell us now?"

"Because I just can't, okay?" she said, cutting her eyes toward Brian with a thanks-a-lot look. "Anybody want shrimp for dinner?"

Brian worked beside her in the kitchen, peeling and deveining the shrimp while she made the salad.

"Sorry," he said after a time. "Guess I got a little overexcited."

"It's all right."

"I thought you were going to tell them when you came home."

"I just want to wait."

"Why?"

She shrugged. The truth, the really terrible truth, was that she didn't want to tell them while Brian was around. Without question, she trusted him with their physical safety, but she knew all too well his emotional obtuseness, and thought the fine calibrations of manner and expression that would make them feel secure when she delivered this news might be beyond his reach. On the other hand, she had no real idea what those calibrations should be, what words she should use. But she knew with a mother's instinct that she would require at the very least a quiet and expansive moment, not the giddy celebratory one that Brian, in his over-compensating way, kept rushing to propose.

"Anyway, you couldn't do any better than Surly," Brian said, keeping his voice low, though Lucy still worried that the children might hear them from the living room and guess what they were talking about. "I hope they put you together with a good core team."

"It's Walt Womack's."

"No shit? Great."

He finished peeling the last of the shrimp and, fastidious as always, put the carapaces in a plastic bag and closed it with a twist tie. "You know, I have to say I'm really kind of surprised. I thought . . ."

"What?"

"You know, that they'd be punishing you to get at me."

"I really don't think that's the way it works."

There was enough testiness in her voice for Brian to throw his hands up in a mock I-surrender gesture. He took the bag of shrimp shells out to the garbage, and in another twenty minutes they were all sitting at the table, neither Lucy nor Brian talking much, or looking at each other, just smiling indulgently at Davis as he told them about how Jeffrey Toomey had thrown up on his desk at school. He made such authentic retching sounds that Bethie almost choked on a shrimp with laughter, and Lucy had to restrain Davis before his fit of silliness spiraled out of control.

The innocent chaos, the poignant illusion of an average American family at dinner, clawed at her heart. Part of her was still in a state of glorious disbelief, constantly having to reaffirm to herself that she had really had the meeting with Shorty, that he had really told her that she was being given a mission; but part of her was aware that in accepting this assignment—in *wanting* it—she was casting a shadow over her family, a shadow whose reach could not yet be reckoned. And she understood that her sudden impulse to buy shrimp and make dinner with her own hands, her reluctance to announce to her children that she would be leaving them on the earth and flying into space, was a way of trying to seize and hold on to a benign normalcy that their family had never really possessed.

When she presented them with their cupcakes Davis used the occasion to ratchet up his giddiness, boinging all over the house in a mock dance of gratitude. Lucy was about to turn herself to the task of settling him down when Brian suddenly scooped him up, grabbed Bethie as well, and announced that he and the kids were going out for a while.

"Going out where?"

"On a secret mission. Right, guys?"

He slipped out the door with a giggling child under each arm. Lucy remained seated on the couch, the house all at once so provocatively still and silent she felt marooned in it. She stood up and walked into the kitchen, reflected for a moment, picked up the phone and dialed her mother's number.

"When?" was her mother's simple response when she heard the news. Lucy could hear her trying to be brave, to be hale and congratulatory, but there was such defeat and dread in her inflection of that one word that Lucy instantly understood she would not have a full night's sleep until the mission returned safely to earth. Her mother was not a fearful person. She had ceded the constant anticipation of tragedy to her more fatalistic husband, and during Lucy's and Suzanne's childhoods she had been indifferent about seat belts and lax about imposing any restrictions on the use of their backyard trampoline, so that sometimes five or six children were jumping at once, knocking their heads together and springing off for a hard landing in the grass. But spaceflight was different, and Lucy's mother would have been a fool not to realize it.

"Not until next September, Mom," Lucy answered. "Between now and then there's almost a whole year of training."

"Well, you know how happy I am for you," her mother said, slowly getting her emotional footing back. "How proud I am. And your father! My God, he would be beside himself. He *is* beside himself, I guess. Somewhere."

Her mother's watery religious impulses had never found expression in their pragmatic household, but after her husband's death she had begun to grope for some sort of intellectually respectable notion of the afterlife, and this was not the first time she had referred to a nebulous counterworld in which the dead might reside. But Lucy could feel it too: her father's approving, beaming presence, as powerful and mysterious as his voice on the economics tapes, all the scattered and inert molecules of his being somehow cohering one final time to witness his beloved daughter's triumph.

"Does Suzanne know?" her mother was asking.

"I'll call her in the morning. I haven't even told the kids yet. So. Are you okay, Mom?"

"I'm just . . . well, you know. I love you and I'm thrilled for you, but I'm just kind of bouncing around all over the place here. Overwhelmed, choked up, nostalgic, *worried*."

"Don't be worried."

"Tell you what, honey. You try not to worry when Davis or Bethie gives you a call someday and announces they're going up in a rocket ship."

"Do me a favor, Mom. Don't call it a rocket ship."

"Space vehicle. Whatever. My God, Lucy . . ."

"What?"

"I just hope you know what a remarkable person you are."

"I'm not so remarkable. But thanks for saying so, Mom."

There was still a quaver in her mother's voice when she said good-bye. Hanging up the phone, Lucy knew she would have to do better with the children. She would tell them tomorrow evening. She couldn't let it go any longer than that, but the moment had to be right, the words somehow steadier than they had been just now with her mother. She wanted to avoid a tone of labored reassurance, to communicate the excitement she felt. She wanted her own joy to touch her children and shelter them from fear.

And it was joy she was feeling, beneath and between her current strata of emotions. She was an astronaut. She was not the sort of person who would lose sight of her goals. But the years of waiting for a mission; the temporal and psychological interruptions of having children; the cyclical tedium of the training flow that kept her yearning sharp but her progress obscure; the haunting question of Brian's status in the program, which she could not detach, try as she might, from his worth as a husband; and finally the stalking shadow of Davis's health: all these distractions had been her companions for so long that they had muted her vibrant ambition to go into space.

A part of her elation, in fact, was the discovery that that ambition was still alive. In her official NASA astronaut biography, there was a paragraph stating that she had dreamed of traveling in space ever since she was a young girl staring up at night into the heavens. But for whom was that not true? Everybody stared up at the night sky, everybody longed to see other worlds. It was not a mystical aspiration that separated astronauts from the rest of humanity, but a grinding need for achievement. Why had Brian wanted to go into space? As far as Lucy knew, he had never had a wondrous thought in his life, but even in childhood he had made it his business to know every constellation, every nebula, the track of every wandering comet. It was the testing of himself—landing at night on a carrier deck, deploying a payload with the satellite arm—that ultimately mattered.

She shared with her husband that relentless need to perform and achieve, but she sensed that the true source of her desire to visit space lay somewhere else. She had seen hints of it during her fieldwork in oceanography, diving on reefs and trying to comprehend the other-worldly life that throbbed all around her, observing from underwater the strange thermoclines and haloclines that split the ocean into eerily distinct planes, like two separate realities abiding next to one another. Hovering underwater in the middle of the blank ocean, she glimpsed infinity in a way that she never had on solid land, and glimpsed as well the poignant limitations of her human perceptions. Once, at eighty feet below the surface, she had come across a tiny fish, a goby, clinging to a piece of coral. It was a sort of fish that rarely swam, that spent most of the day motionless at its station, staring upward, no more capable of reaching the distant vault of the ocean's surface than Lucy was of flapping her arms and flying into the stratosphere. The magnitude of what this fish did not know of what was overhead, an entire creation with continents and cities peopled with air-breathing life-forms whose existence it would never come close to perceiving, had intrigued Lucy. She had been a little high anyway from the effects of breathing compressed nitrogen at that depth, but as she began to surface and the nitrogen narcosis wore off, the understanding that there was a world beyond her knowing took root in a way it never had before. And after her father, on the beach at La Jolla, had suggested to her that she could become an astronaut, she began to think of herself as that goby, somehow casting off the limitations of its biology and rising to the top of the sea and poking its morose, bug-eyed face through the surface for a look around.

To know the thrill of that skyward journey; to experience what true sustained weightlessness was like; to look down on the bright, rotating earth, rising from the cosmic darkness and then subsiding back into it, like a whale's back wheeling into sight from the ocean depths. To see beyond the veil. She had forgotten how much she wanted that. Her instincts as a mother had warred against it, had in fact begun to win the battle. But now she had gotten her mission.

"We got you a present!" Bethie screamed when she ran through the door a half hour later.

"You got me a present?"

Bethie, with an almost delirious smile on her face, handed Lucy a small gift-wrapped rectangular box.

"So what's the occasion?" Lucy glanced at Brian, who was just now entering the house behind his children. She could not help regarding him with a degree of suspicion. If Brian had gone ahead and told the children about the mission after all, she was not sure she would ever be able to forgive him.

"No occasion," he said firmly, his eyes telling her he had kept his word. "We just thought it was time to show you a little appreciation."

"We went to James Avery," Davis said.

"Don't tell her!" Bethie yelled. "It's a surprise!"

Lucy sat down on the edge of an armchair, and Bethie climbed up beside her while she removed the wrapping, revealing, as Davis had blurted out, a box from the James Avery jewelry store in the mall.

"Open it!" Bethie commanded.

Lucy lifted the lid. Inside was a bracelet with a single charm: a miniature silver space shuttle.

"Well, it's just beautiful," Lucy said, as Bethie took charge, removing the bracelet from the box and, with a concentrated frown, slipping it onto her mother's wrist.

"Dad picked it out," Davis said.

"It's because you're an astronaut," Bethie informed her, finally managing with her clumsy child fingers to close the clasp.

"Your father has excellent taste. And he and I have two wonderful, beautiful children."

She would tell them tomorrow night, she vowed once again. She would tell them at dinner, after she'd had the whole day to catch her breath and ponder the least disturbing way to break the news. That meant another day, of course, in which she ran the risk of having Brian seize the initiative, just blurting it out that, guess what, their mother was flying off into outer space; but he would be at work all day himself, at his on-ice job at the Safety Board, reviewing vehicle upgrades.

The next morning she drove Davis to school herself. Bethie would go with Colleen an hour later. She wore her new charm bracelet. Except for her wedding band and earrings, she had never really worn jewelry, and the loose pressure of the bracelet on her wrist felt foreign to her, and maybe a little contradictory to the unadorned, unimpressed professional mien she usually strove to project. But her children had given it to her, and so that was all there was to it.

She caught Davis out of the corner of her eye staring at the shuttle charm swaying from her wrist as she drove.

"This is about the best thing anybody's ever given me," she said, smiling warmly at him, but his attention didn't stray from the charm.

"How come Dad wanted to get you the space shuttle?" he asked after a moment. They were stopped at a light. A block ahead, past a strip mall, was the school, with the yellow buses lined up at the curb and the crossing guards stepping out into the street with their lowered flags.

"Well, because he knew I'd like it. And because going up in the space shuttle is what your father and I do."

"You don't."

"Well, I haven't yet. But that doesn't mean I won't one of these days."

"Are you going up soon?" His voice was suddenly quavering with apprehension. The light was still red. When Lucy shifted her eyes to look at her son, she saw he was staring rigidly ahead, bracing for the answer. It was unthinkable to lie to him.

"Not soon, sweetheart," she said. "In about a year."

"So that's why Dad wanted to give you that charm? Because you got a mission?"

"That's right."

The light changed, and the line of cars began to move forward. Davis said nothing, but when Lucy looked at him his lip was trembling and helpless tears were starting to well up in his eyes.

"Davis? Honey?"

He was doing his best to hold himself together, mortified at breaking into tears so close to school, but in just a moment more he was hiccuping with the effort to hold back his sobs. She pulled out of the line of traffic into the parking lot of the strip mall and unfastened her seat belt so she could hold him, but he fought her embrace and looked woodenly out the window as the tears flowed out of his eyes.

"What's the matter, sweetheart?" she asked, though it was clear to her what was going through his vulnerable mind: his mother soaring into the sky in a tower of flame, heading toward the ultimate darkness of space while he stayed behind, abandoned, on the earth. How could she have ever thought she could withhold this solemn information from him until she was ready to deliver it on her own timetable? Hadn't she learned by now, after seven years of motherhood, that children were alert to every wobble and tremor in the taut family atmosphere? Brian had certainly jumped the gun, with his abrupt congratulatory air and mysterious nighttime shopping trip, but Lucy knew it was she who was to blame for thinking that the longer she postponed her news the more chance she had to somehow make it seem less threatening to her children. Now, caught off guard, she groped and fumbled for words of reassurance.

"It's not for a year," was the best she could do, counting on a child's perspective of the enormity of time to at least temporarily calm his fears.

"I know," he said.

"And I'm only going to be gone eight days, Davis. That's only a week. I've been gone longer than that before. Remember when I went to the Cape last summer? I was gone a whole ten days, and I missed you every single day, but you and Bethie and your dad and Colleen did just fine, didn't you?"

He didn't answer. He furiously rubbed his cheeks with the heel of his hand, still looking away, and when Lucy tried to wipe his tears with a Kleenex he curled up tighter against the door, maybe angry, maybe embarrassed, but shutting her out all the same.

"Are you worried about me going up into space?" she asked.

"No."

"Are you sure?"

"I'm sure."

"Then what's wrong?"

"I don't know." He said this with an explosive, frustrated emphasis, and Lucy backed off, merely stroking his hair with her hand until the crying subsided. The hiccups died away too, and she listened carefully to his breathing, worried that this emotional eruption might trigger an asthma attack. But his breathing was steady, and after a few moments the tears were gone and he announced in a distant voice that he wanted to go to school.

"Are you sure? We can talk a little bit more if you want to."

"No. I want to go to school."

So she took him to school, watching from the car as he walked bravely under the weight of his backpack, its Boba Fett keychain dangling from the end of the zipper. Davis joined the stream of other children and disappeared through the front door, seemingly untroubled now, his inchoate fears absorbed into the activity and routine of a new day at school. Lucy pulled away, one more mother in a long drop-off line of minivans and Suburbans, and then drove slowly to work, to begin her qualification lessons for her mission. She had blown it, she had broken the news to him, somehow, in exactly the wrong way. But what troubled her more than her performance was the fear that there was no *right* way to tell a little boy that his mother was going where Lucy was going—not just to an achingly distant place, but to another dimension. If space was so darkly enticing to Lucy, what must it seem like to a seven-year-old boy? All at once she saw her destination through his innocent eyes, and pictured a realm that was familiar and alien at the same time, infinitely black, infinitely still, the well of nothingness out of which he suspected he had risen into being, the same void that patiently waited to reclaim him and everyone he loved. Why would his mother, why would any mother, voluntarily leave her child to travel to such a place, a place that was as blank as death, and in whose perfect soundlessness his cries to her were sure to go unheard?

Chapter Ten

He was back in business, back in the simulator instructor station in Building 5. Standing in front of his console, speaking through his headset, making notes in the logbook spread open on his desk, Walt felt like a conductor returning to the stage after a listless hiatus. The chatter coming in over the loop was nothing like music, of course, and the four members of his training team, staring at their computer screens with their backs toward him, were nothing like an orchestra. But he was the maestro of this crucial exercise, in which the crew of STS-108, having received their flight assignments and passed their qualifying exams and memorized the Assigned Crew Study Guide, were working together in the simulator for the first time.

They were doing ascents and entries in the motion-based simulator, which from the outside resembled a jerky, boxy carnival ride. It was stationed along with the other simulators in a cavernous warehouse space more or less adjacent to where Walt's team was working. But there were no windows in the control room, and the astronaut crew was out of Walt's sight. They were just voices over the loop, the way they would someday be to the mission controllers monitoring their actual flight in distant space.

During the months of training, Walt and his team essentially played the part of Mission Control, helping the crew rehearse the part they would soon enough be performing for real. Walt's core training team had a straightforward teaching function, but there was a formalized maliciousness to their work as well, an adversarial undercurrent. Not so much today, when the script they were following was boilerplate and short on surprises, but in the months to come not only would the basic exercises become much more complex but the members of Walt's team would take on a role of Olympian mischief, hurling down glitches and malfunctions and all-but-unwinnable scenarios that would make the crew fight for their virtual lives on the flight deck of the simulator. Walt had a plentiful supply of thunderbolts already built into the upcoming scripts, but he made a point of keeping these scripts as loose as possible, so that they adhered to basic themes of ascent and entry, rendezvous and docking, but were overall as accommodating to improvisation as a jazz chart.

Walt glanced at his watch. It was already eight o'clock at night, and they had another two hours to go, with a Transatlantic Abort Landing and an Abort Once-Around on the schedule. He had eaten a donut from a box that Surly Bonds had brought to the pre-brief, but he had not had dinner and was starting to feel the mild ravenousness that was inseparable from the sense of preoccupied well-being that he often experienced in the control room.

This first simulation was, more than anything, a chance for Walt to observe how the crew might function as a team. It was necessarily an imperfect exercise, since two members of the six-person crew—Chuck Nethercott and Patti Halapeska—were not even in attendance. As Mission Specialists 3 and 4, they rode in the shuttle's mid-deck, just below the flight deck, and had no real duties until the vehicle reached orbit. At the moment Chuck and Patti were going through habitability training while the rest of the crew did their ascents and entries. Even with only four people, the flight deck of the motion-based simulator was a cramped and stressful place, particularly so during the first few runs. So far, Walt liked what he saw well enough. As far as mission commanders went, Surly Bonds was pretty close to the gold standard: good-humored, generally imperturbable, a top gun fighter pilot who had seen dozens of his friends auger into the ground but who nonetheless appeared to have coasted through life without an anxious thought.

"Uh," Walt heard Lucy Kincheloe saying to Surly now over the loop. "Before we shut down the APU? I just wanted to check to make sure we got the MPS/TVC ISOL valves closed."

"Oops, my mistake," admitted Tom Terassky, known to the crew as Tom Terrific. This was Tom's first mission as pilot, and Walt expected him to be a little nervous on his maiden sim. He had closed the valves but forgot to call it out, a reasonable mistake in an otherwise nominal ascent. Nevertheless, Walt noted it in his logbook. And by Lucy's name he made a note about communication skills: that "uh" and her hesitant, interrogatory tone about the APU shutoff needed addressing in an environment where sharp, impossible-to-misinterpret declarations were crucial. But he also wrote "Good S.A.," meaning situational awareness. She was alert to everything that was going on, and wasn't afraid to point out a problem to the commander, even though as MS1 she was expected to essentially say nothing during the ascent.

"OMS-two cut-off," Surly was saying. "We have achieved orbit, over."

"Good deal," Walt said. "Let's run it again."

In the simulator, Lucy sat on the right side of the flight deck, in the seat behind the pilot, studying her checklist. It was T plus 2 minutes and 30 seconds, just after the separation of the solid rocket boosters. She and the crew were canted upward in the flight deck, rocketing into a blue sky with scraps of moving cloud that were projected onto the orbiter windows. From her seat behind Tom, Lucy had a congested view of the windows, but it was a better view than she had expected. She had assumed, when she was first named for the mission, that she would be riding down in the mid-deck, where there were no windows at all. But as it turned out it was Chuck and Patti—Mission Specialists 3 and 4—who would be traveling to space in the shuttle equivalent of steerage. Surly had given Lucy the MS1 slot, and so she would be in the center of the action during launch and entry. She would be able to see with her own eyes, when the moment finally came, that she was truly leaving the earth.

Now, of course, she was experiencing only the best approximation of the experience that $100 million or so of taxpayers' money could buy. It was still a pretty good ride, she thought. Brian had told her not to even bother trying to imagine how the actual launch would compare. The real thing was impossible to describe. He had tried to tell her and the kids numerous times, but he ended up either staring into space or falling back on some bled-out term like "awesome" or "amazing."

Anyway, it was not her job to bear witness, much less to invent a vocabulary for the inexpressible. Her job was to focus on the checklist, to monitor the launch procedures and make sure that everything got done. So far, she thought she was batting five hundred. Her communication discipline, when she had spoken up during the last run, had been dreary. She had winced even as the words about the Auxiliary Power Unit had come out of her mouth. Where had that nervous Chatty Cathy voice come from? On the other hand, she had noticed, when nobody else had, that Tom had forgotten to do the callout before the APU shutdown. Surly, in the commander's seat in front of her, had turned and given her an approving wink, and Walt Womack, who never missed anything, no doubt had taken note of the incident in the control room. What had he thought? she wondered. What had he written in his logbook about her?

The flight deck rattled and pitched slightly as the simulator took them soaring into the upper atmosphere, a sensation like riding a powerboat as it slammed across the stippled waves of an open sea. Her eyes bounced all over the clipboard, and it required an effort to isolate the items of her checklist.

They heard Mickey Flato's voice from the control room telling them that they were Negative Return—officially beyond the possibility of a return to launch site. That meant that if Walt's team was going to throw in a malfunction it would probably be for the purpose of practicing a Transatlantic Abort, though it was possible that at this early sim Walt would have pity on the crew and let them fly all the way to Main Engine Cut-Off. But they hadn't made it to MECO yet, and Lucy didn't want to bet it was in the cards for this run either. It was hot in the simulator, her teeth were rattling, and next to her in the MS2 seat, Buddy Santos was starting to sweat so bad that droplets were rolling down his wide forehead and plopping down on his checklist. This was Buddy's first mission as well, and as MS2 he served as flight engineer, with a thousand things to keep track of during ascent. He was a mechanical engineer from a prominent Filipino family that had run afoul of the Marcos regime and fled to the States when Buddy was still in grade school. Round-faced, with a constant conniving smile, he was in on every joke, alert to every breath of gossip, but just at the moment all this personal ease seemed to be evaporating as red lights started blinking on both sides of the console. The training team had just thrown in another malfunction. An electrical buss had gone out.

"You've lost nosewheel steering System One," Buddy blurted out to Surly. "Also Brake Isol Valve One is—"

"Yeah, okay," Surly replied, "but I don't need to focus on those problems right now. How about making a note for the pre-landing brief instead?"

Surly's voice had a faint edge. Coming up on MECO, he had plenty to do in the first place, and this new mal that the team had just tossed him preoccupied him so completely that even legitimate warnings about nosewheel steering and brake valves counted only as distracting chatter. Lucy glanced to her left to take a reading of Buddy's reaction. She could tell he was a bit chastened. The mistake he had made, if you could even call it a mistake, had been exquisitely slight, but it had happened on the first sim, when they could not help gauging each other's performances with exaggerated scrutiny.

Buddy caught her glancing at him, grinned, and shrugged his shoulders in an I-guess-I'm-an-idiot way that she found winning. She was pretty sure he would be her best friend on the crew.

They finished the run with a Transatlantic Abort, and then did two more runs after that, ending in a Return to Landing Site and an Abort Once-Around. After that they were officially through for the night, though after the very first sim, with Surly in a celebratory mood, there was little chance of either the crew or the training team actually going home. Surly announced he was buying drinks for everybody at the Outpost and insisted that Lucy and Tom and Buddy ride with him in his new Hummer.

"Maybe I should take my car," Lucy ventured as they filtered out with the members of the training team into the parking lot. "I'll probably be going home earlier than anybody else and—"

"Hop in," Surly interrupted, making a point of pretending he hadn't heard her. He punched in the security code on the driver's side door of the Hummer, and the members of the crew climbed on board. It amused Lucy that they all, without a thought, sat in their assigned flight-deck places: Tom in the front seat beside Surly, Lucy and Buddy behind.

"Somebody call Chuck and Patti and tell them to meet us," Surly said as he headed toward the main entrance of JSC. "Don't want to leave them out just because they're in the cheap seats."

Tom was dutifully dialing on his cell phone when Surly suddenly put on the brakes so forcefully that the Hummer skidded to a stop in the middle of the road. They all looked at him in puzzlement, but he was gazing serenely past Tom and out the right window, where the great Saturn V rocket lay stretched out on the grass in the moonlight.

"How many times a week do you think we drive by that thing and don't even give it a look?" he announced to his crew. His voice was full of calculated gravity. Lucy suspected he had made this same stop with the crews of the five other missions he had commanded.

They gave the Saturn V a look. It seemed to Lucy like an office building that had gently fallen on its side. It dwindled dramatically in diameter from the massive booster section at the base to the tiny cupola-like command module where the three Apollo astronauts had squeezed together for the greatest voyages in human history. It looked ancient and clumsy, with none of the elegance of the shuttle that had replaced it. It was a machine designed for nothing but brute thrust, for hammering away at the resistant ceiling of the atmosphere. Lucy had met half a dozen or so of the men who had journeyed on this rocket into the moon's orbit. She had met four who had actually flown down to the moon's surface on the Lunar Excursion Module and stepped out and bounded across the lunar dust. They were gaunt, aging men in golf shirts, with hair growing out of their ears and white patches on the skin of their foreheads where dermatologists had burned away emerging skin cancers. They were polite, hesitant in speech, generally unreflective, far more animated talking about their grandchildren than about their Ezekiel-like journeys beyond the world.

The fact that they could not seem to truly share in the wonder of their own wondrous lives had touched her, and haunted her a little. She knew you could not count too much on a trip to space to bring a defining glory to your existence. Brian was proof enough of that. But she also knew that if she ceased believing that it could somehow enlarge your soul, then her justification for the whole enterprise was deeply in jeopardy.

"Proud tradition, folks," Surly said, with that same stagy undertone of awe, as he continued to stare at the Saturn V, an unreachable full moon conveniently stationed in the sky above it. They all concurred with silent nods, though Lucy could not rightfully think of herself as an heir to the men of Apollo. Nobody was going to the moon anymore, probably not during their own careers, maybe not even in their lifetimes. Lucy could defend the reason—the priority of completing the International Space Station so that space could be explored in solid, incremental stages—without quite understanding it. As enthralled and alive with possibility as she felt right now, together with her crew at this benedictory moment, it seemed to her that space travel in her time had lost more in vision than it had gained in viability—that the original quest had been forsaken or forgotten, and that she and the other shuttle astronauts were mostly in the service of keeping the practicality of space alive until a bold new direction could be charted.

"Heavenly Father," Surly intoned a half hour later, bowing his head over the neck of his Corona. "We ask thy blessing on STS-108 and its crew and its instructors. We ask that you watch over us during training and help us learn to respect each other, to count on each other, so that we can perform the awesome mission that has been entrusted to us and return our vessel safely home to your good earth. This we ask in your name. Amen."

He clinked his bottle against each of theirs—they were all here now, Patti and Chuck and all the members of the training team—and then tilted his head back for a long gulp, his Adam's apple bobbing up and down with energetic confidence of its own. Surly Bonds was fifty-two years old, the father of four grown boys from a worn-out first marriage, and two young girls with an austere new wife, the daughter of a famous cardiologist in River Oaks. This would be his sixth mission, his fifth as commander. He had logged almost fifty days in space, along with a spectacular nighttime landing at Edwards Air Force Base and an unsurpassed record for successful satellite deployments.

Lucy felt at home in his company, though this was the second time this evening he had held them all hostage to a Deep Thought moment, and there was the chance that if he didn't rein in his born-again brio it could become a presumptuous distraction. But he knew the shuttle and its systems better than anyone now flying, and he was a genuinely imperturbable space hero. Also in his favor was the fact that Walt, perched on his bar stool around the crowded table, seemed to regard him with amused fondness. Lucy had happened to catch Walt's eye just as Surly was finishing up his prayer, and the message she read in his look was reassuring. Don't worry about it, he seemed to be saying, it's just Surly.

They had already had a debrief immediately after the sim, but the talk inevitably returned to the various runs and how the crew had dealt with the mals. Walt patiently went through it all again, his criticisms seemingly offhanded and unconcerned.

"Right now comm discipline's a little loose," he said, not needing to mention Buddy's overanxious callouts about the failed buss, or Tom's mistake in failing to mention the APU shutdown, or Lucy's own long-winded correction of it. "But it's only the first time out. Another few sims, you'll be reading each other's thoughts."

Nobody was going to read *his* thoughts, though. Sitting there in comfortable silence as the others joked about the sim and baited each other, the team exaggerating the mistakes of the crew and the crew reflecting on the innate cruelty that must have led the instructors into this line of work, Walt had an air of enticing detachment. It was something they all noticed and tried in various ways—Kyle with drunken candor, Sylvia with a kind of motherly fussing, Surly with sideways comradely glances—to break through. It was odd that someone whose whole professional life was about preparing other people to go into space should have the air of consequence and banked awareness that Lucy had not been able to discover in those Apollo moonwalkers.

He seemed comfortable but somewhat out of place in the Outpost, the classic astronaut hangout whose identity, like Surly's, was all about the vanishing heraldry of old-time spaceflight. The bar was a red-painted shack sitting all alone on a vacant lot on Egret Bay Boulevard. In a town where a decade-old building was practically a historical monument, the Outpost struck Lucy as a relic from another time entirely, some unimaginably distant epoch fifty or sixty years in the past, before John Kennedy had blurted out America's intention of reaching the moon, before Lyndon Johnson had decreed that the headquarters of human space exploration be situated in his home state of Texas, when Clear Lake City did not yet exist and all that stood on these lonely stretches of coastal rangeland was maybe a scruffy crossroads tavern or two where cowboys and oil workers and wandering lease buyers could stop in for a beer and a steak.

Inside and out, the Outpost was as rawly constructed a place as a child's clubhouse. Though it was open to the public, it still had the allure of a secret hideout, an ageless meeting place of the society into which she was now at last on the verge of receiving full membership. The wooden walls of the Outpost were crowded with the usual faded mission photos and newspaper clippings. There was an empty space suit hanging from the ceiling. She had been in this bar on dozens of occasions, but now for the first time she felt she had a right to be here.

Sylvia Molina handed her new digital camera to the girl behind the bar, and the team and crew squeezed in together while she uncertainly took a group picture. Sylvia, Lucy guessed, would emerge as the mission archivist, the one who collected the photos and assembled the cartoons and jokes and typewritten quips that the team, after launch, would use to decorate the hall in Building 5 for the astronauts' safe return.

They passed the camera around and they all looked at the tiny picture on the LCD screen. Caught in the full glare of the flash, Lucy's face appeared flat and pale, her smile witless. She groaned and passed it on to Patti, whose flawless bone structure spared her from ever taking a bad picture.

By the time the camera got to Walt, Surly was already passing around something else: an idea for the mission patch he had just sketched out with his mechanical pencil on a cocktail napkin.

"It's just a starting place," he was saying. "But it's got everything in it: *Endeavour,* the station, hell, if you look close enough you can even see the Beta Gimbal Assembly. And check this out: These stars up here? This little constellation? Look what happens when you connect the dots."

While Surly retrieved the napkin from Gary and began to connect the dots, Walt took the opportunity to look at the photo on the screen of Sylvia's camera. He regarded the washed-out, grinning faces, oddly comforted that Lucy had not escaped the harsh reckoning of the built-in flash. Maybe she wasn't beautiful after all. Maybe he could relax and settle down to work.

Gary grabbed the napkin out of Surly's hands as soon as he finished connecting the dots and read out loud the message they spelled: " 'Beyond.' "

"That's the business we're in, right?" Surly explained, keying off their vacant looks. "The beyond business? Beyond gravity, beyond boundaries, beyond fear, beyond whatever."

"I never knew you were a Trekkie," Gary said. "Walt, the guy's a Trekkie!"

Walt smiled and held his counsel, thinking it better to wait and gauge the level of Surly's investment before commenting. He might be a fighter jock, but it was easy enough to hurt his feelings. Surly harbored all sorts of artistic aspirations—Walt remembered a painful period several years ago when Surly had thought he played guitar well enough to join MaxQ—and the older he got the more his cosmic speculations grew. In any case, Walt had seen astronauts in the past who were as dependably incurious and unemotional as robots moping like schoolchildren when their ideas for the mission patch were shot down. This was because the patch was serious business. It was the enduring physical legacy of the flight, a talisman designed by the crew itself, and often encumbered with secret messages and meanings—like the hidden motto in Surly's constellation—that strove to represent something deeper than the mere official fact of the mission's existence.

"I like the idea of the stars spelling something out," Chuck Nethercott spoke up in a diplomatic tone of voice. "I think that's great. I think it's really worth exploring."

"I agree," said Patti.

"What do you think, Walt?" Surly said.

"It's not my call. It's a crew deal. Like Chuck said, maybe you should explore it."

"You're draining my batteries," Sylvia said to Walt, who was still holding her digital camera. He took another glance at the photo, and as he handed the camera back to her he did his best to sweep away a thought that always entered his mind sooner or later: is this the first crew I'm going to lose?

When the party showed no sign of beginning to wind down, Lucy went outside to use her cell phone to call Brian.

"How did the sim go?" he asked. It had been three weeks since she had been assigned to the mission, and he was still wearing his game face, still ostensibly pleased with her success and patient about assuming a suddenly heavy burden of child care. How long this hero-husband mode could last, she had no idea, but at least he understood without her having to explain to him that it was her turn now. And she was cautiously grateful.

"I think it went pretty well. Walt's still talking to us. I thought I'd be home by now, but I'm kind of stuck at the Outpost."

"I'm not surprised. There's usually a party after the first sim. Have you seen Bethie's blanket?"

"Her blanket? She hasn't wanted her blanket for a year."

"Well, surprise, she does now."

"She's not asleep? It's almost eleven."

"I know it's almost eleven, Lucy. I'm the one who's just read her *Horton Hatches a Who* sixteen times. Any idea where the blanket is?"

She had put away Bethie's crocheted baby blanket—or what remained of it—in an archival box that she kept under their bed. Stored away with it were a number of other grubbily precious objects—her father's wallet, the card Davis had made for her birthday three years ago—that she meant someday to transfer to a safe-deposit box at the bank. Now, in full-time training, without a hope of any significant free time until she returned to earth, the thought of attending to such placid motherly chores as storing and filing her children's things was a distant abstraction.

She told Brian where to find the blanket, vowed that she would be home as soon as she could, and walked back into the bar, where to her surprise she was greeted by her colleagues with a raucous cheer.

"I give up," she said.

"You have been entrusted," Buddy replied, "with the most important, the most sacred, the most vital—"

"I'm the patch coordinator," she guessed.

Surly broke out into a grin and handed her the cocktail napkin as he took in the rest of the crew with a glance.

"You all think about what you'd like to see on the patch, get together with Lucy, and give her your ideas. She'll take it over to the Graphics and Reproduction people and see if it flies. Gotta get the patch right, folks. Get the patch right and we're halfway home."

"Speaking of which," she said, "I should be halfway home myself. I've got a little girl who won't go to sleep."

There was a hanging moment. Walt set his beer bottle down on the table and stood up.

"I'll take you back to your car. I'm ready to go home myself."

"I don't want to pull anybody away from—"

"Are you kidding?" Kyle said. "He's always looking for an excuse to leave before the serious fun starts."

"You ready?" Walt asked her. He tossed a few $20 bills onto the table, but Surly grabbed them and stuffed them almost angrily into Walt's shirt pocket, protesting that the evening was on him.

They said their good-byes, and Lucy left the bar with Walt. Once out the door the silence of the winter night, after the high-spirited noise in the Outpost, was like the silence of space itself. Walt pulled on a nondescript windbreaker.

"It's over here," he said, gesturing with his keys to an equally nondescript sedan—a Ford Taurus?—sitting at the edge of the gravel parking lot. As she walked with him to the car, she was aware of his presence beside her in a way she could not quite classify. He was a few inches taller than she was, and his gait—for these few yards they were walking across the parking lot—seemed dawdlingly slow.

"Her name's Bethie, right?" he said. "The one who won't go to sleep?"

"That's right. She's three."

"And how old is Davis again?"

"Seven."

He nodded slowly, and held the passenger door open for her. She slipped inside. It *was* a Taurus, the interior was a pale no-color. There was an empty cup from Wendy's in the cup holder, a round medal of some sort dangling from the rearview mirror.

"That's a Saint Christopher medal," he said when he got in on his side and noticed her looking at it. "A friend of mine is a priest. You met him. Louis. He said that in my line of work if I didn't acknowledge the patron saint of safe journeys I was really asking for it."

"I hope you told him he was committing emotional blackmail."

"More or less," he said, with an amused glance at Saint Christopher. "But there he is anyway."

She was so oddly drawn to him, to his fashionless windbreaker, to his proudly uninteresting car, that even this slight personal detail about the Saint Christopher medal carried a reverberant charge in her mind, as if he had just whispered a confidence about, say, his dead wife. But it was just like her, wasn't it, to feel that she had to gain not just the approval, not just the trust, but the actual love of the teachers who sat in judgment of her? She was amused at the utter simplicity of her own psychology. A woman unhappy in her marriage, endlessly mourning the loss of her father, ready to transform this ordinary man behind the wheel of his Taurus into an emblem of surety and calm and strength.

"So maybe if sometime—" he said, as he backed out of the parking lot, but she never heard the rest of the thought, because just then Tom Terrific came running out of the Outpost and rapped on the roof of the car, saying he might get a ride too, since he wanted to get up early and work out at the gym.

"Hop in," Walt said, and on the way back to the parking lot at JSC Lucy tried not to be disappointed that Tom had interrupted them, or to guess about what Walt had started to say. She had no reason to imagine a private connection of any sort between her and Walt. Everything was about the crew, about the mission, and so she listened with a tolerant smile as Walt and Tom talked about the upcoming sims and joked about the mals the training team had in store for them.

Chapter Eleven

Louis had just finished giving his sermon. Not one of his better efforts, it attempted to link the miracle of the loaves and fishes with the all-you-can-eat buffet at Golden Corral. Walt had struggled to pay attention since Louis never failed to quiz him about the sermon afterward, but now that it was over he could relax into the roving meditative state that the Catholic Mass never failed to induce.

In fact that was probably the reason he found himself in church most Sundays—the opportunity it offered to fall into a trance. Now that training for 108 had begun in earnest, and his days were an around-the-clock cycle of simulator runs, of pre-briefs and debriefs and meetings with his team, he welcomed a little zone-out time. Even so, he could not stop thinking about the crew and its progress so far. After almost a month of simulator runs they were working fairly seamlessly on ascents and entries, mastering every kind of abort, and dealing unexcitedly and efficiently with the mals. After a somewhat rocky and tentative start, Buddy Santos was working out just fine as flight engineer. All he needed to do was sublimate his good cheer and desire to please to a baseline sharpness of manner. Tom Terrific showed promise as pilot, though he was still green and even still a bit in awe of Surly, whose depth of experience and alpha personality could sometimes be intimidating.

The congregation was offering each other the sign of peace, one of the many touchy-feely ecclesiastical innovations that Walt had come to find annoying. Nevertheless, he shook hands with the people around him, nodded his head and smiled, muttered "And with you" when they addressed him with "The peace of Christ be with you." To the right of the altar, the awful folk band started up again, led by a young guitarist with thinning bangs and a wrenchingly sincere smile.

The lyrics were insipid, the melody, if there was one, impossible to locate: a far cry from the oppressive but magisterial hymns ("O Salutaris Hostia," "Tantum Ergo Sacramentum") of Walt's boyhood. Everything about the Mass now was perky and evangelical—from the way the congregation held hands during the Lord's Prayer to the stylized crucifix above the altar, where in place of a bleeding, contorted Christ there was now a fully clothed mild-faced man, his arms spread out along the horizontal span of the cross not because his hands were savagely nailed to it but because he was offering a bland gesture of benediction.

Why do I even care? Walt asked himself. He was not a believer, nor had he ever been, really, not even as a gullible child; and just because the rites seemed so bloodless now did not mean that in their ancient and threatening forms they had served a more legitimate purpose. But by his nature he was more suited to lugubrious reflection than to cheerful inquiry, and there was something his mind and heart answered to in the solemn gropings of that now-vanished church. If he did not believe in God, he did believe in the need to feel awe and to express it, and that for this purpose only the deepest chords should be sounded.

When it came time for communion, he didn't go; he just couldn't take it that far, not without Rachel. So he sat there in his pew, a solitary outsider, as the rest of the congregation walked up the aisle with their hands loosely folded in front of them. In the old days all of the men would have been wearing suits, and no woman would have thought to enter church at all without covering her head with a hat or a scarf or, in an emergency, even a bobby-pinned square of Kleenex. Now no one wore anything more formal than a sport shirt, and though women had not yet breached the walls of the priesthood two female deacons were standing there at the altar by Louis's side, heads proudly bare, as he dispensed the host.

He let his mind drift again, musing ahead to next week's simulator runs, and then following various out-of-nowhere thoughts that were vaguely suggested by his occupation. In one of these reveries, as the band tuned up again after communion, he saw himself as a kind of falconer, never leaving the earth but reaping satisfaction from the sight of his winged comrade spiraling out of sight, trained by him, charged by him, and in some way carrying his consciousness into the heavens.

If he had such an emissary in this crew, it would be Lucy. For the remainder of the Mass, he coasted along on this illicit notion, curious where his mind would lead him, and then aroused and alarmed as he followed his thoughts to their salacious conclusions. Well, so what, he told himself. One of the great satisfactions of his arm's-length relationship with the Church was his renegade conviction that his thoughts were his own, that he was mature and sensible and moral enough to imagine things without carrying them into action. He had begun to suspect, though, that an exquisitely faint breath of reality animated his speculations, that something *could* happen if he were to be so base as to apply himself to the possibility.

It was partly the zealous way she focused on him in the briefing room, the deference in her voice when she spoke to him. Walt was used to the gratifying attention of overachieving students. Nobody worked harder than astronauts to master their task or to make a good impression. What was different was the depth of Lucy's alertness. She excelled through wariness rather than natural confidence, and while she was as professional and good-natured as any crew member Walt had ever worked with, even these traits seemed to him to be directed by a relentless, vulnerable striving.

Several weeks ago, after the first sim, when they had just gotten into his car so that he could drive her home from the Outpost, he had been aware of her assessing glances. Maybe she was just trying to size him up, maybe she subjected anyone with potential control over her destiny to that same covert scrutiny. But the impression he couldn't shake was that there was something more to it, an echo of the helpless and wholly inappropriate interest he had felt toward her since she gave her talk at the church. If Tom Terrific hadn't unexpectedly appeared at that moment— well, nothing would have happened, of course; but in the few minutes it would have taken to drive her back to the Building 5 parking lot they would have entered into a conversation of cheerful banality and the heightened silence preceding it would have been dispelled and forgotten. As it was, that moment had lingered between them, or at least his vanity preferred to think it had. During these early weeks of training, the bond between the core team and the crew typically grew tight, but it was primarily a group bond, an evolving esprit. There was limited occasion for one-on-one discussions that weren't specifically mission-oriented. Out of pride or uncertainty, Walt had not gone out of his way to create such an occasion with Lucy, and he sensed in return a guarded formality on her part.

If this tense shared awareness of each other was not an illusion on Walt's part—a very strong possibility, he had to admit—it was certainly subtle enough to be essentially meaningless. And if it did exist, and was for the sake of argument not meaningless, it was still impossible. As he sat musing in a pew in Our Lady Queen of the Heavens Catholic Church, the word "adultery" resounded so loudly in his mind it was almost comical. A mortal sin, of course; particularly as reckoned by the unfeeling, unrelenting standards of the religion Walt had once known, by the God who preferred to send people to hell rather than see them stumble into an unsanctified bed. Walt didn't care about such cold-hearted decrees anymore, but it was usually plain enough to him what was wrong and what was right, what the sort of man he was would do and would not do.

All at once, his thoughts *were* beginning to seem dangerous, so he tuned back in to the trailing edges of the service. The leader of the folk band was singing but no longer playing his instrument. His hands were raised instead to the heavens like a preacher in a tent revival, and his eyes were shining with dazzlement.

"I can't believe this shit," Louis said an hour later as they stood in front of the church, watching a dark squall line march in from the Gulf.

"Not a good day for the old canoe," Walt replied in a lighthearted voice, but Louis was in a mood, and he kept staring combatively at the clouds.

"We could beat it," he said. "I bet we could get in an hour, maybe two, before it really starts to come down."

"Are you crazy? Do you seriously want to be in a canoe in the middle of the bayou when those clouds open up?"

"Yes, I do, Walt. Come on, let's give it a shot."

"Let's go to a movie or something."

"No. This is our routine. We've already missed the last two Sundays because you had to work. If we miss again today, guess what? It won't be a routine anymore. It'll just be an occasional thing we do."

Walt indulged him to the extent of strapping the canoe on top of

Louis's car and driving out to Bay Area Park, but by the time they got there the storm had already arrived. They sat in the parking lot as the rain blew in horizontally and made surging patterns across the windshield like a lava lamp.

"Give up?" Walt finally said.

"Yeah, I give up. Fuck you."

"What did I do?" Walt said. "I came all the way out here with you, didn't I?"

Louis turned on the ignition and watched the windshield wipers rearrange the cascading water in front of their faces.

"Is something the matter with you?" Walt asked after a moment.

"What? Just because I said fuck? Sorry to shatter your cherished priestly illusions."

"Seriously."

"I'm fine."

"You're not acting like it."

"I'm not acting like it because I wanted to get out on the bayou today. And that's not going to happen, so I have a normal human reaction of being pissed. So give me a fucking break, my son, okay?"

Louis reached into the glove compartment, pulled out a fishing chart of Galveston Bay, and tossed it into Walt's lap.

"As long as we're just sitting here, why don't you take a look at that?"

Walt unfolded the map and studied the ocher expanses of the bay. Louis had drawn a line in red Sharpie that followed the contour of the mainland all the way from Bay Area Park to the mouth of the Gulf.

"Three days," Louis said. "Leisurely pace. The first night we pull up in Texas City, the next night in West Bay, have dinner in Galveston at Gaido's, then in the morning we head out to the Gulf, turn around just past the jetties, and then ride the surf onto the beach. Touchdown. Piece of cake."

"I'm not sure I'm going to have three days free anytime soon, Louis. I've got a mission to train. I don't know from one day to the next when the training manager is going to give us the simulator, or for how long, or for—"

"All I'm saying is give it some thought."

Walt sat wearily back in the car seat, the rain still assaulting the windshield in front of him. It was a nutty idea, and Louis for some reason had decided to deepen his investment in it. Walt had seen him in these moods before, suddenly becoming aware of the confines of his priestly life and beset with a prowling, grudging, unfocused energy. By and by it would pass, but probably not before he picked a fight with Walt, his best friend and safe enemy.

"Let's drive by Krispy Kreme and see if the 'Hot Now' sign is on," Louis suggested, silently conceding that the rain wasn't going to let up anytime soon.

As they drove down Bay Area Boulevard in the rain, on their way to Krispy Kreme, it came to Walt that he and Louis, when they got together, inevitably took on the restless vapidity of teenagers. Walt could excuse Louis. After all, Louis had never really been a teenager, since he had more or less been sequestered in the seminary since the age of fourteen. But Walt had been a full-grown man for decades, and in cruising for donuts with Louis he was starting to feel a certain slippage, a regression from the state he ought to have achieved or the person he ought to have been. Somehow, in losing his wife, or in giving up the fight to have children with her, he had failed to lock himself into adulthood.

"It's not lit up," Louis said gloomily, peering at the window of the Krispy Kreme, where the "Hot Now" sign was unilluminated beneath a steady curtain of rain.

"What difference does it make?" Walt said.

"What difference does it make? What difference does it make if one of your astronauts presses the wrong button and suddenly they're in a different orbit or something?"

"Couldn't happen."

"Don't get technical on me. The point is it's a serious matter. If they're not hot they're just another donut.

"The hell with it," he said, swerving into the parking lot at the last moment. "We might as well be here as anywhere else."

They walked into the Krispy Kreme and each ordered a room-temperature glazed donut and a cup of coffee. They sat at a gleaming white table and studied the archival photos that were hanging on the wall of donut delivery trucks and long-dead men in snappy white Krispy Kreme uniforms. Louis faced the rain as he wolfed down his donut, then swiveled in his chair to stare morosely at the unmoving conveyor belt behind the counter. If the belt had been moving, the donuts would have been hot.

"Get over it," Walt advised.

"No, I'm going to wallow in my misfortunes. I'm going to curse God. So did you ever call that chick?"

"Chick? What are you talking about? Are you seriously using the word 'chick'?"

"Whatever you call them."

"Women. We call them women. We're forty-eight years old, Louis. And anyway, what chick?"

"The one with the bike. You said you were thinking about calling her."

Lauren Bell. The woman from Payloads. He had just seen her the other day on the running trail, stopped to talk to her about her adventures in the Hotter'n Hell hundred-mile bike ride in Wichita Falls. It would have been the ideal moment to ask her out, and in fact it seemed to him from her animated, perhaps exaggerated friendliness, that she was expecting such an invitation. But he had let the moment pass and gone on with his run, second-guessing himself all the way.

"What's the problem with her?" Louis wanted to know.

"I didn't say there was any problem with her."

"Then what's the problem with you?"

Walt didn't answer. He ate the last bite of his donut, wiped the sugar off his fingers, and tossed the napkin into a nearby trash can.

"I mean," Louis said, theatrically lowering his voice, "don't you get horny?"

"This is not an appropriate conversation to have with a priest."

"What? Priests don't get horny? I've got news for you, Walt. Every night when I—"

"Please, Louis. Let's leave it right there, okay?"

Louis shrugged. The rain was starting to let up, with bold streaks of blue sky appearing at the ragged following edge of the front.

"Remember Debbie DiMona?" Louis said to Walt. "I did it with her. Right after my novitiate."

Walt stared blankly at his friend and said, "Really?"

Louis only nodded.

"I didn't know that you'd ever—"

"You could have asked, you know," Louis said. "Sometime during the last few decades it might have occurred to you to ask."

Louis drove Walt back to his car in the church parking lot. The storm had been brief, but like much of greater Houston, Clear Lake City was built upon a subsidence zone, below sea level in some places, and so the water was still axle-deep in the streets, roiling fiercely at the curbside drains.

"Okay, so let me ask *you* something," Louis said when he pulled to a stop beside Walt's car. They had not spoken for five minutes, but Louis resumed the conversation as if the awkward gap had not occurred. "Are you doing okay?"

"Yeah, I guess," Walt said. "I'm not half as pissy as you are, for one thing."

" 'Cause every Sunday I'm standing up in the pulpit, looking out over the congregation, and there you are. And you've got this look on your face like you're expecting something from me, an epiphany or some sort of shit like that."

"I'm not expecting anything, Louis."

"Well, then maybe that's worse. So what the hell are you there for?"

"I thought you wanted me there."

"I do," Louis said. "But you're starting to make me a little self-conscious. I've got to *sell* this stuff, you know? And there you are, out in the congregation rolling your eyes—"

"I don't roll my eyes."

"Figuratively. You roll your eyes figuratively, Walt.

"So I'm just wondering," Louis continued after a moment, "if you're doing okay. That's all. I mean, you give this impression of everything being fine with you, and maybe it is. But if it's not, if there's something you're looking for—hey, that's what I do, you know?"

"Okay," Walt said. "I appreciate it."

"I'm not going to lie to you. I'm not going to pretend I know what it feels like when your wife dies. But I'm skilled in the art of bullshit, Walt. I really am. So if you ever want to, like, talk for real . . ."

"All right," Walt said, drumming his fingers on the door handle. "Thanks. It's a deal."

"Yeah, some deal," Louis shot back, after a moment of annoyed silence. "I miss Rachel too, by the way. You know what I miss most?"

"No," Walt said.

"She was somebody who would take the trouble to talk to a person."

Chapter Twelve

The girl's name was Xochtli, mercifully corrupted to Zokie. She was almost twenty, the daughter of two Peace Corps volunteers who had met and fallen in love in some insurgent village deep in the Yucatán jungle.

"Here it is!" she was saying, bending over the living room sofa and extracting Davis's missing shoe from between the cushions. Lucy decided not to think one way or another about the tattoo—was it some sort of Mayan glyph?—teasingly visible on the small of her back. The girl seemed competent and good-humored, and flexible enough to undergo an interview with Lucy as she scrambled to get her kids ready for school.

Now that Lucy was in serious training for an actual mission, and her schedule more impossible and unpredictable than ever, she needed a babysitter who could fill in the gaps when Colleen's studies made her unavailable. It was Colleen, in fact, who had recommended Zokie, a high school friend who had dropped out of San Jacinto Community College after only one semester and had drifted into as much of a slacker lifestyle as this driven community had to offer.

Brian had already left an hour ago for an early-morning run. It was an indulgence on his part that Lucy could not afford, but it would have been cruel of her to point this out to him, since his career was obviously flatlining and his solitary emotional burdens were great. He ought to have been here, though, not just to help with getting the kids off to school but to give his opinion on Zokie. The girl seemed fine. Just now she had taken the initiative of handing Davis his shoe and complimenting him on his painstaking, infuriatingly slow knot tying. Davis, for his part, regarded her with charmed wariness. Bethie made a point of constantly hovering near Lucy, studying the intruder from a safe distance.

"I'm so sorry we have to talk on the fly like this," Lucy told Zokie as she carried the breakfast dishes into the sink, Bethie clinging to her legs. "But that's kind of the way life is around here these days."

"Oh, it doesn't bother me," Zokie said. "It's interesting."

There was a placid, assured smile on the girl's face that Lucy couldn't quite warm to. She suspected there might be some icy distance between her and her two Peace Corps parents, whom Lucy imagined as crusading and rigid and silently smoldering over the fact that their daughter had taken vengeance on them by becoming a San Jacinto Community College dropout rather than an Ivy League graduate. But Colleen had vouched for her, saying she had a good heart and a sense of responsibility. Just as important, she had worked as a lifeguard in high school and knew CPR and basic first aid. She also had a little sister with asthma, and had not looked concerned at all when Lucy showed her Davis's inhaler collection and handed her a list of emergency contact numbers twenty names deep.

"You want to ride along while I drop them off at school?" Lucy asked. Zokie responded with an affirmative shrug, and in the car she chatted amiably, although less with the children than with Lucy, and mostly about herself: her dim childhood memories of Mexico, her vague aspirations to be a costume designer for the movies.

"We probably won't need you this early in the morning," Lucy told her after the kids had been dropped off. "Usually I'll take them to school, or Colleen will, or my husband. But I thought it'd be a good idea to show you the routine. Things are going to be kind of unpredictable until the launch. And let's see, I think Colleen told you ten dollars an hour?"

"That's right."

"And that's fine with you?"

"Sure."

"Are the seat belts okay in the backseat of your car?"

"Oh, yeah. They're good. No problem."

Lucy had driven back to the house so Zokie could pick up her Jeep Cherokee. Looking at its dinged-up fender and fraying seat fabric held together by duct tape, she had a twinge of concern. But she couldn't buy a part-time babysitter a new car. Overall, the Cherokee looked imposing and crash-worthy, and Lucy had already made clear to Zokie that she expected the children to be strapped in at all times, and Bethie in particular securely wrestled into her car seat.

"So," Lucy said before Zokie got out of the car, "I guess that's it. Is there anything you'd like to ask me?"

"No, I can't really think of anything, Mrs. Kincheloe."

"You can call me Lucy if you'd like."

"Oh, okay," she said, sliding out of the car. "Bye."

Lucy drove off to JSC feeling just the slightest twinge of disquiet. Zokie was fine for the job, completely adequate. But the fact that she wasn't perfect, that she seemed to have no real initiative or any apparent depth to her personality, made Lucy feel like she was cutting corners in a part of her life where compromise should never be considered. And anyway, the problem wasn't the babysitter's qualifications. It was the need for her in the first place, the wall-to-wall child care without which Lucy's mission would be an impossible task.

Brian was doing what he could, cooking dinner for the kids when Lucy couldn't, putting them to bed when she had a late night in the simulator, but Brian's day was full too, not just with his astronaut duties but with the dark contemplation of his career. So far, both of the kids seemed to be taking everything in stride, but Lucy sensed that this morning's hectic introduction of a new figure in their lives only served to confirm that the ground was shifting beneath them, that the stakes were rising.

STS-108 was not a high-profile mission. It was pretty close to the ideal of a routine flight. Lucy and her crew were to launch in *Endeavour*, one of the newer vehicles in the small shuttle fleet. They would dock with the half-completed International Space Station and deliver supplies to its crew by means of a glorified moving van called Raffaello, which would be lifted out of the payload bay of the orbiter with the robot arm and attached to the Unity Node of the station for unloading. Lucy was the loadmaster, responsible for making sure that the contents of Raffaello were faultlessly organized and that everything that moved into and out of the station was accounted for and secured in its assigned place on Raffaello's stowage racks and platforms.

The shuttle would also deliver a number of scientific experiments known as Get Away Specials, as well as a small satellite, and an automatic incubator for studying the effects of microgravity on Japanese quail eggs.

But there was another component to the flight whose thrilling reality Lucy was still trying to process. Surly had given her a spot on the EVA team. She had always known she had a shot at a spacewalk. Her size, if nothing else, recommended her for the assignment. Although space suits were made up of interchangeable components to accommodate various body shapes, smaller women had trouble finding a good fit. Besides, overall strength and size counted when you were outside the vehicle, groping—or, in space jargon, "translating" for sometimes as long as six or seven hours across the exterior surface of the orbiter or along the various trusses of the unfinished space station, encumbered by tools and portable foot braces, wearing a SAFER unit on your back in case the unthinkable happened and you became untethered and had to propel yourself through empty space to grasp the orbiting hardware that was your only possible salvation.

Lucy was to do the EVA with Buddy. Patti was on the EVA team as well, training with them so that she could choreograph the exterior work and communicate with Lucy and Buddy from inside *Endeavour*. The task itself was straightforward. Lucy and Buddy would ride the robot arm high up onto the station's truss structure, where they would disembark and climb up to the top of the truss, tethering themselves against the station like mountaineers on a technical ascent. Once there, they would install two insulating blankets over the gimbals that rotated the station's solar wings.

Because every inching move, each procedural detail of this excursion, would be planned and rehearsed for months, because all official discussion of it was rendered in such an obscuring fog of acronyms and jargon, it required an effort of Lucy's imagination for her to remember that the activity she was scheduled to perform was wondrous. Standing at the end of the robot arm, moving along one of the segments of the station truss, she would be alone in her space suit in the heavens, able to gauge the passage of the earth below her with her outstretched hand, and to confront, in almost naked isolation and vulnerability, the extinguishing nothingness of space.

It was to EVA training that she was headed now, out to the Neutral Buoyancy Lab, where Space Center Boulevard dead-ended in open pastures, with grazing cattle and flocks of blackbirds moving in cyclonic flights from one field to the next. Lucy went through the security gate and parked, then walked through the high-bay area, whose cavernous space was cluttered with mock-ups of the shuttle exterior on which the EVA team trained for contingencies, a word that everyone politely chose not to recognize as a synonym for catastrophes.

She climbed up the stairs next to the hyperbaric chamber and made her way along the deck of the vast indoor pool to the locker room, where she took off her clothes and slipped on a form-fitting diaper—a necessity for someone about to spend six hours underwater—that was maliciously known as a Maximum Absorbency Garment. Over the MAG she pulled on a set of Patagonia long underwear, and over that her Liquid Cooling and Ventilation Garment, a meshwork of capillaries that always made her think of the plastic Visible Woman model kit she had assiduously assembled in seventh grade.

Buddy was waiting for her at the donning stand, sitting on a chair with a blood pressure cuff on his arm, surrounded by the usual chaos of doctors and suit techs and engineers and test conductors and configuration divers.

"So is the new babysitter a keeper?" he asked when Lucy sat down next to him.

"With any luck," she said.

"What'd you have for breakfast?"

Lucy rolled her eyes and mumbled, "Oatmeal." There was nothing that Buddy didn't want to know about, nothing he didn't take in. He already knew both Davis's and Bethie's birthdays, all the details of Davis's medication, all of Lucy's child care travails, and as the doctor moved the blood pressure cuff from his arm to hers he even accurately predicted, based on his perfect memory of her previous readings, what her systolic and diastolic pressure would be.

"Did you know they used to put a Fruit Roll-Up in these things?" he said as he lay down on a mat to begin the process of pulling on the lower torso of his suit. "They'd, like, Velcro it in there next to the Big Gulp, and if you got hungry during the EVA you could just lean your head down and take a bite. Man, those were the days."

With the lower torso and his boots on, he waddled over to the donning stand, from which the hard fiberglass shell of the upper torso assembly was suspended. He scrunched beneath it and wiggled inside, aided by three techs who made sure that the thumb loops of his undergarment were attached and that the drinking tube of his water bottle, known as the Big Gulp, was not jabbing him in the throat.

When Buddy's head popped out of the neck opening, he was grinning at Lucy as if he had just done something remarkable.

"So then what happens?" he continued. "Congress starts cutting back on the space program, and of course the first things to go are the mission to Mars and the Fruit Roll-Ups."

"Are you going to do the running commentary thing again this morning?" Lucy said. She was lying on the mat, pulling on the bottom half of her own suit, an awkward task she had never warmed to, and four or five times as difficult as donning the thick and unyielding wet suits she used to wear when diving in frigid California waters. By the time she had finished with the lower torso and had positioned herself on the opposite side of the donning stand from Buddy, she was already in a sweat, notwithstanding the heroic air-conditioning system of the vast building.

Buddy kept talking until they fastened on his helmet, relating how his great-grandfather had helped build the Corregidor tunnel, passing on some last-minute thoughts he had about the mission patch before Lucy met this afternoon with the Graphics and Reproduction people, singing a few verses from one of the songs on the Afro-Cuban All Stars CD he planned to take with him into space. In another person, the constant jabbering could have been annoying, but it was so much a part of Buddy's infectious personality that it had a soothing effect on Lucy. As the techs wrestled on her gloves and snapped and locked the rings that created a lifesaving seal, she was beginning to feel the faintest intimations of claustrophobia. It was something she kept to herself, of course, and something that would pass—this would be only her third full-scale run in the NBL. But there was a reason the space suit's proper name was the Extravehicular Mobility Unit. It was not so much a garment as a vehicle, and to command its movements and feel at home inside it one had to develop the confidence and feel of a heavy-equipment operator.

She had already had several caution and warning classes in which she had gone over the engineering drawings of the EMU, learning how to read the information on the display and control module on its front, running procedures and practicing malfunctions in the same way the crew did in the simulator.

But the suit still felt foreign to her, both protector and entrapper, with the potential for being as much a tomb as a womb for her vulnerable human body. When the helmet was placed over her head and the connecting rings locked, it always took her a moment to get over the sensation of being sealed inside, to adjust to the unnatural timbre of voices over the loop, to the deliberate circulation of breathing gas, and to the strange soundlessness of the world she saw through the polycarbonate screen in front of her face.

Just now, a few yards away, Patti Halapeska was talking to Tricia, the test conductor, about the task they were about to run. The main event of the EVA was to attach the thermal blankets, but that was not what they would be rehearsing today. Today they would be working on a few follow-up tasks that would take place at the end of the EVA. Once they had attached the blankets, they would be climbing back down the truss to retrieve a protective cover on the S-Band Antenna Assembly so that it could be stowed in the shuttle's cabin, and then Lucy would have the task of installing a lighting stanchion on the exterior of the Unity Node that connected the U.S. and Russian portions of the station.

It would be Patti who would talk them through the EVA, both in the control room during the test runs in the pool and from inside the orbiter when they were doing it for real. The fact that Patti had an abrasive, uninflected voice should not have mattered, but somehow it did. Lucy had joked about it with Buddy—the two of them alone in space, hovering on the edge of oblivion, their only connection to the inhabitable world a woman whose voice sounded like a creaky door hinge.

As she stood on the donning stand while the techs attached the mini workstation to the front of her suit—a metal platform that jutted out from her chest and held all the tools and tethers and end effectors she would need for her spacewalk—Lucy covertly studied Patti through the lens of her helmet. She was commandingly attractive: straight blond hair, cut in a functional bob like that of the outdoorsy women in an L.L. Bean catalog, clear skin, brilliant teeth, and—the birthright that Lucy most envied—an effortless, elegant slenderness. But Patti's eyes were tiny black staring buttons, and her constant powerful focus was indistinguishable from a trance. This distracting intensity, Lucy imagined, might have something to do with the fact that she was unmarried and unattached. No man, or woman for that matter, had been known to penetrate her force field.

That sort of asexual bearing was certainly not something Lucy aspired to, but she could well understand its usefulness for an astronaut. As far as Lucy could tell, when the launch day came Patti would be leaving nothing behind. She would enter space without fear, possibly even without excitement, merely with the same attitude of blank contentment with which she experienced life on earth.

The donning platform, carrying Lucy and Buddy with it, began to move toward the edge of the pool. Lucy flexed her hands in her gloves. Like the rest of her suit, the gloves had a threadbare look. They were bleached and a little frayed by countless hours underwater, the thick plastic on the knuckles starting to peel off. The EMUs they would be wearing on the actual spacewalk would be pristine, but Lucy found the lived-in quality of this suit welcome, since it carried the idea that space would not be a totally denaturing environment, but full of intimate, familiar, workaday things.

The pool she was hovering over now in the donning stand was oceanic. Built in order to train astronauts in an environment that might reasonably mimic the environment they would find in space, it was deep enough and wide enough to hold a full-scale mock-up of the shuttle's payload bay, as well as mock-ups of the modules and trusses of the International Space Station.

Attached to the stand by a shoulder belt, Lucy craned awkwardly forward and looked down at the bottom of the pool, forty feet below, just as her boots began to sink below the surface. The immense mock-ups, from this height, cast their own submarine shadows, splintering the pool into complex gradients of light and texture. They reminded Lucy of the way coral reefs or subsurface rocks looked from above the waterline, their true contours wrinkled and distorted by the uneasy play of light through water. When her helmet began to submerge, she automatically took a useless last breath, though there was of course no interruption to the flow of oxygen. It was like riding an elevator into another dimension. In front of her were the blue reaches of the pool, configuration divers swarming everywhere, as populous as the fish on a reef. Above her, the white umbilicals that provided her with air and electricity for life support and communication lay on the surface in snaky coils, and buoyant yellow float bags—the means by which the config divers ferried tools from one end of the pool to the other—were festively ascending everywhere.

One of the divers—his name was Morris, and he had a florid tattoo of the Virgin of Guadalupe on his biceps—swam up to her and, after she had gotten out her reel and tethered herself to one of the handrails on the exterior of the shuttle's air lock, unfastened the strap that held her to the donning stand. She felt herself floating in neutral buoyancy, a familiar sensation from years of diving, but within the cumbersome space suit there was barely a hint of the soaring freedom she used to feel in scuba gear. She felt instead as bulky and unmaneuverable as a parade float, a helpless, bloated blob clinging to whatever solid surfaces presented themselves.

She and Buddy were underwater for four hours. The time passed slowly: the awkward transit up to the top of the station mock-up, as they tethered and untethered themselves to the handrails along the trusses; all the while the divers following, observant as angels, and Patti's coarse voice hammering away on the loop, going through the checklists, calling out upcoming procedures, confirming settings and directions along the various faces of the trusses. Among the tools Lucy carried was the PGT, a $350,000 ratchet wrench with multiple rotating rings like the lens of a camera for setting speed and torque.

She spent most of the four hours alone with the PGT at the solar array, while Buddy worked twenty yards away from her practicing the retrieval of the protective cover of the S-band assembly. He was below her, but "below" was a term that was meaningless in space, where there could be no consensus about up and down and no such thing as cardinal directions. In this case, Buddy was facing toward nadir, the direction in which the earth was visible, while she was oriented toward zenith, which meant the rest of the black universe. In between were forward and aft, port and starboard, more game attempts to fix a human thought-mark in a void that defied orientation.

The water in the pool was utterly transparent, foreshadowing the unreal clarity of vision she could expect to experience in airless space. The red stripes on the arms of Buddy's space suit—indicating his status as the leader of the EVA team—shone brilliantly at this depth, though Lucy knew if he were to sink a few feet lower the red would become a corrosive green as the increasing density of the water washed out, one by one, the colors of the spectrum. Such unworldly things had already become long familiar to her: red turning to green in front of her eyes, her body weightless and numb, north and south replaced by zenith and nadir. But she still could not imagine what it would feel like for real to look down upon the earth, knowing that her children were beyond her reach on its surface as it slowly coasted from day to night.

Lucy fought to keep her morale from sagging as she continued to close the troublesome hatch brace with the PGT, trying out various settings and torques until both she and the team in the control room were convinced they had finally hit upon the right way to accomplish the task. Patti's flat, procedural voice in her ear was an irritation; it was almost a refutation of the whole idea that there was glory in spaceflight. She never felt that way in the simulator, no matter how hard and exhausting things got, because she was always aware of being under Walt's scrutiny, of needing to be seen and judged by him in the best possible light.

It was almost two o'clock in the afternoon, she hadn't eaten since breakfast, and just the thought of Buddy's discontinued Fruit Roll-Up was beginning to torture her. She kept sipping water from her Big Gulp to try to keep the hunger at bay, chastising herself for eating an abstemious breakfast when she knew perfectly well that all this neutrally buoyant maneuvering tended to leave her famished.

The hunger was a minor distraction, however, compared to the usual background anxiety she felt when she was away from her cell phone. If there was a real emergency with one of the kids she could, of course, be reached, but the thought of such a thing happening while she was underwater in the NBL filled her with a peculiar dread. She did not like imagining all the steps that would be required before she could rush to the rescue of her children: tethering and untethering her way along the trusses to the donning stand, then the slow hoist out of the water, then the necessarily methodical divestment of her space suit, the frantic change from her cooling and ventilation garment to her clothes, then racing to her car across the parking lot, on the way at last to wherever the crisis was taking place.

The question of how she would deal with this anxiety in space, where the notion of any sort of motherly rescue mission was flatly impossible, was something she knew she could not afford to think about. She just had to trust that nothing terrible would happen to her children while she was gone and that the shuttle carrying her away from them would not explode at launch or disintegrate at reentry.

Here on earth, though, she checked for messages as soon as she got out of the water and could reach her phone. Nothing. No urgent calls from Lorelei or Dr. Trimble, no troublesome messages from Brian. All was well. There were only two messages—one from Surly informing her that tomorrow morning's sim had been rescheduled by the training manager for five o'clock in the evening and one from Ernest, the Graphics and Reproduction guy, letting her know that he'd be in the office all afternoon.

Graphics and Reproduction was housed in a one-story building across from the astronauts' gym that looked from the outside like the office of an oil-field equipment company. Inside, though, it was a cheerful hive filled with young graphic designers in trendy eyeglass frames whose workspaces were cluttered with action figures and wind-up toys.

Ernest was one of the oldsters in the office. He was pushing forty, but still hipster-thin and full of slouchy good cheer. The words "The Sky Is Crying" were tattooed on the back of his wrist—a drunken response, he had told Lucy, to Stevie Ray Vaughan's death in a helicopter crash.

Ernest led Lucy to his cubicle and showed her on the screen of his Macintosh the latest version of the much-revised mission patch.

"So what do you think? Do we have a green light from you guys yet? Because I'd really like to take it up to the Ninth Floor and get it approved."

Surly's beloved connect-the-dots "Beyond" motto had long since been revised out of the patch, though there was still a cluster of stars in the sky, each one representing a crew member's spouse or child or parent. (Davis's and Bethie's stars were twin points just to the right of the nose of the orbiter.) Both the orbiter and the International Space Station it was flying to were rendered with an economy that bordered on the impressionistic, and the first of Lucy's many battles as patch coordinator had been to convince the more literal-minded members of the crew that Ernest was right in insisting that not every bolt and heating tile could be depicted.

The patch was an irregular shape, with the tail of the orbiter protruding from its base like a stem and the space station visible above it in a field of mushrooming space. Lucy never tired of reading the names gathered around the perimeter of the patch: Bonds, Terassky, Santos,

Kincheloe, Halapeska, Nethercott. Seeing her name in that terse expeditionary listing thrilled her, made her feel as if she were already a part of history.

"It looks pretty good," she said to Ernest. "Really good. Just a couple things, though."

"Please, please, don't bring up the solar arrays again. This is *not* an engineering diagram, it's a patch!"

"No, we're all okay with not showing the solar arrays. You've convinced us. Calm down. It's the stars. That's the one thing everybody's worried about: that you can't really see the stars. Maybe if you could highlight them with a black border or something."

Ernest leaned forward in his chair and banged his head theatrically on the desk.

"You have a problem with that," she guessed.

He lifted his head wearily. "I have a problem with it because it can't be done. The medium here, in case you've forgotten, is needle and thread. A tiny little black border on a tiny little star sounds great. But you're going to have to do me a favor and tell the crew that there's no possible way to *sew* that. Okay?"

"Okay," she said. "Brace yourself."

"The fucking color gradations again?"

"Look, I know this is hard, Ernest. I mean, after all, you're an artist. You're like Michelangelo on the ceiling of the Sistine Chapel and we're like the pope calling up to you to—"

"Okay, you're starting to overdo it."

"It's just that Surly has got this fixation. He doesn't want the background to be black, he doesn't want it to be deep space. He wants to show how the light keeps changing in low earth orbit."

"Christ, what does he want, a stained-glass window? You tell Surly that if I go back and put all those colors in there, his mission patch is going to look like a Rainbrow Brite sticker."

They bantered on good-naturedly for another half hour or so, then Lucy joined the rest of the crew for a habitability training session, and after that she had a payload meeting in Building 9.

By the time she got home it was seven thirty. Brian had been off work since six, and he had sent Colleen home and driven the kids to get take-out Chinese food.

"We went ahead and ate," Brian said as she came into the house. He was sitting on the sofa, lacing up his running shoes. "I wasn't sure what time you'd be back."

"I thought you already went running this morning," she said.

"I just wanted to do a few more miles."

"We got you General Tso's chicken," Davis said. He was still sitting at the dinner table, which was littered with Styrofoam take-out containers and packets of soy sauce, swinging his legs back and forth as he did his homework. Bethie had clutched her mother around the legs with both arms as soon as she came through the door, and Lucy bent down to pry her off and hoist her into her arms instead.

"So are you in training for a triathlon or something?" Lucy said to Brian as he stood up. She didn't bother disguising the edge in her voice. It was a tone that seemed to suit him just fine, since it gave him the right not to reply or explain himself. He just trotted off down the front sidewalk through the still-open front door.

While he was gone, Lucy got Bethie into the bathtub and allowed Davis to finish his homework on the bathroom floor. She put the toilet seat down and sat there eating her cold General Tso's chicken, smiling indulgently when Bethie demanded that she watch her swim underwater. At the same time she wearily attended to Davis and his homework ("Mom, how do you spell 'about'?"), and the more tired she became the more animated both children grew. They wanted to know everything about Zokie, the unknown figure who now promised to loom so large in their lives. How did she get her name? What did her tattoo mean? Had it hurt to have it put on? What kind of car did she have? Would they get to ride in it if she instead of Colleen picked them up from school?

Lucy did her wan best to answer this barrage of questions. She wanted to think. There was some sort of explosion coming with Brian. For a month, he had done his best to put her needs and her mission ahead of his own brooding concerns, but she knew that such gallantry was an act of will and could not last forever. She had noticed the growing tension in his face and his demeanor all week, but the training schedule kept her so busy and exhausted she had had neither the energy nor the opportunity to sit down with him, as she had learned to do in the earliest days of their marriage, to draw him out and try to defuse his anxiety.

He was home from his run in less than an hour, breathing hard, his face covered with a sheen of sweat even though it was a mild winter evening outside. She told him, trying to put some warmth in her voice, that she would get the kids to bed. He took her up on the offer with no more than a nod, irritating her with his presumption that she owed him. She *did* owe him, but she hated the fact that he was incapable of performing any parental or domestic task without entering it to his account in some cold-blooded mental ledger.

Bethie was down by eight thirty, but Davis, as usual, was more of a problem. Lately, in his attempts to forestall bedtime, he had hit upon the strategy of becoming chatty and revealing. Tonight he lay in his bed, staring up at the Day-Glo stars on the ceiling, and told Lucy all about Mrs. Ortiz's lasik surgery and about the children's-book writer who had come to visit their class, and about his fears about going out for T-ball because he didn't think he could raise his glove fast enough to keep the ball from smacking him in the face. Even though she was on to him, even though all his cozy talk was plainly opportunistic, she had no real choice but to sit there and listen and comment and make soothing remarks. She couldn't run the risk that he might get it into his mind that sitting here beside his bed was not the most important thing in her world.

She listened to him talk for another half hour, all the while listening less to the rush of words than to the timbre of the breath that carried them. Tonight there was not a hint of wheezing or gasping; the perfect soundlessness of his breathing was as calming to her as music.

And after that initial outburst in the car on the way to school, Davis had seemed to have no trouble in accepting the fact of her mission. Lucy had asked Colleen and Lorelei Tran and Mrs. Ortiz to keep an eye on him for signs of emotional stress, but none of them had detected anything. It appeared that he had made a choice to accept his mother's constant reassurances as the simple truth. Now she had to make sure she did not betray his trust by failing to return to earth.

It would have been wonderful, after leaving Davis's room at last, to sink into her own bed and fall instantly to sleep, but as she walked down the hallway she could hear Brian furiously tapping away on the computer keyboard in the spare room they shared as an office. If there was a confrontation brewing, she thought, she might as well face it now. She went into the kitchen for a glass of water and then joined him in the office. He shifted his head slightly to acknowledge her presence but did not speak. He continued composing his e-mail, while Lucy sat silently in the old rocking chair where she had once nursed her babies to sleep. She waited until he pressed the Send button before speaking.

"How far did you run?"

"Three or four miles. Just around the neighborhood."

"We haven't had a chance to talk about Zokie."

"She seemed all right," he said absently. "Maybe a little spacey. What's with that name?"

"I don't know. I guess her parents wanted something exotic."

"Well, they got it."

"Seriously. You feel okay about her?"

"If I didn't, I would have said something. She's fine." He continued staring at his e-mail in-box, deleting ranks of messages. "I can't believe all this spam."

"So what's the deal?" she said.

"What deal?"

"I just want to know if there's any particular reason I'm walking on eggshells tonight."

He took a moment, fixing his eyes on the screen as he scrolled down with the mouse.

"I went up to the Ninth Floor today," he said at last. "I had a meeting with God. I'm just getting tired of this, you know? I needed somebody to lay it on the table. Am I or am I not going to ever fly again? Am I going to spend the rest of my career sitting on one bullshit committee after another?"

He punched the Delete key, zapping half a dozen lines of spam at once.

"So," he said, "God laid it on the table. He told me he'd heard about a lecture position in aerospace engineering at U of H, and if I wanted him to he'd call the dean and sound him out about it for me. Pretty clear, huh?"

He was looking at her now, but this time Lucy felt the need to face away. She put her chin in her hand and stared at a framed photo on the wall of Brian and the two cosmonauts with whom he had been on *Mir*, all three of them floating weightlessly in one of the modules, all of them grinning at the camera in a display of brotherly fellowship. Anyone who knew the history of that tortured mission, Lucy thought, would have known how counterfeit those smiles were.

"So you're quitting the program," she said flatly.

"It's a possibility. Obviously it's a possibility. I was going to ask what you thought about it."

"Really? You didn't ask what I thought about it before you went in to see God Doggett."

"What's the point of me staying around?" he went on, ignoring her comment as if it were the most obtuse objection in the world. "People are already looking at me like I'm a ghost. Everybody knows I'm never going to get another mission, everybody knows I'm not enough of a suck-up to even get a decent job in the astronaut office."

Her fatigue was growing greater with every word he spoke. She was too weary at heart to even respond. But he seemed to take her dispirited silence as deliberation, and he swiveled around in the cheap office chair and rolled toward her a few inches, his voice earnest.

"There'd be some money issues. I don't know what the teaching job would pay, but probably not more than sixty or sixty-five. But I could supplement it all sorts of ways. I could do some speaking. Alan Crumley says he's done some of those Dine with an Astronaut gigs down at the Kennedy Space Center and they pay pretty well."

"Dine with an Astronaut!" Lucy couldn't keep herself from exploding at last. "Jesus, Brian! You really think you're capable of standing in front of a bunch of tourists with a big smile on your face, answering every stupid question they—"

"I might be. I might be capable of a little more than you think, Lucy."

His eyes were feral and challenging now, looking right at her, turning her into the enemy. She was almost ready to give him the satisfaction of playing the enemy tonight, but not quite.

She leaned back in the rocking chair and looked up at the ceiling, evading those eyes that wanted to force her into either agreement or defiance.

"I'm really tired," she said.

"I'm not sure what the point is anymore anyway."

"The point of what?"

He had already wheeled his chair back and was looking at the computer screen again.

"The point of what, Brian?"

"Low earth orbit, okay? When did the whole idea of spaceflight change from actually going somewhere to going around and around? I mean, you have to admit it's gotten to be kind of a joke. When we were kids we had people on the *moon*! NASA had serious plans to go to Mars! Now all they can do is send us up two hundred and forty miles. Christ, that's about as far as it is to Dallas! We build a space station so we can pretend to have a destination. Then we keep the shuttle flying so we can have a way to get back and forth to the station. All it is is busywork. Why hang around for that?"

She couldn't believe he had said that. If she wanted generic anti-shuttle blather she could read newspaper editorials or scroll through Web sites run by disappointed space geeks. It was irrelevant that there was a certain amount of truth to what he was saying, that on her most vulnerable days the goals of the program were never as sharp as the training and procedures necessary to achieve them. What mattered was that his bitterness was so consuming and selfish. It was not enough for him to fail—the whole shuttle program had to fail with him.

"So what are you saying?" Her voice sounded harsh and flat to her, like Patti Halapeska's grating voice coming in over the loop while she was underwater in the NBL. "That I'm a dupe?"

"That you're what? Jesus, Lucy, I didn't mean that."

"Well, maybe if there's no point to my mission, maybe if I'm just doing it out of vanity or whatever, maybe I should quit too."

"What are you talking about? I don't want you to quit." He scooted back to her on the wheeled chair and grabbed her hands with what was meant to be reassurance but which she read as a kind of panic. "Honey," he said, "I didn't mean that. How could you even think I would mean something like that?"

She was too tired not to reassure him. She met his imploring eyes and nodded vaguely, enough of a signal to imply a truce, but nothing more.

"Just do me a favor," she said. "Wait until my mission's over before you decide to do anything drastic."

"Of course. I never had a thought of doing anything until you got back. This is your time. It's your slot. I'm focused on your mission, just like you are."

She left him thinking he had won his point. She didn't care what he thought. She walked into the bedroom and got into bed and quietly wept, drawing the sheet up against her mouth so he wouldn't hear her as he resumed working, after a suitable period of abashed silence, at the computer. No, she could not ever love him again. How could she love a husband who was willing to poison her with his own weakness and futility? She could hear him tapping on the keyboard down the hall, and as she began to fall asleep the tapping became the sound of a small animal—a hamster or a gerbil—scratching obsessively against the glass walls of its cage. But it was *his* cage, she knew even as she drifted into sleep. It was his cage, and this time it was her mission.

Chapter Thirteen

G ive me a sensor problem," Walt said, turning to Sylvia. "Let's make them wonder if they've got a leak in one of the fuel cells."

Sylvia grinned and clicked her mouse, creating a false reading on a sensor in one of the oxygen tanks. She was ready to do some damage. They all were. For almost an hour the crew had been practicing orbital skills in the fixed-base simulator, and under Surly's experienced guidance they were cruising along a little too smoothly, working a little too well together. Here in the control room, the team was getting bored. It was time to pick up the pace and throw in a mal.

Walt listened in as the crew reacted to the caution and warning light that suddenly flashed in the cockpit. It was Tom Terrific's responsibility as pilot to deal with the fuel cell problem, but everybody had an opinion about what was causing it, and Walt decided Surly was being a little too indulgent in allowing an atmosphere of committee speculation. Things could go bad real fast when too many people were working on the same problem.

Since all the astronauts were staring at the same data screen, trying to figure out what had gone wrong with the oxygen tank sensor, Walt decided it would be a good idea to make the screen go blank. He glanced over at Gary, at the DPS console. Gary had anticipated him. He was sitting there looking over his shoulder at Walt, his finger twitching above the mouse, a conniving smile on his face.

"Shall I kill their monitor, Captain?" Gary said in the affectless, alien voice of some character from *Star Trek*.

"Make it so, Mr. Upchurch," Walt said.

The crew took the loss of the data screen in stride, and Walt was impressed with the way Lucy promptly suggested that she and Buddy could take over that particular problem, leaving the commander and pilot free to discuss the thornier issue of the oxygen sensor.

Lucy and Buddy got the screen back online faster than Walt expected, and it was only a few minutes after that that Tom began to understand that he wasn't dealing with a leak but a pressure problem. Just as he was resetting the limits on the sensor, though, Walt told Kyle to throw him a manifold leak, a tricky mal whose source would be hard to locate.

Kyle followed Walt's instructions with quiet eagerness. Outfoxing the crew, handing them problems that if not solved in time could end in simulated death, was part of the appeal of the job, and Walt didn't mind if the team took pleasure in the ritual of destruction as long as things remained seemly. Every so often he would have to speak a calming word when a team member forgot himself and began to rejoice as a particularly vicious mal threatened the crew with oblivion. None of them were immune to such spells of dark enthusiasm, not even Sylvia, but Kyle was the one Walt kept the closest eye on.

Just now, as the crew scrambled to find the source of the leak, hurriedly working their way through the checklists and closing one isolation valve after another, Kyle was enjoying his grim reaper moment. He began to sing, warbling "Lookin' for leaks in all the wrong places" as the fuel for the thruster jets disappeared at an alarming rate.

"Slow the leak down," Walt instructed him.

"Slow it down?" Kyle said in a hurt voice. "Hey, I'm starting to kick ass here, Walt."

"Just give them some time to solve the problem!" There must have been a harsher tone in Walt's voice than he realized, because Sylvia turned in her chair and regarded him briefly with a sharp scrutiny.

For a moment, Walt himself didn't know what he was angry about. Kyle's playful maliciousness wasn't really out of line. There had been plenty of times when Walt had indulged, even encouraged, an atmosphere of doomsday gamesmanship. But Kyle was, uncharacteristically, a bit too much of a presence today. He had come to work a half hour late, slipping into the pre-brief with overwrought apologies. He said he'd had a fender bender coming out of the drive-thru lane at Chick-fil-A, but there were bright welts on the side of his face that seemed more like the results of a real wreck, and his fast-forward demeanor and the way he waved away everyone's concern made Walt think he had something to hide.

But he didn't want to think about it now. He had a sim to run. It took the crew longer than he would have liked to find the manifold leak and power the thrusters again. Even Surly was a little rusty on that one. When the problem was solved, Walt ordered up the death of all three inertial-measurement units, curious to see how efficiently the crew would be able to realign the spacecraft in the manner of all ancient way-farers, by fixing its position against certain guide stars in the heavens. In this case the heavens were a computer image visible to the astronauts through the windows of the orbiter. Walt listened in as they argued with each other about whether or not Canopus was lined up in the overhead window, and whether or not they had the Pleiades coming into view from the front as Surly slowly rolled the ship into position.

"Guys," he heard Lucy saying at last in a voice whose conviction and exasperation pleased him and filled him with troublesome longing. "*Those* are the Pleiades, and *that* is Castor. Just take my word for it, okay?"

After the debrief, as everyone was leaving the conference room, Walt discreetly asked Kyle to hang on for a minute. Kyle unslung the bike messenger satchel he used as a briefcase, tossed it onto a chair, and then took a seat on the conference table itself, a nonchalant posture whose subtle defiance was unmistakable. If Walt sat down in one of the chairs, which he would have preferred, since he had remained on his feet for much of the sim, he would find himself in the untenable position of being on a lower physical plane than the subordinate he planned to con-front. So he stood with his back against the floor-to-ceiling window that looked out on the hallway, where Sylvia happened to be standing at the moment, going over some lingering instructional issue with Tom. She wasn't just standing there by accident, Walt knew. She had picked up on all the day's subtleties and had planted herself there to spy on what was going to happen next.

"Now you've got Sylvia curious," Kyle said.

"Guess we'll have to live with it." Walt smiled. He wanted this to be friendly and companionable.

"You live with it. I've already tried."

So: suspicions confirmed about Kyle and Sylvia. But Walt saw fit to pretend he didn't know what Kyle was talking about. He put his hands in his pockets and stared at his shoes, giving himself a moment.

"I can guess," Kyle said, before Walt could find an opening that sounded right. "I was late, and it was an important sim. And I second-guessed you about the manifold leak in front of the team, in effect questioning your authority. So, if you're pissed—which I think you are, though it's always kind of hard to tell with you—you've got an excellent right to be."

Walt changed his mind. He grabbed the back of one of the chairs, pulled it out from the conference table, and took a seat. It didn't matter to him anymore whether or not he was looking up at Kyle.

"Here's what's on my mind," he began. "Forget about being late, forget about the second-guessing stuff. Basically, I've got no complaints with the way you do your job. It's just that lately I've started to have this uneasy feeling."

"Okay," Kyle said. "I'm listening."

"This is completely between us, okay? I can't prove anything, I don't *want* to prove anything, I don't even want to ask you anything. I just want to make an observation. It seems to me you may have a drinking problem."

"Okay," Kyle said. "Can I ask how you came to this conclusion?"

"It's not a conclusion. I'm just speculating. It's a concern."

"You think I had a wreck because I was drunk."

"I don't know, Kyle."

"But you're not ruling it out."

"I'm not ruling it out."

Kyle's face was flushed now. He stared down at the chair seat on which he had set his feet and started scooting it back and forth on its rollers.

"Well, you know, Walt, I sort of wish you'd gather a little more evidence before you accuse me of being a—"

"I told you this isn't about evidence. It's not about official letters of reprimand, it's not about—"

"Well, what the fuck is it about, then, Walt?"

The hurt and hostility in Kyle's voice were plain, and his eyes had the sort of teary sheen that Walt remembered seeing in the eyes of kids during schoolyard fights.

"This is a one-time-only discussion, okay?" Walt said, his own voice coming out so judicious and reasonable it repelled him a little. "Like I said, I think you may have a drinking problem. I don't know if I'm right or not. I'm not going to investigate. I'm not going to try to prove it one way or the other. But if I start to feel that it's something I have to worry about, that it's something I have to deal with, I'm going to find a way to get you off my team."

Walt paused to give Kyle a chance to respond, but he said nothing. He just compressed his lips in anger and looked at Walt with filmy eyes.

"Because their lives are at risk enough as it is," Walt went on, gesturing with a nod of his head in the direction of the simulator room. "And if we have to focus on anything other than keeping them alive, then I—"

"Can we just do this without all the self-righteous bullshit? Would that be possible, Walt?"

"All right," Walt said. "Let's leave it there. I'll see you tomorrow."

Kyle stood and grabbed his messenger bag and left the room without glancing back, though he said "Bye" under his breath in a way that may have signaled either disgust or appeasement. Walt remained seated, brooding over the conversation, not at all sure he had handled it right but reasonably confident that Kyle would be back in time for the next sim, and that sometime in the next week or so they could talk without Kyle being quite so defensive or Walt sounding to his own ears quite so patronizing.

"So we're all just a little bit curious," he heard Sylvia calling out as he walked past the simulator control room on his way out of the building. He took a step back and stood at the open doorway. She was sitting at her console pretending to inspect the crew training catalog.

"It was a personnel issue, Sylvia."

"I'm a personnel. You can tell me."

"Maybe you should talk to Kyle."

She shrugged. "We don't talk about stuff anymore. Just tell me if the team's okay or not."

"The team's okay," he said.

If the team was okay, he thought as he drove home, if the team was solid, then the crew would be okay. But Walt lived with the knowledge that if he made a mistake in gauging the quality of his team, and if in consequence the team made a mistake in transmitting crucial skills and knowledge to the crew, then the crew could die. Something like that had happened somewhere along the line with the defective O-rings that had doomed the astronauts in *Challenger*. Somebody along the way, any number of somebodies just like Walt, had allowed themselves to sink into a workaday complacency, to surrender to the illusion that their profession, with its Dilbert cubicles and office birthday parties and chatty newsletters and interdepartmental softball teams, was about something other than sending their colleagues off on a lethal journey. When *Challenger* blew up, Walt was only a few years out of graduate school and steadily burrowing his way into the NASA culture. He was not yet a team lead, just a systems instructor working only his second mission. He had been training a different crew, but he knew the crew of *Challenger*, had worked with some of them in the single-system trainers and talked with them glancingly at parties. The knowledge that they had all ceased to exist at the same moment had been, beneath the genuine grief, a dark excitement, a confirmation of a natural malevolence that until then had seemed to be only a kind of rumor. Walt felt that he had been playing a game of chance in which the stakes were politely acknowledged but never actually believed.

He believed them now. And the incident with Brian Kincheloe on the last mission had been a lesson about his own fallibility as an instructor. He couldn't help blaming Brian's lack of judgment at least partly on himself, because judgment was something he was supposed to teach, along with ascents and entries and orbital maneuvers.

He was stopped at a light when he happened to glance down and notice the wrinkled claim form from the drugstore's one-hour photo lab lying in one of his car's cup holders. Walt picked the form up and read the date and time his pictures were due to be ready: two months ago. He hadn't forgotten them exactly; he had just been avoiding them. They were pictures from a disposable camera he had found in the glove compartment a few months after Rachel's death, photos she had taken on the last trip they had made together, to Oklahoma City for her niece's wedding. At the time the thought of seeing those pictures, of having her image tauntingly reappear when she herself could not, had been unbearable to him, and he had almost thrown the camera away. But after a number of months his longing and curiosity had overcome the lethargy of grief, and he had taken the film to Walgreens. Where he had left it for more months still as his courage flagged again.

He had passed the Walgreens every night on his way home from work without stopping, but now he turned in. The encounter with Kyle had left him unsettled, but he was still charged with a certain confrontational energy, an impulse to get unpleasant tasks behind him. At the one-hour photo desk, the clerk had to rummage through a number of cabinets before he was able to locate Walt's long-unclaimed order.

While the clerk was ringing up the bill, Walt slipped the photos out of the envelope and shuffled through them. Rachel had shot most of the film and as a result was present in only a few of the pictures, over-exposed group shots of uncles and cousins posing behind a sofa or in the backyard around a Saint Francis of Assisi bird fountain. In these pictures, Rachel was as anonymous as all the rest of them; so anonymous, Walt thought, she could even still be alive, instead of boldly selected for death. He realized what he had feared was that he would see her face again in all its vibrancy, its sometimes startling beauty, and that that would be too sharp a reminder just now of what he had lost.

He paid for the pictures, and when he turned around to leave, there was Lucy Kincheloe, striding down the candy aisle with her chin tucked in and a concentrated frown on her face, carrying an oversized pastel bag from the pharmacy at the back of the store.

"Oh," she said, in a mildly startled tone. She held up the pharmacy bag as if she were still in the simulator and owed him an explanation. "Picking up prescriptions."

"Picking up pictures," he said.

They walked together out to the parking lot. It was nearing dark, and the mild South Texas winter was hosting its last norther. A solitary gull flew along with the traffic on NASA Road One.

"So what pictures?" she asked him. She was wearing a blue canvas jacket, and as she spoke she lifted its corduroy collar to block the wind, framing her slender neck.

"Just some generic family stuff," he said. He almost responded with "What prescriptions?" but he checked himself. Medication, like income or the state of a marriage, was a private matter. Instead he said, "Nice work on finding Castor today."

"I've gotten into this habit of studying star charts in the bathtub."

"Surly says you've also been spending a lot of time in the single-system trainers."

"Whenever I have an hour or two. It's important for me to understand better what everybody else on the flight deck is dealing with. You know how it is—you get into your little mission specialist world and forget somebody's got to actually fly the thing."

"Well, it's paying off. Good call on that mal with the data screen. I was glad to see somebody take the initiative on that."

She nodded a thank-you. Then the two of them stood there, oddly suspended, and watched the wind send a cardboard box skidding across the street.

"So," she said. "Generic family stuff. Like a reunion or something?"

He handed her the photo envelope so she could judge for herself. She looked through the pictures rapidly, conscious of him watching her.

"Pretty generic," she said. "But that's a good picture of you."

She held up one of the photos. Walt was standing by himself in a field of stylized metal chairs, a sober expression on his face. He remembered that when Rachel had taken the picture, her eyes had been red from crying.

"That's at the Oklahoma City bombing memorial," he said. Walt had meant this comment to be explanatory, not chastening, but the playfulness he had thought he heard in Lucy's tone was suddenly compromised.

"It's still pretty good," she said. She put the picture with the others and took a step back and handed the envelope to him as formally as a process server. They fell into step as they both ambled toward their cars.

"So what's going on with Brian?" he asked. He thought he heard her sigh; at any rate, she leaned back against the door panel of her minivan and looked off contemplatively in no particular direction.

"It's kind of cold out here," she said. "Do you want to go over to that Starbucks and get a cup of coffee? Do you have time?"

"Sure."

"Let me make a call and I'll see you there in a minute. Would you mind ordering me a latte with skim milk?"

She was holding out a five-dollar bill to pay for the latte, but he waved it off with a tired look and left her in the parking lot with her cell phone while he walked over to the Starbucks in the adjacent strip center.

"Working out some babysitting logistics," she said when she joined him at a miniature table in the back of the café. She pulled off her jacket and draped it over the chair. Underneath, she was wearing a white mock turtleneck.

"It may take a minute," Walt said, nodding toward the counter, where two Starbucks employees were frantically making complicated coffee drinks. The place was busy, the roar of the espresso machine was constant, but most of the customers were dashing in and out, and only a few of the tables were occupied.

"That's all right," Lucy said. "I don't think I'm in a huge hurry."

She dug her cell phone out of the pocket of her jacket and set it on the table—the reflexive gesture of a person who felt she had to be ready for anything.

"I don't know," she said. "I guess the real answer is he's feeling pretty isolated."

It took Walt a moment to catch up to the fact that she was talking about Brian, responding to the question he had asked a few minutes ago in the parking lot.

"I've seen him get into those moods before," he said.

"I'm not sure we can get away with calling it a mood. It's starting to look like a permanent condition."

"Grande cappuccino and skinny latte!" the kid at the counter yelled. Walt stood up to get their coffees. When he came back Lucy was staring absently at a table on the other side of the café, where three youngish engineers with JSC badges were gathered around their Bibles, earnestly discussing with each other some issue of faith.

"He's been talking to God," she resumed.

"Brian?" Walt glanced once again at the Bible study group.

"No, not that God," she said. "God Doggett. Brian sort of confronted him about whether he had any future here. And God sort of said no. I guess in a way it was something Brian had to do. Make somebody come out and say something for once. But I just . . ." She took a sip of her coffee. "I just wish he could, you know, figure out how to *be* around people."

"Do you think it'd do any good for me to talk to him?"

"That's a nice offer, but I don't think he's that interested in talking to anybody. Anyway, what would you say? I mean, be honest: is there really any reason to encourage him to stay in the program?"

She tossed this question off, but her eyes had a probing look as he searched for something other than an honest answer.

"Not necessarily," he finally had to admit.

"And of course he's a little bit jealous about my mission," she said. "I don't really blame him for that. Everybody's human, right? But it just makes things that much harder."

Walt watched her peel apart the plastic lid of her latte cup.

"I probably shouldn't be talking about this with you," she said.

"I'm glad you are. I like to know what's going on with the crew."

"Don't think I'm distracted or anything."

"Okay."

"But he was so completely human!" one of the Bible scholars blurted out in an exuberant voice that made his whispering colleagues suddenly uncomfortable. "I mean, come on: 'Let this cup pass from me'? If that's not human, what is?"

Lucy glanced at Walt, and they shared—he thought—a furtive moment of bemusement, after which she became self-conscious and willed her hands to stop destroying the coffee lid.

Then she said: "Your wife was in some of those pictures."

"In only a few of them. She was usually the photographer."

"I recognized her. Not that I knew her. But I remember meeting her at that party you guys had after the integrated sim for Brian's mission. She was nice."

"I'm glad you thought so."

"I bet everybody thought so."

"Pretty much," he said.

"I didn't mean to bring up anything that's—"

"No," he said. "Everybody sort of assumed from the beginning that I was the kind of guy who wouldn't want to talk about it—about her. And so I didn't, just to make everybody else feel comfortable. But it feels good every now and then just to have somebody bring her up in conversation, to hear somebody say her name."

They were silent for a moment, listening to the espresso machine, as noisy as a locomotive. Lucy sat back in her chair, her spine straight, and took a deliberative sip of her latte. Walt assumed she was either about to diplomatically change the subject or look at her watch and remind herself it was time to leave. But instead, as the storm cloud of noise began to dissipate, she came back to Rachel.

"Sylvia told me about it. About what happened." Her voice was neither too casual nor too solicitous.

"Sylvia was there," Walt said. "She and Rachel were good friends. They'd gone to the mall together. Rachel was standing at one of those kiosks buying a new battery for her cell phone. She was talking to this salesclerk, this kid, and he was telling her that she was using the charger in her car too much, that she was draining her battery—anyway, that's what Sylvia remembered. And then it just happened. Sylvia called me right after she called EMS, but by the time I got to the hospital there was no brain activity. I suppose I'd heard the words 'pulmonary embolus' before, but I wasn't any more prepared than that."

He didn't tell her what he'd guessed since: that all those doomed pregnancies, all those fertility drugs, all that manic effort to create life might have been what had killed her. There was a link between pregnancy and sudden death from blood clots. He had read it in a newspaper headline but had chosen not to torture himself by reading the whole article. It was over, she was dead. He did not want to think about how in boldly and tirelessly reaching out for what she wanted most, Rachel had doomed herself. He wondered now if she had had any real idea of the risks. Probably; she had been an obsessive consumer of medical information. Walt still had, filed away somewhere, her meticulous pregnancy journals and lists of questions for every doctor visit. But there had always been a quiet daring about her. It was hard now for Walt to understand that he had had no daring of his own to match it.

"That kid is still working there," Walt said to Lucy. "Every once in a while I go to the mall, and I walk past that kiosk, and there he is. He's got a little goatee and these accountant's glasses, that retro-hip look or whatever you call it. And I think: that was the last person Rachel ever talked to, probably the last person she ever saw. The poor kid. It must have really freaked him out."

"Not as much as it freaked you out," Lucy said.

Walt felt an obligation to pull the conversation back from whatever self-indulgent brink it was heading to: bathos, pity, an unseemly display of what he hoped she would consider manly grief. At the same time he did not want to surrender the tone of intimacy that seemed to have so naturally arisen between them.

"You get over things," he said. "Everybody has things they have to get over."

"Sure," she agreed. "You know something? I want to get over this mission."

He could tell that his own puzzled look must have alarmed her. "I don't mean that I'm not thrilled about it. That I'm not counting every minute till launch. But I want it to happen and then I want it to be behind me. I want to see my kids' faces when it's over. I want to hold them. I want to come back from the Cape and take a long bath and think about what it was like to have flown in space. Should I be telling you this? I don't have doubts, I really don't. It's just that every once in a while . . . every once in a while . . ."

She leaned forward and whispered in a voice too low for the Bible group or anyone else to hear.

". . . I'm scared out of my mind."

He did her the favor of smiling, so that she knew he understood she was speaking with self-effacing candor rather than from a sudden loss of nerve.

"Everybody is," he answered.

"I bet they don't tell you about it."

"Doesn't matter. Everybody is."

"The kids are the hard part, of course. Sometimes I can't get it out of my head: if I didn't come back, what would they think of me? Would they be able to forgive me?"

"The point is you are coming back."

"I know I am, and I know that's the point. Are you aware they have a Christa McAuliffe doll at Toys R Us?"

Walt wasn't aware; he shook his head.

"I better go relieve the babysitter," Lucy said. She picked up her cell phone off the table, slid it back into the pocket of her jacket, and then looked at him again.

"I'm a hundred percent committed. You understand that, right? I'm not afraid of this mission, I have no doubt about my ability to perform."

"Of course I understand that."

"It's just that every once in a while," she said as she stood up and slipped on her jacket, "it's nice to talk to somebody."

Chapter Fourteen

Surly's wife was named Cheryl, but he called her Paloma. She was requisitely slim, and the frames of her glasses were bold and artistic and flattered her sculpted face. Lucy had never met her before and had expected her to be constrained and maybe a bit haughty, but if she was slumming here in her River Oaks mansion—entertaining the awestruck members of the crew and the training team—it was artfully unapparent. She threaded her way from one guest to the next, knowing all about them, congratulating everyone on the six-month sim as if she had as much invested in its successful completion as they did.

The house where Surly and Paloma lived was brand-new, constructed of native limestone, with plank floors made from ages-old cypress trunks that had been preserved under the mucky bed of the Sabine River, and with solar heating and rainwater catchments and all the other righteous details of indigenous architecture. It was a warm night, and the party had flowed from the spacious rooms of the house itself out onto the patio, where a catered enchilada buffet had been set up. The backyard was vast, dominated by an ornamental Mexican fountain that had been built by two artisans from San Miguel de Allende who now lived in Paloma's guesthouse and whose genius, she said, she was determined to introduce to the world at large.

Paloma had managed to put even Brian at his ease, Lucy noticed.

Her husband was standing now in a rustic arbor beneath the leafy bower of a magnolia tree, talking to Paloma and Surly and Patti about whether or not the new space plane that had been designed to replace the station's outdated Soyuz escape capsule would ever actually be funded.

Lucy herself stood at the edge of the patio with Mickey Flato, sipping a Dos Equis.

"When you come right down to it," Mickey was saying, "it was a thing of beauty."

Lucy clicked her beer bottle against his. She liked Mickey. He was earnest and understated in a way that made this declaration about how moved he had been by the six-month sim seem touchingly out of character. But it *had* been beautiful: an intense marathon session with a very difficult script in which the crew had worked so flawlessly together that Walt and his team had greeted them at the debrief with applause. Already she was feeling nostalgic. The six-month sim was a wistful high-water mark, the beginning of the end of stand-alone training, that phase of the flow in which the crew and the primary team worked together in privacy like musicians rehearsing a chamber piece. Soon enough it would be time for the full orchestra, the integrated sims in which the crew would perform not just for Walt's team but for fifty or more flight controllers with new scripts and new merciless mals.

Mickey's wife, Eve, joined them and gazed with longing at the seductive backyard, with its tranquil lap pool and garden paths and carved stone benches placed at strategic meditative points.

"Sigh," she said. "Just give me one-tenth of this yard. Just give me one square foot."

Lucy knew that Eve and Mickey and their two-year-old daughter lived in a characterless apartment complex across the parking lot from a thirty-eight-screen multiplex near the Sam Houston Tollway. Eve was studying to be a dental technician and, at an impromptu party the crew and team had put together last month, had confided to Lucy the guilt she felt at having to put her daughter into day care, and the never-ending background terror she'd lived with ever since the day of Mickey's cancer diagnosis. She and Mickey were young and strapped and scared. Lucy found herself envying them anyway. They were easy together, solid, and the tribulations they faced did not seem to be driving them apart but rather binding them together with a cohesive clarity.

"Everyone," Paloma announced, standing next to a grave middle-aged Mexican chef. "Gilberto tells me that dinner is ready. So everybody please get your plates and sit wherever you want, and whatever you do don't let your food get cold. We are *completely* informal."

Lucy lingered where she was, finishing her beer as Mickey and Eve drifted over to the buffet. She noticed Walt and Sylvia standing by themselves on the other side of the lap pool, deep in conversation, Walt staring down at the black tile of the pool as Sylvia confided something to him, her face so close to his she could have been whispering into his ear.

"So," Buddy said, standing beside Lucy now with a full plate of food. "I see it hasn't slipped your notice either."

"What?"

Buddy nodded in the direction of Walt and Sylvia. "You think about it, it's been staring us in the face for six months."

"I'm not following. Something's been staring us in the face for six months?"

"Come on. Reach deep."

"Walt and Sylvia?"

"Yes. Excellent."

"No!" she said, wanting her tone to sound exasperated and amused and skeptical, to mask the watery sense of betrayal that had suddenly arisen out of nowhere. In an effort to prove to herself that she shared Buddy's detached curiosity, she bantered with him for a few minutes more, feigning a delicious gossipy interest, even going so far as to declare, "Well, good for them!" in a tone that sounded, at least to her ears, ringingly authentic.

So that was the end of *that,* she reflected when they were all seated and eating their flan and Surly was making a speech praising everybody for their impeccable performances in the six-month sim. That was the end of an absurd little flurry of . . . something. By now she had worked her way around from feeling hurt to feeling contemptuous of her own vulnerability. She did not want to dwell on how she might have reacted if the tremors of attention she had felt in Walt's presence had turned out to be justifiable. It was a relief, in a way, that she no longer had to think about that, or to ponder the consequences it might have brought to her family—if she had been weak and selfish enough to ever let it go that far.

In just minutes, she was back in familiar power-ahead mode, thinking about the endless tasks before launch, making a point not to glance at Walt but to keep her attention on her husband, who was seated next to her, listening with outward good cheer to Surly's remarks. Out of politeness to Paloma and her apparently revered chef, Brian had eaten a bite or two of his flan, and then had pushed it discreetly forward a few inches as if out of the range of temptation. But his self-control when it came to such a frivolous consumable as dessert was now so complete that Lucy doubted very much that he even remembered what temptation felt like.

"And if I'm not mistaken," Lucy heard Surly say, "I believe our beloved patch coordinator has a presentation to make."

Lucy stood and walked over to one of the stone benches flanking the patio, where she had left the small plastic bag she had brought to the party.

"I just want to say," she announced to the group as she opened the bag, "that if you have any complaints, if you have any changes, if you have any last-minute thoughts, I'll be very happy to hear them. But there's one thing you should know: it is now officially too late to do anything about them."

There was hearty applause, and then she reached into the bag and pulled out the completed mission patches and walked around the table, passing them out to the members of the crew first, and then to the training team. The astronauts accepted theirs in silence, testing the texture of the weave with their thumbs, staring thoughtfully at the bright colors and emblems. Lucy had given the patch the same hushed inspection when Ernest had handed her one that afternoon in Graphics and Reproduction. It must be the same feeling, she reflected, for an author receiving the first copy of his book, or a singer listening for the first time to her recorded voice on a CD, or a small-business owner whose ad in the Yellow Pages provides the first confirmation that his enterprise is no longer a private dream but something whose existence has been boldly announced to the world.

Chuck Nethercott was studying his patch with the intensity of a jeweler appraising a diamond. Chuck was a mild-looking man in his forties with a Ph.D. in mechanical engineering. Before joining NASA, he had been an Army Ranger in the Gulf War and had played some sort of key, dangerous role in maintaining the stability of Sarajevo's water supply when the city was besieged by the Serbs. On the STS-108 crew, however, he was most notable for his strategic invisibility, doing his work quietly and competently, always happy to be included but never pressing himself forward. To a degree, Lucy guessed, his detached demeanor was the result of his assignment; since he and Patti were stationed during launch and entry in the windowless mid-deck, their presence had not been required in the many ascent-and-entry sims that Lucy had found to be such a bonding experience early on in the training.

But by now there had been enough sims in the fixed-base simulator involving all of the crew, and so much other training in so many areas, from habitability to EVA, that Chuck and even Patti had started to feel like family. And the patch she had just handed out to them would be as cherished down the years as a family crest.

She saw Walt give the patch a cursory glance and slip it into his shirt pocket as he exchanged a comment with Janine Nethercott, Chuck's equally unimposing wife. A mission patch was nothing new to Walt, of course, but Lucy couldn't help taking his lack of absorption as a gesture of dismissal. She glanced at Sylvia; she could sort of see it. Sylvia was a few years younger than Walt, but she was smart and kind and maybe sexy and wholly appropriate. And what business was it of Lucy's in the first place?

It was only nine thirty on a Friday night and people were in a lingering mood. To good-natured groans, Surly produced a guitar and began to strum the opening chords to "House of the Rising Sun."

"Okay," Paloma announced. "There's *got* to be an alternative to this. Anybody want a tour of the house?"

Out of courtesy, Lucy went along with Paloma, leaving Brian on the patio to listen to Surly's tortured singing. Walt stayed behind too, along with most of the members of the training team and Buddy Santos, who with Gary leapt right in to lend their caterwauling harmony as Surly segued from "Rising Sun" to "Ghost Riders in the Sky" and then the theme to "Rawhide."

Sylvia got into the spirit as well, and a stern look from her told Walt he'd better join in on the chorus. The correct lyrics sprang alarmingly to mind—"Don't try to understand 'em, just roll 'em rope 'em brand 'em"—but he had no singing ability, and his voice sounded so leaden he was afraid the rest of the singers would come to an appalled stop as soon as they noticed it. But they didn't. Sylvia and Kyle had their arms around each other as they sang. Maybe it was just camaraderie or maybe something had reignited there. For a few days after Walt confronted him, Kyle had avoided his eyes and gone about his tasks with a spiteful, exaggerated compliance, but that attitude had soon dissipated, and there had been no recurrence of the original problem. Indeed, Sylvia had told him, during a hushed conversation they had had beside the pool before dinner, that Walt's reprimand had been such a shock to Kyle that he had even warily signed up for an AA meeting.

"Rawhide" led Surly naturally enough from Frankie Laine to Johnny Horton, and he began a frontal assault on "The Battle of New Orleans," demanding that everyone join in. But the song was obscure enough that the younger members of the team had never heard it, and as Surly was chastising them about their ignorance Walt noticed that Brian was slipping discreetly away, wandering out into the yard to follow the winding flagstone path that meandered through Paloma's garden.

When Walt joined him, Brian was looking at the mission patch in the weak illumination of a solar light.

"What do you think?" Walt asked.

"It's all right," Brian said, fanning the edge of the patch impatiently against his fingertips. "I've never understood why people get all worked up about this kind of thing."

Walt shrugged in semi-agreement.

"So I guess she's doing pretty well," Brian observed.

"Yeah, pretty well. Hard to imagine the crew without her."

"I'm not surprised."

"You should be proud of her," Walt said lamely. In talking to Brian, he always felt a need to rush into the silence with a comment, no matter how vacuous.

"I didn't say I wasn't," Brian replied, though whether this was a rebuke or a simple statement was, as was so often the case, impossible to discern.

Brian looked down at the grass and then shot him a glance. Brian had a confiding look in his eye, a rare gleam of trust that Walt found himself grateful for.

"Did Lucy tell you I'm reevaluating?"

"No," he lied. "Reevaluating what?"

"Pretty much everything. Thinking about teaching, maybe."

Walt said nothing; he nodded his head slowly. The group on the patio was now attempting to sing "You've Lost That Lovin' Feelin'."

"So did you end up catching a lot of shit over it?" Brian asked.

"Over what, Brian?"

"You know, that business with me and the switch. I never exactly apologized to you about it."

"Don't worry about it."

"It just seemed like a reasonable thing to do at the time. I was awake, Bill was asleep, the way Ground had presented it to me I thought—"

"Come on, Brian," Walt said. "All that's over."

"I know, but you put your trust in me and I let you down."

"Time to change the subject," Walt insisted. They endured another chorus in silence; Surly continued to belt out the song over his slipshod guitar strumming, but with every note his voice grew flatter and hoarser.

"Do you think it's even possible for him to feel embarrassment?" Walt asked.

Brian smiled. For a moment Walt thought he might have pulled him out of his gloom. But then Lucy came out of the house, her body so tense with alarm that the singing on the patio stopped cold. "Where's Brian?" Walt heard her ask. Her voice was taut, her features rigid. Her fingers were clenched around her cell phone. Someone pointed to the backyard, where Walt and Brian were standing, but by then Lucy's husband was already jogging toward her across the grass.

Chapter Fifteen

Zokie was in the emergency room when they arrived, sitting with Bethie in a hard plastic chair, trying to read the exhausted child to sleep. The moment Bethie saw her parents, she leapt out of Zokie's lap and ran to Lucy, holding out her hands and sobbing, "What's happening? What's happening to Davis?"

"It's all right, honey," she said. "It's all right. You don't have to worry. He's going to be fine. Now I'm going to have Zokie take you home and put you to bed, okay?"

"No!" Bethie's voice was hurt and defiant, and she dug her tiny fingernails into Lucy's arm with cruel insistence. The chaos and fright of the child only reinforced the methodical clarity that had been governing Lucy's mind ever since she had answered Zokie's emergency call forty-five minutes earlier. All those hours in the simulator, she realized, had had a spillover effect on her maternal consciousness. She felt conditioned and unsurprised, ready to regard Bethie's terror as a minor mal that could safely be bypassed for the moment while she dealt with the greater danger of her son's health.

Lucy quizzed Zokie in a firm, procedural voice, allowing Bethie to continue to cling to her, until she had a reasonably clear sense of what had occurred. Zokie told her she had taken Davis and Bethie on a short walk down to the neighborhood park just after dinner. Davis had been pushing Bethie hard on the swing when all of a sudden he began to feel tight and anxious.

"He was having trouble getting his breath, and he looked kind of scared, so I just picked him up and carried him home. And then I checked his level and it was 180 and he was wheezing real bad by that time and then he started crying. So I thought I'd better call you. And then I just took him to the emergency room like you said."

Zokie herself looked a bit pale, and there was a wobble in her voice as she recited these events. Lucy reassured her, and praised her calm efficiency, though she knew that if Colleen had been in charge tonight instead of Zokie she probably would not have allowed Davis's swing pushing to accelerate, as Lucy suspected it had, into hyperventilating hysterics.

"You did just fine, Zokie," Lucy told her. Brian helped her wrestle Bethie back into the girl's arms and then the two of them walked into the emergency room. They found Davis lying in one of the curtained-off rooms set up in radial fashion around the nurses' station. He was pale, even his lips had no color, and Lucy could hear the wheezing in his lungs and the tremulousness in his voice when he said, "Hi." He raised his hand in a kind of wave. There was an oxygen monitor attached to his finger. He meant the greeting to sound manly and offhanded, but he was helpless to keep the tears of relief from flooding his eyes as he saw his parents striding forward to embrace him.

Lucy kissed his clammy forehead while Brian bent down and squeezed his shoulder. Lying in his hospital gown in the vast white bed, straining for breath, his eyes wide and teary, Davis looked so vulnerable that Lucy felt a collapsing sensation in the center of her body, as if he had just been torn away from her nurturing womb.

"Sweetie, give me a number," she said.

"Six."

"We've given him two treatments already," said a young doctor who just now sauntered into the room. She introduced herself as Dr. Schweighofer. She was pleasant and confident, but Lucy could hear in her voice a hint of concern. "We'll give him another one in a few minutes, but if we don't get the results we want I'd like to admit him and get him started on some steroids. I called Dr. Trimble, and of course I'll keep him up to speed with everything we're doing."

She looked from Lucy to Brian and then clasped her hands together and gave a curt, conclusive nod of her head. "Sound good?"

"Sounds good," Lucy heard herself idiotically repeating, though she knew, just from looking at Davis, that another dose of albuterol from the machine would not be enough to restore his breathing to the safe zone.

"It's going to be a long night," she told Brian when the doctor left. "You'd better get Bethie home and get her to bed and let Zokie go. I'll stay with Davis."

"You sure you can do that? What's your day like tomorrow?"

"It doesn't matter what my day's like, Brian. I'm his mother and I'm going to stay with him."

She hadn't meant this to sound quite so self-righteously defiant, but that was the way Brian took it, and he looked at her across the boy's bed with an aggrieved expression that bordered on hostility.

"I only meant that I could stay with him instead. I wasn't suggesting we leave him all alone in the hospital. Jesus, Lucy."

"I'm sorry," she conceded, glancing guiltily down at Davis, who was following this dispute with nervous looks from one parent to the other as he struggled for breath. Lucy understood that fear was making both her and Brian shrill and even more impatient with each other than usual. Her instinct was to push her husband away, to banish him from the force field of motherly power she felt she needed to create in order to protect her child. She thought he had no strength to lend her; his own anxieties about their son, his nervous comments and attempts at reassurance, were simply in the way. For the second time that night, she thought wistfully of how, in a better marriage, Brian would be her full partner in crisis. They would be working together in precise coordination, and their fears for the health of their son would result in fellowship, not fretful bickering. If she could have that sort of relationship with her crew, with her training team, why was it so impossible to achieve it with the man who was supposed to be her life's companion?

"Maybe you could call Surly for me," she said to Brian, in what she hoped he would regard as a conciliatory tone. "Just give him an idea about what's going on. I've got habitability training at ten. I probably won't be able to make that, but the rest of the schedule might still work out."

"All right. I can shift some things around myself and come relieve you. Just let me know."

"I don't think we'll be here that long," she said, smiling down at

Davis. "I bet we'll be out of here in the morning, won't we, sweet-heart?"

In another hour she was alone with Davis in a private room, pred-nisone trickling into his veins from an IV tube. She sat beside him holding his hand and running her fingertips against the grain of the whispery hairs on his forearm. His breathing was a little better, though he was still jittery from the albuterol and he didn't feel like talking. He wanted to watch television, but the hospital's cable menu was limited, and there was little to watch besides twenty-four-hour news stations and late-night talk shows. Davis finally settled on an old movie, *Youngblood Hawke,* and stared feverishly at it long enough to fall asleep. It was after midnight by then, and Lucy did her best to sleep as well, though the hos-pital chair was as unyielding as a school desk and her son's harsh breathing kept dragging her vigilant mind back into consciousness.

Throughout the long night a nurse would come every few hours to wake him and administer more medicine, and he would fight and squirm and finally settle back into sleep until it was time for him to be roused again. During one of these interludes, at about three in the morn-ing, when sleep appeared impossible for her, Lucy turned on the TV, keeping the sound off so that she would not disturb Davis's fragile doz-ing. She caught the last scenes of a comedic western starring Frank Sina-tra and various members of the Rat Pack, and then the beginning of a movie called *The 300 Spartans,* about the battle of Thermopylae. The silent images flashed on the tiny wall-mounted screen with hallucinatory incoherence and force, Joey Bishop somehow logically giving way to King Darius, the Spartans' fight to the death the tortured continuation of a slapstick shoot-out in a desert canyon. The washed-out Technicolor scenes began to seem the indistinguishable parts of a despairing dream. Love was caustic, life absurd; the Persians were massing, and she had to lay down her life to stop them, though she could not make her weeping, desolate children understand why. All she knew was that it was all somehow her fault, that she had destroyed their bright world for a rea-son that was supposed to be noble but that kept insistently revealing itself as selfish. As the enemy advanced toward her in their armor, as she knew herself to be facing a fool's death, breath came to her in labored spasms.

She willed herself awake. There was a tincture of daylight at the window, Doris Day was now holding forth on the silent television screen, and Davis was at last peacefully asleep, breathing shallowly but evenly, the color back in his face. At that moment she heard a polite rap at the door and Lloyd Trimble walked in. Trimble was a fervent Aggie and made a point of comporting himself like a cowboy doctor, wearing pressed Wranglers or boot-cut slacks and sometimes even a bolo tie. He was sixty-five, but his thatchy brown hair and lean build made him look ten years younger, and he was still fit enough to run in the Houston marathon.

"Don't wake him up," Trimble said, slipping across the other side of Davis's bed and unwinding his stethoscope. "How long has he been asleep like this?"

"A couple of hours."

As Trimble listened to Davis's lungs through the stethoscope, the child's eyes fluttered open.

"Hi there, partner," the doctor said. Lucy saw Davis glance nervously to his right, to see if his mother was still there. She took his hand and squeezed it while Trimble studied a chart.

"Well, the last reading we got was pretty good. We'll check his peak again in an hour or so, and then I guess you can take him home. That okay with you, Davis?"

"Can I go to school?"

"Better stay home today. Veg out. Watch some videos. Okay, bud?"

Davis nodded wanly. Trimble gave him a friendly rap on the forehead with his knuckle and turned to go.

"I'll be right back, honey," Lucy said to Davis and followed the doctor out of the room. She shut the door behind her.

"You did the right thing getting him to the ER," Trimble told her. "Low as his peak was, he needed a little boost."

"How serious was this, Lloyd?"

"Well, it needed attention. I wouldn't call it a life-or-death situation. He's fine now. You're the one who's looking a little ragged. You get any sleep at all? You know, if you'd asked for a bed they probably would have been glad to bring you one."

"You know I have a mission, right?" she asked him, after a distracted silence.

"Yeah, of course I do, Lucy. Congratulations, by the way."

She could tell she was keeping him. He stood there in the corridor in the universal hurried posture of doctors, his hands in his pockets, his weight shifting onto his back foot, as primed to make an escape as a sprinter in a starting block. Even so, she took her time in asking her question.

"Should I go?"

Trimble shifted his weight back in her direction.

"Should you go on the *mission*?"

She nodded. He walked over to the other side of the corridor and leaned against the wall and stared down at his boots as he knocked the heel of one thoughtfully against the toe of the other.

"I'm not sure I'm the one you should be asking a question like that," he said finally. "The point is, Davis had an episode, it was a bit scary for you, and now he's fine. We're going to keep on top of his asthma, and someday he's going to grow out of it. In the meantime, in the short term, he'll have some days when he's not up to speed, maybe every once in a great while something of an acute nature like we've just had. So I guess if you want my opinion, you stay prepared for a crisis, but you don't put your life on hold *waiting* for it."

"Okay," she said, "but in terms of his general condition."

"His general condition is no different than it was six months ago. It might even be better. It was an *episode,* Lucy. Go on the mission, okay? He'll be in good hands here on earth."

He pushed off against the wall and walked over to her and gave her an awkward hug of reassurance, a gesture she didn't need. It irritated her to think her distress was so visible that Trimble felt he had to address her concerns with fatherly comfort rather than hard information.

Davis had gone back to sleep, and as she sat by his bed sipping a cup of coffee that one of the nurses had brought her, her morale began to revive. She turned the sound up on the TV and watched the first few moments of *Today,* the waving out-of-towners in Rockefeller Center, the cheerful banter of Matt and Katy and Al judiciously giving way to somber headlines, the pleasant illusion the show conveyed that all America was rising together in hope and good humor to confront a difficult world. She looked at her son's sleeping face. In another day or so it would grow noticeably fuller and rounder from the steroids that were flooding through his veins, but at least he was breathing now with merciful ease, no panic or struggle in his expression as his chest rose and fell beneath the hospital blanket.

He woke up on his own a few minutes later, talkative and content in his drowsy helplessness, taking it for granted that he would find his sleepless, vigilant mother beside him.

He was given a last dose of albuterol an hour later, and his docility ebbed away as he began to grow jittery and demanding. But just as he was making a face at his breakfast tray, Brian arrived with a bag of chorizo-and-egg tacos.

"I talked to Surly," Brian told her as she dripped salsa onto her taco. She was ravenous, and the thick homemade tortilla was warm against her palm. "Your morning's clear. Habitability's been moved to two, and nobody had any problem shifting the EVA session to tomorrow afternoon. I got Bethie to school and Colleen can stay till seven, and Zokie's on deck if we need her after that. Okay?"

"Okay," she said, and went so far as to kiss him to show her gratitude. Brian's nature was generally inflexible, but he had the potential to shine bright in emergencies. And because it had fallen upon him to take command of his wife's logistical crises, he had a heartening air of consequence this morning that briefly stirred her affection.

Brian stayed in the room as Lucy filled out the paperwork for Davis's release, and then went out to get the car and bring it around to the hospital entrance. Lucy had not thought to ask Brian to bring fresh clothes, and so she had Davis put on the jeans and rugby shirt he had been wearing when Zokie took him to the emergency room, and then she walked beside him as a nurse pushed him toward the lobby in a wheelchair. He was still shaky from the profound assault of his all-night medications, but he was happy to be leaving the hospital and regarded the wheelchair ride as an unexpected benefit.

Brian was waiting with the minivan at the curb, and he gave Davis a high five as the boy slid out of his wheelchair and climbed through the open panel door into the backseat. The bright midmorning coastal sun worked its evaporative magic, at least for a moment or two, on Lucy's imagination. Davis was safe, the terrors of the night had passed, the doctor's judgment that she had every reason to live her life in confidence rather than dread made moral sense to her. But as she buckled her seat belt she saw herself being strapped into the flight deck of *Endeavour,* and she felt an actual shudder in her body. The sureness of catastrophe—of "contingency"—was suddenly as real to her as it had been in last night's movie-induced nightmare when she had gripped her sword and waited to advance in the fatal battle against the Persians, all the while her children wailing from somewhere behind her, pleading with her to stay and protect them.

"Why can't I go to school?" Davis said as they pulled out of the parking lot.

"Because you have to rest," she said. "You don't want to have another attack."

"But I'm not going to!"

"I know you're not," she said, turning in her seat to face him. "But we have to be sure. And that's why you're going to stay home today with Colleen and rest."

He made a point of sighing and grumpily folding his arms. Lucy was glad the instinct to return to school was so strong in him, that he was still invested in a personal image of health rather than one of illness and self-defeat. But she also could tell that his defiance was minimal. The hospital stay had scared him, and his mother's stern voice, telling him exactly what he must do, excused him from the effort to appear heroic.

"Is that a deal?" she said.

"It's a deal," he answered wearily. He still seemed just a bit pale to her, and she reached out her hand to feel the skin of his cheeks.

"You don't have to keep doing that, Mom," he said. "I'm okay. Dad, tell her I'm okay."

"You heard the man," said Brian.

Lucy smiled at her son in the backseat. His skin was cool, after all, and there was more color in his face than she had thought. She was about to turn around when she saw Walt Womack through the rear window of the minivan. He was getting out of his car in the parking lot, carrying a gift-wrapped package and walking toward the hospital entrance.

"There's—" She caught herself before finishing the sentence. She didn't know why.

"There's what?" Brian asked, as he merged out into traffic.

Lucy turned around in her seat and faced forward as Brian turned onto NASA Road One. "Nothing," she said. "I just thought I saw somebody."

Chapter Sixteen

What had happened to Lucy?

That was the topic of conversation that naturally emerged as Walt and Sylvia took a walk together along the JSC jogging track. Walt would have preferred to run. The training schedule defied regular hours—the simulators might be available to his crew at eight a.m. one day and at ten p.m. the next—and so of course the idea of a predictable exercise routine at this intense stage of the flow was hopeless as well. Walt had never been a jock, but over the years he had developed a metabolic dependency on his four-mile runs, and as a consequence mere walking felt pointless and sluggardly. But Sylvia had invited him, and she was immune to exercise anxiety. She just thought taking a walk would be a pleasant thing to do.

It was four in the afternoon. They had just finished a series of emergency de-orbit runs in the fixed-base simulator and had a two-hour break before what promised to be an all-night session in the motion-based simulator. The mild coastal winter had given way to a barely perceptible spring. The oaks along the path were in leaf again, the woodland shade fuller. A week ago, Walt had made his annual shift from long-sleeved to short-sleeved shirts, though most winter days had been so warm that the difference was largely ceremonial.

"She missed that callout this afternoon," Sylvia was saying. "And have you noticed how she seems to lose her way in the checklists lately?"

"I've noticed."

"She's really off her game, Walt. When we first started training she had the Flight Data File down cold. She could practically recite it. Of course, how can you not be distracted if your kid is sick?"

"She'll be back up to speed in a few days."

"You think so?"

"Sure I do. Remember when Elise Trube's mother was dying? She had a few wobbly days there."

"Yeah, but then her mother died and it was over. A kid with asthma, though, that's chronic. Not to mention her husband."

They walked on for twenty more yards. Several astronauts, running hard, passed them on the trail, waving backward as they disappeared around a bend in the trees.

"What about her husband?" Walt decided to ask.

"Nothing. It's just that Brian can't be the easiest guy in the world to live with. All that negative energy oozing out of every pore."

"He tries."

"Does he, do you think?"

"Yeah," Walt said. "I think he tries."

"Good for him, then. Anyway, what do I know? I've never been married. Husbands are still mysterious beings to me."

They made the loop and ended up where they'd started, near the astronauts' gym, gossiping along the way about Surly's wife and the dumbfounding elegance of their life in River Oaks, and about what areas the crew still needed work in to prepare them for the first of the integrated sims.

Sylvia took a sip of water from a bottle she had been carrying in her hand the whole walk, and offered it to Walt.

"The deal is," Sylvia said, "things hit her pretty hard, don't they? Lucy, I mean. She's got that depth-of-feeling thing going on, and you never know if that's an asset or a liability or what."

"She has stuff she has to wrestle with," Walt said. "That's not a bad thing. It keeps her strong. It keeps her aware of how much she has to want the mission. Also, when it comes to the crew, she's sort of the center of gravity. You've got Surly on one hand, who's like this astronaut action figure, and on the other hand you have Buddy Santos, who's practically a stand-up comic. You take Lucy out of that equation and—"

"Who said anything about taking her out of the equation?" Sylvia looked genuinely surprised. "I was just saying maybe somebody needs to help her snap back into focus. Remind her to make her callouts a little sharper. And you being team lead and all, and such an adorable personality to boot—"

"Okay," Walt said. "I'll talk to her."

But it was Lucy who was in touch with Walt first. She called him on his cell phone the next evening as he was pulling into his parking place at his condominium.

"I just wondered," she said, "if you might have a moment in the next day or two to sort of talk."

"I can talk now," he said.

"I was thinking in person."

"I know," he said. "I meant I could meet you now."

"Can you hold on a minute?"

Walt heard her on the other end of the line conferring with a young woman he assumed to be a babysitter.

"Okay," she said when she came back. "Sorry. Now would be fine. Are you still at the center?"

"No, I'm at home. But I could drive back there and meet you in the briefing room. I don't think anybody's using it right now.

"Or," he heard himself saying, "you could just come here."

"To your house?"

"It's not really a house."

There was a puzzled stretch of silence on the other end.

"It's a condo, I mean."

"Oh," she said. "Sure, I guess I could come over there. If it's no trouble."

"I've got stuff to drink. I don't think I have much food in the refrigerator at the moment, but if you're hungry, if you want to have dinner or something, I could go out and—"

"Oh, no," she said; her voice had a note of mild alarm in it. "I'm not hungry. But if *you* are . . . Look, I'm sure this can wait till tomorrow if you'd rather—"

"Come over here," he said in his team lead voice, as if he were correcting her during some flustered mistake in the simulator. "Hold on— I'll give you the address."

. . .

It was strange to see a woman standing in the living room of his condo. It was strange to see anyone here, really. Louis was the only person who ever came around, and then it was just to swing by when it was his turn to drive to dinner or to one of their canoe outings. Walt noticed Lucy glancing around, and the way her eyes seemed to settle on nothing at all confirmed his suspicion that the place was characterless. Rachel had picked out all of their furniture, with only grunting affirmation on his part. Walt had always supposed she possessed good taste, and he had had no reason, since her death, to change his mind. But the truth was that none of the things she had bought at Penney's or Dillard's or Restoration Hardware held much sentimental value for him now, or much interest. Living alone with these chairs and sofas and coffee tables, he found them as generic and expressionless as if they were still lined up in the department store showroom, as if no human form had ever made an imprint on them.

"To begin with," Lucy said, slipping her purse off her shoulder and taking a seat on the sofa. She set her elbows on her thighs and clasped her hands, in a posture that was both businesslike and supplicating. "To begin with, I want you to know that I've been more aware than anybody that—"

"Don't sit there," Walt said. "Let's go out on the deck."

He led her through the sliding patio door out onto the small deck that looked over Clear Lake. There was no wind at this hour and the water was flat, and the fading light gave it a sheen as bright as an oil slick. In the marshy fringe at the edge of the water, a night heron was on patrol.

Walt ushered Lucy to one of the plastic Martha Stewart deck chairs he had bought at Kmart.

"I've got some red wine," he said. "I've got beer and Dr Pepper."

"Maybe just water, thanks."

He went into the kitchen and returned with two glasses of ice water. Then he went back and poured some tortilla chips into a bowl and brought them out along with a widemouthed jar of salsa.

"So," he said, taking a seat at last, "let's hear it."

She took a sip from her glass as she stared out across the lake without looking at him. He had to make an effort not to stare at her. The rich evening light brought the same radiance to her skin and hair that it brought to the water's surface, and it gave the planes and contours of her face a sculptured completion.

"Okay," she said. "It's plain to me, as it has to be plain to you, that in the last few days I haven't been all that sharp. Nobody's said anything yet, not even Surly, but I just wanted to get ahead of the curve on this. I wanted to make a sort of announcement, to make sure you understand that I have very high standards of achievement for myself that I have every intention of meeting."

Her declamation delivered, she took another drink of water. She crossed her legs and nervously pumped one foot up and down, her heel rhythmically slapping against the leather inner surface of her sandal. The sandals were open-toed. Her toenails were unpainted, and carefully but squarely trimmed in a way that Walt found touching.

It was up to him to respond, and he knew she was expecting something more than bland reassurance. She wanted, he thought, to be challenged.

"Are you afraid you're going to be dropped from the mission?" he said.

If this rattled her, she didn't let it show, though her foot continued to pump up and down. And she made a point of not meeting his eyes as she silently surveyed the little balcony.

"You should have some plants out here," she said.

Walt took a chip and dipped it into the salsa. A brown pelican coasted right in front of them, three feet away, its knowing eyes level with theirs. Walt gave her all the time she needed.

"Everybody knows that you said something to Kyle," she finally said. "Something to the effect that if he didn't shape up he'd be a risk to the success of the mission and you'd get rid of him."

"It's not the same situation, Lucy."

"I know it's not. But I made a mistake the other day when I told you I was scared. I know you pretended to wave it off, but I can tell you haven't by the way you look at me. And I know I've been a little preoccupied lately with my son's asthma. So I was worried that you'd put all that together and start to have doubts. And like I said, I'm here to tell you you shouldn't."

"What do you mean," he said, " 'the way I look at you'?"

"I don't know. I can just feel the scrutiny, that's all. The judgment, whatever."

"Look," he said, "if I had doubts I would have already talked to Surly. You would already have been asked to pull yourself off the mission. But I don't have doubts, because I know you'd rather die than screw up. And if I've been looking at you that way, I'm sorry. I wasn't aware of it."

A Jet Ski came ripping across the surface of the lake; its reverberant whine caused a great blue heron standing in the mud of the shoreline to lift its wings in annoyance and fly off. Lucy kept her eyes trained on the irritating little vessel as it disappeared into the marshy distance where the sun was setting, leaving behind a roiling echo.

"Have you ever had anybody pull themselves off a mission?" she asked.

Walt shook his head. "Do you want to quit?"

"No!" she declared. "God, no. It's unthinkable . . . or it would be if I hadn't thought about it."

She smiled at him, nervously; trustingly, he thought. He stood up and walked into the kitchen and brought back a bottle of wine and two glasses.

"I just wanted water," she said, but allowed him to open the wine and pour it into her glass. It was almost dark now. The beacon of the lighthouse on the other shore had been illuminated while he was in the kitchen, and the few boats still out on the lake were discernible only by their running lights and by the industrious humming of their engines. The Jet Ski had not come back, nor had the heron.

"It can get cold out here still, if you want to borrow a sweatshirt or something," he told her.

"Give me a break," she said. He was glad for the intimacy her chiding tone implied. "Don't even utter the word 'cold' when you're talking about this place to a Yankee. But you were born here, right?"

"Close. Houston. I grew up in Spring Branch."

"Well, your biochemistry is bound to be semitropical. Put on a sweatshirt if you need one. I've got to be going anyway."

She looked at her watch but seemed to draw no conclusions from what it said, since she continued to sit in the plastic chair, taking her first sip of the wine.

"Do I have the right to do this?" she said. "That's the big question. That's the one that keeps looming."

"I can't answer that," Walt said.

"Of course you can't. But I like the idea that I can say it aloud to somebody. That I can talk to somebody about what it feels like to see my little boy lying there in a hospital bed fighting to breathe, and both of us knowing that in a few months I'm going to leave him."

"Maybe you need to remind yourself you're only leaving him for eight days," Walt said.

"I know. But instead I keep reminding myself it could be forever."

She turned her chair around a bit, scraping its plastic legs against the concrete surface of the patio, so that she could face him.

"I'm not really saying any of this," she said.

"Any of what?"

Walt heard her give a soft, rueful laugh. He watched her take another sip from her wineglass, feeling he now somehow had the right to regard her plainly rather than furtively.

"That's what I mean," she said.

"What?"

"That look."

Walt did not turn his eyes away; he let her do that, after a deliberate moment or two. She shifted in her chair and looked away from the deck into the illuminated living room, which to Walt's eyes suddenly seemed like an empty stage set.

"You should also have some pictures on the walls," she said.

"Well, if you decide to pull yourself off the mission you can always become an interior decorator."

"No, I take that back. Don't change a thing. There's something blah about the place that's kind of becoming."

She gave him the same assessing glance she had just given his drab environs.

"Were you different before? When your wife was alive?"

"Was I less blah? Probably not by much."

"Were you happy being married?"

"Are you not?"

She shrugged. "Every once in a while, between Brian and me, there's a glimmer of what it's supposed to be like. That's about the best I can say. What about with you and Rachel?"

"It wasn't perfect, Lucy."

"More than a glimmer, though, I bet."

He nodded. More than a glimmer.

"Wasn't perfect how?" she asked him.

He told her about the crucial struggle of their life together, how Rachel had longed for children and how Walt, armed with cruel reason, had unknowingly turned himself into her antagonist.

"I would have been like her," Lucy said. "I would have gone to whatever irrational limits were out there. I wanted children as much as I want to go into space. More, even. What do you think you would have been like as a father?"

"Adequate."

"Better than that," Lucy declared.

"Since it's a moot point, I'll defer to your judgment."

"You might still have kids with somebody."

"I think that would feel wrong," he said. "She'd wanted it too much. It'd feel like a betrayal."

"You could say that about being alive in general."

"You could."

"What about Sylvia?" she decided to ask.

"What do you mean?"

"Does she want children?"

The look of puzzlement on his face was unexpected, and awkwardly gratifying.

"Is there some sort of rumor?" he said.

"I wouldn't call it a rumor. It's more like an assumption."

He gave a brief, weary laugh. She watched him as he looked out over the dark water.

"Incorrect?" she said.

"Incorrect."

"I wouldn't have brought it up if I hadn't thought it was common knowledge."

It hadn't been common knowledge, it had only been gossip from Buddy Santos. But it had fit somehow, and she knew she had brought it up for some sort of churlish confirming reason of her own.

"Whatever you could do to set the gossip record straight," he said, "I'd appreciate it. None of us needs that sort of distraction in the middle of the training flow."

She held up her hand in a mocking pledge. Neither of them seemed to feel particularly abashed. Lucy took advantage of the direct, half-chiding tone that had arisen between them and asked the question she had been holding back.

"I saw you in the hospital parking lot the other day when we were leaving. What were you doing there?"

"Visiting somebody," Walt said. "Or trying to. Hold on a minute."

He stood up and walked into the condo, disappearing into the bedroom and returning with the gift-wrapped package Lucy had seen him carrying in the parking lot.

"You'd already checked out," he said, setting the present on the table. "I wasn't sure what to do with it. It seemed awkward just to show up at your house. He doesn't even know me, really. Maybe you should give it to him and say it's from you and Brian. It's some sort of Lego thing. The box said ages five to seven, but it may be too young for him."

"It won't be. And I'm going to make sure he knows it's from you."

He was still standing. She rose from her chair and walked around the circumference of the circular plastic table and embraced him. Walt was aware of her open hand compressed against his spine, the faint pressure of her lips just below the lobe of his ear. Her face sank to his shoulder and rested there a moment, and idly, even innocently, he stroked the back of her head until they both reasoned their way out of each other's arms.

"I don't know what you would call that," she said.

"A collegial hug."

She laughed, and briefly and familiarly touched her hand to his chest, a gesture that thrilled him more than the ambiguous embrace they had just exchanged.

"I'm sorry," she went on. "I come here to convince you how professional I am, and I end up doing—whatever this is."

"There's nothing to worry about," Walt said. He started to clear the table and she eagerly joined in, following him to the kitchen carrying the chips and the salsa jar. She screwed the lid on the jar and put it in the refrigerator, and while he watched she poured the rest of the chips back into the bag and fastened it with a plastic clip and opened the door to the shallow pantry and set it inside. She looked about for something else to do, but Walt was already rinsing the wineglasses in the sink, and when he turned around they found themselves decisively facing each other in the confined and brightly lit kitchen.

"I'm not going to do this," she said.

"I'm not either."

She retrieved her purse and headed down the hallway toward the door, but then she turned and walked back toward him, and then past him, out to the deck where Davis's present was still lying on the table. On the way back she planted herself in front of him as if she meant to say something that had just occurred to her, but instead she just extended a finger and touched one of the middle buttons of his shirt. "Oh, hell," she whispered, when she could think of nothing to say. Then she turned and walked out the door, leaving him standing alone in the hallway.

Chapter Seventeen

Because Lucy was obsessively early for every appointment, she found herself standing alone in the lobby of Building 2, where she was scheduled to meet a writer from *Texas Monthly*. Spanning the wall above the entrance to the auditorium was a gigantic mural that she had never taken the time to study before, an outdated and rather feverish vision of the future of spaceflight.

She could tell from all the busy space activity on the right side of the mural—astronauts zipping in and out of the shuttle with their rocket packs, a mammoth space station as big as a city under construction in the background—that this vision was a product of the hopeful 1980s, before the *Challenger* disaster and the continual erosion of the budget for manned spaceflight had caused the program to shrink and lose its way. This confident painting seemed wrenchingly naive to her at the moment, with its triad of martyred astronauts—Grissom, White, and Chaffee—who had died in a launch pad fire during the early Apollo days now proudly resurrected and looking out at the unstoppable industry all around them. Among the people gazing heroically up to the heavens was a single woman astronaut positioned to the side of the central figures, her helmet in her hands and her hair in an antiquated flip.

What kept Lucy from bristling at the image of a woman as a quaint variation in a robust male fantasy were the earnest tertiary figures stationed at the very bottom of the frame: flight controllers and trainers in their suits and white shirts and glasses. Though it had been three months since that night in Walt's condominium, and though they had both been wise enough to let nothing come of it, she had a habit now of looking for Walt everywhere, of seeing him in every context. She was amused and touched, but maybe a little angry too, that in the bombastic scale of this painting he and his colleagues were forlorn marginal players. She thought Walt, with his Dockers and his pen-and-pencil set, should be the colossal figure in the middle of the canvas, in the same way he seemed to be slowly becoming the stable center of her own life.

"Am I late?" the writer from *Texas Monthly* said as she opened the glass door and scurried across to Lucy with her hand outstretched. She said her name was Jeannette. She was maybe fifty, stylish, scrutinizing, a bit jittery. She had just come into the air-conditioning from the August heat and was busy dabbing perspiration from her hairline as Lucy reassured her that she was on time.

Lucy led her into the LBJ room, a small conference room down the hall, decorated with photographs of Lyndon Johnson in a hard hat inspecting the construction of the space center that was being built in his name.

"So what I'm hoping to do," Jeannette said, after complimenting Lucy on her earrings and issuing a few bromides about the August heat, "is just talk to as many women as I can, try to get a sense of—well, what it's like, of course, to fly into space—but also how you find your way as a woman in a culture that's so historically male. I mean, all these acronyms, all this vestigial macho *terseness*."

Was she asking a question? Just two hours ago, Lucy had emerged from an eight-hour integrated sim, in which not just the crew but two different shifts of mission controllers had trained together in a highly detailed and realistic run-through of the first day of the mission. She had no problem with terseness. After months of training for this mission she had developed a longing for clear, measured, uninflected speech. To her, it was the sound of security, the soothing cadence of people who knew what they were about, who knew how to run through the procedures and talk their way through and out of danger.

Lucy listened as the writer ruminated for another sentence or two. She was intelligent, maybe incisive once she actually got her words down on paper, and there was something amiable in her floundering approach, her apparent need not just to interview Lucy but to somehow enlist her. But by and large her restlessness and lack of focus made Lucy nervous, since in the world she inhabited these were fatal flaws.

Nor could Lucy quite respond to the undercurrent of gender grievances she was starting to detect in the interview. Jeannette was maybe ten or twelve years older than Lucy; the feminist struggles of her generation were still evidently personal and immediate, and perhaps she was unwilling to believe that a woman could succeed in this "culture" without essentially being co-opted by it. Lucy was abundantly aware that she herself was not a pioneer. The painting she had just been gazing at confirmed that fact. She had entered the program at a time in the history of spaceflight when the idea of women astronauts was already so firmly established as to be mandatory. There were problems still, of course, systemic male biases and presumptions common to most professions, but she did not care to advertise them to a stranger. Nor was she eager to let her interviewer know that most of the barricades she faced seemed to be pointedly of her own making.

"Oh, that's sweet!" Jeannette suddenly said, boldly reaching out and taking Lucy's wrist so that she could examine the shuttle charm on her bracelet. "Does everybody get one of these?"

"My husband and kids gave it to me when I got assigned to the mission," Lucy explained.

"You have kids? How old?" When Lucy told her, one eyebrow notched up in interest. "So young," she said. "I have a daughter who's starting college next year, if she can ever motivate herself to actually fill out the applications."

Lucy smiled, but asked no further questions about Jeannette's daughter, since she knew from experience that would lead her to expect a reciprocal candor from Lucy herself, something she wasn't ready to supply. The trick in these interviews was to strike a tone of cordiality but to guard against any inadvertent revelations, any hint of a chaotic internal life.

She answered the reporter's gently intrusive questions about what it was like to tell your children you were going into space, how you assuaged their fears and how you dealt with your own. To her own ears she sounded, as she meant to sound, brisk, unreflective, *terse*. Of course you think about it, she admitted. How could you not? You feel a certain anxiety, but an anxiety so mingled with anticipation and excitement it would be a mistake to call it fear. You focus on the confidence your training has brought you, and you take care to communicate that confidence to your children, not as a strategy to keep them compliant and unaware but as an opportunity to pass on values, to show them how to boldly face a challenging task.

It was pure poker-faced NASAspeak, but she believed it, much of it. For the last few months she had felt that she was on the team again, her mood high, her time and attention so completely absorbed that she had even forgotten to notice the oppressive coastal humidity. This was due mostly to a summer-long suspension of bad fortune. Because Davis's health had held steady, the whole family had begun to stand down from a perpetual crisis footing. Brian was working uncomplainingly at what they both knew was a dead-end job on the Safety Board. His hours were reasonably flexible and predictable, which made her outrageous training schedule more bearable for all of them. The children had spent a good deal of the summer in various scheduled activities—swimming lessons, classes at the children's museum, a day camp for Davis at the Armand Bayou nature center—and for the first two weeks of August they had gone to visit Lucy's mother in Massachusetts. Now Davis was already back in school, assigned to a class with one of the best third-grade teachers, and, even with her schedule of wall-to-wall training, Lucy had managed to carve out time to take him to the first day of school and to show up with Brian for back-to-school night. Bethie, meanwhile, was due to start pre-kindergarten in another week or so, and Lucy felt that the excitement of being in school would help to insulate her from the anxieties that would inevitably gather around the launch, which was now only two months away.

There was a serenity to being so passionately involved in such a complex endeavor. She was working harder than she had ever worked in her life, but it felt more like she was gliding, borne along on a powerful purposeful current. The change had come after that night three months ago at Walt's condominium. Davis's asthma attack, Brian's simmering petulance, her own growing disquiet about whether she had the right to be both a mother and an astronaut—all this had brought her to a ragged pitch of doubt. Maybe, she thought now, she had been close to some sort of breakdown, given the uncharacteristic, almost predatory way she had sought Walt out and confided in him and almost launched an affair with him as they stood face to face in his tiny U-shaped kitchen.

But there had been no affair; they had not allowed it, and neither of them had spoken of that moment in the months since. It had helped that they had entered a different phase of training, in which the one-on-one intimacy between the primary team and the crew was dispersed somewhat. The integrated sims were much bigger productions, with a Simulation Supervisor and a flight director and a CapCom and dozens of controllers all running the simulation from the actual Mission Control room. In the integrated sims, the primary team was no longer at center stage. Though Walt still had significant input in writing the scripts, advising the SimSup as to which areas the crew still needed work in and suggesting fruitful mals, he and his team took a backseat during the integrated sims themselves. Sequestered in a room off the main Mission Control floor, they no longer ran the show but simply entered the mals ordained by the SimSup and his team.

The rest of her training schedule—for the EVA, for her loadmaster duties, for emergency evacuation procedures, for conducting the scientific experiments, for a thousand other details—had intensified as well. There were periods of two or three days when she didn't see Walt at all. But she was aware of him. When she woke up in the morning at five thirty her first gauzy thoughts were often of him, and as she dressed for her workday she was conscious that she meant her appearance to attract and sustain his notice. She had grown accustomed to a feeling of buoyancy that was based, she knew, only on an intimation; only on a reawakened conviction that it really was possible to be in love, to feel not just warily supported by someone but backed up in every moment and gesture of your life. Just the poignant thought that Walt— in another life, in another universe—could have been that person for her, that perhaps he would have *liked* to be, had helped to soothe her turbulent thoughts for an entire summer.

"Will your children be at the picnic today?" the woman from *Texas Monthly* was asking her.

"Excuse me?" Lucy said. The question was so unexpected and its tone so strangely invasive that her first instinct was to hide behind a fog of confusion.

"I understand there's a picnic today for all the people who took part in the big simulation you just did. I asked the Public Affairs Office if I could be a fly on the wall, and they seemed to have no problem. It seemed like a good chance to talk to people."

"Sure," Lucy said. "That's a good idea."

"And I'd love to meet your kids. And your husband."

"Brian's supposed to pick the kids up after school and meet me there," Lucy said carefully. "You're welcome to meet them, of course, but in terms of—"

"Oh, I didn't mean *interview* them," Jeannette said. "I wouldn't dream of trespassing on your privacy like that. But just seeing you with them would be interesting for me. I'm just looking for that little extra human something, you know?"

The picnic was at Challenger 7 Memorial Park. The park was just west of the freeway, at the end of a road leading through undeveloped pasture. Lucy had not been to Challenger Park often—most of the picnics and beer busts and barbecues that took place during training were held on the JSC grounds—but over the years she had taken Davis or Bethie there a few times to various birthday parties and school outings. Neither of them had ever bothered to ask how the park had gotten its name, or had asked about the black granite marker sitting on the summit of a little mound near the entrance, where the names of the *Challenger* astronauts were incised.

When Lucy drove past the memorial today she glanced in its direction for only a moment and then kept her eyes straight ahead. She did not want to think about Christa McAuliffe today, this close to launch. She did not want to think about the techs giving the Teacher in Space an apple as they helped her through *Challenger*'s hatchway, or about her New Hampshire high school students gathered in front of a television in the school auditorium for the deadly launch, or about Christa's own children shopping at the souvenir emporiums of Cocoa Beach on the day before liftoff, proudly buying T-shirts and buttons with their famous mother's picture on them, not knowing they had seen her for the last time.

What happened to Christa McAuliffe's children would not happen to hers. This was the simple assertion she must at all costs believe. If she did not, if she did not have sufficient confidence in the shuttle systems or in the training of herself and her crew, if she did not have faith in her own destiny, the destiny that her ravaged father had revealed to her that evening on the beach in La Jolla, then she was worse than a fraud. She was a mother willing to sacrifice her children to her own outrageous ambitions.

To give too much heed to the *Challenger* monument as she drove past would be to give credence to her darkest doubts, and she would not do that. She kept her eyes focused ahead, on the parking lot and the striped tent where the mission controllers and trainers and crew members and their families were standing in a food line, or throwing Frisbees or playing softball. Scanning the gathering, she found her family quickly enough. Brian and Davis and Bethie were all sitting on the ground eating fajitas, protecting their plates against a nosy dog. She got out of her car and started toward them, but she was not through looking. Walking through the crowd, waving hello and trading quips with the controllers, she searched for Walt as well. She discovered him in the distance at the edge of the softball game, talking to Jeannette, the woman from *Texas Monthly*. He had his hands in his pockets, laughing softly as he talked, as open with the writer as Lucy herself had been wary.

Jeannette was furiously writing in her notebook, trying to keep up as she chuckled along with him. She wore the same light green Banana Republic T-shirt she had been wearing that afternoon when she interviewed Lucy. The summer light, even at this late-afternoon hour, was harsh. It caught Jeannette's middle-aged features in its full unflattering glare, and yet Lucy saw there was something lively and good-naturedly conniving about her that Walt had noticed and was responding to. Lucy was not directly aware of being jealous, but she felt herself growing protectively alert, irritated at Walt for talking so freely to a woman that Lucy had chosen to regard as threateningly intrusive.

Bethie saw Lucy first and ran to her, just barely managing not to capsize her flimsy paper plate of fajitas and rice as the unknown dog loped along opportunistically beside her.

"Daddy told us to go ahead and eat, but I wanted to wait for you," she said.

"Daddy told you the right thing. He knew I was going to be late."

"This dog's trying to get our food!"

"Hold on," Lucy said. "I'll save you."

She hefted the girl in her arms and said "shoo" to the dog, who looked up at her for a moment as if his feelings had been deeply hurt and then continued to trail along beside them as she walked over to Brian and Davis.

She was with her family, at a celebration of a successful effort by a team of which she was very much a critical part, with the dream of her journey to space accelerating to reality; but one look at the preoccupied expression on Brian's face was enough to collapse her bright mood into a familiar fretful wariness. Something was going on with him. Something had happened.

But she couldn't just demand that he immediately share his gloomy thoughts with her, not at a public gathering like this, not with the kids so innocently content. So she just smiled at him as if she had detected nothing, and then bent down and gave Davis a kiss and asked him about his day.

And then Jeannette was there, smiling, her notebook closed so that Lucy would know she was making good on her promise not to "interview" the kids. Lucy introduced her to Davis and Bethie, and she crouched down to their level and spoke to them in a delighted voice, with a manner so sincere and unaffected that it forced Lucy to assess her own mothering temper on the spot and find it by comparison shrill and put-upon. When Jeannette had bantered with the children for a few moments, she turned her attention to Brian, peppering him with predictable but perfectly agreeable questions about his own spaceflight experience and the novel challenges of a two-astronaut household. She was chatting, not interviewing, her notebook still closed.

But even so, Brian froze her out, answering her questions with flat, declarative sentences, refusing to meet her curious eyes, until finally she took the hint and gave him a curt "Thanks so much for your time" in return and then politely wandered away.

Lucy looked at her husband with alarm. She herself had been less than forthcoming with Jeannette earlier in the day, feeling protective of her privacy and afraid to venture into the speculative realms where she knew this particular writer wanted her to go, but she had at least presented a congenial front. Brian, for some mysterious, brooding reason of his own, had decided not to even bother to try.

Whatever the reason was, Lucy decided she didn't want to hear it just now. She just wanted away from him. His self-absorption not only shut her out, it actively repelled her.

"Watch the kids," she said, in a tone she was sure sounded as disgusted as she felt. "I'm going to get something to eat."

"Okay," he muttered, but she had already turned her back and stalked off toward the fajita line. She was gathering her paper plate and utensils when Buddy Santos walked up and stood beside her, sipping a foamy beer from a plastic cup.

"So everything's okay, I hope," he said.

"What do you mean?"

"I just thought I'd check up on you. My understanding was that it was sort of a bombshell deal."

"I have no idea what you're talking about."

"Oh, shit." Buddy's face was suddenly slack with embarrassment.

"Buddy, what?"

"Look, Lucy, I'm sorry, but you better talk to Brian."

"Is it *about* Brian?"

"Just talk to him, okay? I'll catch up with you later and we can hash it out."

She let him wander away and turned her eyes sharply back to Brian. He was still sitting on the ground with the children, laughing a little at the persistent dog but with an underlying sulkiness that it was impossible for her to miss, or to forgive. There was no way in hell she was going to ask him what was going on, when everyone else in the world except her seemed to know about it already.

There was Walt, standing by himself now, watching the haphazard softball game that was taking place at the edge of the picnic field. Walt was dressed in the same casual uniform as the rest of the men here—jeans, polo shirt, a pair of worn-down running shoes. He had gotten a haircut, she thought, either that or the gentle perspiration that was inevitable in this heat had caused his hair to lie flat. He was an okay-looking man, his hair full enough, his jaw firm enough, his body on the slender side except for the faint thickening at his middle-aged waist. But she thought of him at that moment as beautiful, beautiful in this accidental pose of solitude, beautiful in his bearing and authority.

She walked toward him wanting to fall into his arms but reminding herself that she would of course do no such thing.

"What happened with Brian today?" she said.

"He hasn't told you?"

"No."

"I don't know if I should—"

"Yes, you should, Walt. Please."

She allowed him a moment to consider. She heard the ping of an aluminum bat as Mickey connected with a pitch and began showboating around the bases.

"What I heard was that he'd been making a lot of noise about how pointless his job on the Safety Board was, that he thought it was all just busywork and they weren't making any meaningful decisions about safety or anything else. Anyway, this afternoon he was in the middle of some long, boring meeting and he just got up and walked out and went to Shorty's office and told him he wanted to be reassigned. Shorty got pissed off. He said, okay, fine, you're on Crew Equipment. You can guess how that went over. So—he quit."

"He quit?"

"He told Shorty he wanted out of the program. Shorty said that would be no problem."

She could feel herself trembling with anger. Walt extended his hand and touched her elbow.

"Steady," he said. "There's a lot at stake right now, Lucy."

She turned and looked at her husband. Someone had brought out a big bakery box of cupcakes and Davis and Bethie had run over to get one, leaving Brian sitting on the grass alone. No one approached him. No one talked to him or tossed a Frisbee to him. Lucy knew that deep in his soul he took satisfaction in his isolation and failure, in the fact that he had finally thrown away the one thing that made him special. He had quit. He was no longer an astronaut. She had known this day was coming, but he had promised it would not come before her mission, and she had been naive enough to believe his resignation would be the result of an orderly and dignified transition and not a temper tantrum.

It seemed to her she was in control of her own emotions as she left Walt and walked over to Brian and sat down next to him on the grass and stared straight ahead. She could see the stubby black monolith commemorating the *Challenger* crew.

"Okay," she said. "I know about it now."

"I didn't see any reason to ruin the picnic for the kids. I was going to tell you when we got home. I'm sorry. I should have remembered how fast gossip travels around here."

"It's two months till my launch," Lucy said. "How am I supposed to deal with this?"

"You don't have to deal with it. I will. I think that U of H job might come through. Maybe not till next year, but until then maybe I can get some kind of short-term consulting contract."

"Well, all your glowing references ought to help out there."

He whispered, "Oh, fuck off," and stood up and started walking to the parking lot.

Lucy sprang to her feet and caught up to him, searching for something to say in rebuke or in rebuttal. Nothing came to mind, but she kept dogging his steps anyway, and when he unlocked his car and got inside she found herself holding the door open so that he could not close it, so that he could not shut it in her face.

"What are you doing?" he said.

"I don't know what I'm doing, Brian. All I know is that at launch minus two months my husband just quit his job without bothering to say anything to me about it and then told me to fuck off when I happened to ask. So I'm standing here trying to find out what the hell is going on."

"What's going on is I'm supposed to be an astronaut! I'm supposed to be in space! And I know I'm never going to fly again and I guess I had one bullshit meeting too many, okay? Then when I said something to Shorty, he tried to put me on Crew Equipment. I'm not going to do it, Lucy. I'm not going to spend the rest of my career in Crew Equipment training other astronauts about where to stow their dirty laundry and how to color-coordinate their fucking meal trays! Shit, here come the kids."

Lucy looked up and saw Davis and Bethie running toward their parents in the parking lot and held up her hand and called out, "Wait. Wait a minute. Stay right there!"

The harshness of her voice brought them to an abrupt halt. They stood there, twenty yards away, staring at their parents, and other people were staring too. Lucy knew she had better let it go, but her anger toward Brian at the way he'd betrayed her and humiliated her had a momentum of its own.

"You could have stood it for another few months," she told him. "You could have done that for me. Unless"—and the thought became clear to her only as she uttered the words—"you didn't want me to go. Unless you were so jealous you were trying to sabotage my mission."

"Jesus Christ, Lucy!" he shouted. She had given up wrestling with him for the car door, but she was still gripping it slightly, and now as she heard the violence in his voice and sensed the tension in his arm as he tightened his fist around the armrest, she instinctively let go. He slammed the car door with furious force, so hard that the clear pane of the window burst into a spiderweb pattern of shatterproof glass that stayed suspended in place for a moment before tinkling down onto the asphalt.

The sounds of the door slamming, of the window breaking, were percussive. Lucy's first thought was of her children, and when she looked in their direction she had no firm idea of how to address the fear and bewilderment in their eyes. Absurdly, she shrugged and smiled, as if Brian breaking the car window was no more than a laughable misstep.

Brian was as stunned as she was.

"Go on home," she told him in an absent voice, and he took her up on it, his tires making a crunching sound when they passed over the broken glass on the way out of the parking lot.

Lucy walked calmly back to the picnic, swatting away a stray piece of glass or two that had landed in the folds of her clothes. She noticed that Jeannette, the woman from *Texas Monthly*, was standing with her back to her and writing in her notebook. Walt was headed in her direction, but Lucy met his eyes and managed with a look to inform him that later would be a better time.

"What are you crying about?" she said to Bethie, sweeping the little girl up into her arms. "It was just a silly window."

Chapter Eighteen

They could have met in the briefing room, or for a drink at the Outpost, but Walt's instinct was to suggest someplace out of the way.

"What about the parking lot at Bay Area Park?" he asked.

"The parking lot? Are we hiding out or something?"

"I don't know," Walt said.

He got there first, an hour or so after dark. He parked facing the boat slip where he and Louis came to launch their canoe. The park was almost empty except for a few boys lingering on the monkey bars and arguing about arcane details from some movie that Walt finally decided must be *The Matrix*. The night was dark and windless, and except for the boys' high-spirited debate and the soothing passage of cars along Bay Area Boulevard there was no sound.

He waited for almost thirty minutes. The thought that she might not be coming filled him at first with relief. He could feel the tension draining from his body, the sense of peace he experienced when he woke from a troubling dream to realize that the transgressive things he thought he had been doing had in fact been illusory and that his understanding of who he was and how he behaved was true after all. Not that he was consciously venturing into forbidden territory tonight. He still chose to believe that his relationship with Lucy was more or less appropriate; more or less nominal. Nothing had yet occurred between them that could be judged by a fair-minded observer to be seriously out of bounds. He was still, it could be argued, very much in the role of instructor, of counselor. What had happened yesterday at the picnic had so clearly unnerved her that he had not just a desire but a duty to call her, to lend his support, to hear her out, to do his best to calm her anxieties so that she could proceed with her mission with as few emotional complications as possible to leave behind on earth.

He stared at the oncoming traffic as it approached the bridge spanning the narrow bayou just before the entrance of the park. A minivan approached, its turn signal flashing, and Walt felt an ambiguous surge of anticipation that immediately canceled out his mature resignation of a moment before. The minivan, though, drove right past him and up to the playground. The woman behind the wheel called out to the boys to get in the car, and they leapt down from the monkey bars and slid open the panel doors, one of the boys demanding to know if his friend could spend the night and the mother wearily saying, "We'll see" before driving away, leaving Walt alone in the park.

His cell phone rang.

"Are you still there?" Lucy said. "I'm so sorry I'm late."

"Where are you?"

"I'm just about to turn in."

She was crossing over the bridge, slowing down for the turn. He watched her gliding up toward the boat landing in her minivan; the sight unaccountably hypnotized him, as if the movement of the vehicle bearing her to him was a working of nature, as mysterious and serene as the silent flight of pelicans across this saltwater lake.

When she pulled to a stop beside him and got out, he reached across the seat and opened the door for her. She slid inside, said "Hi" as casually as if they were passing in the hallway in Building 5, and then launched into an apologetic recital of why she was late: Davis's lost school binder, Bethie's meltdown over her favorite T-shirt that she had just discovered had shrunk in the dryer, the need for Brian to rent a car because the window on his could not be repaired until the next day.

"And I look like a wreck, of course," she said. She was wearing a T-shirt and cargo shorts, and her hair was pulled back haphazardly and fastened with a plastic clip. She sat with her back against the passenger door, facing him, studying him, a helpless smile on her face. He told her she didn't look like a wreck.

"I'm coming over there," she said.

She slid over on the bench seat and set her head against his shoulder and grasped him tight around the trunk of his body with both her arms, but neither of them took it any farther than that as they stared in silence through the windshield.

"There's something in the water," she said.

"Where?"

She pointed to the bottom of the boat slip. A few yards out from where the water met the concrete, something thick and undulating was moving. In another moment a four-foot-long alligator emerged onto the ramp and began cautiously padding upward until it reached a level patch of grass.

"Maybe it's looking for a place to nest," Lucy said in a whisper.

Walt could think of no better reason why an alligator would crawl out of the water like that and shuffle around inquiringly in the grass. After a moment it seemed to lose interest in investigating the terrain and simply winched itself down on its meaty legs and lay there on its belly staring out at the dark water of the bayou.

"I kept hoping you'd call last night," she said, after they had spent five minutes staring at the alligator without comment.

"I didn't know if it would be a good idea."

"It probably wouldn't have. It was probably better that you waited till today. I was a mess last night. Of course by the time I got home Brian had switched to super-contrite mode, so I didn't even have the satisfaction of a real fight. Do you think I should divorce him?"

"Don't ask me that," Walt said.

"Right now I can't stand the sight of him. The thought of him."

Her lips were inches away from his face. Walt could feel her breath as she spoke, and an unruly wing of hair that had escaped the clip at the back of her head whispered against his cheekbone.

"This is strange, isn't it?" she said.

"Yes," he admitted.

"What are our ground rules? Do you have any idea?"

"No."

"I don't particularly want you to kiss me. I don't want to make love. Are we still in agreement that that would be a mistake?"

"You've got your children to think about. You've got the mission. We'll just sit here and watch the alligator."

Why was that the wrong thing to say? Why did such reasonable and reassuring words cause him to sense, as she fell into a neutral silence, that a life's opportunity was in danger of being lost? Walt had the suspicion that in trying to win her trust with the cautious response she seemed to be soliciting he had in fact lost it. In accommodating her rather than challenging her, in accepting with defeated silence the stasis that bound them both, he was failing her in ways she had yet to calculate.

So he cast aside the rules they had just set down and kissed her. She opened her mouth to his and grasped his hair tight in her hand and pulled him even closer, and it was only after a full minute that she finally asked him to stop and then backed away again to the passenger door.

"I just want to think," she said. "I want to think this through."

She extended her leg and set one foot familiarly on his thigh. He touched her ankle, just above the rim of her tasseled athletic sock. There was little moonlight, but her bare legs were still lustrously visible. Walt waited for her to speak again, to offer the thought-out observation he knew was coming. He knew that whatever she said, measured against the anguished, unreal desire he was feeling at the moment, was bound to be comically pale. But he would have to listen if he was serious about saving them both from what would plainly be a grievous mistake.

"I just don't see what the purpose would be," she said at last. "I don't want to have some *affair.* Do you?"

"Not if you put it that way."

"If we were in love, maybe. If you were everything to me. If I could be sure I was everything to you."

"What if that were true?" Walt said.

His question startled her, thrilled her, so much so that she had to pretend she hadn't really heard it.

"And even then," she went on, "how could I do that to Davis and Bethie? They love their father. They love our family!"

Walt could not rouse himself to argue. He admired her love for her children, he admired the terms she seemed to be implicitly setting: all or nothing, no turning back. Could he meet those terms? Was he man enough to put his own desires so boldly in play, to face the moral and emotional consequences of violating not just the bonds of a marriage but the happiness of two innocent children?

"When you put it that way," he said finally, "I don't know what we're doing out here."

"We're indulging ourselves a little bit," Lucy admitted. "We're creeping up to the edge. We're trying to get a glimpse of how beautiful it would be."

"And what do you think?" he pressed her, because at the moment he was feeling confused and destructive. "*Would* it be beautiful?"

"Oh, yes."

They turned over that thought in silence for a long moment more, and then Lucy pulled herself to a sitting position again and leaned over and kissed him innocently on the lips.

"Good night," she said.

"Good night."

They stared at each other with mournful intensity, until their own star-crossed mopiness began to strike them as humorous and they broke into sputtering laughter. Walt took some gratification in this display of self-knowledge and adult irony, but not enough. It still hurt when she took his hand and kissed it and stepped out of the car. She lingered there, glancing once more at the alligator, which had still not moved, and then bent down to speak to him one last time through the open passenger window.

"You're all right?"

"I'm fine."

She got into her car and turned on the ignition and rolled down the window so she could look across at him. The dashboard lights in the minivan illuminated her face as she smiled sadly in good-bye, then put the car into gear and backed away.

Chapter Nineteen

The International Space Station orbited the earth at a height of 240 miles and a speed of 17,500 miles per hour. It was 146 feet long, an ungainly assemblage of odd-shaped components—cylindrical living modules, rectangular solar arrays, cone-shaped air locks and mating adapters—that gave this fantastically engineered craft a look of haphazard inelegance. In the dream Lucy was having, the station was worse than inelegant, it was malevolent. Its hard surfaces and jumbled structural themes seemed like a deliberate mockery of organic coherence, a silent inhuman rebuke of everything made of flesh and blood. The only thing recognizable about it was its spreading solar arrays, which reminded Lucy of the unmoving wings of a dead moth.

The dream unfolded like a simulation. Lucy was on the flight deck of the shuttle, running through her checklists, positioning her body so that she could see past the commander's and pilot's positions to the forward windows, through which she watched the moth growing ominously larger as they approached. Lucy sensed something wrong, some glitch in the software, some leak somewhere in the thruster system. For some reason her children were on board, below her in the mid-deck. She could not see them but could hear them deliriously laughing as they floated about in weightlessness, unaware of the impending collision that only she could avert. She frantically paged through the checklists, but as soon as she drew near to solving the problem the checklist branched into multiple new subcategories, and she didn't know which one to follow. She steeled herself and chose one at random, and it too soon diverged, sending out tendrils of procedures for shuttle systems whose properties she had never heard of or even imagined. She was lost in the checklist like a child lost in a smothering forest, unreliable paths leading off in every direction. She desperately listened for Walt's patient voice to break in over the loop, explaining to her what she should do next, reassuring her that it was only a simulation. But she didn't hear his voice, and the evil form of the space station kept drawing closer as her frantic mind grew hopeless.

It was when she began to hear the screams of her children from the mid-deck—Bethie calling out to her that she was afraid and that Davis couldn't breathe—that she woke. Lucy was practical about nightmares. She had trained herself when she was a girl not to regard them as omens, and as an adult she had not much patience with the whole idea that there was any benefit in "interpreting" them. They were the discharges and spasms of an overstimulated brain, their themes were either glaringly obvious or hopelessly cryptic, and in any case they could be dismissed without fear of some sort of cosmic penalty. In the first few minutes after waking this morning, however, she had to ride this dream out. It still clung to her, and it took a while for her to be able to safely accept that it had not been real. Staring at herself in the mirror as she brushed her teeth, she found that she was close to weeping with relief.

It was almost six, the early-morning light barely making a showing through the screen of pine branches in the backyard. When she walked out into the den, she found Brian sitting on the edge of the sofa where he had slept, tying the laces of his battered running shoes.

"Hi," he said.

"Hi," she answered, and that was it. After the incident at the picnic, they had both naturally fallen into a kind of power-saving mode, shutting down all systems of their marriage—conversation, for instance— that were not critical to its immediate operation. Everything was tabled, by mutual unspoken consent, until after her mission returned to earth.

But everything unpleasant in her life, even the horrid dream from which she had just awakened, was something she observed now from a euphoric distance. She had pulled back from Walt last night—she had *had* to—but the feeling of being desired by him lingered; if carefully nourished, if not thoughtlessly acted upon, it might linger the rest of her life. But she wanted to act upon it, of course, she wanted to give herself over to Walt Womack with the same forceful, defining yearning that she wanted to travel into space. The two desires were to some degree insep- arable in her mind: the man who was training her for spaceflight was providing her at the same time one more touchstone on earth. What would it be like to come back to him, she dared herself to wonder; what would it be like to come back to him and not to Brian?

In this bright mood, as she drove to JSC in the early morning along broad streets that had not yet filled with traffic, she imagined herself in the body of a falcon, sweeping along at the top of the sky, weary but exhilarated from flight. Almost unnoticeable from this height, in the earth-wide panorama below her, stood the patient man from whose glove she had launched herself and to whom she was now returning. The two of them, she and the man, were partners in exploration. He himself could not leave the earth, but in some mysterious way she could not stay aloft without him, and the rapture of her flight could not be considered apart from the satisfaction of settling once again on his padded glove, of having journeyed back from the edge of infinitude to a beloved and familiar perch.

She hoped that this mood would stay with her all day, that she and Brian could maintain their discreet avoidance of one another without an outburst of anger. It was an important day. It was launch minus two weeks. In a week she and the crew would be going into quarantine, unable to see anyone who did not have a Primary Contact badge. It was impermissible for children to receive PC badges, since the main purpose of quarantine was to keep the crew away from colds and infections that might compromise the mission. So in a week she would be saying good- bye to Davis and Bethie, and this evening she planned to talk to them and help them understand what would be happening as the launch day approached. She had to do it right. She could not be emotional or appre- hensive. In the last few weeks, neither of the kids had demonstrated any outward concern. After Brian broke the car window they had eagerly accepted Lucy's fictional explanation that there had been a hairline crack in the glass already and that their father had not really slammed the door as hard as it seemed he had. Like Lucy and Brian, their children were in power-saving mode. They seemed to know instinctively that the less they thought about their parents' bitterness toward one another, about their mother's upcoming mission, the greater was the possibility that these things did not truly exist.

She would not see Walt today. She had an appointment with a NASA dentist at eight this morning, to make sure there were no untreated cavities or nascent abscesses that might cause trouble during the mission, and then a final EVA run that would last until five or six. She would see him tomorrow, though, in the pre-brief and debrief for one of the final integrated sims. They would glance at each other in the crowded room, as the SimSup went over the tasks and contingencies and procedures that were now as familiar to her as her own heartbeat. From time to time, as she drove to her dental exam, a flurry of panic raced through her. Had she been foolish to break it off last night? Would Walt, after her refusal to pursue a futile possibility, decide—as he had every right in doing—to withdraw from her? She didn't think so, but at the same time she was aware that she was asking him for something she had no right to expect: that he would love her even when it was hopeless to do so, that he could continue to want her in the full realization that they could never have each other. Lucy had allowed a door to be opened that she could never walk through, but the thought of that door being subsequently closed was a torment.

"Did you ever listen to that CD I made you for your PPK?" Buddy Santos said to her a few hours later as they were walking together into the NBL from the parking lot for their EVA briefing.

The PPK was the Personal Preference Kit, made up of the individual items and talismans that each astronaut chose to carry in space. One night several weeks ago, Lucy had asked each of her children to choose something that they wanted their mother to take. Bethie had gotten out her crayons and drawn a picture of their house on Purple Plum Court, with four smiling stick figures standing out front. Davis had impulsively tossed the Milo Thatch figure he had been playing with into Lucy's lap. He had meant it as a charged gesture of indifference—with his boy's pride, he wasn't going to be maneuvered into a sentimental moment. But Lucy had understood that this odd little plastic man, with its floppy yellow hair and round-framed eyeglasses, was somehow a precious gift.

"Did you?" Buddy repeated.

"I haven't really had that much time, Buddy," she said.

"I knew it. For your information, though, it doesn't take that much time. You can listen to music while doing other things. For instance, it's been reported that some people even listen to music while driving their cars."

"Okay. I'm sorry."

"I thought I knew you. I thought we were EVA buddies! Let me ask you this, have you ever even cared about music?"

She had to admit she hadn't, not in the way he meant; probably not in the way most people did. She knew the names of songs and the names of the bands that had been popular when she was in high school. She had listened to them and danced to them and from time to time had felt music as she supposed it ought to be felt, as a mysterious natural beneficence like sunshine or sex or friendship. But she had a tendency to forget, for long stretches at a time, that music even existed. She was in one of those periods now, she realized, relentlessly preoccupied with the mission and her troubles with Brian and her worries about Davis and Bethie. She and Brian, come to think of it, did not even own a stereo, just a little boom box they had bought for the kids and that they never thought to use to play anything other than *Sesame Street* tapes. What music did Walt listen to, Lucy suddenly wondered. What music would they listen to together?

"Well, just so you'll know," Buddy was saying, "you've got an expertly selected greatest hits selection in your PPK, should you ever choose to give it a shot. Beethoven, Miles Davis, Riders in the Sky. Nobody does 'Home on the Range' like Riders in the Sky, by the way. The way Too Slim's voice breaks on that one verse line?" Buddy suddenly began to warble:

> Where the graceful white swan goes gliding along,
> like a maid in a heavenly dream.

"Tears your heart out, doesn't it?" he said.

"I don't want my heart torn out."

"I even included some John Denver. Not my personal taste, I hope you understand. I'd rather listen to Alvin and the Chipmunks. But it's catchy, it's cosmic, and to your unsophisticated ear it might—"

"Okay, Buddy," she said. "Thanks."

"Can you believe this?" he said. He was standing at the door of the NBL, holding it open for her. He had the biggest grin on his face that she had ever seen.

"What?"

"We're really doing it, aren't we? We're really going into space."

"Looks that way," she said, basking in Buddy's infectious, uncomplicated enthusiasm. He had his own problems, she knew: a sister with multiple sclerosis, an infirm father whose spirit had been broken by his exile from the Philippines, and like all of the crew a just-detectable undercurrent of anxiety about how he would perform on the mission, and whether he would return from it. But his optimism was not a bluff, it was a secure tenet of his personality. Lucy counted on Buddy's presence to remind her that her mission to space was a glorious opportunity and not, as she had sometimes felt, a grim duty.

After dinner that evening she sat with the children in the living room and talked to them about what would be happening in the next three weeks. A week from today, she told them, she would be going into quarantine at JSC.

"It's kind of like a motel," she said. "The crew lives there for a few days before we take off for the Cape. Remember when Daddy did that before his mission?"

"I remember," Davis said with a calculated air of disinterest. He was scrunched up against her hip on the couch, playing with one of his action figures, doing his best to pretend that his mother's upcoming launch did not concern him at all. Bethie sat serenely in Lucy's lap, sucking her thumb. She had just come from the bath. Her hair was still damp and the cotton sleeper she wore was so freshly laundered it was still warm from the dryer. From where she sat, Lucy could see Brian in the kitchen as he rinsed off the dinner dishes and loaded them into the dishwasher. He did so with a hypnotic economy of movement, setting each plate and glass into place as if they were pieces in a puzzle that he was solving with an unhurried finesse.

Her children were peacefully gathered up against her, clean and scrubbed and warily attentive. Her husband was uncomplainingly doing the dishes. But Lucy could not keep from registering this moment of domestic contentment as a pang, a loss. Every night with her family should have been like this, instead of the usual frantic arguments about bedtime, the half-grudging manner in which she read the children their stories, the spoken or unspoken recriminations with Brian adding tension to what should have been every calming ritual. The drowsy perfection of the scene before her only served to drive home how rare such scenes had been, how much she had let slip away. If the shuttle exploded on liftoff or burned up on reentry, there would not have been enough such evenings to gain a proper hold in her children's memories. They would recall their mother as a hurried, driven, preoccupied woman who one day just disappeared into the sky.

"I don't want you to go to quarantine," Bethie said when she took her thumb out of her mouth.

"Don't be stupid," Davis told his sister. "Quarantine's awesome. They have bowls of M&M's and they get to watch movies."

"We still have to train," Lucy said. "We have to train up until the time we fly off to the Cape. And you know why we train so much, Bethie?"

"Why?"

"To make sure that nothing can go wrong. That nothing can happen that we don't want to happen."

Brian turned the faucet off in the kitchen. He kept his back to her, still facing the sink, listening.

"And everyday when I'm in space," Lucy said to Bethie, "I'm going to look at the beautiful drawing you made me."

"Can we watch TV for just fifteen minutes?" Davis said. His voice was flat and almost hostile. He was holding this mission against his mother in a way that he could not measure or articulate. Lucy remembered when he had broken down in the car on the way to school the morning she first told him about the mission. He had tried to hold himself apart from her then, as well, but his fears had broken to the surface. In the months that had gone by since then, he had gotten better at keeping his vulnerability hidden, at punishing her by denying her the chance to comfort him.

"You certainly cannot," she answered, then spoke to him in a warmer voice. "And everyday I'm going to look at Milo Thatch and think of my beautiful boy."

She kissed Davis on the forehead.

"It was so nice of you to let me take him."

"It was no big deal," he said.

"I promise not to lose him."

"Whatever," Davis said, shrugging, twisting out of her arms, moving away from her and her hollow reassurances. "I don't care."

Chapter Twenty

The integrated sim that took place the next day was a bit more ragged than anyone had anticipated. One of the mals, a slow leak in a helium tank that pressurized the thruster system, kept the ground controllers scrambling for a solution longer than it should have. As a result the briefing room afterward was crowded, and the conversation so focused and contentious that it required all of Walt's and Lucy's attention. Walt had been expecting, or at least hoping for, a more relaxed sim, a lull every now and then in which the unconcluded business between Lucy and himself could at least be silently resumed with a look or a whispered word. But it was impossible. Their eyes met once or twice during the briefing, but neither of them dared more than that, since the concentration in the room was so intense that any glance between them that was not freighted with problem-solving energy would be immediately discovered for what it was.

But what was it? The more technical the conversation grew, the more heated the discussion became between the crew and Ground about who should have spotted the mal first, the more Walt began to worry that the moments with Lucy in his car had taken place only in his imagination. Lucy was the only one who could provide confirmation, and the deeper she was drawn into the briefing the more a kind of absurd panic took hold of him. When he looked in her direction again he saw her frowning in concentration over something Surly was pointing out in the pages of the Flight Data File. She was wearing one of the maroon crew shirts, the mission emblem elevated by the gentle slope of her breasts. Her hair was loose today, falling forward along the sides of her face as she bent closer to study the FDF. That was when she looked up at him, just for an instant, and relieved his concern. There was no real message in her look that he could make out except that perhaps she wanted confirmation too, and to assure herself that he was still standing there on the other side of the room.

The meeting ran late, it was four o'clock, and a woman from the Public Affairs Office was waiting impatiently at the door with a van parked outside to rush the crew over to Building 2 for a press briefing. Lucy gave Walt a furtive, helpless look as she raced down the hallway on the heels of the PAO woman. It was a ridiculous time to try to come to terms, Walt knew: the last week or so of training, with quarantine looming, the pace on every front accelerating, fears and doubts and distractions growing riotously.

Even under normal circumstances, this was not his favorite phase of the training flow. It was not just that he felt somewhat sidelined by the greater authority of the SimSup during the integrated sims, or apprehensive that some problem might be discovered there that he had not thoroughly covered with the crew during stand-alone training. It was more a sense that the show was coming to an end. He had often speculated that it must be akin to the experience of a theater company as a play nears the end of its run and all the intimacy and magic expended in the common cause of its production inevitably begin to dissolve.

This sense of deflation was entangled, when it came to the space business, with a sense of dread. This was the time when it usually hit Walt, just before quarantine. He had done his job the best he knew how, but he was sending the crew off, perhaps, to die. It was going to happen sooner or later, he knew it was: some malfunction among one of the shuttle's millions of parts, like the frozen O-rings in the solid rocket boosters that doomed *Challenger,* or some minor mistake by a crew member or a flight controller that grew into a catastrophe, was statistically inevitable.

Leaving JSC today, he had to work to keep this sense of background morbidity from sharpening into panic. It had always been personal; by the end of training the members of the crew were always his friends—even if, like Brian Kincheloe and a few others, they were sometimes difficult friends. But the fear of something happening to Lucy stirred up not-so-old memories of an emotion starker than grief. He did not want to experience that emotion twice, that savage foreclosing of present and future happiness that had been a lasting imprint of Rachel's death. Nor would he feel entitled to experience the same emotion if Lucy died. It would be presumptuous, it would be an affront not just to Rachel's memory, but to the legacy of despair that ought to be hers alone.

Louis called him on his cell phone.

"Get me out of here," he said. "I'm down in Galveston for some bullshit conference and they're about to put us on a bus and take us to a retreat center where a bunch of Guatemalan nuns are going to feed us taco salad."

Galveston was forty miles away in rush hour traffic, but Walt had nothing better to do at the moment and no better strategy to keep himself from surrendering to pointless apprehension. When he got to Galveston Louis was waiting for him on the curb in front of a church just off Broadway, wearing a Hawaiian shirt.

"Where are we going?" Walt asked as Louis got into the car.

"Someplace where I don't have to see any priests."

They went to a shrimp joint on one of the piers built out over the Gulf beach, arriving in time for sunset, feeling the world quiet down all around them as they drank beer and ate fried redfish and gazed through the gaps in the floor at the mild breakers trailing shoreward beneath their feet. A sign requested diners not to feed the seagulls, probably because the wooden rail around the open-air restaurant was already covered with speckled bird droppings. Louis, on his third beer, took it upon himself to ignore the sign, tossing an occasional French fry out over the water to watch a gull swoop down and catch it in midair.

"You're making her nervous," Walt said, nodding toward their teenage waitress, who was watching them as she served another table, trying to decide whether or not to walk up to Louis and point out the infraction.

"She needs to get over herself," Louis said, tossing out another fry, but so offhandedly the gulls did not notice in time and had to chase it all the way down to the surface of the water. He was in an inexplicable growly mood.

"What was the conference about?" Walt asked him.

" 'A Moment of Crisis, a Moment of Healing.' Throwing up yet?"

Louis looked out at the horizon, where the moon was rising in lingering daylight above a flat green sea.

"Sometimes I wonder what I got myself into," he said. "Remember that movie we saw when we were kids? *The Cardinal?* With Tom Tryon being all macho and tortured and getting beaten up by the Klan and stuff? And women driving themselves crazy because they can't have him?"

"I remember."

"Well, it ain't like that."

"Not surprised," Walt said.

"Yeah, you're such a know-it-all. You never get taken in by anything."

It sounded like he meant the comment to sting. Walt let it pass. He watched Louis take another long sip of his beer and contemplatively twirl his coaster on the salt-stained tabletop.

"Don't mean to take it out on you."

"Whatever," Walt said.

"It's just that I've spent the last eight hours hearing about all the fun my fellow priests have been having with teenage boys. 'A challenge to our community of faith.' Yeah, no shit. It used to be, when you'd be out wearing your collar, you'd get these kind of interested glances, you know? 'Here comes a man of God, how cool is it to be him?' Now people just sort of look away, because you might be a child molester. I think I actually heard somebody spit behind my back the other day."

"Come on, Louis."

"It's true. The guy behind me at the ATM. And he wasn't just expectorating, Walt. He was commenting."

Louis finished his beer and set the empty bottle in front of him and folded his arms as if in contemplation of it.

"Here's what it comes down to," he said. "What if I'm in the wrong business?"

"The wrong business?"

"It's not just the creepy crawly stuff. The child abuse. It's something else. For a long time I've just been feeling—what? A little bit stupid, I guess. Here I am with my one and only life, you know?"

"What do you mean, you're losing your faith or something?"

"I wish. At least losing your faith sounds dramatic. That's what Tom Tryon got to do."

"Everybody gets bored with their job sooner or later."

"Yeah, but I don't have a job, Walt. I have a vocation. This is who I'm supposed to be. What do I do, just tell myself I made a mistake? It turns out I'm not me after all?"

"Lots of people leave the priesthood, if that's what you're talking about here."

"Yeah, they leave, they marry ex-nuns, they grow their idiotic goatees, they find some pissant progressive job somewhere, they become walking clichés."

"Everybody's a walking cliché, Louis."

Louis shrugged. He checked to see that the waitress had her back turned and threw another French fry to the gulls.

"Cut it out," Walt said. "Obey the rules."

"Have you been listening or not? Obeying the rules is how I got into this. Obeying the rules is how I ended up wasting my life."

Walt gauged the silence as Louis picked up the check and studied it through his reading glasses.

"Have you talked to somebody about this?" he asked finally.

"I just talked to you."

"No, I mean somebody who would know how—"

"Don't worry about it," Louis said. "It'll pass. You're in for fourteen dollars."

"That include tip?"

"What? You think I'm going to stiff the waitress just because she's a control freak?"

They walked back along the sidewalk at the top of the seawall to Walt's car. It was dark now and the moonlight showcased the foamy crests of the breakers, which at high tide were overwhelming the remnant strip of beach at the base of the seawall. Louis asked Walt a few questions about the mission and asked if he was going to the launch.

"Probably not," Walt said. "There's not that much point anymore with all the security. It's better just to say good-bye here."

The words "say good-bye" sounded forceful and final in a way he hadn't intended, and the helpless brooding started again: what if indeed she didn't come back? What if these few days before she went into quarantine were all that was left, the only chance they would ever be given?

Even before Louis had started in about wasting his life Walt had been feeling the same looming possibility for himself. The opportunities that arose in life were not always tidy, not always right. But it had to be a mistake—a kind of moral surrender of its own—to accustom yourself to turning them down.

"Then maybe that would be the perfect time for our amazing canoe adventure," Louis said, interrupting this tumbling thought.

"Maybe," Walt answered distractedly. It appeared that Louis was not going to ever allow this fantasy expedition to die its natural death.

"A resounding maybe," Louis said, "from our fearless space pioneer."

"What's the matter with you tonight?" Walt said. The mocking edge in Louis's voice was starting to convince him that his friend was really angry.

"What's the matter with me, Walt? Gee, thanks for listening. Want me to recap?"

"What I mean is how is all of this my fault?"

"Because I'm trying to hold the line here. I'm doing my best to actually believe all this crap I'm dispensing every day, while my best friend just hangs back and watches in amusement, from his *skeptical distance,* and then when push comes to shove, when it's the worst day of my life and I'm angling for a little support, he won't even agree to go on a fucking canoe trip."

Louis was not yelling, but his voice was shrill enough to carry, and Walt could see heads turning in their direction from the pier they had just left.

"I didn't realize it was the worst day of your life," Walt said.

"Okay, figure of speech. But if you'd been listening maybe you would have put two and two together."

"Look, I'm really sorry," Walt said. "We'll do the canoe trip."

"I don't want to do the canoe trip."

"Well, what do you want, Louis?"

Louis stopped walking; he sagged as if Walt's response left him not just exasperated but physically exhausted. For a moment he stared out at the Gulf as the offshore wind tousled his matinee-idol hair.

"You know, you're always creeping up to the edge of things," he finally pronounced. "You've been doing that all our lives, creeping up to the edge and then slinking back, and I'm kind of sick of it. Stop asking me all these nitpicky questions about Jesus and God and just go ahead and be an atheist, okay? If you don't want to paddle a canoe out into open water, quit leading me on about it. Now that I think of it, it's no accident that your job is sending other people into space while you keep your own feet planted on the ground."

"Wait a minute," Walt said. "So now I'm supposed to be an astronaut?"

"I bet it never even crossed your mind, did it?"

"No."

"My point exactly."

Walt instinctively gave a short laugh, as if this sudden bleat of resentment was just another variant of the insulting banter they had been exchanging since fifth grade. But Louis didn't laugh back.

"And either be my friend or just stop pretending," Louis said.

Walt was truly astonished. "I'm *pretending* to be your friend?"

Louis saw fit not to answer. They walked on in uncomfortable silence until they got to Walt's car. Louis gave Walt directions to the retreat house where he was going to spend the night, and where he would spend the next day continuing to hear about strategies for dealing with predatory priests.

"Who was the girl in that movie?" Louis said as they drove up to the entrance.

"What movie?"

"*The Cardinal.* Was it Romy Schneider?"

"You want to talk about all this or not?"

"No, let's leave all the important stuff tragically unaddressed."

Louis had cracked open the door, but not far enough to trigger the overhead light. He looked through the windshield, where a solitary priest could be seen sitting on a bench beyond the curved driveway of the retreat house, staring up at the stars and anachronistically smoking a pipe.

"Maybe I'm just remembering wrong," he said after a while, "but it was different when Rachel was alive. She kept you in touch somehow. Without her around you have this tendency to be all careful and calibrated. Like you've got this checklist: 'Expend X percent of total available emotional energy on best friend. Check.' "

"All right," Walt said. "I hear you. I'm sorry. I didn't realize any of this was going on with you until tonight. Listen, why don't I try to carve out some time and—"

"Yeah, why don't you *carve out some time,*" Louis shot back. "Why don't you do a feasibility study while you're at it? Why don't you put together a task force to—"

"All right," Walt said. "I tried."

They watched the priest fervently puff on his pipe. In the heavy night air the smoke lingered in an unmoving cloud above his head.

"Anyway," Louis said finally, "thanks for coming down. Without you around to get mad at, there's no telling what I would have said to those Guatemalan nuns."

Walt said he was happy to be of service. He thought about saying more, but he was angry himself now and not in a mood to stand down from this confusing argument. When Louis grunted a half-apologetic "check you later"—another bygone idiom from their shared youth— Walt returned it with his eyes straight ahead.

He drove back to Clear Lake in an intolerable mood. If Louis had meant to leave him feeling confused and amorphously guilty, he had pulled it off perfectly. It was plain enough that Louis was going through some sort of faith or career crisis. Walt was not willing to subscribe to the idea that it was somehow his fault, the result of some supposed failure of nerve or empathy, but he was riled all the same by Louis's angry urgency. He felt some version of it himself. The anticipation he had been feeling all during training, that he and Lucy were meant for each other, would ultimately have each other, had been eclipsed by apprehension. Apprehension that it was not true after all, that this rapturous prospect would disappear before he could reach out to grab it.

He drove to her neighborhood. He knew the name of her street but not the address, so he just cruised up and down, staring at the houses and wondering which of them might be hers. It was an unremarkable suburban development, and its very anonymity struck Walt as enchanting, as guileless and devoid of pretensions as she herself was. He passed a family out on an after-dinner stroll, and for a moment he thought it might be hers, but there were three children instead of two, with a huge standard poodle striding out in front like a show horse. He looked for her in the little neighborhood park, where a few children and their parents were still lingering on the playscape and swing sets. He wasn't sure how hard he was looking. He had no plan for what he would do if he saw her. He was in a state of agitation that felt new to him, unpredictable.

When he remembered that she would not be home yet, that at this hour she would still be in the pool at the NBL for her final EVA run, he drove out of the development and back onto El Dorado Boulevard, meaning to go home and go to bed and give this irrational energy a chance to discharge.

He passed a solitary figure jogging along the sidewalk in the opposite direction—running more than jogging, and with competitive fervor. Even in the dark, Walt knew it was Brian right away, from the glowering expression on his shadowy face, from his righteously sweat-soaked T-shirt and uncompromising stride. He had obviously been on a long, solitary jaunt, churning over the injustices that had been visited upon him, and was now running back toward his home.

This unexpected sighting filled Walt with annoyance, with anger. Here was Brian once again, fighting his perpetual struggle against his own happiness, a battle into which Lucy and their children had been unfairly conscripted. Brian's scowling expression as he ran along the side of the road presented Walt with a feeling of justification for what, he now understood, he was about to do.

When he reached Space Center Boulevard, he turned right instead of left, which would have taken him home. He drove to the end of the road and parked at the far end of the almost vacant lot outside the NBL. He rolled down the window and turned off the engine of his car and waited there for another twenty minutes until he saw her emerge from the building with Buddy and Patti. Walt prayed the three of them would separate, and they did, each going to their own cars. He watched her wave to her EVA comrades as they drove off. It was the way she lingered there at the door to her car, pretending to fumble with her keys, that made him realize that she had not just seen his Taurus in the parking lot, but had been looking for it since the moment she left the building.

Chapter Twenty-one

She got into the car without saying a word. She looked at him briefly, with a frown of deliberation on her face that Walt found almost too exciting to bear. She looked down at the floorboard and then reached across the seat to take his hand.

"I can plausibly be gone for a couple more hours," she said. "If I call Brian and lie to him."

Walt didn't think it was seemly to advise her, but he waited tensely while she made her decision. She got out of the car and closed the door and dialed a number on her cell phone. Walt watched her walk in tight circles around the empty parking lot as she talked. The conversation took longer than he expected it would, but when she got back in the car she was calm.

"So Buddy and Patti and I are all meeting for drinks to go over the EVA one last time. It's a bonding kind of thing."

"You think he believed you?"

"Are you nervous?"

"Pretty nervous," he said.

"I knew you'd come," she told him. "I knew this would happen. Somehow or other it would happen. Are we going to your place?"

"Is that all right?"

"Don't ask me. Tell me."

"It's all right. It's going to be all right."

"Okay. I'll follow you over in my car. I'm going to park a block or so away just in case somebody we know comes cruising by and gets the wrong idea. Or the right idea."

Walt drove slowly home, glancing in the rearview mirror every few seconds to make sure she was still following him and had not lost her will. The deliberations and doubts, the surges of resolve and hesitation that had been ruling his mind all day and for much of the past weeks had all suddenly vanished, and he was left with the sort of ecstatic calm that the astronauts he trained had often reported to him experiencing in the seconds before liftoff, when there were no more choices to make and nothing left to do but surrender to the unthinkable force that was about to rip you away from the earth's gravity.

When he pulled into his covered parking space he saw her veer off down a side street. He climbed the stairs to his condominium and took the keys out of his pocket and opened the door: every move he made seemed unhurried and orchestrated to him. Though his body was alive with thrumming urgency, he felt no haste. Indeed, he was aware of each footstep, of each moment expanding to accommodate his swelling sense of serenity. He seemed to have slipped out of the stream of true time into some swirling eddy where every unbelievable instant was being captured even as it took place, and would remain lazily present for as long as he wished.

Walking down the dark side street, with the soles of her running shoes whisking against the asphalt, Lucy was in a quiet cocoon of her own. Brian did not enter her thoughts. She was even managing somehow not to think about her children. With every step she took, she was bringing them all closer to a potentially devastating reckoning. What she was doing now could shatter her family. But if she was about to commit such a grievous wrong, why did she feel not merely justified but deeply content?

Walt had not closed the door to his condo but had left it several inches ajar. The sight of that half-closed door, its silent welcome, filled her with a desire she could not distinguish from outright happiness. When she pushed it open she saw him standing there in the entry hall, facing her, waiting for her, his hands in his pockets. The overhead light in the entry hall was harsh, and it touched her that in his muddled inexperience in matters such as this he had not thought to dim the light or turn it off.

Lucy closed the door behind her and leaned against it and looked at him. He was wearing his usual pleated khakis, a pale blue short-sleeved Oxford shirt.

"Do you want anything?" he asked. "Something to drink?"

"I don't want anything," she said.

She stepped forward and he took her hands and gently twined her arms behind her back as he kissed her. Then she rested her head tight against his shoulder, aware of the smell of the laundry starch in his shirt collar and of a trickle of sweat running down his cheek and into her hair.

"Are you having any trouble believing this?" he asked her.

She nodded. She didn't want to talk, afraid that the sound of their voices would startle them back into the universe she was trying, at least for this one unreal moment, to evade. So they made their way into the bedroom mostly in silence, with only a fondly chiding comment or two, and a heartfelt but stammering declaration of appreciation on Walt's part as he watched her undress at the side of the bed in what she prayed was flattering indirect light from a hallway bathroom.

Of course an unwelcome clearheadedness assaulted them both afterward. They were old enough to have anticipated this tidal retreat of euphoria, but foresight was only foresight; it was not a remedy for the reality that now lay so inevitably exposed. Lucy was married to Brian, and it didn't matter that this fact struck them both as wrenchingly unfair. They would have to surrender to it and go their separate ways, or face it head-on and deal with the consequences.

But now was not the time for a head-on confrontation, not when Lucy was a week away from launch. Walt lay in the bed that he and Rachel had shared for over ten years, feeling the heat of Lucy's naked body against his own. Everything about her was unfamiliar—the size of her breasts, the span of her shoulders, the texture of her hair, even the shape of her teeth—but at the same time he felt mysteriously accustomed to her body.

He moved his arm slightly so he could look at his watch, nervously wanting to know how much time they had left, but she grabbed his hand and held it there.

"Don't," she said.

She shifted her head out from under his chin and tilted it upward to kiss him.

"I don't have to go yet," she explained. "Unless you want me to."

Walt shook his head against the pillow. He stared at the unmoving ceiling fan above the bed, the blades flexing a little even in the still atmosphere of the room.

"Can we talk about what's next?" she whispered. "What's next between us?"

"All right."

"I don't mean about the future, nothing that big. Just between now and the launch."

"I want to see you again before you go into quarantine."

"I want to see you too. How can we manage it?"

"You have a day off beforehand, don't you?"

For a moment she didn't answer. She traced the veins on the back of his hand with her fingertip.

"I need to spend that day with my family," she said. Then she whispered, "I'm sorry."

"Don't be sorry," Walt told her. "Of course you should be with your family."

"Maybe there'll be a chance tomorrow,' she said.

"I don't have a sim scheduled. I'll be in my office part of the day. If you have a gap between things, call me. Maybe we can find a few minutes."

She nodded, her head resting on his chest now.

"When I get back from the mission, there'll be more than a few minutes," she said. "I promise."

She lifted her head an inch or two off his chest and looked around the room. There was an eight-by-ten photograph on top of the dresser, the silver frame gleaming a little in the imperfect darkness. Lucy could not make out whose image rested inside the frame, but of course it would have to be Rachel. There was one other picture on the wall, barely discernible as a generic photograph of the shuttle lifting off at nighttime from Pad 39A at Cape Kennedy. Other than that, there were several blank walls, a closet door, a squat bookcase with several dozen volumes, most of them—judging by the width of their spines—probably dutiful histories and biographies from the Book-of-the-Month Club. There was a nightstand by the bed with an alarm clock and another thick book about the building of the Panama Canal, and nothing else in the room but the clothes they had scattered on the floor or over the single office chair that seemed to have no function other than to take up space. If there was a purpose to this blankness, some sort of ascetic principle at work, Lucy could not discern it. To her, the room just seemed lonely and negligently bare, and her heart stirred for the uncomplaining man who inhabited it.

They were both wonderfully quiet now. She could hear the steady tap of his heart and the almost inaudible snare-drum sound of her electronic watch as it ruthlessly whisked away each irrecoverable second.

"What about the Cape?" Walt said after a while. "I'm assuming Brian and the children are going down to watch the launch."

"Yes."

"I could be there too."

She thought about it for a long time, still listening to the time sweep away.

"Would you take it wrong if I said I didn't want you at the launch? The thing is, I don't know if I'll be able to focus, knowing you're going to be there, trying to find some way to see you alone when we both know that'll be impossible. I've got to think about the mission. I've got to think about doing the job you trained me for."

Walt said that was fair enough. In a way he was relieved. The thought of being with her in the beach house on Cape Canaveral where the astronauts and their spouses and friends gathered just before the launch suddenly did not seem like a good idea. He could have no visible claim to her, no way to touch her or speak to her except in ways that now seemed perfunctory and one-dimensional. Meanwhile he would be helplessly positioned to witness her and Brian at a charged emotional moment, and the thought of such a scene taking place made him feel, now that all the markers had so abruptly changed, disheartened and even angry.

"I want to know you'll be thinking of me, though," she said, as he was brooding over this point.

"I'm not going to be thinking of much else. I'm not sure I like the idea anymore of you going into space."

"Losing your nerve?"

"Maybe. I never had any reason to lose it before."

She accepted this statement in peaceful silence. Her eyes welled up. She did not know if she was starting to cry because of the natural warmth of Walt's words—the sort of flat expression of affection she had never really heard from Brian—or because of some other item on her ever-growing roster of bewildering emotions.

"Are you all right?" she asked him, because his thoughtful silence was beginning to feel solemn.

"I'm fine. I'm happy."

"Don't be happy," she said.

"Why not?"

"Because it's pretending."

This time she was the one who looked at her watch.

"I thought we weren't supposed to do that," he said.

"Twenty minutes," she told him. "I can't stay any longer than that. I really can't. Are you going to tell anybody about this?"

"Tell anybody? No."

"Not even your friend? The priest?"

"Do you want me to tell Louis?"

"Of course not. I just thought maybe you'd need to talk to some-body. If you had to, I wouldn't mind. I trust you."

But she knew, of course, that he would not tell anyone, and neither would she. The risks were too significant, the ultimate meaning of this strange moment too unknowable. There would be no chance of making a coherent assessment of where to go from here until after her mission. There was something lovely about no one but the two of them knowing about themselves, but something lonely as well, as if this shimmering, mirage-like interval would evaporate without someone else in the world to witness it.

It was eleven o'clock when she left. Walt wanted to walk her to her car, but she insisted on going alone, and so he watched her from his open door, which looked out upon the courtyard of the condominium complex, as she walked away. The street where she had parked her car was lined with townhomes that backed up to a canal where the owners kept their boats and from which they gained access to the waters of Clear Lake. The moon shone brilliantly onto the calm water of the canal, and illuminated Lucy as well until she disappeared beneath the fronds of a streetside row of palms. In time he heard the muted sound of her car door opening and closing, and then saw her headlights sweep around the corner as she drove back in her minivan toward NASA Road One. The sight of her driving away created a surge of wistfulness in Walt that was close to physical weakness. It was as if she were already drift-ing on orbit in the darkness of space, and there was no longer any way for him to reach her.

Chapter Twenty-two

"This should all be fairly perfunctory," Jimmy Sladek announced as he slid a thin pile of documents across the polished conference table to Lucy and Brian. "Just a quick review, make sure there's nothing you want to add, nothing you want to do differently."

Jimmy was their lawyer, a short and compact man of sixty who wore tailored suits and collected antique panoramic photographs. The document they were reviewing was their will. It was a familiar procedure. She and Brian had gone over the will just before his last mission, and now that it was her turn to go into space prudence dictated that they do so again.

"Brian, as you know, is the executor," Jimmy said, pointing across the table with the tip of his Mont Blanc ballpoint to the provisions he wanted them to notice. "In the case of your death, Lucy, he would also of course continue to raise the children, unless something, God forbid, happened to him, in which case you've designated your sister, Suzanne, as guardian and also as trustee. That's still the case, I assume?"

"That's right," Lucy said, with a brief glance at her husband. She had won this point years ago, when they had first made out their will. Brian had not put up much of a fight to have either of his brothers—one the head of a prosperous restaurant-supply company, the other a veterinarian, both childless and divorced at the time—named as guardian, but

she knew it was a buried sore point with him that she had not encouraged much discussion about the matter before putting forth Suzanne as
the obvious candidate. But Brian betrayed no lingering resentment now,
and he had no comment on any of the other provisions of the will as
Jimmy made his brisk and amiable way through its particulars.

Lucy did her best to keep herself on the surface of things, laughing at
Jimmy's occasional witticisms, nodding her head in agreement with
some sensible minor proposal he recommended about the beneficiary
designation for her retirement plan, making small talk—on the way
out of his office—about the three-foot-long panoramic photo of early-
twentieth-century Galveston bathing beauties that hung next to the
door.

"I'm sure you'll have no need of anything we've discussed today,"
Jimmy said as he said good-bye, but his reassurances were so blatantly
rhetorical that even he seemed a little embarrassed. He knew the odds
well enough, she supposed, otherwise he wouldn't be taking her hand in
both of his and looking her in the eye in a way that was unsettlingly significant and sincere.

But as she walked back to the car with Brian she found that the
effort to repress the horrors of what this meeting had represented—her
poor bewildered children facing life without a mother—had left her in a
tremulous emotional state.

"If it blows up at launch—" she said as Brian was turning on the
ignition.

"What?" he said.

"If it blows up at launch, if you even feel that something's not quite
right, get them inside as fast as you can. I don't want them staring up at
the sky, trying to figure out what's going on, like those poor kids had to
do with *Challenger.*"

"Come on, Lucy."

"*Listen to me, Brian!* I want to talk about this. We've never really
talked about it, and we need to."

"All right," he said. "Let's talk about it." He turned the ignition off.

"If I die, I want you to be the one to tell them. I want them to hear it
from you. And don't put it off. It'd be even more horrible if they saw it
on TV, or just overheard somebody talking about it. They're going to
have to be able to trust you to tell them the truth."

"Lucy, honey, I know it's kind of freaky, having to go over the will
like that. But the chances of anything happening are pretty remote."

"They're not that remote, and we both know it. I don't know if they'll need any sort of grief counseling or not. You'll have to play that by ear. The important thing is for you just to be near them, you and Suzanne and my mother. Would you mind if my mother stayed with you a while?"

"Of course not."

"Routine is going to be the most important thing for them, I think. Going back to school, seeing their teachers, seeing their friends. If Davis's asthma starts to—"

"Jesus Christ," Brian said. "Are you sure you even want to go?"

"Don't you dare ask me that," she said. "I never asked you that."

"All right. I'm sorry. Take it easy."

The look of hurt and confusion on his face was strong enough to convince her that she had stepped over the line into irrationality. She apologized, and when he waved the apology away she felt a twinge of tenderness for him, for his befuddlement and innocent concern.

"As long as we're talking about this," he said. "It would be hard on me too, you know? Losing you. I might not be able to deal with everything as efficiently as you think I should. It might hurt too bad."

"I know. I should have thought about that. I'm sorry."

"Just for the record," he said.

They drove together back to JSC and talked about nothing while she tried without success to stop meditating upon the possibility of her own annihilation. What kind of parent would Brian be without her influence, she asked herself, glancing over at him as he drove, his profile etched against the bright midmorning sun. Would his sharp edges and punishing rigor and simmering sense of martyrdom make the house intolerable to his children? And if he remarried—*when* he remarried—what if the wife he would clumsily select turned out to be some humorless automaton or outright bitch? Maybe that was her greatest fear, the idea of some unworthy and unfeeling woman stepping in to become the mother of her children.

It was unfair to Brian to speculate this way, she knew. He would do the best he could, he was doing the best he could now. Was it guilt over what had happened between her and Walt last night that was spiking her anxiety now, and robbing her of any charitable thoughts toward her husband? She could do nothing about the guilt: it was there, it would always deservedly be there from now on. But if she wanted to quell the anxiety, if she wanted to feel remotely complete and secure, she knew she had to see Walt again before she went into quarantine tomorrow night.

As it happened, it was not that hard a thing to do. Late that evening, there was an unexpected gap in the pre-quarantine flurry of activities when a crew meeting Surly had called ended up being rescheduled and then scrubbed altogether, and when Lucy called Walt's cell phone he was already at home, waiting for her.

So for the second time in two nights she lied to Brian, telling him the truth about the scrubbed meeting but fabricating a late-night solo session in the single-system trainer so that she could go over, one last time, her duties during ascent. He didn't question her. He identified with her last-minute jitters—he had been through them himself—and told her he would get the kids to bed.

They met at Walt's condominium again. She parked in the same place she had parked the night before, and though they were just as rushed tonight there was no momentum wasted, no hovering at a brink from which they had already jumped. All that tormented deliberation was behind them. It freed her, and excited her a little, to realize that the damage was already done, that she and Walt were now alone in the frightening and unfamiliar reality they had allowed themselves to create. They made love with the covers thrown back, their bodies boldly exposed to one another, no patience for furtiveness or shyness. But when it was over, and the breeze from the ceiling fan was too telling on their bare skin, they dressed and walked into Walt's living room, which, unlike the bedroom, and the hallway where he had been waiting last night to kiss her, still had something of a neutral charge. It remained a nostalgic vestige of the chaste world they had left behind, a room still inhabited by the ghosts of their previous noncriminal selves. Lucy could not carry the illusion much farther than that. She found she still had the need to be physically close to him, impossibly close, as they lay on his couch and looked out the sliding glass door at the smooth, dark lake.

"We're going to see each other while I'm in quarantine, right?" she asked him.

"Not like this."

"I know that. But we'll see each other."

"Sure we will."

"And when we happen to look in each other's direction, when we happen to catch each other's eyes, we'll know what the other one is thinking."

"Tell me what you'll be thinking."

"No. I don't want to say anything out loud. Not until I get back from the mission."

"You're right," he said. "Don't think about anything but the mission. After it's over, we can sort all this out."

She was lying against him, and she could feel his arms tighten, cinching around her chest with a possessive strength that pleased her. She watched the lighthouse beacon on the far shore as it moved back and forth like a scanning eye, slowly surveying the black water below. The eight days of her mission were beginning to seem less like a stretch of time than a physical gap like the lake that was spread before her, not a destination in itself but something she had to cross to reach something else. But what was she trying to reach? What was it she would be coming home to?

She told Walt about the visit to her lawyer, the exchange with Brian afterward, how close to the surface her fear was running now that the mission was imminent. She talked about this fear without inhibition. She had guardedly broached the subject with Walt before, but the openness and trust with which she now spoke felt new to her.

Walt offered a few words of bland reassurance, but mostly he just listened. And even as she poured out her misgivings to him, his presence strengthened her. She could talk to Walt this way because both of them understood that her resolve would in the end be a more powerful force than her doubt. She would go on the mission, she would take the risk that must be taken. There was no question of that, there had never really been. She had just needed a way to remind herself.

"I better go now," she said.

"I know," he whispered.

She twisted around on the couch to kiss him. She went into the bathroom to straighten her clothes and comb her hair, and when she came out she kissed him again, and they clung to each other all the way to the door, and when she finally walked through it she had not yet let go of his hand.

When she caught sight of Walt's priest friend walking toward them, ten feet away on the open-air corridor leading to his front door, her hand jerked backward as if she had just received an electric shock.

"Hello," she said, in as unconcerned a voice as she could summon. "Father Louis, right?"

"Actually, it's Father Mondragon. My order does the last-name thing. But in any case it's Louis to you. Hey, Walt."

Walt greeted Louis with a confused, abbreviated wave as the three of them stood awkwardly at the open door of his condominium. Louis was holding a ten-gallon bucket of popcorn that was almost as big as a trash can, and he had a stalled smile on his face as they all did their best to talk past the incriminating moment that Lucy was pretty sure he had just witnessed.

"Lucy's going into quarantine for her mission tomorrow," Walt explained.

"Wow, big moment," Louis said. He set down the bucket of popcorn and clasped her hand with a pastoral warmth that Lucy, despite her anxiety at this unwelcome meeting, felt a little beguiled by. She liked him. She understood why he was Walt's friend.

"I'm going to be praying for you and your crew," he said. "And for your family while you're up there."

"That's really kind," she said.

"You're going to do great," Louis went on. "I could tell, that night you came to the church, that you're somebody really special. Well, I guess by definition all astronauts are special, aren't they? Anyway, there's something about you."

He had talked himself into a corner, and Lucy thought she saw him blushing in the imperfect illumination of the porch light.

"Thank you," she said, and touched his arm, a gesture that she hoped was not considered forward in relation to a celibate priest. "I better get home. I've got a lot of work to do before tomorrow."

"Would it make you uncomfortable if I asked to give you a blessing before you go?" Louis said. "I know you're not Catholic, and you might feel that—"

"Louis." There was an irritated undercurrent in Walt's voice.

Lucy ignored him. "It wouldn't make me uncomfortable at all," she said. "I'd be touched."

"All right," Louis said. "Do me a favor, Walt, and back up a little bit. I need some room to get my mojo working.

"Almighty God," he said, as he touched the top of Lucy's uncertainly bowed head, "we ask that you accompany your servant Lucy and her companions on their journey to the heavens. Let them see the light of your protection even in the blackness of space, and let that light guide them home again safely to their families. We ask this in the name of the Father, and of the Son, and of the Holy Spirit. Amen."

He made the sign of the cross and then let his hand rest tenderly for a moment on the crown of her head, a consoling touch that called forth tears from her wellspring of boiling emotional complexity. She thanked Louis, with a sincerity she had not anticipated feeling. She said good night to him and then to Walt, trying for a timbre of guiltless comrade-ship as she gave Walt a perfunctory hug and told him she would see him in quarantine.

Walt waited to say anything until she had gone down the stairs and he could hear her footsteps as she walked up the street where her car was parked.

"What's the deal with the popcorn?" he finally said to Louis.

"It's for you. I got it at Office Depot. Don't ask me why they sell popcorn at office-supply stores. They just do.

"Anyway," Louis said, scooting the bucket toward Walt with the toe of his foot, "I was an asshole the other night, so here."

"Thanks," Walt said.

"There's three different kinds of popcorn in there for your snacking pleasure."

"You want to come in?"

"No, this was just a drive-by mea culpa thing. So assuming my apology is accepted, I'll be on my way, all the while saying nothing about things that aren't any of my business."

"That would be much appreciated," Walt said.

But Louis didn't leave. He remained where he was, silent, listening to Lucy's distant footsteps.

"You could've talked to me first, that's all I'm saying."

"We both know what your opinion would have been."

"I'm that predictable?"

"Come on, Louis, you're a priest."

"I'm not talking about that. Let's just say for the sake of argument I don't even give a damn about your soul. I would still have expected you, as my friend, to say, 'Hey, Louis, something's troubling me, I think I'm heading into some deep water here, let's go have a Shiner Bock and talk it over.' "

"I'm sorry it didn't play out like you thought it should."

"That's a reasonable expectation, Walt. To be consulted."

Louis was trying for a tone of exaggerated reasonableness, but it was hard to miss the anger in his voice. He was looking at Walt in a way he rarely did: straight on, not bothering to cut his eyes away in ironic evasion. Everything was for real now, everything was suddenly on the table.

Walt wasn't accustomed to looking Louis in the eye, and he wasn't interested in a staring contest. He glanced down at the absurd bucket of popcorn, then up past Louis's shoulder toward the night sky, where a few stars managed to shine bright through a pale wash of light pollution.

"She's married, Walt. She has two kids."

"I'm not going to talk about this with you, Louis. You can take your popcorn back if you want."

"Oh, no," Louis said over his shoulder as he walked to the stairwell. "No way. That's a gift. That's a fucking gift from me to you."

Chapter Twenty-three

Bethie was shrieking. The child had planted herself in the hallway at the entrance to Lucy and Brian's bedroom, pleading to some unknown tormentor in a voice shrill with terror.

"No! No! Please! Don't put me in the oven!"

In an instant, Lucy sprang from her own troubled sleep, bounded out of bed and across the room, and lifted the screaming girl into her arms. But in the confusion of her night terror Bethie pushed against her, trying to escape.

"No! I don't want to go in the oven! Mommy! Mommy! Don't let her put me in the oven!"

"Sweetheart." Lucy spoke to her in as calm a voice as she could muster. "It *is* Mommy. I'm here. I'm not going to let anything happen to you."

The sound of her mother's voice caused Bethie to stop struggling. Her screams gradually subsided to whimpers as Lucy held her close and stroked her hair and kept murmuring reassurances.

"She okay?" Brian said sleepily as Lucy carried her over and put her into bed with them. Lucy nodded her head and then looked at the bedside clock. It was three thirty in the morning. It only took Bethie a moment more, lying next to her mother's body, to fall asleep.

"When I came home," Brian whispered to Lucy, "she was watching some Hansel and Gretel show on TV with Zokie. That's probably what caused her to have a bad dream. One of those creepy Eastern European things that are dubbed and the colors are all faded."

If it had been that creepy, Lucy wanted to ask, why hadn't he turned it off, instead of what he no doubt did, which was to leave Bethie in front of the television with Zokie while he went out for his inviolable evening run? But she didn't ask, of course, both because it was a bad time for rancor and because she was all too aware of where *she* had been last night. While Bethie had been falling asleep, as her unconscious fears began to coalesce into a nightmare about a ferocious witch, Lucy had been lying in Walt's bed. And now it felt cruelly appropriate that in Bethie's terrified nighttime delirium she had mistaken her own mother for the witch that was trying to force her into an oven.

Bethie had sunk into a peaceful sleep now, and Brian was lightly snoring again on his side of the bed, but Lucy knew sleep was no longer an option for her. This was the last day. She and Brian were going to spend it with the children, and then she would say good-bye to them. She would still be in Houston for another three days, until it was time to fly to the Cape for the launch, but during that time she would be quarantined with the crew in their quarters at JSC.

Part of the rationale for quarantine, in addition to the primary concern for colds and infections, was to give the shuttle crew a chance to change their sleeping patterns to conform to those of the crew members on the space station with which they would be docking. Leaving the earth meant leaving behind the earth's reigning diurnal rhythms, a terrestrial understanding of night and day that did not apply in space, where time was trackless and bewildering and therefore had to be meted out from Ground in Houston.

Lucy had wanted to get a good night's sleep, since the first order of business once she entered quarantine tonight would be to stay awake with the crew as long as possible in order to get this process underway. Walt would be there. One of the rituals of quarantine was that the primary training team joined the crew on that first night of sleep shifting in a kind of farewell slumber party. Maybe it would be a comfort to have him there as they all sat up and watched movies and talked until dawn; maybe it would be a torment. In any case, there on the threshold of her dream of entering space, she would be sleep-deprived, ragged, away from her children, and sealed off from the sustaining intimacy she had just discovered with Walt.

She got out of bed, hopelessly wide-awake now. There were so many things for her to feel nervous or guilty about that her mind skittered from one to the next like a needle on an old-fashioned record. The groove it finally settled in was the scene last night at Walt's front door. If Louis had felt obligated to pass judgment on her, he had kept the obligation to himself. The blessing he had given, she knew, was genuine. She was not a religious person and had not felt, or at least had resisted feeling, the settling upon her of some sort of spiritual protection. But she had felt the bestowal of Louis's caring concern, and it had carried a charge. That charge, she theorized, was what Catholics meant by grace. But she didn't know if she could parse the difference between godly contentment and the illicit peace she felt with Walt. How were you supposed to behave when sin itself felt like grace? She worried about Walt, because the true-enough torments of right and wrong she was experiencing had to be, in his case, at least shadowed by issues of salvation and redemption. She had not lingered after she left them last night. She had needed to get home to her children, and in any case she had had enough pride—or enough apprehension—to keep herself from eavesdropping on their conversation.

While the rest of her family slept, she took a shower and washed her hair, and put on her jeans and a souvenir T-shirt from a 5K run that had been a fund-raiser for Davis's school. The T-shirt was deliberate, as were the unsuitably girlish earrings that Bethie had picked out for her last birthday. She was going to record a video for the kids. If she died, they would be watching this video over and over again for the rest of their lives, and they would see the care their mother had taken to include these tokens in her final words to them.

In the last week she had bought a new battery for the camcorder and a new video cartridge, and had sketched out what she had wanted to say on a piece of notebook paper and made a point of safeguarding time after breakfast today to record her message. But it was even better to do it now, she decided, even though it was still long before daylight and the house was dark and lonely and her sense of dread correspondingly more acute. The fogginess of sleep had worn off, her thoughts were clear, and except for a single mockingbird outside, calling out from tree to tree in a piercing voice, there was quiet all around.

She closed the door to the den, turned on the lamp at the end of the sofa, and set the camera up on a tripod. When she was sure that the focus and framing and lighting were adequate—thanks to her astronaut training, video photography was among the things in which she had become proficient—she sat down and recorded a message for Davis and then one for Bethie. She told them stories about the days they were born, about the first time they had smiled at her, the first words they had said, the time Lucy had held Davis in her arms and showed him the faint moving light in the night sky that was the *Mir* space station in which his father was orbiting the earth, the time an elderly woman came up to the family as they were eating dinner at Luby's cafeteria and pointed to Bethie in her high chair and said, "That is the most enchanting child I have ever seen."

In both messages she told about how a precious dream had been fulfilled for her when her children were born, and how she could not imagine ever feeling more complete or more happy than she had at those moments. But she told them also about the power of her dream to fly in space, to do something that few people, men or women, had ever achieved; and how when you have a dream that feels so right and so strong it means there is something meaningful and undeniable at work within you, as powerful as an artist's need to paint or a musician's instinct to organize sound into rhythm and melody. She said she would miss her children while she was in space, and she hoped they would miss her too, but she told them they should be proud when *Endeavour* lifted off and climbed into the sky, proud not just because their mother was flying into space but because she had had a dream strong enough to take her there, and because someday they would have such a dream for themselves.

She ended with assurances about how much she loved them, how much she would be thinking of them while she was gone, the things they would do together when she got back. It was important for her words not to be too momentous, not to sound like a farewell.

Bethie's message was easier to record. The simple, soothing notes of reassurance came naturally to Lucy, and would be taken at face value by her trusting daughter. With Davis, she had to take into account his greater acuity, his suspicion that her great adventure in space was in reality a selfish errand. She felt the need to defend herself somehow against these silent charges, but she could neither address them directly nor dwell on them in her own mind, for fear they might turn out to be true. All her talk about living out your dreams, when she tried to imagine this video through Davis's eyes, sounded hollow to her. But it was true, and she could not help it if the truth sometimes sounded like some sort of bland rationale.

She played the messages back, watching herself through the little hinged viewing window on the camcorder, and could not think how to do it better. It would have to be enough. In any case, once they docked with the station she would be able to use the IP phone while she was on orbit, and would be able to talk with them in a way that wasn't quite as gravely ceremonial. The tapes were not the only communication her children would receive from her while she was gone, but the carefully chosen words she had recorded and the carefully mustered feelings were the bedrock sentiments she needed to make sure they heard.

By the time she had finished it was almost six in the morning, but still solemnly dark outside. As she was labeling the tapes the door to the den opened and Brian appeared. He was wearing a pair of jeans and the T-shirt he had slept in.

"You been up all this time?" he asked.

She nodded and held up the tapes. "I'm going to put these right here," she said, setting them on the bookshelf. "I thought the kids could watch them after the launch when they come back from the Cape."

"What did you tell them?"

"You can watch with them."

"Did you make one for me?" he asked.

"Do you need one?"

Brian shrugged. He could have been joking, but nevertheless it struck Lucy as significant that she had not even thought to tape herself telling her husband how much she loved him and how much she looked forward to returning to him.

"So what's the plan today?" he said.

"I go into quarantine at seven tonight. The rest of the day is family day. Whatever the kids want to do. We should get them up in an hour or so."

"This is our last chance, then," Brian said.

"Last chance for what?"

She had not noticed the subtle downshift in his voice, his awkward attempt at seductive insinuation. It was their last chance to make love before she went into quarantine and then blasted off into space. That was another thing she had not thought of.

"Bethie's in our bed." She worried that the declarative tone in her voice would make Brian think that she was looking for obstacles, which of course she was.

"I can move her," he said, with an odd smile.

She told him in as pleasant a voice as she could summon that she would be there in a minute, after she had put the camera and the tripod away. Then she sat there in the dark den, stalling and thinking. It was one thing not to know if she loved her husband. It was another thing not to want to sleep with him at the last opportunity before she left the earth in a tower of flame, after having betrayed him two nights running with Walt.

She did not feel weak with guilt, as she would have expected, but strong with a sort of predatory power. Strong enough to be kind to Brian when she joined him in the bedroom, withholding a secret that she realized could shatter him. She presented him with the body he had grown glumly accustomed to, but a body whose worth was now known to her, because another man, a better man, had desired it. It was strange how her treachery opened the way for her to feel generous, even loving, toward Brian. Maybe it was just the tenderness people feel toward those they are leaving, those they suspect they have outgrown.

The whole day, at least until this evening when Lucy went into quarantine, was open to them. Over breakfast, she asked the children what they wanted to do. Davis said AstroWorld, Bethie cluelessly seconded his suggestion, and in a few minutes more the four of them were driving west on 610 in the family minivan. They spent the morning riding Diablo Falls and the Serpent and soothing Davis's frustration when he discovered he wasn't tall enough yet to ride the Mayan Mindbender. When they were through with AstroWorld they drove over to Westheimer and had lunch at the Cheesecake Factory, and then Lucy and Brian took them to FAO Schwarz and let them each pick out a toy. It was a day of outrageous indulgence. If it had not been for the ticking clock Lucy could not help hearing, it would have been a day of great contentment as well, the family all on the same team, all determined to make a happy memory together, Brian tolerant and uncomplaining.

On the way home in the late afternoon both children fell asleep, and Lucy stared at them in silence from the front seat as Brian drove.

Bethie's sleepwalking terror last night had been frightening, but it seemed to have evaporated in the morning sun, and Lucy thought she had more or less succeeded in portraying the mission to Bethie in a way that made it seem like a grand adventure and not a looming threat. But Lucy knew, after last night, that Bethie was able to cling to that version only during the daylight hours. At night, obviously, murky threats were stalking her sleeping mind. But all children had nightmares, whether their mothers were astronauts or not. As dearly as Lucy wanted to, she could not patrol her daughter's dreams.

Davis's fears were more conscious, though he was doing his active best to hide them, both from himself and from her. His resolve not to show vulnerability complicated the expression of his other emotions, giving him a hollow gleefulness at some moments and a sullen indifference at others. His authentic feelings were too dangerous to expose. Lucy understood this. She had no idea what to do about it, except to reassure him by casual words and gestures, and to hold her own emotions in check so that he would not perceive these last hours together as a dangerous threshold.

A little over two weeks, she kept reminding herself; that was all. Eight days to launch, assuming the launch wasn't postponed, which was as likely to happen as not; eight days in space, and then back again. Two weeks, three at the outside, and she would be back home with her children.

All that remained was to say good-bye. Lucy had wanted the moment when she would leave her children to feel as casual, as workaday, as possible, and so she had taken Buddy up on his offer to ride with him in his car to the quarantine quarters. She had asked him to swing by at six forty-five and honk the horn, as if he were just picking her up for a routine meeting or some crew function at the Outpost.

She had just finished playing Candy Land with the children when she heard Buddy's horn. The game was too young for Davis, and he was ordinarily contemptuous of its simple rules and slow pace, but this evening he seemed to find it soothing, and Lucy watched the way he stared at the tokens on the board as if he could somehow hold them in place and stop time.

"Okay," she said in a lilting voice, "it's time for me to go." When the time comes, she had been telling herself for the last several months, don't overdo it. Don't let them see fear or regret or guilt, just smile and kiss them and tell them you love them and walk out the door with such confidence there can be no question in their vulnerable hearts that you will be coming back.

"So how long am I going to be gone again?" she asked them.

"Two weeks!" Bethie called out obediently, though there was a tremor in her voice now, and a wild, wary look.

"Two weeks and I'll be home again. And the two of you and Daddy are going to come to Florida and see the launch and if you look really really hard do you know what you might see?"

Davis looked away, not willing to play this game. But Bethie, her eyes starting to fill up with tears now, said, "What?"

"You'll see me waving at you through the orbiter windows. You'll see me waving at you when we take off and waving at you again when we come home."

She glanced at Brian, who was standing next to the door holding her suitcase. "And guess where you and your father and Nona and Aunt Suzanne are going the day after launch?"

"Where?" Bethie said. Lucy was now relying solely on her for a response, since Davis had become predictably distant and mute.

"Disney World!" she told them triumphantly. "Is that okay with you?"

"It's okay," Davis said, with a lack of enthusiasm that sent a chill through her.

"But we want *you* to go with us!" Bethie blurted out.

"I will some other time, sweetheart. I promise. Now give me a huge hug."

Lucy had to hold her breath to keep from crying as she gathered Bethie in her arms and told her that she loved her, and then did the same with Davis. Bethie was crying now, and holding on to her leg, but Davis took his sister's hand and pulled her away.

"Let Mom go," he said.

She kissed them both again and walked toward the door listening to Bethie's suddenly bewildered weeping and—worse—to Davis's stoic silence.

Brian walked with her out to the curb, where Buddy was sitting grinning behind the wheel of his T-Bird.

"They'll be fine," Brian told her.

"Promise me?" she said. She had stopped holding her breath, but every nerve in her body was taut with the effort not to dissolve into heartbroken weeping.

"Of course I promise," he replied. "I'm their father. I'm not going to let anything happen to them. If you don't believe that, you'd better stay home."

"I didn't mean it like that," she said. "I'm sorry."

"I'm just pointing out that you can trust me."

She didn't have to say good-bye to Brian now. With his Primary Contact badge, he could come and go during quarantine, and she would see him when he came down to the Cape before launch. But nevertheless she kissed him with a warmth she had not expected to feel.

"The kids take it okay?" Buddy asked her as they drove off.

"Okay enough," Lucy said. There was music playing on his car stereo, Marcia Ball singing some sort of anthem from the Louisiana bayous.

"Do me a favor," Buddy said. They were passing the HEB where Lucy shopped for groceries for her family, the shoe store where she had bought Davis his first pair of lace-up shoes, the Little Ballerina Dance Academy in whose introductory class she had just enrolled Bethie. "Do me a favor and tell me where we're going. I just want to hear somebody say it."

"We're going to space, Buddy."

Buddy laughed out loud, overcome with exuberance and delight. Lucy too was enraptured at the thought of what awaited them, but at the same time the characterless exurban landscape of Clear Lake City was beckoning her back with heartrending force.

Chapter Twenty-four

Walt drove over to the quarantine facility at about nine o'clock that night, several hours after the crew had checked in. He found the team already there as well, except for Mickey, who had caught an ear infection from his young daughter and would have to stay away until the doctors certified him as no longer contagious.

The crew was sitting at a table in the brightly lit common room, signing a mountain of crew pictures and laughing and talking in such high spirits that they all spontaneously cheered when they saw Walt walk in.

"The man who made it all happen!" Surly said, as he leapt up from the table and gave Walt a manly, backslapping hug. The rest of the crew hugged him as well, Lucy more shyly than the others, but with a twinge of pressure from her open hand against his shoulder blade, a possessive gesture that no one could see but that registered in every welcoming nerve of Walt's body.

"So what's the plan?" he asked them.

"Ask Gary," Surly said. "He was in charge of renting the movies."

"We will begin our cinematic explorations," Gary announced, "with *Marooned,* in which three astronauts including Gene Hackman and the incomparable Richard Crenna find themselves stranded in space. We will continue with *Capricorn One,* a superb paranoid thriller from the seventies about how the sinister National Aeronautics and Space Administration fakes a Mars landing to dupe an unsuspecting American public. From there we will—"

While Gary continued to reel off the list of movies he had rented for the evening, the entertainment that would keep the crew awake until dawn in the first phase of their sleep-shifting procedure, Walt casually made his way to where Lucy was standing. He kept his hands in his pockets, but allowed his arm to brush up discreetly against hers.

"How did it go?" he whispered. "The kids all right?"

"It went okay. It was hard. Did you and Louis get a chance to talk?"

"Sort of."

"Everything okay?"

"It's okay."

"You sure?"

He nodded vaguely and drew their attention back to Gary, who was expounding on the glories of *The Fifth Element,* the movie he predicted they would start watching at about four thirty a.m. Gary was in geek heaven, here in this dorm-like space where everything—from the oppressive fluorescent lighting to the bowls of M&M's and pretzels scattered about to the wide-screen flat-panel TV—was consciously designed with an all-nighter in mind. Sylvia had gone to the trouble to have the mission patch blown up into a wall-sized poster, but otherwise the crew quarters had the air of a sterile, transient place, with only a few generic space photos for decoration.

The crew and the training team had dinner together at the long table in the dining room—spaghetti and salad and garlic bread, followed by chocolate cake. After that Surly broke out his guitar and treated them to a song he had written, titled "The Ballad of STS-108," made up of tortuous half-rhymes and music that Walt was pretty sure had been stolen from some ancient TV western.

During the good-natured groaning that followed, Gary ordered everyone to take their seats, and they all settled down in front of the television and watched the first movie, the crew wisecracking their way through it as they busied themselves with signing more crew pictures or checking their e-mail on their laptops.

Walt stared at the TV screen, at the primitive special effects as the stranded space capsule orbited the earth. He paid no attention to the story, or to the smart-ass commentary from the space professionals in the room. But the TV seemed as handy an object as any on which to keep his eyes focused so they would not drift helplessly in Lucy's direction.

"Are you feeling all right?" Sylvia asked him. She was sitting next to him on the crowded couch, eating a piece of the chocolate cake.

"What do you mean?"

"I don't know, it's like you're actually watching the movie or something."

Walt leaned forward and scooped up a handful of freeze-dried peanuts from the bowl in front of him. "I'm just thinking about the mission," he said. "I'm thinking we should have run that manifold leak problem a few times more."

"You've got opening-night jitters. You always do."

She patted him on the arm and got up to get a beer. Walt took the opportunity to look again in Lucy's direction and fleetingly meet her eyes. He saw that she thought Sylvia might have discerned or discovered something, and in the instant afforded them by this glance he tried to reassure her. He was on a down cycle: a little apprehensive, a little concerned that he might have overestimated the intensity of what had been going on between him and Lucy. There was just no opportunity, in this high-spirited group environment, to confirm it. There was too much at stake on too many fronts.

What if he had thrown her as much off balance as she had him? The guilt he felt over betraying Brian had been pesteringly small in the passionate moments he and Lucy had spent together, but every hour he was apart from her it was growing more relevant and acute. For Lucy it would certainly be worse. While she was sitting here waiting to be launched into space she had to be thinking, thinking hard, about what would happen to her family now. What Walt feared was that she was not just thinking but calculating, edging toward a pragmatic realization that Walt was someone she simply could not afford.

How could he blame her? By allowing himself to fall in love with her, he had thrown her far deeper into emotional turmoil than she had been before, and this new level of distraction might incalculably increase the physical danger for her and her crewmates.

He sank further into these reflections as *Marooned* came to an end and *Capricorn One* began, with Gary once again introducing the movie. His exegesis, after three or four beers, was even geekier and loopier. Walt kept his seat, although most of the other people in the room were wandering around by this time, talking in small groups and ignoring the movie. He watched Kyle walk up to Lucy and fall into an animated conversation with her, with an ease that he himself seemed to have forfeited. Kyle was drinking a soft drink—he had brought his own six-pack of Mr. Pibb—and as far as Walt could tell he was still rigorously on the wagon.

Walt stood up and ambled over to join them. Lucy greeted him with a casual welcoming glance, shifted a little to give him an opening in the conversational circle.

"We were just talking about Bob Poteet," Kyle said. "Remember how he was so terrified he was going to have to pee while he was strapped in on the launch pad waiting for liftoff that he didn't drink anything for like two days before? He's so proud of himself for not having to use his MAG, but then two days later he's on orbit and he gets kidney stones."

"I remember," Walt said. "Poor old Bob."

"Moral of story," Kyle told Lucy, "your maximum absorbancy garment is your friend."

He drained the last of his Mr. Pibb and drifted off to observe the domino game that Surly and Chuck Nethercott were now playing on one of the big tables in the common room. Walt and Lucy found themselves with a moment of relative solitude, but they both knew there was too much to risk by taking advantage of it.

"I'm getting sleepy," she said.

Walt looked at his watch. "It's after midnight."

"You don't have to stay to the bitter end, you know. You can leave before it's time for us to tuck ourselves into bed."

"I think I'll stay and watch whatever the last movie is."

The Fifth Element," Lucy said.

Walt looked around the room, gauging how far they were from the rest of the group, wondering if he could say something marginally intimate without being overheard. But Lucy guessed what he was thinking and said, in a whisper, "Better not."

They both looked away at the television screen, neither daring to speak or venture a revealing look. But Lucy's cautionary words, along with the fond, plaintive expression in her eyes when she said them, were proof enough that he wasn't alone in this weird emotional limbo.

He needed this conviction to see him through the night, which finally ended just before dawn, when he and the rest of the team dragged themselves out of the crew quarters with sleepy good-byes and drove to a hole-in-the-wall restaurant on Highway 3 to eat migas before going home.

The training was not over, even with the crew in quarantine. For a few days more, up until the time they left for the Cape, there were still ascent and entry sims to run, but with guards clearing the halls as the quarantined crew walked through Building 5 and escorting them into and out of the van in which they now had to travel, the chances for any sort of private conversation between Walt and Lucy were remote. It was not until the afternoon that the crew at last gathered at Ellington Field to fly off in their T-38s for the Cape that they had even a fleeting chance to speak again.

It was a miserably muggy mid-September afternoon. Walt and his team stood in a group on the tarmac with the sun beating down on them as the crew walked out of the Flight Ops building on their way to the jets. They were wearing flight suits and holding their helmets. Walt had never seen Lucy in a flight suit and was disturbed by the sexy air of intrepidity it gave her. She was not lean; her womanly hips were an awkward fit for the suit's trusswork of straps and buckles. But she looked strong and confident, striding without apology beside Patti Halapeska, whose rangy body seemed to Walt boring in its flawlessness.

There was no elaborate ritual for saying good-bye, just hugs and fervent handshakes, expressions of thanks from the crew and jokey admonitions from the training team.

"Don't you guys screw up," Walt heard Sylvia telling Buddy as she clung to him in a hug. "Don't make us look bad." There were tears in her eyes, as there always were. They all felt proud and sad and apprehensive, helplessly aware that some slight mischance or miscalculation at any time during the mission could mean that the crew would not be coming back.

Walt said good-bye to each of them in turn. Lucy was not last, since they both wanted to avoid an obviously climactic scene. But her eyes were moist when she embraced him, and before she let go she whispered in his ear, so softly that no one else could possibly have heard, "My darling."

Then she turned and walked with Surly to the T-38 the two of them would be flying to Florida. Walt stood there with the rest of the team and watched as she strapped herself into the student's seat behind Surly. Tom Terrific and Buddy Santos were in another jet, and Patti Halapeska was flying a third, with Chuck Nethercott seated behind.

It took only a few minutes for the little squadron to taxi onto the empty Ellington runways and roar off into the pale September sky, and when they had disappeared Walt walked with Sylvia back to where their cars were parked behind the Flight Ops building.

"This is ridiculous," Sylvia said as she wiped the tears from her cheeks. "Think what I'd be like sending my kids off to college or something."

Walt put his arm around her.

"It was better when we used to go to the Cape and see them off there," she said. "It wasn't quite so all of a sudden. If my mother weren't coming to visit, I might even take some personal time and go down there myself. Even if my heart was in my throat, I always liked to watch the launch."

Walt joined Sylvia and the rest of the team for a beer at PeTe's, and lingered long enough to have an early dinner with them. Afterward he drove south on I-45, took the Bay Area Boulevard exit, and found himself, for no particular reason, walking down the air-conditioned corridors of Baybrook Mall. Maybe I need a new pair of shoes, he thought, and he went into an upscale shoe store and spent $125 on a pair of brown walking shoes featuring what the salesman described as a "patented lacing system." He walked out of the store wearing them, their cushioned soles giving his steps an alien springiness.

He hadn't needed a new pair of shoes, he realized. He had bought them in a kind of trance. And now he was haunting the mall in the same sleepwalking way. He was entering one of those spells in which he didn't know what to do with himself, and this time the sensation of aimlessness was close to panic. Teenage girls walked through the mall in their hip-hugger jeans, their pierced navels gleaming, their phones to their ears. In the food court a bored employee was holding trays filled with free samples of teriyaki chicken on toothpicks.

"Want one?" he said to Walt, almost imploringly, as if he were a beggar rather than a profferer. To be polite, Walt took one, but the sweet glaze and the fatty morsel of chicken thigh repelled him and he discreetly spit it out into his hand and tossed it into a trash can.

The cell phone kiosk where Rachel had spent her last conscious moment had been converted in the last few months into a venue for selling novelty pet items, including handmade dog collars and scuttling hermit crabs. Walt stopped there, realizing only at that moment that it had been a kind of destination. He stared down at the crabs in their aquarium tank as they crawled through the sand bed, clumsily sidling up to each other in their painted shells.

"Aren't they cute?" the girl at the kiosk said brightly. "They're only $7.99."

Walt gave her an amiable look, not quite able to actually smile. He stood in his new shoes and looked past the girl to the Old Navy display window on the other side of the corridor. If Rachel had been facing in this direction when the blood clot caused her to lose consciousness, that's what she would have seen.

The girl was still looking at him expectantly. He felt as if he owed her some kind of explanation, that he was honor-bound to tell her that he was not interested in a hermit crab but was only standing here because this was the place where his wife had died.

"Excuse me," he said. He walked away, past the buttery bakery smell of Auntie Anne's pretzels to the mall entrance outside of which he had parked his car.

He had an urge to call Louis from his cell phone to see if he wanted to go out and drink a beer together and talk things over after all. But it was too late for that. He was under the impression that he and Louis, at least for the next few weeks, were no longer speaking.

He went home instead, and sat in a chair and watched a documentary on the Discovery Channel about underwater archaeologists excavating the sunken remains of Cleopatra's palace. And while he stared at the screen he kept remembering Lucy's whispering voice in his ear and her jet disappearing into the sky.

He went to bed and woke up in the morning at six o'clock. He brushed his teeth and dressed, then got his suitcase out of the closet and threw in a week's supply of clothes. In another hour he was driving east on I-10, the familiar route that would take him without deviation all the way to Florida.

Chapter Twenty-five

He had made this trip, from Houston to Cape Canaveral, more than a dozen times back in the old days when the whole team would go down together and hang out with the crew and wait for the launch. But since the new security measures had gone into effect after 9/11, the crew was isolated from everyone but their family members and closest friends, and the pre-launch contact and camaraderie between the trainers and the astronauts had dwindled to such an extent that it was no longer worth the trip.

It felt odd to be driving alone past the familiar freeway strip of carpet and tile warehouses east of Houston, where giant inflated gorillas sitting atop used-car dealerships waved their arms slowly in the torpid breeze; past the refineries around Buffalo Bayou and finally to the first glimpse of marshy nature where the interstate passed over the confluence of the Old and Lost Rivers. He called Lance Briscoe on his cell phone to let the flight manager know he was taking a few days of personal time. He thought he owed it to Sylvia to tell her something as well, and so he left a cryptic message on her answering machine telling her he had had a sudden impulse to drive to Florida. He thought about calling Lucy. He would probably be able to reach her at the Ops and Checkout building at the Kennedy Space Center, where the crew was now quarantined, waiting out the three days to launch. But he checked the impulse.

She had made it plain she didn't want him there, that she wanted to focus on the mission and that his presence would be a distraction she didn't need. He assumed that calling her on the phone would amount to a violation of the same precept. He had agreed to be forbearing, and he would.

So what was he doing? Why was he driving eight hundred miles when he was certain he was not even going to see her or talk to her? All he knew was that in his restlessness his routine environs had suddenly become intolerable to him, and that there was something soothing in just the idea that he was in motion, that he was headed, mile by mile, closer to where Lucy was. In another few days, there would be no point in toting up such measurements of terrestrial progress. She would be accelerating around the world in a way that made distance and proximity irrelevant. In her separate reality, traveling at unthinkable velocities, floating in weightlessness, she would be as unreachable as if she had ceased to exist.

"Gee, thanks for inviting us," Sylvia said, when Walt answered his ringing cell phone.

"It was just a spur-of-the-moment decision," Walt told her. "I barely had time to invite myself."

"You're behaving in increasingly un-Walt-like ways. Plus you're kind of hurting my feelings."

"Sorry, Sylvia."

"Okay, so level with me. Were you planning to eat at Prejean's?"

Prejean's was the Cajun restaurant in Lafayette where the team always used to stop for lunch when they drove down to the Cape.

"I hadn't thought about it," Walt said.

"Because you better not. Not without us. You can just eat at a damn Burger King or something. You know what?"

"What?"

"I'm taking a deep breath here."

"Okay."

"I get the impression you're having an affair with Lucy Kincheloe."

Walt fumbled for some way to respond.

"Don't worry," Sylvia said. "It's not general knowledge. It's just spectacular intuition on my part. And of course I'm not going to tell anybody. Where are you, anyway?"

"Just coming up to Orange. Almost to Louisiana."

"Mind if I say something?"

"No."

"Never mind."

"What?"

"Just, you know. Here I always was."

Walt saw the humpbacked bridge in the distance that spanned the Sabine.

"If you say it never even occurred to you," she went on, "I'll kill you."

"It occurred to me. It just never—"

"No, let's not talk about it anymore. You've got your mind on other things. But swear to God, Walt, I'm not kidding about Prejean's."

So he didn't stop for lunch in Lafayette, just kept heading east until Baton Rouge, where he stopped and filled up with gas and ate a McChicken sandwich from McDonald's. From Baton Rouge he detoured onto Interstate 12, though if he had been with his team they would have stayed on 10 and taken the longer route through New Orleans, where they had often spent the night and risen early in the morning to dawdle over beignets and chicory coffee at Café Du Monde before hitting the road again. But today he bypassed New Orleans, picking up 10 again at Slidell and then leaving it to follow the coastal road through Bay St. Louis and Pass Christian.

It was almost dusk now. The houses and antebellum mansions on the left side of the highway were obscured in the deep shadow of live oaks, and on his right the great, slack expanse of the Mississippi Gulf lay still as a playa lake in the desert. There was a yellow Waffle House sign every three miles, and as he drew nearer to Gulfport he saw the vast casinos looming in the distance through the misty atmosphere. Before he reached them, he pulled over at one of the anonymous motels lining the highway and checked in.

He ate dinner down the block at one of those ubiquitous Waffle Houses, and then walked across the highway and took off his shoes and waded out into the warm water, which was only inches deep and near the peak of a languid low tide, so that the farther out he walked the more the ocean seemed to be almost evaporating before him. The tranquillity of the water, compared to the turbulence of the Texas Gulf, was foreign and a bit unnerving. He felt as if the world had suddenly stopped moving. The wind had died, and the birds had come down out of the sky to roost silently in the branches of the oaks across the highway. Even the traffic had thinned out, and the casinos in the distance looked like empty, extravagant ruins from a livelier age.

The lugubriousness that had stolen over his life after Rachel's death, and that had lifted as he drew closer to Lucy, was threatening to settle in again. Driving to Florida was nothing more than an inchoate attempt to escape the already suffocating reality of Lucy's absence. Walt understood too well that this absence could, due to one of the mals they had trained for, or one that had not yet occurred to anyone, be total and permanent.

Three more days until launch. If the launch window was met, if the mission went as planned, then eight more days until she came back. He didn't think he was being naive to speculate that Lucy's return to earth would mark a serious reconfiguration of both their lives. He'd seen the evidence in her eyes and heard it in her voice. But he did not disregard the obstacles, the wrenching emotional business that lay ahead for both of them. If they were in this for real, Walt would have to stand by her as she separated from her husband, he would have to stand by his own sins with an unwavering conviction. He would have to win the tolerance and affection of her children, without anticipating that they could ever really trust him or love him. He had set all this into motion, and if he did not follow through with it he would feel as stranded as he did now on this listless beach, where the water was so heavy and still it would not even allow a wave to arise and slap against his legs.

Come back. The words formed in his mind with such force that he realized he had spoken them audibly. He was glad Louis wasn't there to hear, since he would have insisted Walt had uttered not a plea but a prayer.

Chapter Twenty-six

It was L-1: launch minus one day. Lucy stood alone on the back deck of the astronaut beach house, watching the sun as it set subtly over the dunes. She was holding a plate of shrimp but had not touched it because of a sudden apprehension that shrimp were highly perishable things, more likely than other food items to produce food poisoning or anaphylactic shock. She knew she was being neurotically cautious, but it was not impossible that the launch could be scrubbed because of a bad shrimp. In any case, she was not the only crew member in the same state of mind. Buddy Santos had declined to go for a run on the beach with her yesterday out of fear he might trip and sprain an ankle. Tom Terrific would barely touch solid food, thinking it might make him more susceptible to space sickness. Even Surly Bonds, the veteran shuttle commander, had had a moment of alarm when he bit down on a dried cherry and thought for a moment he had cracked his tooth on the pit.

She had never known anything quite like this hovering state of anticipation, the sense that everything in her life had become defined by and predicated upon a climactic moment she could not be sure would even arrive. During her pregnancies, the endless wait for labor to begin had created a similar state of suspension, but with childbirth there was always the certainty of a conclusive outcome. An unanticipated weather pattern, a flight of birds that might momentarily confuse the radar, a mechanical failure or the suspicion of one: there were an almost limitless number of things that could delay liftoff and cause STS-108 to miss its narrow launch window. Launches were postponed more often than not, and sometimes missions were scrubbed entirely. "Don't believe anything till you're pullin' g's," Surly had told them time and again during the preceding weeks. When the big liquid-oxygen tank was burning and propelling the shuttle off the pad, when the force of the ascent was splaying your face and mashing you back against your seat, then you could reasonably assume that you were actually going into space. But even then it would not be until eight minutes later, at MECO—Main Engine Cut-Off—when you could be sure that you had arrived.

Surly had counseled them to assume that the launch would be postponed, to fully expect that at launch minus twenty seconds there would be some warning light somewhere that would shut the whole thing down, and that after waiting in suspense for two and a half hours the crew would be required to leave the orbiter and ride in the van back to the O&C building and wait around in quarantine for a day or a week until the problem was fixed or the weather had cleared up enough for another attempt.

Ever since they had come down to the Cape, Lucy had been working on her mental resilience, rehearsing how when the CapCom broke in to tell them that the launch had been postponed, she would shrug her shoulders and sigh, but not bitterly, just more out of a sense of routine exasperation. But there was nothing routine in her life now. Her relationship with Walt was as unreal in its own way as the prospect of tomorrow's launch—more so, because she had not trained for it, and had not dared to dream of it.

A gull flying above the deck cocked its head, expressing interest in her plate of uneaten shrimp. Lucy set it on the salt-stained rail and walked away and watched as the gull descended in cautious stages to grab the shrimp off the plate one by one. Then she looked off past the dune grass to the distant shape of the Vehicle Assembly Building, looming like an office tower through the coastal haze. She could dimly make out Pad 39A as well, where the shuttle stack, with the orbiter and external fuel tank and solid rocket boosters was already in place.

Buddy came out on the deck and joined her for a moment in staring at the pad. He didn't say anything, and his uncharacteristic silence felt reverential.

"Surly is summoning the clans," he said finally. "I think he's got one of his group hug things in mind."

Lucy followed Buddy back into the beach house. There had been several parties and gatherings here since the crew had come down to the Cape, but this was the final such occasion, and the last time Lucy and the others would see their spouses until they returned to earth. The mood had been reflective when Lucy had walked out onto the deck with her plate of shrimp, and it was even more so when she returned, with Surly standing in the middle of the spacious living room holding Paloma's hand, and the others crowding into place around him as he bowed his head and gathered his thoughts. Brian was there, of course, carefully keeping himself at a wary distance from her. She knew he had deliberately not followed her when she wandered out onto the deck alone, and in a way she resented his too-fastidious regard for her privacy. A more intuitive man—Walt, for instance—would have known that what she was craving right now was not isolation but comfort and contact.

The astronaut beach house was a homely place for a group about to embark into the exotic realm of space, but that was the tradition. Crews had been gathering here for decades, in this wind-stripped structure set up on stilts, with cracks in its walls through which the fine sand drifted and the Atlantic wind sang. Compared to the sterile air-conditioned crew quarters where they had been spending most of their time, it was a sagging, decrepit place, open to the sound and grit and weather of the world they were leaving. Lucy loved the beach house. They all did.

Standing with Paloma in the center of the room, Surly embarked upon one of his good-old-boy homilies, praising the crew for their team-work and fellowship, expressing gratitude to the families for allowing the astronauts to follow their dreams, presuming once again to call for God's blessing upon their voyage. When he had finished, Surly broke out several bottles of his favorite champagne, a vintage from the Texas Hill Country named Victory or Death, with a picture of the Alamo on its label.

They toasted the mission and their families; they toasted the training team back home in Houston. The champagne, for all its Texan pomposity, was surprisingly good, but Lucy did not dare take more than a few sips for fear it might bring on a headache. Afterward, husbands and wives began to pair off to say good-bye. Neither Buddy nor Patti was married. Patti had brought her sister, but Buddy had decided on this last night to come alone. His family had come down to the Cape, but his father was frail and his sister was in a wheelchair, so they had said their good-byes earlier. Buddy was now standing in the kitchen talking with two astronauts, Jeff Graham and Luke Applebome, who had been assigned to be the Family Escorts for the crew of STS-108. Everybody on the crew knew, however, that in the event of a disaster Jeff and Luke's official designation would instantly change from Family Escort to Casualty Assistance Officer. They would be the ones who would hustle her children away to seclusion, guard them from the media, bring them toys or games in a hopeless attempt to distract them. And hence Lucy could not help regarding them as specters.

"You want to go for a walk on the beach?" Brian asked her. They had barely spoken during the beach house party, not because of any fresh grievances but simply because neither of them any longer had much to say that the other would want to hear. But of course she went with him. He was her husband, and this was the day before her launch.

They climbed down the stairs of the house and made their way through a few shallow dunes and across the wide beach to the water's edge. Lucy took off her sandals and walked along the foamy margin left by the retreating waves. Brian kept his running shoes on. He was wearing a T-shirt and khaki shorts. He walked along beside her with his usual tense gait, leaving the impression that her own dawdling stride was holding him back and that if he were alone he would break into a heedless run.

They talked about the children, of course. They were with Lucy's mother and sister at the moment, staying with them at a big, sprawling hotel in Cocoa Beach with a swimming pool that had a waterfall.

"They're doing just great," Brian said before she could ask again. "Your mother let them both sleep in her bed last night, and she took them to one of those surf shops this afternoon and bought them all sorts of touristy junk."

"You make sure you keep an eye on Davis during the launch. He's working real hard at acting like it's no big deal, but he's under a lot of stress."

"I know, but I'm watching him every minute, and so are your mother and Suzanne. We've got doctors on-site, and we're five minutes from an emergency room if he has an attack."

"I think he'll be okay once we get to MECO. The actual launch is going to be the worst time for him."

"There's not going to be a worst time," Brian said.

"He knows about *Challenger*. He's seen the pictures of it blowing up."

"Look, Lucy, he's going to be fine, it's going to be a great mission, you're going to have the time of your life."

He put his arm around her, something he had not done in a while. She felt a stab of pity for him, because of what he did not yet know. Despite herself, she found herself responding to Brian's touch. When he put his arm around her shoulder, she put her own arm around his waist. There had never been all that much magic between them, but a little of the old affection came back. Now that Walt had reminded her what love was supposed to be like, she could not pretend anymore that she had ever felt the full strength of that particular emotion with Brian, but there had been a closeness in the beginning, if nothing else, a comradely satisfaction and a sense of common purpose. So somewhere within her current skein of emotions there was a thread of wistful regret.

The sound of the waves on the beach was thunderously soothing. As they walked, ghost crabs streaked across the sand ahead of them, pale and silent. They passed the spiky inflated body of a puffer fish that had washed ashore, and farther on Lucy saw the broad tracks that a sea turtle had made in the sand as it lumbered out of the ocean to lay its eggs. The turtle was probably nearby digging out a nest at the base of the dunes. During her oceanographic studies Lucy had observed nesting sea turtles in Mexico suffering and grunting under their own huge weight as they devotedly laid their eggs in the sand, nearly as out of their element in this gravity-bound world as she would be tomorrow in space.

They had gone a hundred yards or so down the beach when Brian stopped walking and stood and faced her. Over his shoulder she could see the lights of the beach house nestled in the dune grass.

"What?" she said, because the look on his face was so solemn and purposeful.

Brian took the wedding ring off his finger and held it out to her.

"Here's what I'm thinking," he said. "I know it's too late to get this approved for your PPK, but it's small enough that nobody's going to mind if you just put it in your pocket. I want you to take it to space, and then I want you to bring it back to me."

She took the ring. It was a thin silver band, not very expensive. They had picked them out together at a jewelry store in the mall.

"All right," she told him, in a blank tone of voice.

"I know I haven't exactly earned the right to expect that you'll think about me up there. So maybe this can be kind of a reminder to you that I'm still your husband. That I love you and want you to come back. And maybe when you do, we can start over again and make things better."

She was startled into silence by this quasi-romantic outburst, and she did not resist when he drew her into a dramatic farewell kiss. She would carry his wedding ring into space—how could she say no?—but the idea of starting over again with him when she returned had no more appeal to her than starting high school over again.

But she gave Brian credit for surprising and unsettling her, for driving her to the point of confused tears as they stood on the beach with the waves foaming around their ankles. In his own mind, she suspected, he had succeeded. He had reaffirmed his love for her, he had made a bold gesture of the sort that people make in movies, he had put himself back in play.

But that was in *his* mind, not hers. Part of her resented him for the effort he had made, because since Walt had come into her life she had begun to regard Brian's self-absorption with something like satisfaction. It was part of the case she had assembled against him, the evidence that would ultimately give her the moral justification to deceive him, perhaps ultimately to leave him. The last thing in the world she wanted him to do right now was *try*.

It was nine o'clock by the time she was back in her room at the Ops and Checkout building. The celebrations, the parties, the good-byes were over. It was time to settle in and try to go to sleep so that she could be ready to wake in the pre-dawn hours for launch. Lucy made one last call: to the hotel in Cocoa Beach where her family was staying. Her mother answered the phone. She was not tearful. She seemed to understand what Lucy needed from her, permission to be confident and unafraid, and though the conversation was warm and loving it was also brisk, as if they were both maintaining the fiction that Lucy was simply going on a long road trip. Suzanne, her sister, was an ob-gyn whose clinical armor Lucy had counted on for keeping the family's spirits on a steady keel, but when she came on the phone there was a flutter in her voice and she was almost unable to choke out the final "I love you."

But the children, to Lucy's great relief, were exhausted from a day at the pool and happily preoccupied with the video that Suzanne had rented them.

"We're watching *Shrek*," Bethie told her. "And we've got it on Pause."

"I won't keep you long, honey," Lucy told her. She listened as Bethie told her about their outing that afternoon to the beach, how the salt water had stung her eyes and the waves had knocked her down, and how it wasn't nearly as much fun as the pool. Lucy listened to the innocent chatter. Safe in the indulgent custody of her grandmother and her aunt, Bethie seemed to have forgotten all about the launch, or to have willed herself to, and that was just fine with Lucy. Davis, as ever, was a more complicated case, still speaking to her in a disinterested monotone, but his voice tightened a bit near the end of the conversation, when she told him for the fiftieth time that week how much she loved him and how she couldn't wait to see him again.

She was a wreck, as she'd known she would be, when she hung up the phone. She sat on the bed in the unadorned space in which she was quarantined. She heard voices from down the hall, Buddy and Tom Terrific laughing with the astronaut escorts, their excitement uncontainable.

She had to at least hear Walt's voice. She picked up the phone and called his home number, got his businesslike voice-mail greeting, then hung up without leaving a message and called his cell phone.

"It's me," she said. "I'm violating my rule. I'm calling you."

"You ought to be asleep already," he said. "What time are they going to wake you in the morning?"

"Three o'clock. What are you doing?"

"Staring at the TV."

"But you're not at home. I called your house."

"No, I'm in a motel. In Titusville."

"You're *here*?"

"Close enough."

She took a moment to absorb this. "You flew all the way to Florida?"

"Drove."

"Why?" she asked, and then in a hopeful quaver, "Because of me?"

"Because of you," he answered. "I knew you didn't want to see me. But I just wanted to be near. I wanted to be in the vicinity."

"I don't know what I was thinking when I told you not to come," she said. "I wanted you to be here."

"I'm here."

"It's too late to see you, Walt."

"I know. It's all right."

"Are you going to watch the launch?"

"Of course."

"Where from?"

"I've got a pretty good view from here. It's close enough."

There was a silence. She sat there on the edge of the bed holding the phone. She told him she loved him, heard him say it back, and in a moment more they whispered good-bye and she hung up the phone. She felt a serene current pass through her body, but it was followed soon enough by a stab of turmoil as she remembered the careful farewells of her children, and the face of her husband on the beach tonight as he handed her his wedding ring and entrusted their marriage to her safekeeping.

Chapter Twenty-seven

She sat in her seat in the Astro Van, almost immobile under the weight of her orange pressure suit, staring out the window toward the Atlantic beach. There was a faint suggestion of dawn, but it was no competition for the xenon floodlights that unnaturally illuminated the stack at Pad 39A. The Rotating Service Structure, the huge hinged tower that covered the shuttle when it was upright on the pad, had been rolled back, revealing the vessel that would transport Lucy to space. From this distance the orbiter itself was poignantly small, a stubby-winged parasite attached to an orange tank of liquid fuel as tall as an office building, with the two smaller solid rocket boosters on either side.

Buddy, seated behind her in the van, rapped on the back of her head with his knuckles. When she turned around he said, in a whisper, "Are you believing it yet?"

She shook her head. Buddy's were the only words any of the crew had spoken so far on this short drive. Everyone was silent and reflective. They had been ever since breakfast, which only Surly had eaten with any appetite. Lucy and most of the rest of the crew had drunk only a token glass of orange juice, worried that solid food would enhance their susceptibility to space sickness. No one had had coffee, since they would be sitting upright in the orbiter waiting for launch for a minimum of two and a half hours, and the last thing any of them wanted was to have to urinate into their maximum absorbency garment.

Lucy's bladder was already giving her nervous signals, but she had expected these twinges and was hopeful she could ignore them until lift-off, at which time they would surely be forgotten. She focused on the view outside the van window. The beaches and wetlands that made up the Kennedy Space Center were a wildlife sanctuary, and as they drew closer to the pad she caught a glimpse of an alligator floating in a water-filled ditch along the side of the road, the ridges on its back glistening in the creeping daylight. A few yards ahead she saw geyser-like clouds of dirt erupting from a hole in the ground. From a wildlife tour of the Cape she had taken during her astronaut training days, she knew this was probably the work of an unseen gopher tortoise, industriously enlarging its burrow.

In another hour or so, Brian would be waking the children up. Then they and Lucy's mother and sister would be taken to the top floor of the Launch Control Center, where Davis and Bethie and the children of the other crew members would, according to tradition, draw pictures of the mission on a dry-erase board that would later be hung in the hallway.

Walt, in his motel across the Indian River in Titusville, would be getting up as well. He hadn't told her exactly where he would watch the launch. No doubt he had his own vantage point, away from the crowds on the beaches or along the causeways. It didn't matter where he watched it. She wouldn't feel so alone knowing that his eyes were on her when the liquid-fuel engines ignited.

The security guard at the last checkpoint saluted as the van climbed the concrete slope that led to the launch pad. Lucy got out with the others. It was a humid morning, and sweat was already pooling at the neoprene collar around her neck. They all stood there for a moment as they stared up at the stack, as spray from the condensed water cascading down the outside of the external tank cooled her face. Built though it was by men and women, the space shuttle seemed to Lucy too colossal to be grasped through a human prism. Its beauty was almost beyond the range of her perceptions as well: the rust-colored orange foam of the external fuel tank was suddenly sumptuous and complex, like the unexpectedly rich hues hidden in the drab scales of oceangoing fish. The white solid rocket boosters flanked the liquid tank with a majestic symmetry and presence that seemed imposed by nature rather than decreed by human design. Indeed, the whole assemblage, frosted with chemical ice, glistening and seething and groaning on the pad, reminded Lucy of some remote mountain peak, nearly impossible to climb, shrouded in its own unruly weather.

They scaled the peak in the elevator built into the scaffolding of the gantry. They rose in silence to the 195-foot level, where they disembarked and walked along the catwalk toward the hatch where they would enter *Endeavour*. On the way, they lingered, looking out over the railing at the day breaking over the Cape. The Banana River causeway was a solid procession of headlights: people coming to watch the launch. In the flaring light, Lucy saw flocks of shorebirds wheeling above the beaches and marshland below them. Despite the noise of the elevator as it descended and the baleful moans of the wind threading itself through the gridwork, despite the almost organic sounds emanating from the explosive liquid core of the external tank, Lucy could hear those birds: the belligerent barks of gulls, mixed in with rapid-fire trills from the terns circling the stack, and below it all the mournful questioning tone of some unseen early-morning wanderer.

"Last chance to pause and reflect," one of the techs who greeted them said as he pointed to the dismal little toilet off the catwalk. Lucy had hoped she could avoid this cumbersome last-minute pit stop, but the needling sensation she had been feeling on the van ride had suddenly blossomed into a full-scale need to pee. It was the same for all of them. The techs waited patiently while they took turns. Lucy and Patti went into the cramped space together, helping each other unzip their suits and zip them back up again. When they had all emptied their anxious bladders, Surly instructed them to write their initials in the frost covering the oxygen supply line leading into the orbiter. It was one of those odd little traditions that had begun for no real reason but would be dangerous now to ignore.

After that they waited on the catwalk until they were called in turn into the White Room that abutted the orbiter hatch. The techs in the White Room were soothingly friendly and efficient. They helped Lucy into her parachute harness and lumbar pad and sealed on her helmet as they teased her about whether or not she had dared to eat breakfast and telling her she should be glad she was an astronaut and not a cosmonaut, because the most sacred tradition before a Russian spaceflight was not anything as simple as writing your name in the frost of the O2 line. You had to climb down out of the bus that drove you to the launch pad and, in full view of the assembled space workers, unzip your suit and urinate on the right rear tire.

The techs were dressed in sterile white bunny suits. The room was glaringly white, and in this unnatural enclosed space, with her snoopy hat and helmet muting her hearing, Lucy felt less as if she was about to embark on the adventure of her dreams than to undergo a dangerous surgery. She was grateful for the small talk and the jokes, for the way the techs distracted her with laughter as they solemnly triple-checked all the connections and seals upon which her life depended.

When they were through it was time for her to crawl through the crew hatch, through the mid-deck and then on to the flight deck. She had practiced this many times in training, and she was used to the heavy, ungainly pressure suit, but even so it was still jarring to her to move through these horizontally designed compartments when they were pointed at a ninety-degree angle toward the sky.

She was greeted on the flight deck by Larry Contreras, an astronaut from Lucy's class who was still waiting for his first mission, though his lead guitar work and raspy vocals had made him the dubious star of MaxQ, the astronaut band. Like the techs, Larry was dressed in a bunny suit. He was serving as a Cape Crusader on this flight, helping to get the crew into place and settled.

"Looking gorgeous," he said to Lucy as she stood on the aft bulkhead that served as the floor of the upended flight deck. She smiled at him through her open visor, breathing heavily after crawling through the hatch in her cumbersome suit. The air in the cockpit was warm and stuffy, and the circulating fans did little but push it around.

Surly and Tom Terrific were already strapped in, staring up at the sky through the cockpit windows, facing the two thousand switches of the control panel. With Larry's help, Lucy heaved herself up into the MS1 seat behind Tom. They were both sweating. The seat was cramped and hard, a thin cushion over an unforgiving steel frame. Larry handed her her communication cable and oxygen hose. He adjusted the fit of her helmet and guided her through her comm checks.

"How are you feeling?" he asked her. "Raring to go?"

"Raring to go," Lucy repeated as she opened the visor on her helmet, noticing the condensation that had briefly formed on the inside.

She felt her heart beating with a steady insistence that she thought at first was caused by the exertion of getting into her seat, but which she finally had to recognize was just outright fear. The air was still thick, but now that all the hoses were attached, chilled water began circulating through the ventilation garment she wore beneath her pressure suit, and as her body cooled the sense of being trapped began to ease. She felt calmer after Buddy was strapped into the seat beside her, and calmer still when Patti and Chuck had been settled into place in the mid-deck. She could not see Patti and Chuck but could hear their voices on the loop, and the knowledge that the crew was together gave her a familial sense of comfort.

"Well, I guess it's time for my boot heels to be wanderin'," Larry said as he reappeared on the flight deck, the sweat still glistening on his forehead. He had obviously rehearsed this lighthearted exit line, but it didn't quite work out—Lucy heard his voice catch and saw him blink hard to clamp down on a tear that was forming in his eye. She couldn't blame him for being emotional at the enormous thing that was about to happen to these six people in his charge. He shook each of their hands in turn, and was bold enough to give Lucy an awkward kiss on the top of her helmet before he whispered "godspeed" and left them alone on the flight deck.

"I think he likes you," Buddy said.

"Shut up," Lucy answered him.

Not long after, Lucy heard the crew hatch close and Ground confirm it with Surly. They were alone now, the six of them, alone in the massive vessel that in a few hours' time was scheduled to erupt with the force of a volcano and drive them through the atmosphere. Soon there would be no one within three miles of them, except for the rescue crew stationed in a protective bunker a mile away. Lucy stared upward, looking between Surly's and Tom's shoulders at the sky, now vibrantly blue with the full morning light, a few inconsequential clouds straying in from the ocean side of the Cape. The weather was good, the updates from Ground were positive.

"You know what, space cadets?" Surly said to the crew over the loop in one of the lulls when the voice of the Orbiter Test Conductor was not passing along information or running through checklists. "I think this is really going to happen. I think we're going to get off the pad on our first try."

Lucy knew there were still a thousand things that could scrap the launch: a minor radar anomaly, a sensor warning, an unexpected weather complication. But the conviction was growing in her that it was going to take place, that nothing would stop it, that the launch was not just on schedule but ordained. Part of her wanted to surrender to that conviction, to take comfort in the fact that fate was overriding every choice she could make and every apprehension she could feel. But there was also a part that would not deliver herself so passively, and that was the part that kept envisioning her children in their room at the Launch Control center, the dutiful way they would be drawing their pictures on the dry-erase board before they were taken outside to stare at the billowing flames and feel the shaking ground as the engines of their mother's spaceship ignited. It was the part of her that thought of Walt following the countdown from his motel room in Titusville, having driven eight hundred miles just to be closer to her when the unthinkable moment he had trained her for finally arrived.

She listened as Surly and Tom, from the commander's and pilot's seats in front of her, admired the pristine switches of the *Endeavour* cockpit—so different from the worn, constantly used switches in the simulator. She listened to Buddy anxiously humming phrases from some song she couldn't quite place, and to Patti's and Chuck's good-natured complaints from the mid-deck about the spectacular view of the storage lockers they would have during launch.

At this point in the countdown, there was not much for the crew to do except lie on their backs in their rigid seats and try to distract themselves with talk. When Lucy became aware of her own silence she thought of Christa McAuliffe. She had once listened to the tape of the pre-launch cockpit banter of the *Challenger* crew, Judy Resnik complaining about how her butt was numb, Greg Jarvis offering to give her a massage, Dick Scobee, the commander, breaking in with an authoritative observation every now and then about the wintry Florida weather outside. It was the same sort of high-spirited and nervous commentary that Lucy was listening to today, but what had struck her at the time she heard the tape and what came back unwelcomed to her memory now was Christa McAuliffe's near-total silence. She had not joined in the conversation; she had seemingly drawn no consolation from the jittery fellowship of her crewmates, but had sunk into a contemplative isolation at her station in the windowless mid-deck. What had she been thinking about during this sustained silence? Had she been wondering about the children who would soon be motherless, and the cheerful reassurances by which she had betrayed them? Only once on the tape had Lucy heard Christa speak. She had said, as the winter wind whistled outside, sweeping the frost off the fuel tank so that those looking out the cockpit window thought it was snowing, "It'll be cold out there today."

Next to her, Buddy shifted in his hard seat. "I've got to pee again," he said. Lucy told him she didn't need to know that, but as soon as he had announced it she felt once again the pressure of her own bladder. It was all right. She would rather concentrate on physical discomfort than on the dread that could steal over her if she allowed herself to dwell on the wrong thoughts. Her back was starting to ache, so she squeezed a bit of air into the inflatable lumbar pad. The slight shift in position that resulted helped her back, for a moment at least, but sharpened the urge to urinate. She felt a bit hollow as well, and was starting to regret that she had skipped breakfast. Her mouth was dry. She told herself it was because she had been avoiding liquids, but she suspected it was really from fear.

Another hour passed, the countdown moving smoothly toward the automatic hold that would come at nine minutes before launch. Lucy listened as Surly talked to the woman monitoring the Ground Launch sequencer, watched as the Abort light brightened and dimmed on the console in front of him as Ground conducted an abort check. Lucy reviewed the emergency escape procedures printed on a card Velcroed to her sleeve, though of course she had long known them by heart. She also knew that, if there was a sudden fuel leak or fire while they were still on the pad, it was a benign fantasy to think she could release herself from all the straps binding her to her seat and drag herself and the eighty-five pounds of space suit she was wearing to the escape basket outside the gantry before being incinerated in a vicious explosion.

Buddy started humming again, just a few bars of some improbable tune—was it "Blue Eyes Crying in the Rain"?—and then he drifted back into silence as the callouts from Ground grew more frequent and the communications discipline began to tighten.

It was happening. At T minus 9 minutes there was a built-in hold for ten minutes. Lucy checked to make sure all her straps were tight, glanced again at the emergency egress card. She no longer registered the pressure in her bladder. The pains in her back were still there, and there were now cramps in her upended legs, but none of it mattered any longer.

"*Endeavour,*" Lucy heard the GLS voice say over the loop, "countdown clock will resume on my mark. Five . . . four . . . three . . . two . . . one . . . mark . . . T-minus nine minutes and counting."

"Roger," Surly answered, with a delighted bounce to his voice. "We see the clock running."

Buddy reached over and gave Lucy a congratulatory punch on the shoulder.

"On our way, Lucy-goosey," he said. Through the open visor of his helmet, she could see the disbelieving smile on his face, and just a hint of the terror that lurked beneath it. She meant to reply in the same awestruck tone, but when she opened her mouth she found that she was incapable of forming any words at all. She took a long sip of water. It helped a little, enough to allow her to utter a reply, but almost immediately the tissues of her mouth felt numb and dry again. When she tried to swallow, her throat constricted in a parched spasm. She could feel the fear leaching all the moisture out of her body.

In a few moments she could feel the cockpit vibrating as the three main engines at the base of the orbiter began to gimbal into their launch positions. At T minus 2 minutes they closed their visors, and the cool oxygen that circulated around Lucy's face momentarily distracted her from the suffocating dread that threatened to claim her. But after that things began moving too fast for any emotion, much less any purposeful thought, to linger more than an instant. She saw the data flowing across the computer screens, she heard Surly's voice acknowledging the closing of the oxygen vents and the retraction of the Oxygen Vent Hood, she felt the whole ship lurch and sway as the computers made one last check of the steering controls.

She thought she had prepared for everything, but the pitiless swiftness of the countdown clock caught her by surprise. Someone seemed to be tossing each of those irrecoverable seconds, perhaps the remaining seconds of her life, indifferently away. Then all at once time was up, the main engines were igniting, and something more powerful and savage than she could have ever believed existed took control of her life. It was not just the liquid hydrogen burning in the external tank, not just the powdered aluminum in the solid rocket boosters reacting to an instantaneous igniting dart of flame, that propelled the shuttle off the pad. It was something with a determinative force and will, some *being* on its own errand, no more concerned with her existence than it was with the scattering shorebirds or the tortoise she had seen that was surely now quaking in its burrow.

The roar as they cleared the tower blanketed every sound except for the steady tinny voices she heard through her headset, bulletins from the ground about the trim of the engines and the upcoming roll maneuver. The vibrations that assaulted them were so strong, so much stronger than she could have imagined, that for an instant or two she thought the orbiter might be coming apart. She looked at the computer screens, but the effort of trying to focus on the jittery data they displayed gave her an acute sense of vertigo, and she closed her eyes for a moment to dispel it.

It took a conscious effort, with the monstrous g-forces that were bearing down on them, for Lucy to even open her eyes again. This time she glanced at the pocket mirror she had strapped to her knee so that she could see through the orbiter's overhead windows. *Endeavour* was just beginning the backward roll that would help throw it into a high eastward arc, and through the little window she caught a blink's length impression of whitecaps slouching onto the beach where she and Brian had been walking the night before, and then almost before the image had formed on her retina it was gone, replaced by a scatter of white as the shuttle blasted through a cloud deck.

The ship rattled even more as it bored past the sound barrier and traveled along in its rough envelope of supersonic air. The g's mashed her back in her steel seat, holding her in place with the steady, malevolent intent of a strangler. Straining to breathe against this phantom assailant, she thought about her son in his asthmatic struggles, understanding for the first time how he must see the disease not as an affliction but as an active enemy.

This empathetic thought had barely formed before *Endeavour* lurched violently and she heard a tremendous cannon-like boom and tendrils of yellow flame streaked across the cockpit windows. It was SRB Sep, the empty solid rocket boosters blowing themselves away from the orbiter as it continued to climb with the remaining fuel in the liquid tank. Surly had warned them not to mistake this violent event for the shuttle itself blowing up, but the jolt was ragged and cataclysmic enough for Buddy to reach out and grab her arm and not loosen his grip until the jagged ride turned suddenly silken and the oddest silence Lucy had ever known visited the cockpit. The view through the windshield, through the overhead windows projected in her pocket mirror, was of a deepening spectrum field, a shading to seductive black. They were high now, almost into space, in a realm where the air was too thin for sound to carry. The three engines at the base of the orbiter were still roaring, but Lucy and the crew couldn't hear them anymore. The sound of *Endeavour* forcing its way through the thick atmosphere had stilled as well, though they continued to climb, more insistently than ever. The gravitational pressure holding her in her seat continued to be intense, but in the silence and stillness it had changed from a malevolent force to a protective one, a firm and gentle hand, almost maternal, holding her down until she could be released without harm.

"Houston," she heard Surly calling to Mission Control, his voice intimate in her headset. "Roger. Press to MECO."

MECO: Main Engine Cut-Off. This was the milestone Lucy had been praying to reach, the moment when they could detach themselves from the external tank and its lethal explosive potential. *Challenger* had blown apart long before it reached MECO, with the children and families of the crew watching, but *Endeavour* was now far out of sight. If something went wrong now, at least Davis and Bethie would not have to witness it.

"MECO on time," Surly called out to Mission Control. The hand that had been pressing down on Lucy's chest gently withdrew. Lucy noticed that her arms were now hanging suspended above her lap, and the cords that had tethered the checklists in the cockpit were floating tendrils. A mosquito that had boarded the shuttle before the hatches were closed was now with them more than two hundred miles above the earth. Lucy watched it turning frenzied loops in front of her visor, doing its bewildered best to fly in weightlessness.

One last violent spasm rocked the orbiter as the empty fuel tank was blown away, and then there was the thrust of the Orbital Maneuvering System engines driving the craft the rest of the way into orbit. The OMS boost provided a final reminder of gravity, shoving Lucy back into her seat again and sending the mosquito tumbling downward. When the burn was over it was quiet again, except for the laughter and congratulations of the crew. It was only then, when the incredible g-forces had vanished, that Lucy realized she could lift her head and look out the orbiter's overhead windows. They were flying upside down, but in the weightlessness of space, in the unframed infinitude to which they now belonged, up and down had ceased to be relevant. The windows were filled with a scrolling panorama of cloud and sea and glimpses of rumpled landforms and sharply defined continental edges. All of this coasted toward a horizon constantly renewing itself with prismatic light, and beyond the horizon a biblical darkness, deep and total. This was the earth she had left only eight minutes ago, but which was now a lifetime away.

Chapter Twenty-eight

Walt watched Lucy's launch from a little waterside park at the edge of Highway 1 in Titusville. The motel where he was staying was a decrepit tourist court from the 1950s whose only modern amenity was a claim to free HBO, though the television in his room was snowy and staticky except for the local CBS affiliate. Nevertheless, the motel was only a few blocks from the shoreline, and just after sunrise he walked down to the park and joined the people with their coolers and lawn chairs who had already gathered there to watch the launch.

The Indian River was more a broad coastal lagoon than a river, and across its expanse he could see the tower of the Vehicle Assembly Building rising above the sand of Merritt Island. With his binoculars, he had a hazy but adequate enough view of the distant launch pad, and as the sun rose he listened to the countdown commentary from the radio of one of the families who had come to the park.

Some of the onlookers had brought their breakfasts, bags of Egg McMuffins from McDonald's or donuts and cinnamon rolls from the bakery down the street. Seeing them break out their food made Walt realize he was hungry, and he thought about walking down to the bakery himself—there was plenty of time—but some sort of superstitious hesitation prevented him. It seemed more fitting for him to be hungry, and to remain standing instead of being comfortably seated on a lawn chair, when the fate of Lucy and the crew he had trained was about to be determined. With his terrible burden of knowledge about everything that could go wrong, he dreaded launches, and he dreaded this one most of all. He wanted it to be over—and soon enough it was.

The people in the park cheered when they saw the brilliant flames billowing on the flat, featureless island across the water. Even at this distance, the ground shook, and the gulls that had been standing on the concrete rim of the little seawall were frightened into flight. Walt watched as the shuttle rolled onto its back and seemingly headed out across the ocean rather than straight up into the sky. Everything was nominal. Remembering that *Challenger* had blown up after seventy-three seconds, he could not suppress the conviction that every instant *Endeavour* stayed intact represented new evidence that it would make it all the way to MECO.

He thought of Lucy in that fragile cockpit, at the apex of that violent white contrail. He was frightened, of course, but also disturbed in a metaphysical way, as if she had not just disappeared in a human conveyance but had fallen through a mirror, traveled into a parallel world where she could never be reached. After only a few minutes some of the people in the park began drifting back to their cars, but Walt stayed until he heard the voice of Mission Control on the nearby radio confirm the separation of the solid rocket boosters, and later of the external tank.

She had survived the hazards of launch and made it to MECO. She was in space. Walt left the park and walked across the crowded highway, and it was not until he got back to his motel and reached into his pocket for his room key that he realized his hands were shaking.

He checked out of the motel and filled up his car with gas. It was almost eleven by then and he still had not eaten, so he stopped and had a grouper sandwich at a little fish shack on the Banana River that he and his team had discovered several years earlier. The traffic was oppressive; his was only one of thousands of cars trailing inland from the Space Coast after watching the launch. He didn't care. The slow procession toward Orlando gave him time to daydream, to think of Lucy, touchingly weightless now as she worked to stow away the seats and reconfigure the cockpit from launch to orbit mode. He thought of how her hair would look, no longer following the contours of her face as it did on earth but suspended and slightly teased by the nearly total lack of gravity. She might be space sick. It was a common malady, and in all his years of training crews Walt had never developed a clear instinct for who would be susceptible and who would not. The thought of Lucy retching in space, of weightlessness bringing her chronic nausea rather than otherworldly joy, aroused in him such a poignant solicitude that he could feel tears backing up behind his eyes.

He turned on the radio and kept it tuned to a talk station, where there would be regular hourly news and urgent bulletins if anything disastrous happened to *Endeavour*. When the news came, there was not even a mention of the launch, and over the hours there were no bulletins, just Rush Limbaugh with his inexhaustible grandiloquence, and then Dr. Laura hectoring her callers as they stammered on the line trying to defend the disasters they had cluelessly made of their lives. Some of the callers were not defensive; they were all but mute, waiting for Dr. Laura's belligerent voice to confirm for them the shame they already felt.

Walt knew that he himself would have no case if he were to pick up his cell phone and call Dr. Laura. She would accuse him of putting his own desires and needs ahead of Lucy and of her children, of pretending to support her when in fact he was exploiting her, betraying the trust that was the foundation of his position as team lead, unforgivably adding to her inventory of emotional distraction and distress at the most vulnerable moment of her life. What could he say in response, except to observe that the distinctions that were supposed to exist between selfishness and selflessness were no longer clear to him, and that love itself now seemed to be an aggressive force rather than a static good?

From Orlando he drove north on 75, the spaced palms giving way to thick pines as he rose from the simple limestone platform of the Florida basin into hummocky terrain. When he caught I-10 again he drove relentlessly west, still monitoring the radio for disaster reports late into the night until he finally made himself pull off at a motel in Baton Rouge.

"Everybody's really pissed at you," Sylvia told him when he called in from the road the next morning. "They couldn't believe you just took off and went without us."

"I know. I'll be back this afternoon."

"Good. You can come to our little meeting."

"What little meeting?"

"I took the liberty of crowning myself acting team lead. And since I didn't know when you were coming back, I thought the rest of us had better get together and start planning how to decorate the hall."

"That was smart."

"I know it was smart, Walt. Let's do our best not to patronize, okay?"

"About that other conversation we had."

"What I recall about that conversation is that it featured a topic—well, actually, two topics—that neither of us needs to discuss again."

Walt could usually tell when Sylvia was angry or just acerbic, but the tone she was taking at the moment was slippery. He felt reprieved when the connection started to break up, and told her through the static that he would try to get back in town in time to make the meeting. To salve his conscience, he pulled off the interstate in Lafayette, drove up to Prejean's just as the lunch rush was ending, and bought the whole team a take-out order of gumbo and crawfish fettuccine.

He made it back to Clear Lake by four o'clock. He didn't bother to go home, just went straight to his office cubicle in Building 4 South. He turned on his computer and sorted through his backed-up e-mail. Among the messages there were already four from the *Endeavour* crew, one from Surly thanking Walt on behalf of the whole crew for a great job training them for the mission, and giving an update on how splendidly nominal everything was going so far; another thank-you note from Tom Terrific essentially repeating the same sentiments; one from Buddy Santos that read, in its entirety, "Walt, I am so space sick," and was punctuated with a little happy face graphic with its smile turned down in a nauseated frown; and one from Lucy.

"Dear Walt," she wrote. "We're here! We're all fine, except for Buddy, who's pretty sick and had to have a shot of Phenergan. I'm not even going to try to describe what it's like up here, how it feels to be weightless, how much more glorious the view is than I could ever have imagined. I wish you could see this and experience all this. It's not fair that you can't, since you're the one who got us here. We all love you. We all miss you already. Lucy."

E-mail messages from the shuttle were downloaded and forwarded by the psych support office, and they could not be counted on to be private. Lucy knew this, and of course so did Walt, so he was not surprised or disappointed by the tone of this message, by the fact that it had been written in a way that would not look suspicious to prying eyes. But the code she was using was clear to him. "We all love you. We all miss you already" was too fervent a conclusion to a comradely message. She was speaking for herself, or so Walt needed to believe. I love you. I miss you already.

Before he left the building he walked into a conference room and stood in front of a television playing the live feed from orbit on the NASA Channel. It was the second full day of the mission, and most of the members of the *Endeavour* crew were on the reconfigured flight deck. From the looks of things, they were about to power up the shuttle's docking system for its rendezvous tomorrow with the space station. Walt watched with a kind of entrancement as Lucy drifted in and out of the frame in her maroon mission shirt and utility shorts with their multitude of Velcro straps and attachable pockets. Like the others, she wore only socks on her feet, and the casualness of her attire contrasted winningly with the severity of her expression as she studied a checklist. Walt could make out Buddy hanging about in the background where Chuck was stationed at the rear instrument panel, testing the controls of the robot arm. Buddy hovered in the background looking game but grim; apparently not quite recovered from his bout of space sickness.

Lucy was never close enough to the camera or in frame long enough for Walt to get the sustained look he craved, but from what he could make out her coloring looked good and she hovered and tumbled through the chamber with assurance. He had guessed right about her hair: it formed a suspended but unmoving frame around her head. Her face had the familiar puffiness that came from the fluid shifts that human bodies undergo in weightlessness. Her cheeks were fuller, the tautness in her expression that came from dutiful concentration no longer quite as apparent. When she was not moving, her body reverted to the fetal crouch common to the human form in the absence of gravity, when there was no up or down to align itself to.

"Don't think that's going to help," Gary said a few minutes later, when Walt walked into the conference room in Building 4 where Sylvia had convened her meeting. He was carrying two giant plastic take-out bags of Cajun food, and he set them on the table, which was already almost covered with photographs and drawings and notes.

"It needs to be warmed up," Walt said.

"We refuse to accept your lame attempt at an apology," Gary continued as he sorted through the bags. "What kind of gumbo is this?"

"Chicken and sausage," Walt said.

"Their seafood gumbo's better."

"Well, then don't eat it," Walt said, as he caught Sylvia's eye. She looked away, still a bit annoyed and not wanting him to see her smiling.

"There's a microwave in the break room," Mickey announced. He gathered up the bags and they all followed him down the hall, heating up their food in turn and then returning to eat it in the conference room.

It had been a sacred tradition since Walt had first come to work at JSC that the primary training team decorate the hallway in Building 4, where the astronauts had their offices, for the crew's return. Everyone on the team religiously kept note of embarrassing comments or flubbed callouts in their logbooks, and there was a wealth of pictures as well— Surly cutting up at the big party at his house in River Oaks, Buddy earnestly sitting on the space potty during habitability training—for which wise-ass captions would be required.

As they settled into their work sorting through the quips and compromising pictures, as they ate their gumbo and the crawfish fettuccine, no one said anything more to Walt about his solo drive to Florida. Walt made suggestions or contributed details from his own logbook when it felt appropriate, but for the most part he sat back and let Sylvia run the meeting.

When they were through for the day he went home and ran through the cable stations until he found the NASA Channel again, and watched Lucy and the crew for another hour until the coverage shifted from live footage of the shuttle to a children's documentary about Space Camp.

During work the next day he was never far from a monitor, and he watched Surly and Tom on the flight deck as they meticulously guided *Endeavour* toward its rendezvous with the space station. The docking went flawlessly, Surly flying the orbiter in a careful quarter circle around the bristly station, stopping three hundred feet ahead of it and then slowly inching back toward the docking port, Lucy doing her part by punching the buttons that locked the latches between the shuttle and the station once the two craft were joined.

No problems with the launch, none with the rendezvous and docking. All that remained, all that Lucy and the crew had now to survive, Walt reminded himself as he ran around the winding track that evening, was the completion of the spacewalk and then reentry and landing five days later.

He always ran with his cell phone in his hand when a mission was up. He had gone a mile at a faster pace than usual when it rang, and when he stopped abruptly and walked off the track into the trees his breathing was erratic.

"It's me," she said. "Can you hear me, Walt?"

"What loop are you using?"

"I'm on the IP phone in the Node. It's private, though I think we're near the end of this comm pass. The signal may cut out any minute, but this is the only time I could get the phone without anybody around. Did you get my e-mail?"

"Yes."

"I hated that it had to be so vague. Did you understand what I was trying to say?"

"I understood," Walt said. "I watched you all day."

"Oh, God, my face is so puffy. I look like a Cabbage Patch doll. It's so beautiful up here, Walt. Why can't you be here too?"

"I'll be here when you come back."

"You promise? Because I'm thinking about that a lot, you know. Seeing you again. You sound out of breath or something."

"I'm out for a run."

"We're coming up over the West Coast. Maybe in a few minutes I'll be able to look down and—"

The line went dead, as she had predicted. Walt knew there was no chance of another comm pass until the next orbit, and even then the chances of her having enough time or privacy to try to speak again were remote. But the sound of her voice from space, the knowledge that she had needed to talk to him as much as he needed to talk to her, brought a sustained surge of energy to the rest of his run.

He went home and took a shower and then went out again, carrying the *Houston Chronicle* he had failed to read that morning. In the cafeteria line at Luby's, Carmen greeted him as usual in Spanish and presented him with his LuAnn Platter and its spiritless centerpiece of baked cod. He sat down by the picture window, squeezed lemon into his iced tea, set his phone on the table in case she was able to call again, and leafed through the paper. On the bottom half of the second page of the metro section, there was a headline he passed over at first but that drew his eyes back: "Coast Guard Comes to Aid of Shipwrecked Priest."

Chapter Twenty-nine

She was dreaming that her father was alive after all, and had come into her room and shaken her and Suzanne awake and insisted they come out onto the lawn in the middle of the night. "This time it's really going to happen, girls," he told them. "I promise." She didn't care if the meteor shower took place or not. Just seeing him again made her weak with happiness.

But as it happened the meteor shower was real, not just another of her father's hopeful forecasts. Brilliant contrails of light went streaking across the perfect darkness, moving from one end of the sky to the next but mysteriously never disappearing. In fact, Lucy found that by moving her head a few degrees she could almost hold them in place, as if they were shining fish swimming against a powerful current. In her dream, she began to wonder why this was the case, and as she brought her reasoning mind into play she found herself disappointingly awake. The dream had evaporated, but the meteors were still there. They were radiation flashes, caused by particles bombarding her retina when the shuttle's orbit brought them briefly out of the protection of the Van Allen radiation belt.

She was fully awake now, but she did not want to open her eyes, drawn to the beauty of the flashes and the lingering solace of the dream. When she did finally open them, she found herself staring at Tom and

Patti on the other side of the mid-deck, hanging upside down like bats in their sleep restraints. After three days in space, however, "upside down" was no longer a meaningful term to her. In zero gravity, people were just naturally inverted relative to one another, but there were no clues—a pooling of blood in the head, for instance—about who might be in the correct position and who might not. She glanced at her wristwatch, set to Mission Elapsed Time: 03:10:13:18. Another two hours before they were scheduled to be woken up by Ground. It was the day of her space-walk and she needed as much rest as she could get, but she was awake and alert now and there was no point in trying to will herself back to sleep.

Everyone in the crew was sleeping in the mid-deck except for Surly. It was warm here, closer to the heating elements for the experiments in the payload bay, and because there were no windows it was consistently dark, whereas in the cockpit there was the glare of the rising sun every forty-five minutes as the orbiter made another circuit of the earth.

There was something ghoulish about the appearance of her crew-mates as they slept in weightlessness, the unreal manner in which their bodies occupied different planes, the way their arms floated in front of their bodies as if slowly grasping at some sluggish phantom in their dreams. As quietly as she could, she unstrapped herself from the cocoon-like sleep restraint and floated out. There was no sound except for the hum of the ventilation fans and the odd background tinkling whose source it had taken her almost two days to discover: the constant wind-chime effect of floating D rings and zipper handles coming into contact with one another.

She felt clammy after a night in the sleep restraint and would have liked to change her clothes, but she was afraid that opening her locker would wake someone up, particularly Buddy, who would be her EVA partner today and was finally sleeping soundly after his ordeal of space sickness. Anyway, changing any item of clothing, even her socks, was a daunting prospect in weightlessness. With nothing to hold steady against, with every casual brush against a wall panel or bulkhead send-ing her caroming in the opposite direction, getting dressed for the day could easily take forty-five minutes.

Since the closest sensation to weightlessness was being underwater, she had had to cure herself of a natural tendency to propel her body from one place to another using the breaststroke. You could not swim through nothingness. There was no resistance, nothing to be disturbed or dynamically countered, and so you just hung there insanely waving your arms. To make motion happen, you had to push yourself away from stationary objects with just the right amount of force and a correct approximation of where your body's center of gravity resided.

Lucy's center of gravity, she had determined, was just above her hips. The trick was to push off in such a way that you didn't deviate from this crucial axis. If you reached out and grabbed something in mid-translation, if you surrendered to your childhood flying fantasies and extended your arms like Superman, you were likely to create some unwanted rotation that would send you pinwheeling against an unyielding bulkhead.

She decided now to translate herself up to the cockpit, away from the dark mid-deck and her sleeping crewmates, whose arms were still waving and blindly groping, like the tentacles of sea anemones. Just a slight amount of flexion against the floor sent her drifting toward the open hatch between the two decks. She kept her hands at her hips, where they were much less likely to be indiscriminately used and create an unplanned rotation. Even so, she had to correct her course several times with slight finger pushes before she went sailing through the opening with clearance on all sides.

Surly was asleep on the flight deck, wearing a headset and a satiny eyeshade to protect himself against the intermittent sunrises. It was dark now, the sun was beyond the rim of the earth they were orbiting, but in another few minutes it would be rising again in an accelerated version of the night-and-day cycles by which life on the surface of the planet was defined. For now, Lucy looked down on a trackless darkness, far away from any human-generated lights, that she realized was the Pacific Ocean. At an altitude of 240 miles, the crew of *Endeavour* could not see the planet in its entirety as the old Apollo astronauts had on their long voyages to the moon. The earth was close enough to fill the frame of the orbiter windows. To Lucy, it was like a vast, steadily unscrolling map, shockingly vivid, rich with never-ending layers of detail.

She watched lightning pulse within the cloud cover over the dark Pacific, spidery tendrils of light weaving crazily across hundreds of miles. The lightning seemed to be blindly searching for something. It excited the atmosphere into which it reached, so that there was an oceanic chain reaction of pulsing light. When the clouds finally drifted past, Lucy could see an even eerier, steadier glow emanating from the sea itself, and she guessed that it was a gigantic bloom of bioluminescent plankton.

Her back was hurting her. Like everyone else, she had grown an inch or so taller as the absence of gravity caused her vertebrae to stretch out, and the strain on the surprised muscles of her back was constant. Her natural posture now was a kind of floating crouch, which together with enough Advil made the pain bearable. She needed to go to the bathroom, and it would be a good idea to do so now, before the rest of the crew started to wake up. But the thought of the cumbersome steps required to pee—floating back down to the mid-deck, positioning herself on the toilet seat and engaging the thigh restraints to hold herself in place, attaching the vacuum cleaner–like hose, turning on the motor—made her weary, and she was reluctant to spend this precious free time emptying her bladder when she could be gazing down upon the loveliest sight a human being could see.

She put on her Walkman earphones and punched the Play button as *Endeavour* coasted toward the California coast and the brilliant thread of lights that represented the still-sleeping cities of Los Angeles, Long Beach, San Diego, and beyond them the less intense illumination of the Baja Peninsula. She listened to "Sunshine on My Shoulder" as the first tissue-thin bands of light began to appear on the horizon. Buddy had been right about John Denver, about how his corny awestruck songs would sound just right to her undiscerning ears, would provide her with a personal sound track of folkie majesty.

So she hovered there, alone and at peace, listening to the song and gazing down on the rapturous sights below her. The bands of color appearing now above the eastern rim of the earth were exquisitely thin but so true and vibrant and sharp that she felt as if she had never really seen color before and that her vision on earth had been muzzy and muted. There was a flaring of indigo just before the sun rose, then stratum after stratum of bewitching blues, then oranges and reds, and then finally all at once the powerful sun itself, instantly illuminating the continental mass below as if someone had just turned on a reading lamp.

She looked down at a thick canopy of clouds over the California coast, the movement of upper-level winds detectable in their contours, the same way that wind stood revealed in the shapes of waves or the slip faces of dunes. Farther south the clouds dispersed, and she could make out the texture of the ocean's surface near the shore, bands of current and patterns of wave diffraction, and a stippled patch parallel to the coast that she guessed might be caused by a massive migrating pod of whales. Passing over the continent now, she saw river channels and hypnotically geometric irrigation patterns, and up ahead the basin and range country repeatedly rising and subsiding like bunched fabric. The contrails of jets were everywhere, crosshatched above the clouds.

Crossing over Texas, she saw the shelf of the Edwards Plateau beneath a thin screen of cloud, then Dallas and Austin and San Antonio strung out along I-35 like ancient strongholds built on the banks of a mighty river. And there was Houston to the southeast, its industrial haze spreading out over the Gulf, the Trinity River emptying into Galveston Bay. Lucy was living her life now according to Mission Elapsed Time, and it was hard for her to gauge what hour of the morning it was down there, whether Walt was just now rising or already at work.

She could make out the great alluvial fan near New Orleans where the Mississippi River endlessly spilled its sediments into the ocean, and at the same time the translucent water fanning out behind the reef ridges of the Florida Keys and, even farther eastward, the Bahamas. In one God-like glance, she could see the lonely distances that Walt had traveled to see her launch and to return home. She could see the outline of Cape Canaveral and the scattered inland lakes of Central Florida.

That was where her children were, on the last day of their stay at Disney World. Brian had spent two days with them there before flying back to Houston, no doubt desperate to escape the enforced lightheartedness that ran so contrary to his temperament. But Lucy's mother and Suzanne had stayed on, tirelessly accompanying the kids as they rode every ride in the Magic Kingdom and Epcot, bringing them home late at night when the parks closed to their lagoon-side room at the Polynesian Resort. Lucy had talked to Davis and Bethie twice on the IP phone and had e-mailed them every day since she had been in space. She knew all about Davis's exhilaration at being tall enough to ride Big Thunder Mountain Railroad, about Bethie's meltdown during a "Character Breakfast" when she felt the menace of a seven-foot-tall Goofy creeping up to her from behind. "I want you to come home early," Bethie had pleaded to her mother over the phone after recounting this moment of terror. "I want us to go on It's a Small World together."

Lucy managed to talk Bethie past this teary moment, and mercifully the connection held all the way through the conversation. But now, as she looked down at the Florida peninsula slipping away and the dark cloud-flecked Atlantic taking its place, she felt a sharp longing for this mission, glorious as it was, to be over. She knew better than to give in to this flagging enthusiasm. She had to fight against it, against the danger-ous conviction that she was on the wrong ride, that she should be back on earth with Bethie, floating with her in a gentle lagoon past ranks of cherubic robots singing "It's a Small World."

That treacly anthem came into her head now and wouldn't leave, forcing out John Denver's enraptured salute to the Rocky Mountains. Lucy took off her headphones and dug into one of her utility pockets and took out the Milo Thatch figure that Davis had entrusted to her. She held it in her palm and then gently withdrew her hand. The figure wob-bled in midair, staring up at her through thick goggles with a creepy, knowing grin. She reminded herself to take a picture of it before reentry, to prove to Davis that his little plastic effigy had been her companion on this distant voyage. She looked forward to returning it to her son, mys-teriously charged by its journey to space, the way a rosary might be regarded after being blessed by the pope. And there would be another thing to return: Brian's wedding ring. In his touchingly obtuse mind, he seemed to believe that their shared experience of space travel could somehow belatedly consecrate their marriage, could provide a sense of magic it had never had in the first place. But it was too late for that.

Lucy closed her fist around Milo Thatch and put it back into her utility pocket. Then she turned an effortless somersault, rotating her body until she was looking out the overhead windows at the space sta-tion that was now docked to the orbiter through the air lock in the open cargo bay. The station rose from *Endeavour* in a stack of gleaming cylinders, with the wide-spreading solar arrays fanning out to the sides, as long from end to end as office buildings. The rectangular arrays no longer seemed to Lucy like malevolent moth wings. At the moment, with the sun flashing on them and turning them golden, they made her think of gigantic wafer cookies. In space, she had noticed, her imagi-nation tended to be a little riotous, not quite willing to observe the distinction between dreaming and conscious thought.

She saw a figure drift past the lighted window of the station's near-est module, the U.S.-built Destiny Lab. Somebody was awake in there as well, one of the three members of the station's Expedition crew. That crew, which had already been in space two months and was scheduled to remain for three months more, had been overjoyed to see the astro-nauts of *Endeavour,* the Russian commander giddily ringing the bell when the shuttle had finally docked and greeting each of them with a crushing bear hug when the air lock was opened and the two vessels joined. The day after the docking had been filled with frenetic, long hours involving the lifting of the logistics module out of the payload bay of the shuttle with the robot arm and attaching it to one of the nodes of the station. Lucy had also had to oversee the transfer of her and Buddy's EVA suits from *Endeavour* to the station's air lock.

At the end of the day—or what the Mission Elapsed Time clock defined as a day—the crew of the station and the crew of the shuttle had eaten together in the service module, nine people weightlessly hanging about in every possible configuration as they ate the slices of reasonably fresh pizza and the frozen Dove bars that the *Endeavour* crew had delivered to the station.

Only one of the Expedition crew members was an American, an astronaut named Glen Dippie who in a previous life had been the Navy's youngest submarine commander. He was forty-five, with a slim, spider-monkey body that seemed perfectly at home without gravity. Lucy had always found him polite and calm and profoundly boring. He played the harmonica, but his repertoire was limited to bygone oddities like "Wabash Cannonball" or "Believe Me, If All Those Endearing Young Charms."

The commander of the Expedition crew was Konstantin Iossel. He was as powerful as Glen was slight, with a wrestler's body and a bottom-heavy face. He was quiet and calibrated. Lucy's impression was that he was a little morose, a naturally gregarious man whose morale was subtly beginning to fade after two months of confinement on the station and three yet to go. Or maybe she was just reading into his pensive expression the homesickness that she herself would have felt had she been in his place. There were astronauts and cosmonauts who were untroubled by the thought of long-duration space flight. Brian, with his natural bent toward solitude, had been one, and he might have passed a contented time on *Mir* had it not been for his eagerness to be perceived as a martyr to other people's incompetence. But it had not been all Brian's fault. He had been offered little in the way of psychological preparation for such an extreme mission. Nowadays the Expedition crews trained together for two years, learning one another's deficits and capabilities during grueling camping trips and forced marches in sub-zero weather.

Lucy supposed that, with the right preparation, she would be able to endure the claustrophobia of a months-long mission to the space station, but already she was missing her children, desperate to be reassured that Davis's asthma was in check. And after only four days the desire to see them again, to lift them in her arms and prove to them that she had survived just as she said she would, had already imposed on her vital concentration.

Today, above all days, she needed that concentration. Her spacewalk was scheduled for eight hours from now, and she felt like an actor waking to the cold reality of an opening night. To be sure, she knew her lines. For months in the pool at the NBL, she and Buddy had practiced every move, every turn of every bolt, every tethering point. The torque settings she would be using, the resistance she would be feeling as she operated her outsized ratchet wrench, were all precisely stored in her memory.

She and Buddy had spent an hour last night after dinner moving clutter out of the station's air lock, from which they would step out into space. They had checked all the batteries and regenerated the carbon dioxide scrubbers for the space suits and inspected the connections in their cooling garments.

She was running through the remaining items on the checklist—from the order of the tools on her portable workstation to the precise placement of the straw in her drink bag so that it would not tangle with her headset cord—when Ground came in over the loop playing the day's wake-up song, the Proclaimers singing "I'm Gonna Be." Surly, hearing the first chord, shifted awake in his sleep restraint, broke into a grin, and took off his sleep mask. When he saw Lucy floating on the other side of the cockpit, he nodded good morning and said, "That's for you, you know."

"What do you mean?"

He answered her by singing along with the chorus. "I would walk five hundred miles, and I would walk five hundred more . . ."

Surly rubbed the sleep out of his eyes. "But you're going to walk a hell of a lot more than five hundred miles today."

She ate a granola bar for breakfast as she floated with Buddy and Patti in the mid-deck and went over for the thousandth time the script for the EVA. Patti drank hot coffee and consulted her checklist, her mouth pursed thoughtfully around the straw leading from the aluminum drinking bag. Lucy ignored her own craving for coffee. She and

Buddy would be out on their EVA for close to six hours, and the last thing she needed was to start the day with a diuretic beverage. She did allow herself a few sips of reconstituted orange juice—its flavor, like that of most foods eaten in weightlessness, strangely muted, as if she had a head cold. And she helped herself to another granola bar as well, taking on calories to avoid bonking during the physically demanding space-walk.

After breakfast they left *Endeavour* and entered the station, passing through the modules that were attached end to end like the cars of a pas-senger train. As she glided through the Lab, the first of these modules, Lucy could see all the way to the Russian-built Service Module a hun-dred and fifty feet away. The station had the ambience of a storage locker, one long continuous corridor surrounded by interchangeable panels and storage racks, with footholds and handholds and Velcro straps everywhere to secure objects that would otherwise float away. Lucy was beginning to grow used to the notion that there was no top or bottom to these rooms. When she had first entered the station she had felt a need to orient herself as she might have on earth, to think of one plane, which had vents running along it, as the "floor," and its opposite, where the light fixtures were placed, as the "ceiling." But such distinc-tions no longer made any real sense to her. Even the controls for turning on the lights had been changed on some previous mission from toggle switches to push buttons, because the inhabitants of the station were confused rather than reassured by earthly reminders of what was up and what was down.

The schedule called for Lucy and Buddy to do an exercise pre-breathe to purge their bodies of nitrogen, so that they wouldn't get the bends in the depressurized atmosphere of the air lock or during their spacewalk itself. The stationary bike was set up near the rear of the Ser-vice Module, in the space occupied the night before by the dining table, which was now stowed away. Lucy put on a full-face mask and breathed pure oxygen as she pedaled furiously for ten minutes. The background noise of the station's multitudinous fans and pumps receded, replaced by the serene ebb and flow of high-octane air. The natural apprehension she was feeling about the spacewalk started to evaporate as well, as her thoughts, in their oxygen bath, gained clarity and optimism. Sweat trickled past her hairline, and she could feel it pooling above the seal of the face mask. As she worked harder, forcing the nitrogen out, the lens began to fog and the view became dreamy. Vassily Akimov, the third member of the Expedition crew, was in her line of sight, his stocking feet clamped into a foot restraint as the rest of his body levitated in front of a computer workstation. Past him, she could see all the way through the open hatches back to the Lab, and the force of her exertion as she pedaled the stationary bike made the long, interlocking corridor ahead of her flex slightly up and down like the wing of an airplane in flight. And she tried to push out of her mind the thought that this narrow tube, this fragile vibrating wand, was the only thing shielding her from the crushing nothingness of space.

After she was through with the pre-breathe, but still wearing the oxygen mask, she toweled the sweat from her arms and forehead. Trailing the long, snaking air hose, she decided she'd better visit the little hutch that housed the station's toilet. But she had already sweated most of the moisture out of her body, and the microgravity flailing required to close the door and maneuver herself down onto the cold metal seat kept the perspiration flowing. It probably wasn't worth the trouble, she decided, as she cranked the thigh restraints toward her and listened to the airflow motor. But a bathroom break was a line item in the pre-EVA schedule, and she preferred to take advantage of it rather than run the risk of having to think about peeing into her MAG a few hours later as she clung like a barnacle to the outside of the station.

Next, she joined Buddy in the equipment lock, the first of the two chambers making up the air lock that was their portal into space. In the lowered pressure there, they removed their oxygen masks. Patti was there with them to help them put on their suits.

"Come to think of it," Buddy was saying, as Patti pulled the sleeves of his long underwear to straighten out any troublesome wrinkles, "there are a lot of walking songs. Want me to run through them?"

"No," Lucy said. Buddy had entered his familiar chatterbox mode, trying to purge himself of anxiety by keeping his mouth running. Lucy was locked into a contemplative silence. She wanted to focus every grain of her awareness on the awesome task ahead, but she kept thinking of Bethie being startled by that man in the Goofy costume, how right it would have felt to be there and take her daughter into her arms until she came to understand there was no threat.

"Okay," Buddy said, "for starters, there's Nancy Sinatra singing 'These Boots Are Made for Walkin'.' And then you've got Fats Domino with 'I'm Walkin',' Professor Longhair doing 'Walk Your Blues Away,' Ernest Tubb with—"

"You both sure you burped the air out of your drink bags?" Patti broke in. "You don't want any water bubbles floating around inside your visor."

"We're good," Lucy said, and as Patti began to lock the connectors of their space suits and click their helmets and gloves into place even Buddy fell silent. The clock was running down, and the unreal task was drawing closer.

"Wish I could go out there with you guys," Patti said at last, her flat voice suddenly filled with emotion and her eyes shining with moisture in her famously inexpressive face. She had them all suited up now. On their backs they wore emergency backpacks whose nitrogen thrusters would be the only hope of keeping them from drifting away forever if somehow they came untethered from the station trusses.

Patti gave them each an awkward hug and then ushered them into the much narrower crew lock and closed the hatch. Now it was just Lucy and Buddy, bobbing foot to head in the confined space, listening to the shwooshing sound of the air disappearing, replaced by nothing—just the soundless emptiness of space itself.

When there was no air in the chamber, they tethered themselves off. It was Lucy's job to open the hatch. She did so, and saw the world passing beneath her. There was an instant of panic when she pushed out, as if she could fall straight down onto those distant clouds and the khaki-colored continent beneath it. For a moment, as she groped for a handhold on the outside of the air lock, she felt a heart-stopping flurry of disorientation, but this was soon replaced by a blessed conviction of flight that was beyond anything she had ever dreamed.

Chapter Thirty

She sailed above the earth at 17,500 miles an hour. Though she was tethered to the outside of the station, though the suit itself was a miniature spacecraft of its own, and though she was encumbered with a mini workstation that extended from her chest like a TV tray, with safety reels and body restraint tethers and a portable foot restraint that weighed fifty-five pounds on earth, she felt oddly unconstrained. Indeed, facing the universe in this intimate way, she felt almost naked.

She and Buddy moved along the handrails as they had a hundred times in the NBL pool. This was different. Water had density, but space did not, so that every movement she made seemed too quick, too exaggerated. As she reached for the next handhold, she was aware of the fatal possibility of a never-ending follow-through. The earth passed below her with alarming velocity. She felt she did not have time to pause and factor out what part of the planet she was looking at. She forced herself just to keep inching forward along the outside of the air lock, clinging to the station like Ahab in *Moby-Dick* clinging to the whale as it dove and rose again and again.

She and Buddy made their way to the platform at the end of the station's robotic arm, secured themselves to it, and rode it as it extended upward to the base of the vast winglike solar arrays. At least Lucy thought of the direction as upward, since they were moving away from the face of the earth, away from what in space station terminology was known as nadir, and toward the ominous-sounding and infinitely black dimension called zenith. As they rose, she called out instructions to Glen Dippie, who was operating the robot arm, to yaw them a little to port or starboard, her voice sounding calm to her own ears, her comm discipline sharp. She was facing Buddy. She could not see his expression beneath his golden visor shield, but she assumed he was wide-eyed and grinning.

The ride on the end of the robot arm was unsettling at first. Lucy was overcome for a moment or two with the sensation that she could topple off the platform and fall, but soon she was able to process the idea that there was nowhere to fall, no way to plummet down to the distant earth or to be launched into the cold darkness of space. Every attitude and inclination was the same. The danger was not in falling but in drifting away from the refuge of the station if for some reason your attention dissolved and you forgot to tether yourself as you were translating along a truss. Other things could go wrong as well, of course: a disastrous air leak in the suit, for instance, or a failure of the heating or cooling system, which could lead to frostbite or worse. An EVA could come to an end because of something as small as a water bubble that appeared inside your helmet, picked up some of the irritating anti-fog soap from the inside of the visor, and positioned itself painfully against your exposed eye.

Even with this catalog of disasters firmly in mind, she was not afraid. She had been terrified at launch, she now felt free to admit to herself, but this was different. She had done enough ocean diving and enough training in the NBL pool to feel comfortable, even serene, in hostile environments. She had faith in the suit, in her EVA partner, in her own focus and relentlessly honed skills. As she rose higher at the end of the arm, on her way to the work site at the P-6 truss just beneath the port wing of the solar array, the exhilaration she experienced was more ordinary than otherworldly, the satisfaction that came from mind and body bearing down on a complex but finite task.

The arm could take them only so far. When they reached its end, they tethered themselves to the truss and clambered up the handholds until they reached the cylindrical gimbal that rotated the array's portside wing. As they were installing the first thermal blanket over the gimbal, the foreshortened day came to a close. Lucy could feel the sun's warmth leaving, even in her temperature-controlled suit. The temperature outside, she knew, was now minus 165 degrees. Her hands were chilly as they applied torque against the gimbal bolts in their semi-flexible space gloves. The sun's withdrawal did not leave them in total darkness. They had their helmet lights, and the outside of the station was brilliantly illuminated, blocking out the light of the stars that would otherwise have suddenly appeared. Despite the wealth of artificial light, Lucy understood how her morale could collapse if she let herself dwell on the fact that she and Buddy were now floating on the dark side of the earth. With the glare of the sun gone, they could lift their visors, and she was glad. She felt less alone being able to look at Buddy's face. Between callouts from Patti, as they worked to secure the blanket, he looked up at Lucy and smiled. Then he began to mouth the words to a song, exaggerating each silent syllable so that she could read his lips: "These boots are made for walkin'."

Great. So now she would have the voice of Nancy Sinatra in her head for the duration of the spacewalk.

The sun rose again before they had finished with the portside blanket, and it set and rose yet again before the starboard blanket was in place. When they had finally finished, Buddy held up his hand for a high five. They touched their palms carefully, but even so the reaction it generated could have sent them both soaring out into space if they had not been tethered to the truss and winched into place at the work site with body restraint tethers.

Lucy was tired now, and starting to grow hollow with hunger, but there were another two hours left in the EVA.

"Both blankets are on and secure," Lucy reported through her headset to Patti.

"Excellent," Patti said. "You guys are doing a superb job."

"Now we're translating down Face One, on our way to the antenna assembly."

They were five stories above the rest of the station, creeping back toward the air lock with movements as slow and orchestrated as those of a couple of tree-dwelling sloths. The sun appeared again and Lucy turned off her helmet lights and closed the visor against the glare. The sunrise washed over the station and the orbiter that was docked to it, bringing out colors that were even more intense and alluring than those that it called forth from the earth itself. Lucy saw the Mediterranean passing below, the spray of islands trailing the Greek peninsula, the hinge of the Bosporus.

They stopped halfway down to retrieve a protective cover for the S-Band antenna assembly that had been removed during a previous mission and stored in a bin attached to the truss. It took only twenty minutes, and the task was no more difficult or unwieldy than it had been in the pool, but Lucy was still struck by how hard she was working. Her hands within her gloves were cold and starting to cramp, and the mental effort of trying to determine how much force was required for her to start or stop a particular motion was far more wearying than she had expected.

By the time they made it back to the air lock she was ready for the EVA to be over. There was only one more job, the installation of a lighting stanchion on the Unity Node. Buddy stayed on the zenith side of the Node while Lucy worked her way over to the open hatch of the air lock to change out her tools. She was tethered to the handrail below the hatch, but before she went inside for the new tools she took just a moment for herself, gazing down at the world below her as the sun rose yet again in fiery gradations of prismatic light, once more highlighting the silvery surfaces of the station and the white tilework skin of *Endeavour* where it was docked at the end of the Destiny Lab. Craning her head around, she could see Surly and Chuck waving at her through the aft flight-deck windows of the orbiter. She waved back, and smiled to herself, tired as she was, wondering how she would ever be able to put this moment into words for her children, for Walt.

And all the while Nancy Sinatra was still singing in her head. She laughed at the absurdity of that as she began the movement—a simple push against the handrail—that would vault her into the open air lock.

"And one of these days these boots are gonna—"

A jaw-rattling tremor traveled up her arm and ripped her hand from the rail. The planet that had been so placidly coasting beneath her a moment ago was now viciously spinning as she struggled to locate some kind of reference point and frantically sorted through the possibilities of what might be happening to her. In one whirling pass she caught another glimpse of Chuck's aghast face in the orbiter window, and noticed that Surly was already in motion. Whatever violent thing had occurred had taken place in the noiselessness of space, but there was a tuning-fork sound as her suit absorbed its vibrations. As she spun uncontrollably, she saw an iridescent plume, made up of something that in the world of gravity would have been a liquid, settling calmly like a veil over her cartwheeling body.

"What was that?" Lucy heard Patti calling out over the loop. No one was answering. No one knew. Meanwhile Lucy kept violently spinning. Patti and Buddy were both barking out her name now, but for the moment Lucy couldn't answer. She needed all her concentration to bring her bewildered mind back on track. Was she still tethered to the station? She grabbed the reel with both her hands as she spun and pulled it toward her. There was resistance. That meant that even though she was momentarily out of control she was still attached, not drifting off into space.

"I'm all right," she sputtered, holding on to the reel as if it were the saddle horn on a bucking bronco. "Something knocked me off. Give me a minute to get back."

She reeled herself in, still spinning, but knowing now at least where she was headed. She didn't know what had happened and didn't want to think about it right now. She closed her eyes to shut out the visual assault of the horizon coming at her from all directions. The last thing she needed was to be sick and throw up in her suit.

At last she had pulled herself back far enough that she was able to reach out and grab the handrail. She drew herself close to the surface of the air lock and held on tight with both hands until she was able to open her eyes with some conviction that she would now be seeing things from one plane at a time.

"Buddy? Are you okay?" she said into her headset. She was out of breath. She felt as if she had just run six miles at a dead sprint. There was enough sweat pouring down her face that she worried it could short out her headset.

"I'm all right. Are you?"

"What happened?"

"We're working on that," Patti replied.

"I'm coming around to where you are," Buddy told Lucy. He was out of sight on the starboard side of the air lock.

"I think you'd better stay where you are," she said, remembering the veil of iridescent matter she had passed through as she tumbled. "I think I may have gotten hosed by something."

"Hold on," Patti said. "We'll be right back to you."

It was only then that Lucy thought to look at the orbiter. She could see a slow trail of something escaping from one of the OMS pods, which housed the engines that powered *Endeavour* in its orbital maneuvers.

"Something hit one of the OMS pods," she reported to Patti.

"We see it," Patti said. "You guys hold on a sec and we'll get back to you."

Lucy kept her grip on the handrail, watching the ominous migration of fuel from the pod. That was what she had been sprayed with: mono-methyl hydrazine. Some sort of micrometeoroid, some piece of orbital debris, had slammed into the pod and created what appeared to her to be a massive leak of the precious fuel *Endeavour* would require to return to earth.

"*Endeavour* and *Alpha:* Houston on the big loop." The voice was no longer Patti's. It was an astronaut named Woody Farabee, who was serving as the mission CapCom. "We've got a contingency we need to work through fast. So here's what the flight directors have come up with. Buddy, start making your way down the stack as fast as you can. We want you in the payload bay. As soon as we can undock and depress you'll enter *Endeavour* through the shuttle airlock. You can't go through the joint air lock because it's contaminated with hydrazine. Surly, we've got to maneuver the shuttle away from the station immedi-ately. We don't want to dump any more fuel on it than we already have. Go to the Joint Expedited Undock and Separation Procedure."

She had a grim awareness of where this was heading. It was not only the air lock that was contaminated. She was too.

"Okay, Lucy, we're going to ask you to stay outside a while and bake till the hydrazine's gone and it's safe for you to come into the sta-tion. Surly's going to undock, isolate the leak, and come get you on the next orbit."

"Did you get all that?" Patti asked her. "Sound like a plan?"

"Got it. Sounds like a plan," Lucy said robotically.

"They're going to swap you out for Vassily, just till we get the prob-lem solved. Nobody wants to get into a situation where we have four people in the station and only room for three in the Soyuz."

The Soyuz was the station's lifeboat, a miniature Russian spacecraft the size and shape of a diving bell. There were three contoured seats in the Soyuz. If an emergency happened on the station and there were four people on board, one of them would have to be left behind.

"No problem," she said. "Tell Houston I'm sorry to have to kick Vassily out." She was trying for a tone of nonchalant heroism, but her own voice in her ears was still shaky with dread.

In fifteen minutes the shuttle had undocked and was pulling away. It dropped silently downward, like a flat stone falling through clear water.

She could see Surly's and Tom's faces looking up at her through the overhead windows of the flight deck. Surly raised his hand, his thumb up in a gesture of determination as the shuttle sank lower and lower. We're coming back for you, the gesture said.

Yes, please, Lucy thought, as the sun set again and she continued to hang there, contaminated and alone in the dark shadow of creation. Please come back for me.

Chapter Thirty-one

O
h, come on," Louis said. "I wasn't 'dehydrated.' I was just thirsty."

"The paper said dehydrated," Walt said. They were in Louis's office in the rectory. As he spoke, Louis used the remote control to scroll through the special features on the new collector's edition DVD of *Ben-Hur* he had just bought.

"Somewhere on here there's Leslie Nielsen's screen test for Messala," he said.

"The paper said dehydrated," Walt repeated.

"Am I responsible for the sorry state of journalism? Here it is. What if Leslie Nielsen had ended up playing Messala instead of Stephen Boyd? The world might have turned out to be a different place."

"Not likely."

"Oh, yeah? Think what would have happened if they hadn't turned down Ronald Reagan for *Casablanca* and given the part to Humphrey Bogart. Maybe the Berlin Wall wouldn't have come down."

They watched the scratchy screen test, neither of them saying anything as the buffoonish star of *Naked Gun* delivered his lines with explosive sincerity. Walt was worried, and angry. Louis had been side-stepping the issue of his disastrous Galveston Bay adventure ever since

Walt had shown up unannounced a half hour ago at his door. Even now, Walt knew only about as much as he had read in the article he had come across in the paper. Louis had embarked, all on his own, and without telling a soul, on the canoe trip he and Walt had been contentiously talking about for a year. According to the article, a Coast Guard patrol boat had discovered Louis sitting on an abandoned wellhead on a tiny spoil island a few miles north of Dollar Point. He had somehow lost his canoe, along with the food and beverages he had packed for his voyage to the Gulf, and had been baking in the sun for hours.

"Can I at least ask about our canoe?" Walt said.

"Our canoe is fine. I'd tied it up to the wellhead and was just going to take a break and eat my lunch. Then the wind came up and, well, you know how I was never that good with knots in Boy Scouts? Anyway, the Coast Guard guys were kind enough to go find the canoe and pick it up for me. I was never 'shipwrecked.' The ship wasn't wrecked."

There was a dinging sound from the microwave and Louis stood up to retrieve a bag of popcorn. His lips were chapped, and he was deeply sunburned on the back on his neck. He opened the bag and let the scalding cloud of steam escape before holding it out to Walt. Walt took a handful. It seemed to be some sort of peace offering.

"One of the Coast Guard guys was Catholic," Louis said. "He goes to Christ the King."

"That's nice. Did he think you were an idiot?"

"No, he happened to be in awe of the fact that I was a priest. As too few people are these days, I might add."

Louis punched a button on the remote, highlighting the Play Movie option on the DVD menu. They watched the opening credits of *Ben-Hur*, the music of the score growing louder and more triumphant as the camera tightened on Michelangelo's painting of God touching his finger to Adam's.

"Remember when your parents took us to this when we were little kids?" Louis said.

"You could have at least told me you were going to go all by yourself."

"I don't know what came over me. I guess I momentarily forgot I was supposed to report my every move."

"In my opinion, this was kind of serious, Louis."

"Serious how?"

"I don't know. You tell me."

Louis punched Pause. The screen froze on Charlton Heston's grimacing face.

"What are you worried about, Walt? That I'm going to—what?—commit suicide or something? If I'd meant to do myself in, do you think I would have loaded up that canoe with a giant bag of Twizzlers?"

"I just think we ought to talk," Walt said.

"Good for you. But for your information I've been counseling people all day. I've already put in a full shift of getting to the bottom of things. Maybe we could quote-unquote talk tomorrow. Right now I want a little *Ben-Hur* time."

Walt decided to back off. He watched the movie with Louis. He had nothing better to do. After a few minutes the edgy silence between them disappeared and they lapsed into the comfortable routine of staring at the images on the screen and trading comments as they had done since childhood.

"Check this out," Louis said, as they watched a thirst-crazed Heston gaze up in wonder at the unseen face of the man—Jesus—who was offering him water. When a Roman soldier tried to intervene, Jesus stared him down and he skulked away.

Louis paused the DVD and turned to Walt. "You know what? I think this is where my vocation came from. This scene right here. I remember thinking that was so cool, that somebody could make a gnarly dude like that back off with just a look. I thought if I was a priest I'd have that look."

Louis stared wistfully at the Roman soldier's chastened expression on the frozen screen.

"So okay," he said after a moment, "as long as you want to talk about serious things."

"Don't bring that up, Louis. I think I know your feelings about it."

"Her mission going okay so far?"

"It's fine."

"So what about when she comes back?"

Louis waited for an answer and when Walt didn't have one ready he pressed the Fast Forward button until he came to a scene where Ben-Hur was chained to an oar in a Roman warship.

"Here's where they get rammed," he said.

"I don't want to explain anything," Walt said finally. "I don't want to try to justify anything to you."

"Fair enough. Don't try."

"I'm happy to talk about it if we can have a rational discussion."

"You know me. I've got all this medieval stuff going on. Sin and responsibility and—"

"Okay, forget about it."

"I'm not kidding, Walt. What about when she comes back? What's the game plan?"

"The game plan is I'm serious about her."

"Good, because breaking up a family is serious business."

Walt stood and walked to the window and looked out at the empty church parking lot, where a young father was teaching his son how to ride a bike. Louis continued to watch the ancient sea battle on television as if he and Walt had merely fallen into a cordial silence. After a while Louis turned his head and caught Walt studying the kitschy 3-D picture of Jesus and his sacred heart that hung over his desk.

"Do me a favor and toss that into the trash," Louis said.

"Why?"

"It's a little sophomoric, don't you think? Not really fitting for an individual of my stature in the community."

Walt didn't bother to throw the picture away. Louis shrugged and pressed the Play button on the remote.

"Don't turn that on again," Walt said.

"It's my TV, not yours."

"I said I was ready to have a rational discussion."

"Okay, you begin," Louis said, turning off the TV and tossing the remote across the room. "Tell me what you think I should hear. Tell me the reasons you decided to commit adultery with a woman who has two small children."

Maybe Louis was not just righteously angry, Walt decided. Maybe he was jealous as well. Walt had detected something in the way his friend had given Lucy that blessing the other night, something Walt would not have noticed if he had not known Louis all his life. He had brought his priestly juju to bear because, at least in part, he wanted Lucy to notice him, to take him seriously. As much as it had been a genuine prayer of a spiritual representative, it had also been a forlorn display of a man caged by celibacy, entangled in a vocation whose magic was wearing thin. Walt was pretty sure that Louis had always been true to his vows, though it was hard not to share the general attitude that willful deprivation had no currency anymore, brought no particular good into the world. All it did was make people like Louis more solemn and confused and isolated.

"I think you need to take some kind of a break," Walt said gently.

"Yeah, I can see where you might want to shift the conversation in that direction, since the last time I checked we were talking about your epic screwup."

"I mean it."

"What kind of a break do you mean?"

"I don't know. Isn't there some sort of sabbatical you could get? Can't you take some sort of leave?"

"Tell you what," Louis said, this time with real bite. "I think I'm going to just take a leave from you."

Walt had nothing to say to that. It was time to go. But before he could walk out of Louis's room in emphatic silence his pager went off.

The moment Walt walked through the door of Mission Control, Lance Briscoe swooped over to him, took him by the arm and drew him over to a relatively unoccupied space against the wall where the mission plaques were hung. Every console in the room was occupied, the flight controllers staring nervously at their screens, twenty people talking on the phone at once.

"Here's the deal," Lance said to Walt. "Something hit one of the pods on *Endeavour*. It's bleeding fuel like you wouldn't believe."

"They're not still docked?"

"No, they're out of there. Surly did an expedited undocking."

"They isolate the leak?"

"That's the big problem. They can't. We thought it was only the starboard pod, but some of the spall must have hit the interconnect. They're leaking from both sides. If we don't bring them down now they're not going to have enough fuel to come home.

"But here's the other problem," Lance went on. "Lucy's still hanging on the stack."

"What!"

"She got hosed by hydrazine. She has to stay out there and bake. They were going to pick her up on the next orbit, but now we've just found out about this damage to the interconnect."

"She can't stay," Walt said. "There are only three seats in the Soyuz. If something happens to the—"

"We had her and Vassily trade places."

"What are you saying? You're going to keep her up there for what—a month?—with no station training?"

"You want to know the truth, Walt? After this deal we're probably going to have to ground the fleet for a while for an inspection. My guess is it's going to be more like four or five. You're the team lead. You trained her. I need an answer fast. Can she do it?"

"She can do it," Walt said.

"Is she going to freak when we tell her?"

Walt knew what Lucy would want him to say.

"No," he answered.

Lance nodded his thanks and turned around and walked over to Woody Farabee at the CapCom station.

From time to time, as she hung tethered to the outside of the air lock, the CapCom would break in and give Lucy an update. They had somehow managed to patch him through so that he could speak to Lucy directly. Surly and the crew were working with Ground to isolate the leak, shouldn't be too much longer, just hang in there and enjoy the view while you're waiting.

"Thanks, Houston," she would say. "Everything's nominal here. Tell Surly and the crew to take their time and not worry about me."

But the calm words were essentially a script she was reading. They didn't reveal—she hoped they didn't reveal—an apprehension that was slowly growing into terror. She took a sip from her drink bag, flexed her hands inside her gloves to keep them from cramping. It was twenty minutes after the latest sunrise: midday. She looked down on a landmass she didn't recognize, some portion of the African coast, obscured by clouds. The planet that had been so bewitchingly distant an hour before now seemed tauntingly unreachable.

Keep your thoughts disciplined, she told herself. Keep them positive. The shuttle was coming back around to get her. In another hour or two she'd be inside with the rest of the crew. Lucy was pretty sure the damage had only been to one of the OMS engines. It was a serious contingency, but there would still be plenty of fuel for another rendezvous and docking, enough for essential orbital maneuvering and the de-orbit burn that would take them back into the earth's atmosphere. No doubt the mission would have to be cut short because of the fuel loss, but there was nothing to be done about that.

As far as she could tell, there had been no damage to the station itself, but as soon as Vassily came back on board, the station flight controllers would probably order a fly-around in the Soyuz to inspect the exterior of the stack. In the meantime, Lucy busied herself with inspecting the immediate area for any dents or craters in the hull shielding. It was possible that whatever had hit the shuttle might have hit the station as well, or that the force of the initial impact might have created a dangerous spall storm of dislodged metal.

She saw nothing, and there was no indication that the station was in any distress. It continued to coast around the world, with Lucy attached. She watched the sun set again, and turned on her helmet lights against the aggressive darkness. She felt newly vulnerable. Space was filled with orbital debris, from exhausted satellites to random bits and pieces of metal to dust-sized particles of aluminum oxide. There were millions and millions of pounds of such material in orbit, fragments of booster stages or spacecraft that had broken apart above the atmosphere in years or decades past and were now cruising around the earth at the same hypervelocity as the station. Many of these remnants, the bigger ones, could be tracked on radar, but there were trillions of smaller pieces of debris, varying in size from a grain of sand to a golf ball, that could not. Everyone understood that the odds would someday favor a serious incident, and that day had apparently arrived.

As she floated in darkness, Lucy could not keep her mind away from the thought of this lethal rain. During her spacewalk, when her concentration had been so tight on the tasks at hand, she had not had the mental leisure to worry about orbital debris or anything else. But now, idle and alone, she felt the way she had sometimes felt as she surfaced from an ocean dive, overcome by a sudden sense of menace, an awareness that a tiger shark could materialize out of the gloom in a blink and tear off her leg. Back then, her imagination had had to fight back the sea; now it had to fight back the universe itself. She was a lolling target. A piece of invisible debris the size of a paint flake could tear a deadly hole in her suit, could come smashing through the helmet of her visor.

She stared into the blankness, imagining *Endeavour* coasting silently back to her, her crewmates waving to her through the windows. If everything was nominal, shouldn't that have happened by now? Where was the shuttle? Too much time was passing, she thought. No one was talking to her, just Woody Farabee breaking in every few minutes and saying, in his CapCom voice, "Hanging in there, Lucy?"

She answered in the same unconcerned timbre, working hard to keep her voice level. She wished it were Walt talking to her, the only person she knew whom she did not have to convince of anything, of her courage or skill or love. She could tell Walt the truth, that she was afraid, that she was starting to have a despairing sense that the shuttle wasn't coming back.

"Uh, Lucy," Woody said finally, "we're going to need you to do something for us."

"Go ahead, Houston," she said.

"It's kind of a lot to ask."

Lucy tightened her grip on the handrail. Her body was almost perfectly still now, soaring along at unthinkable speed, a speed that was possible only because she and the station were in constant free fall around the circumference of the earth. She did not want to respond; she did not want to hear what was required of her, because she knew what it would be.

"Go ahead, Houston," she repeated.

"*Endeavour* is losing fuel from both engines. They've got to do a de-orbit burn and come home right away. So we're going to need you to stay on the station."

There was no point in asking how long. She knew how long: months. A wave of disbelief, of panic, traveled along her body. She tried to answer before the wave had passed, and discovered she could not make a sound. She took a sip from her drink bag. The water was suddenly icy.

" 'Fraid that's about the only option we've got," Woody said, as the silence expanded.

"Roger," Lucy was finally able to say. "Understood."

"We know it's not an optimal situation, but we got a lot of people down here who know you can do it, Lucy. And we're going to get you home as soon as we can."

She saw *Endeavour* now, below her in a lower orbit. She saw the flare of its de-orbit burn as it used up its last reserves of fuel to travel back to earth. In another hour—only an hour!—Surly and the crew would be home. They would be with their families. She commanded herself not to think about that, about Davis and Bethie. She had to finish baking off the hydrazine. She had to begin to prepare herself for the unknown months ahead.

Another accelerated orbital day came and went, and then finally she was inside the air lock with the outside hatch closed. She waited while the atmosphere was depressed, and then the hatch to the crew lock opened and she found herself looking at Konstantin Iossel and Glen Dippie, two men she barely knew. Their welcoming smiles struck her as obligatory, and she understood that their shock was as great as hers. The crewmate with whom they had trained for two years, with whom they had lived on the station with exquisite coordination, and upon whose crucial skills they had relied, had suddenly disappeared and been replaced by a frightened changeling.

Konstantin unlatched her helmet and pulled it off. She nodded a weary, heartbroken thank-you. No one said anything. Lucy was aware of a smell: something metallic, burnt, faint. She detected it in the fabric of her suit when she had finally wriggled free of it and was floating there in her sweaty liquid cooling and ventilation garment. The smell lingered for a minute or two more—a teasing chemical suggestion at the vanishing edge of her olfactory range. She knew what it was. Other astronauts had spoken about it, the smell that sometimes seeped inside after an EVA. It was the smell of space itself. The smell of nothing, the non-world in which she was now to make her home.

Chapter Thirty-two

She used the IP phone in the Unity Node to call home.

"Oh my God, Lucy," Suzanne said. "Are you okay?"

Lucy said that she was, and she heard Suzanne calling out to whoever else was in the room, "She's okay! She's okay!

"We've been watching it on CNN," Suzanne said to Lucy when she spoke into the receiver again. "Nobody's really telling us anything."

"I don't want the kids to see any of this on TV," Lucy said.

"Of course not. Don't worry. They're down at the playground right now with Colleen. We keep the TV off when they're in the house."

"Where's Brian?"

"He went over to Mission Control to try to find out what's going on. Lucy, how long do you think you're going to have to stay up there?"

"I don't know yet."

"Hold on a minute, Mom's grabbing the phone."

"No, wait. I think I'm about to lose the connection. Tell Mom I'll try to call back in an hour, and ask her to have the kids there so I can talk to them."

There was a silence on the other end of the line, and Lucy knew that the KU band that provided the signal for the phone had gone down for the rest of the orbit. She was not sure how much Suzanne had heard, but hoped that she had managed to get through the information about the kids. She was desperate to talk to Davis and Bethie, to explain the situation to them before they heard something about a space disaster on TV.

She took off the phone headset and hovered in the center of the Node, rehearsing what she would tell them. She pictured the living room of their house where Suzanne had just been speaking to her on the phone. She saw the not-yet-unpacked suitcases from the trip to Disney World scattered about, Davis's and Bethie's backpacks hanging from a peg on the kitchen wall, the Disney souvenirs that their indulgent grandmother had no doubt bought them lying about on the floor. What time was it in Houston? She had left the wristwatch that was set to earth time back in the shuttle, along with everything else—her clothes and toiletries, her food and the contents of her PPK, everything but the liquid cooling and ventilation garment she had been wearing when she stepped into the crew lock and that she was still wearing now. It took her a moment to extrapolate from Mission Elapsed Time, which was displayed on a digital readout in the Node, that it was almost four o'clock in the afternoon. When the children came back from the playground they would be hungry. Bethie would not have had her nap. It would not be a good time to break the news, but she did not have much of a choice.

"Get through to them?" Glen said as he hung discreetly at the entrance to the Functional Cargo Block, which adjoined the forward edge of the Node.

"Not to the kids. I'm going to try again on the next pass, if that's okay."

"No need to ask permission," he said. "You can use the IP phone whenever you want. In the meantime, I've got some clothes for you."

He was holding out one of the Expedition crew polo shirts and a pair of shorts. "They probably won't fit that well, but they're clean at least."

"I hate to take your clothes."

"Don't worry about it." Glen smiled at her. His body was so small and lean and tensile, so accustomed to life in weightlessness, that he seemed to hang in the center of the module by dynamic tension alone. For a passing moment, his presence had a hallucinatory charge, as if he were not a man but some sort of grinning arboreal mammal staring at her with enormous night-seeing eyes. Even as she nodded her thanks to him for his hospitality she had to fight back tears of hopelessness.

"Where's Konstantin?" she asked.

"Up in the Service Module, pulling his thoughts together. Trying to figure out if we can still run the experiments and stuff without Vassily."

"I can help," she said.

"Oh, I'm sure we'll put you to work," he replied. "First we've got to get you settled in. You good for an interview in a couple hours? The media's going crazy down there, apparently."

Lucy nodded, smiled. From his perch in midair, Glen gave her a thumbs-up. He pivoted as sharply as a startled fish, pushed himself forward with expert economy and soared back to join Konstantin in the Service Module.

"Lucy, we've got somebody here who wants to talk to you," she heard Woody saying over the speakers of the S-Band loop. She grabbed a portable mike and answered, rashly thinking it would be Walt's soothing voice she would hear next. It wouldn't matter that she would be talking to him over the S-Band, which, unlike the IP phone, was not private. If she could just hear his voice . . .

But it was not Walt. It was her husband, speaking to her from Mission Control.

"You doing okay up there, Lucy?" he asked lamely.

"I'm okay. Don't say anything to the kids yet. I'm going to call them on the phone on the next pass."

"You got it. We're all rooting for you down here."

We're all rooting for you down here? Was it possible for even Brian to be this tone-deaf in speaking to his imperiled wife? She knew he was on the spot, that he was speaking on an open loop in a room filled with flight controllers, but she could have reasonably expected he would not put his elaborate self-consciousness ahead of her own quite visible needs. This was, she realized, about as far as he had ever been able to go emotionally: a supportive team member instead of a husband.

"Everybody on *Endeavour* okay?" she asked, letting him off the hook a little by deflecting the conversation away from the one-on-one intimacy he was afraid to offer.

"Wheels down an hour ago. They'll all be back to Houston tonight."

"Good," she said. She meant it, of course. Her relief that they were safe was powerful, but the memory of the shuttle burning back into the atmosphere, leaving her behind, carried with it an ineradicable twinge of abandonment.

Brian fumbled for something reassuring to say; Lucy, finding the silence intolerable and threatening, rushed in to fill it. "So," she asked stupidly, "how was Disney World?"

It was the same question she asked Davis when she was able to reach him on the IP phone an hour later. She could hear in his voice that he was in a wary frame of mind, called in early from the playground with his sister, told not to leave the room because his mother might be calling any minute from space. He told her about the Twilight Zone Tower of Terror at MGM Studios, and about how Suzanne had talked the conductor into letting him and Bethie ride in the front of the monorail. Lucy by this time had changed out of her liquid cooling garment and into the shorts and T-shirt that Glen had given her. Even with an elastic waist the shorts were too big, and she had to hold them up with one hand as she floated in the Node. She listened, probing for the moment when she could change the subject. She had to talk to both Davis and Bethie before this twenty-minute comm pass was over, and she did not want an abrupt curtain of silence to fall on either of them.

"Listen, sweetheart," she said, finally interrupting, "there's something I need to tell you, okay?"

"Okay." He said the word in a wait-and-see tone. She knew he was bracing himself to hear some sort of betrayal.

"We had a little problem during the EVA today," she said. She related it all as calmly as she could, not leaving much out, since she needed to be in charge of this conversation and thought the more she told him, the less he would interrupt her with frightened questions. There had been some damage to one of the engines of the shuttle. Just to be on the safe side, it had come home early. Just to be on the safe side, she said again, they thought it was better for her not to go back with *Endeavour* because fuel had gotten on her space suit. So for the next little while she was going to need to stay on the station. She told him not to worry if he saw something about it on the news and they made all this sound dangerous. "It's just that," she repeated for the third time, "to be on the safe side they decided—"

"When are you coming home?" he asked.

"Honey, we're working on that. I'm not sure yet."

"Will you be home for my birthday?"

His birthday was a month from now. There was no way.

"Davis, sweetie," she said, "I'm sure going to try, because there's nothing in the world that's more important to me. But if I can't, then we'll just have your party a little bit later, okay?"

"Okay." She heard the wobble in his voice. He sounded so small. He sounded so alone on the vast earth revolving below her.

She told him again that she was in no danger, that there was no reason to worry about anything at all. He was going back to school tomorrow, and she told him to be sure and have his binder ready and to set a good example for Bethie by eating a good breakfast in the morning and getting dressed in plenty of time.

"And, Davis, if you feel tight, if you're having trouble breathing, you tell someone right away. Do you promise me?"

"I promise."

"Promise again," she said.

"I promise."

"Because this is very important," she said. "You know how important it is, don't you?"

It was one thing to be left behind in space, to be stranded for months in an orbiting mobile home with two men she barely knew. She had faced down the acute terror of the accident, and she knew she had no choice but to endure the unearthly span of time ahead of her. But the thought that her child might be sick, that she could not reach him or take care of him, rose up in her now with a dread she could barely contain.

"Do you want to talk to Bethie?" Davis said. She knew that the dread was rising in him as well, and that his only strategy to contain it was, like her, to pretend that there was nothing special or terrifying about this conversation and that the sooner he got off the phone the sooner the secure life he was accustomed to could resume.

Telling Bethie was no easier. As Lucy spoke, as she listened to the bewildered sniffling on the other end of the line, she remembered the night before she had gone into quarantine, when Bethie had been sleepwalking and screaming in her sleep, trying to escape a witch that wanted to throw her into the oven. Lucy could not shake the conviction that that dream had been her fault. Why had she not allowed herself to see, before it was too late to do anything about it, that Bethie's life was ruled by a chronic submerged fear that her mother's love and shielding power were inconstant, that at any moment she might disappear and leave her child to the mercy of marauding witches?

"But I want you to come home *now*!" Bethie was sputtering. "You *said* you would!"

"Sweetheart, I know," Lucy said. "But I'm going to come home very soon."

"How soon?"

She danced around that point as nimbly as she could, telling Bethie that there was another shuttle flight almost ready to go, and that they would come up and get her and bring her home. She urgently repeated the reassurances she had given to Davis: there was nothing to worry about, everything was going to be all right, don't pay attention to anything she might hear on TV or at school. She had to speak quickly because she could sense the comm pass was about to end, but she also knew these consoling words could not be rushed. They had to be enunciated, driven home with steady maternal force. Perhaps she succeeded, at least a little. She had to believe that, even though Bethie was still tearfully pleading with her when the connection went down.

Chapter Thirty-three

"S tranded Astronaut to Husband: 'So How Was Disney World?' "

That was the headline in the *Houston Chronicle* the next morning. A similar testament to Lucy's heroic flexibility was featured in every paper and on every cable news show, and now she was doing her best to demonstrate that same quality during a live interview.

Walt was watching in one of the conference rooms in Building 5 with the rest of his team and the five weary and shell-shocked astronauts of STS-108. The crew had gotten back to Ellington last night to an abbreviated version of the usual welcome-home festivities. Walt and his team had not even had time to finish decorating the hall in Building 4, but even if they had, nobody was in a mood for celebration. The mission had not been a failure, exactly—the important EVA tasks had been completed, and the crew of the station resupplied—but its abrupt termination, and the wrenching necessity of leaving Lucy behind, had left everyone in a deflated mood. The crew and the team had naturally gravitated toward one another this morning, shutting themselves up in this conference room away from the demands of the press and the more heartfelt but still burdensome concern of the rest of their colleagues at the Johnson Space Center.

Even Buddy was far from his usual irrepressible self as he watched Lucy floating in the Destiny Lab, answering questions from the interviewer as the second-and-a-half transmission delay made her appear lost and distracted. Buddy and Patti feeling, Walt knew, something akin to survivor's guilt, having been ordered to leave the other member of their EVA team behind. Nor was Surly happy. He had performed with his usual imperturbable skill in bringing *Endeavour* home, and there had even been an admiring profile of him in the *New York Times* this morning, but Surly had a disappointed side that could show through sometimes when the pressure was finally off. And since landing he had been working through a profane catalog of the problems that had beset the mission—"Fucking micrometeoroids," "Fucking interconnect valve"—with the exuberance of someone who had just discovered cursing.

"We're all having to make do," Lucy was saying on the television screen, flanked by Glen Dippie, who was smiling eagerly, and by Konstantin Iossel, who had a distant and stoic look on his face. "For instance, I don't even have a toothbrush at the moment. And as you can see, I'm wearing hand-me-down clothes that don't exactly fit."

The shorts and shirt she was wearing were charmingly oversized, and made Walt feel nervous with desire. He had not talked to her since the accident. He had not expected to. He was not a flight controller and would have no business communicating with her from Mission Control over the S-Band, and her precious time on the private IP phone would naturally be devoted to her family. He could not call her, of course. He supposed in the next few days they would be able to provide her with some sort of e-mail access, but their e-mail communications would have to be guarded to at least some degree.

"I just want to tell my kids I love them," Lucy said when the interviewer asked if there was anything she'd like to say to anyone back on earth. "And my husband, of course. And to let them all know I'm doing just fine and I'll be doing even better once I can find a toothbrush. And I want to thank Glen and Konstantin here for taking in an orphan, and to send my love to the crew of *Endeavour* and to a wonderful training team. Especially our team lead."

Especially our team lead. Did he actually hear those words or just will them into being? Sylvia, sitting beside him at the conference table, jostled her shoulder against his, knowing the secret that no one else in the room did. Walt hoped that Lucy had once again been speaking in code, that she hadn't been just kindly acknowledging a job well done but whispering to him across the gulf of space that she had not forgotten him, that she needed him. He had triple-checked that morning to make sure his cell phone battery was charged. He was confident that she would call soon, the next time she could commandeer the IP phone and assure herself of privacy. But every hour that his cell phone didn't ring was another hour in which that confidence, along with the battery, began to discharge.

"Good for her," Surly announced emphatically when the interview was over. "It's a hell of a damn thing, but she's sure making us all proud, isn't she? Walt, can I talk to you a minute?"

They went into an empty control room next door while the others drifted out into the parking lot.

"Can you do me a favor and run this over to Brian?" Surly said. He was holding a medium-sized Ziploc bag with the word "Kincheloe" written on the outside in black Sharpie. "This was what was in Lucy's PPK. I made a point of getting it out of the orbiter and bringing it home with me from Kennedy. He'd probably like to hold on to it till she gets back."

"I think he'd rather you gave it to him. You're the commander."

"I can't just hand it off, not without spending some time with him. And you wouldn't believe all the interviews the PAO has lined me up with. I've got to fly off to New York in an hour to talk to Katie Couric. You mind?"

Lucy's sister answered the door. She was holding a phone to her ear, and she gave Walt an apologetic smile as she ushered him inside. "All right," she was saying, "just call Dr. Broomfield and ask him, as a favor to me, if he'd mind taking a look at her records."

She covered the mouthpiece with her hand and whispered "Sorry" to Walt as the voice on the other end kept droning on. She was slight and athletic, her hair darker, her features sharper than her sister's. But Walt saw a resemblance right away in the shape of her eyes and the line of her jaw, in the nervous, solicitous concern for the visitor she was keeping waiting. She was pretty, or maybe not. In any case, there was something warm and commanding about her that Walt found unnervingly familiar.

"I'm Suzanne," she said, when she finally was able to get off the phone. "Lucy's sister."

"I'm Walt Womack," he replied as he took her hand.

"Walt? Lucy's instructor?"

He nodded. To his surprise, she embraced him. Her arms tightened around his back, and there was a fervent and grateful look in her eyes when she drew back.

"She's told us about you," she said. "How kind you've been to her. How important."

There was no evidence in Suzanne's uncomplicated expression that Lucy had told her any more than that, but Walt was struck by the thought that if she had, he might have been pleased. His affair with Lucy still felt like he had imagined it, and never more so than in this house, where he had never before set foot, and where the evidence of her life without him was depressingly vivid. Suzanne led him into the open kitchen, where Lucy's mother and the girl—Bethie—were pulling an elastic wad of dough out of a mixing bowl onto a floured countertop.

"We're making tea cookies," Lucy's mother said, wiping the flour off her hand so she could offer it to Walt. "They were Lucy's favorite when she was Bethie's age."

Lucy's mother's name was Carolyn. She was physically imposing, a bit stout, with Lucy's broad shoulders, but with blue eyes that were vulnerable and searching. In her fleshy, guileless face he could see what Lucy might look like in twenty years were it not for the fierce winnowing drive that Walt suspected she had inherited from her father.

The kitchen in which they were standing was oddly tormenting to him. The cordless wall phone, the photos attached to the door of the refrigerator with magnets, the stack of worn cookbooks below the microwave with Post-it notes marking recipes Lucy had tried: all this was too revealing of a part of her life—in fact, the greatest part of her life to date—that might be forever closed to him.

Lucy's mother and sister looked to him as an authority, and he did his best to put them at ease about the ordeal she was going through. He had trained her, he reminded them. She was resilient, she was steady, she was philosophical. She had demonstrated all this by her behavior during the EVA accident. She was not in danger on the station; she was just marooned there. She would make the best of it.

Bethie listened intently as this curious stranger who knew so much about her mother held forth in the kitchen. From time to time she patted the forgotten dough with her tiny open palm. Hearing the talk, Davis wandered in from the living room, the video game he had been playing forgotten. Walt said, "Hey, Davis," trying to mimic the casual and open way he had observed when adults who were comfortable with children spoke. Should he initiate a handshake? Should he risk embarrassment by holding up his hand for a high five that might not even be returned? In the end he did what felt most natural, just touched the boy lightly on the shoulder, so lightly he did not even seem to notice.

And then Brian came in the front door, his T-shirt drenched from a long run. When he saw Walt his face tightened in alarm.

"Is she all right? Did something else happen?"

"Everything's fine," Walt said. "There's no news." He held up the PPK bag. "Surly just wanted me to drop something off for you."

Brian looked at the bag and nodded, relieved. He set his cell phone down on the kitchen counter—like Walt, he had been carrying it even on his run, in case Lucy called—and opened the refrigerator and took a long gulp from a bottle of some sort of energy drink. He put the bottle back in the refrigerator and closed the door and turned to Walt and said, "Come on back."

Brian led him back to the spare bedroom that had been turned into an office. It was mostly Brian's office, Walt thought, judging by its utilitarian sparseness, the charmless computer hutch from Office Depot and the obligatory crew photos and framed mission patches on the wall. It was the sort of unthought-out male space in which Walt himself lived, in which he knew he could not continue to live anymore.

Brian beckoned him to a rocking chair, the only other chair in the room.

"I should have asked you if you wanted anything to drink," he said. "Do you?"

"I'm fine."

"Sorry if I looked a little startled when I saw you there. I never know from one minute to the next what I'm going to hear or who I'm going to hear it from. I thought maybe there'd been another accident and she was . . ."

"She's fine," Walt said. "At least as far as I know. Your information's probably a lot more current."

"Don't assume. Just because I'm her husband it doesn't mean they're going to remember to keep me in the loop. I've been camping out at Mission Control just to remind them they need to talk to me."

He looked at Walt. His predatory face suddenly looked slack and vulnerable.

"She's going to be okay, isn't she, Walt?"

"She's going to be okay."

"You would know, right? I mean, maybe even better than me. What she's capable of."

"I don't see how I could know that better than you," Walt said.

"You've got that team lead thing. You can read people. I'm sort of deficient that way—at least that's what everybody seems to think. Especially Lucy."

"You're under a lot of stress right now," Walt offered.

Brian acknowledged this fact with a slight tilt of his head. He put the PPK bag on the desk and leaned back in his office chair, thinking.

"Maybe she'll do better up there than I did on *Mir*. Glen Dippie's pretty easy to get along with. I don't know about the Russian guy, but he probably is too. The thing is, nothing can really prepare you for being shut up in such a small space for so long. At least we can talk to her. She's called three or four times on the IP phone."

"It's good you're in touch," Walt said, trying not to think about the fact that she had not found time to call him.

Brian shifted his attention to the PPK bag.

"It's kind of spooky, having you bring that to me. It's like it's her effects or something."

"Except she's not dead," Walt said, with a sharpness in his voice he didn't quite intend.

Brian glanced at him, caught by his tone, and then leaned forward and opened the bag.

"Maybe I should leave," Walt said.

"No, that's all right."

Brian poured the contents of the bag out onto the desktop. There was a CD with the names of various artists written by hand on a little card visible through the transparent cover: Beethoven, John Denver, Miles Davis. This evidence of Lucy's musical taste came as a surprise to Walt. They had never discussed music, and once more he felt jealous of the things about Lucy that might be common knowledge to others but were still unknown to him.

Walt watched as Brian read through the selections on the CD and then handled the other objects: a child's crayon drawing of a smiling family in front of their house; an action figure from some cartoon Walt didn't recognize; and a tiny jeweler's bag. Brian opened the drawstring on the bag and shook out a ring.

"That's our wedding ring," he explained, holding it up. "I went on a walk with Lucy out in front of the beach house the night before the launch. I asked her to take it up and bring it home to me."

Walt said that was a nice gesture. He said he was sure Lucy was touched by it. His instinct was to offer this difficult man whatever solace he could, but the thought of that intimate beach scene agitated him. Of course Lucy had had to say good-bye to her husband, and even though their marriage was badly frayed, of course they had spoken of things that could not ever be any of Walt's business. He had no right to feel hurt or betrayed, to assume that Lucy's thoughts would have been solely of him both before she went into space and now that she was marooned there.

But she was thinking of him. At three a.m. his cell phone rang, and before he was awake he had already thrown back the covers and sprinted out of bed and grabbed the phone from the top of the dresser, where it was carefully recharging. He stared at the keypad of the phone in sleepy bewilderment until he was awake enough to remember how to answer it.

"Walt?" Her voice was as thin and quavery as a child's.

"I'm here." But he wasn't there, quite yet. He was still fighting his way to consciousness. "Just give me a minute . . . Is that you?"

"I need you," she said. She was quietly sobbing. "I'm trying to be strong, but I'm so alone. I'm so frightened. I can't do this."

"Yes, you can."

"It's *months,* Walt."

"I know."

"My children think I've deserted them."

"No, they don't. I saw them today."

"You *did*? Where?"

He rubbed his eyes and told her how he had gone over to her house to give Brian her PPK.

"I don't have anything from the kids anymore," she said. "Not even a picture of them. Everything was in there. Even Brian's wedding ring."

"I know. He showed it to me."

"Don't think about that," she said. "It doesn't mean anything."

"Of course it does, Lucy. It has to mean something."

"Why didn't I take something of yours up with me? We should have thought of that."

"I know."

"You haven't forgotten about me, have you?" Lucy said.

"I was thinking you'd forgotten about me."

"God, no. I wanted to call you, but every time I tried to get to the phone Konstantin or—"

"It's all right."

"I love you."

"I love you too."

"It's so lonely up here, Walt. I can put on a good front, I think. At least for a while. But I've got to believe you're—"

Her voice abruptly skittered into another register. He heard her talking to one of her crewmates about some chore listed in the Execute Package that she might be able to take care of. "Sure, absolutely, no problem. I can do that," she was saying, and when she got back to the phone her voice had a counterfeit steadiness.

"Can I get back to you later?" she said. It was clear that either Glen or Konstantin was still in the Node with her.

"I love you, Lucy," Walt said. "I'm going to be here when you come home."

"I appreciate that," she said, in the businesslike tone she was working so hard to achieve, as hard as she worked at everything. "That's really nice to hear."

Chapter Thirty-four

Tears did not fall in space. Without gravity, they simply hovered at the rim of Lucy's eyes, gaining volume as she wept, and when she wiped them away they drifted around her head as perfect spheres. She found these little floating globes of sorrow fascinating, the way they lingered and seemed to comment on her passing moments of despair.

As far as actual crying went, though, she thought she was handling herself pretty well. On the phone with Walt, her fears and heartbreak had shone through, but that had been weeks ago. She had not lost her composure again, though the tears from that conversation with Walt were, she suspected, still wandering aimlessly through the various modules of the space station.

She had known from the first that she could not allow herself any extended feelings of self-pity or resentment. Brian himself, surprisingly, had made this point to her, during one of the private calls over the IP phone in her first few days aboard. Self-pity and resentment, of course, had been the emotional hallmarks of his own tenure on *Mir*, just as they were the poisons he had brought to their marriage. After his robotic performance over the open loop from the control room—"We're all rooting for you down here"—when she was so desperate for an intimate and strengthening voice, she had more or less vowed just to let that affectless, unloving tone be the rule from now on. She was tired of hoping for something more.

But in their first conversation over the IP phone, he had apologized, with the directness and sincerity he could sometimes summon. "I didn't mean to sound that way, so wooden or whatever. All these people were staring at me in Mission Control, I felt like I was onstage."

And in the private conversations they managed to have every other day or so, he made a point of not sounding that way. She had always liked him best, always respected him the most, on the rare occasions when he had let her into his thoughts and allowed her to imagine that they shared not just a marriage but a career. When Brian was not feeling useless, he could be generous. And now he had a store of authentic experience of his own to share with her, experience that no longer had to be just a sour memory but could be put to use in her behalf.

"I've had a lot of time to think about it, and I know exactly what I did wrong on *Mir*," he told her. "I know exactly how I did my part in turning that mission into a failure. It was because I started to feel sorry for myself. And I'd been *trained*. I was *supposed* to be there, not like you. But none of that mattered. I wanted to feel sorry for myself because everything wasn't going right at every minute, and so that's what I did.

"Are you still there?" he said, after her surprised pause.

"I'm still here."

"So I guess what I'm saying is don't let it eat at you that you're there. Just accept it. The kids are going to be fine. You don't have to worry about them. All you have to do is focus on getting along with Konstantin and Glen and keeping yourself busy."

Even though this was fairly obvious to her, it buoyed Lucy's spirits to hear him say it, speaking to her for once as if she were not an emotionally demanding partner but a colleague truly in need of his counsel. He kept up this tone in the twice-daily e-mails he sent her after the techs on the ground managed to set up an address for her.

"The worst thing you can do," he wrote in one of his first e-mails, "the very worst thing, is to think about how long you're going to be up there. The time will pass. It will. But you have to let it pass at its own rate. You just have to settle in and let the current carry you."

"Think about the day in front of you," he wrote a few days later. "Don't think about anything but that. How am I going to keep busy? What can I accomplish today? When you don't have anything specific you need to do, wear yourself out on the bike or treadmill. You need the exercise not just to slow the loss of bone mass but to help get you to sleep at night. You have to sleep, Lucy. Your morale depends on it. If you can't sleep, though, don't worry about it. *Do something* instead. Look out the window and study the earth. Learn every river system, every mountain range, track the storms building over the oceans. You've got to keep your mind occupied. You've got to keep it obsessed, not with worrying what's going on with us but with specific, productive goals."

He had advice as well for dealing with her crewmates. "This is where I really screwed up," he wrote. "I wouldn't let myself be part of the team. I was the odd man out from the beginning, and I just decided that if that was the role I'd been handed that was the role I was going to play. Big mistake. You've got to love these guys, Lucy. I'm sure Konstantin's got all sorts of Russian mannerisms and attitudes that are going to drive you up the wall, and Glen's probably not going to get all that more interesting the longer you know him, but you've got to think of them both as your best friends in the world. You've got to respect them. They might be a little cool to you at first. That's natural. Konstantin in particular is probably going to feel superior to you. That's okay, let him. Don't judge him. Just do everything you can to keep busy and make yourself part of the team."

Walt wrote her too, of course, but e-mail was not secure enough for either of them to write in a way that wasn't fundamentally guarded and evasive. Shortly after she was stranded on the station, the weather in Houston took on a monsoonal cast, with one stationary downpour after another. Because of the danger of lightning strikes, the router was often shut down, making the IP phone inaccessible for much of the day. The times when the phone was available, when neither Konstantin nor Glen was hovering about, were scarcer and scarcer. Sometimes, late at night, she still managed to get through to Walt, but she was beginning to understand she could no longer count on hearing his voice.

In these few weeks she had made herself at home as much as she could. Konstantin had assigned her to Vassily's vacant sleep station in the Service Module. It was a closet-shaped indentation next to the toilet. There was no door, but she was used to the camping-out feel of the shuttle, and anyway this tiny dark alcove felt private to her. Konstantin slept in a similar stall just across the aisle of the Service Module, and Glen far down at the other end of the station in the Lab. The walls of Lucy's sleeping station were still covered with photos of Vassily and his wife and teenage sons in the familiar environs of Star City, or on family trips throughout other parts of the world. Lucy gathered, from the pictures, that the whole family shared some sort of fascination with ancient civilizations, because here they were in the Forum in Rome, or at Stonehenge on a drizzly day, or climbing up ladders to the cliff dwellings of Mesa Verde. Before she fell asleep at night these photos sometimes melded into a vivid, hypnagogic travelogue, an Indiana Jones movie in which Vassily and his family intrepidly roamed the earth, searching for some secret, crucial artifact. The action was enhanced by the radiation flashes that continued to bombard Lucy's sleep, and by Konstantin's bombastic snoring across the aisle.

Her first days on the station had been frantic. She had needed emergency training in how to get in and out of the Soyuz and use its comm panel in the event they had to evacuate. She had to make sure she would be able to squeeze herself into Vassily's form-fitted seat liner and be able to wear his Russian-made space suit. Then Konstantin had had to undock the Soyuz and do a tense fly-around to determine that the station itself had not been damaged by the space debris that had crippled *Endeavour.* It was only after these urgent survival matters had been settled that Lucy had remembered that among the supplies *Endeavour* had brought to the station in the MPLM were clothes for future Expedition crews. She spent the better part of a working day tracking down with a bar-code reader which of the dozens of white storage bags held the clothes and then retrieving the bags themselves from the least accessible parts of the module. The racks and bags that had to be shifted around weighed nothing, but then neither did she, and the fact that she could bring no countervailing mass to bear made the effort oddly more strenuous than it would have been on earth. In the end, with sweat pouring into her eyes, she had located four or five changes of clothes that would fit her reasonably well, as well as a supply of sanitary napkins. What she could not find was a toothbrush, and so she had to make do with Vassily's and its worn-down bristles.

She had his running shoes as well. The shoes were far too big for her feet, but she needed them to work out on the bike and the treadmill, so she had filled in the gaps with foam she had scavenged from the lining of one of the station's toolboxes. For most of the mission day, however, she went barefoot. Because she habitually anchored herself in weightlessness by slipping her feet under the straps and footholds that were abundantly placed throughout the modules, she soon developed odd-looking calluses on the tops of her toes.

Food was a problem. It was plentiful enough, but each member of the station crew had selected his own menus, and Lucy inherited Vassily's store of jellied herring and reconstituted borscht. Glen took pity on her, offering to share his own American meals until they ran out and they would both have to fall back on the dreary Russian cuisine, but Lucy took the high road and refused, claiming she was indifferent to what she ate. It was a lie, but one for which Glen—judging by the look of relief on his face—was clearly grateful. She knew from Brian's e-mails and from her own survival instincts that she had to get along with both her crewmates, to win them over, and it would not be a good idea to start off by demanding a portion of Glen's precious store of palatable food. In two months a Russian Progress vehicle, an unmanned resupply craft, was scheduled to be launched, and Lucy was assured she could choose the menus she wanted loaded aboard. In the meantime, there were enough snacks on board—pretzels and tortillas and M&M's—to subsist on when Vassily's food packs looked particularly unappetizing. And there was, blessedly, an abundance of salsa. In space, where everything tasted muted and monotonous to her, she found that spicy condiments were a real hedge against depression.

Full fellowship with her crewmates would be slow in coming. She had understood that fact the moment they had opened the hatch after she was stranded in the air lock. Konstantin and Glen were courteous and welcoming, but they were still in shock from the sudden loss of Vassily, with whom they had trained so long and shared so much. And in terms of the actual functioning of the station and the experiments, she was simply in the way. The systems and protocols on the station were much different than they were on the shuttle, and Konstantin and Glen, who had to take over Vassily's duties just to keep the craft running, had no time to train her.

At first Konstantin avoided the topic of how she might help. "No, no," he said with a note of chivalrous dismissal as they ate their dinners together in the Service Module. "Please. You are guest in our home."

The more she insisted she be given something to do and shown how to do it, the less hospitable he seemed. His natural presence was grave and solitary. He was happiest, Lucy noticed, when the day was just beginning, after he had read the Execute Package and talked with

Ground during the Daily Planning Conference. He liked to know what was in store, what had been completed, and what there was still to do. A crisis would not faze him, Lucy guessed. He had the experience and the methodical cast of mind to be confident that there was a solution for every contingency. He was happy when Lucy discovered the extra supply of mission clothes, encouraging when she figured out how to adapt Vassily's oversized shoes to her feet. He wanted her to feel comfortable. But he seemed to think the problem of her presence on the station had already been solved, and he was not pleased to be reminded that it hadn't.

In the end, when he finally capitulated to her badgering, he gave her the most menial jobs on the station: wiping down the hatch seals and handrails, changing out the filters, vacuuming the lint and debris and wandering food particles from the ventilation ducts. They were the sort of tasks an untrained crew member should have been given, and she was happy to do them. Even replacing the filter and waste bags on the toilet, the foulest job of all, made her feel purposeful and helped keep her mind away from darkly contemplating the endless months ahead.

She had thought that life on the station would be claustrophobic, but to her surprise it was not. She grew more proficient at weightlessness every day, and sometimes when there were idle moments she would time herself as she flew from one end of the station to the other, from the Russian Service Module all the way to the U.S. Destiny Lab. With a good push-off, she could make it all the way, adjusting her trim as she went. There was no wasted space in the station, no ceiling above her head she could not reach. In weightlessness, everything was accessible, and she was intrigued by the way the cramped modules seemed to open up to her and expand as she flew through them.

It was not her closed-in vessel that she found threatening, but the black infinity surrounding it, and the unreachable earth below, and the immensity of time through which she would have to pass to see her children again. Three months, four months, she didn't really know. At any rate, a multitude of days that it would be foolish to try to count down. Brian had told her, and she knew it to be true, that she could drive herself insane that way.

She had to give Brian credit. In her first days on the station, when she was still overwhelmed and disoriented, he had taken the initiative to gather up the family photograph albums and take them over to the psych support guys to have them scanned and uploaded to her. The computer at Vassily's vacant workstation had become hers, and before she went into her hutch at night to sleep she slipped her feet into the foot restraints and hovered there before the laptop screen, e-mailing the kids and then staring at the photos with such brokenhearted concentration that she sometimes felt as if she were already dead and sorting through the memories of a life she had realized too late had been blessed and happy, and to which she could never return.

She stared at the faces of her children and, as Brian instructed, at the face of the earth. She devoted herself to her maintenance jobs and helped out wherever she could as Konstantin and Glen tended the experiments on board. For hours every day, she worked out on the treadmill and the bike to keep her bone mass as constant as possible and to purge her mind of restless thought. She ate her Russian food without complaint. She listened to Konstantin's stories of growing up in a three-room flat in St. Petersburg where two families lived along with a harsh old woman who was a dentist and kept an office during the day in a closet no bigger than Lucy's sleeping station; how during the White Nights, after all the angry screaming in the flat had finally subsided along with the dentist's drill, he would sit at the window and read stories of Soviet space heroes by the light of the unsetting sun until two in the morning. She listened to Glen reminisce about his submarine days ranging beneath the arctic ice for six months at a time, and endured his cheesy harmonica playing and his good humor. In the Unity Node next to the Lab, where the perpetual noise of whirring fans and cycling pumps was the least detectable, she watched movies on DVD with her crewmates—*Forrest Gump* and *Mission: Impossible* and *Ocean's Eleven*.

In this way the moments struggled by, and two weeks passed, and then three, and Lucy began to prepare herself for the call telling Davis she would not be able to make it home for his birthday. She had been planning his birthday party anyway, sending Brian e-mail bulletins that, just to make sure, she copied to both Colleen and Zokie. She told him the names of the kids to invite, how to find their addresses, what time to book the party at Laser Tag, which bakery made the yellow cake with chocolate frosting that Davis liked.

"You can't go wrong with action figures," she wrote to Brian. "He can disappear for hours playing with them. I'd rather he played with something like that than video games—they're more solid and they seem more like a birthday present somehow. I've heard him talk about something called the Justice League of America. Maybe you could send Colleen or Zokie to Toys R Us to see if they could find some sort of Batmobile or rocket ship or something and then get the action figures for it and wrap them up separately. Maybe one video game wouldn't hurt, as long as it's fairly innocuous and not some sort of street crime fantasy. And there's that candy place in the mall where you can get gummy spiders—his favorite. And don't forget to take Bethie to get a token something for him as well. It's important for her that she feels she's participating in her brother's birthday."

When it came time to tell Davis she could not be there, she simply did the best she could. When she called, Colleen answered the phone, for which she was grateful. Lucy's mother and Suzanne had long since had to go home, but it was good to know that there was a female presence in the house, someone with an instinctive understanding of how to comfort a disappointed and frightened little boy. Davis took the news stoically enough. The fact that his mother would not be home for his birthday was more a suspicion confirmed than a cruel surprise.

"Honey, I'm so sorry." As the words came out of her mouth, they sounded aggressively inadequate, as if they were meant to wound as much as soothe. "If there was any way for me to be there, you know I would. Being there for your birthday means more to me than anything."

"It's not more important than being in space," he said quietly. His aim was precise. If he had not been rehearsing this very line, he had clearly been brooding on some similarly effective way to hurt her back.

She refuted what he had said as calmly as she could, knowing that a protesting outburst on her part would only spotlight her own guilt and the truth of the charge. And of course the charge *was* true, or at least partly so. She knew that, and had always known it. She had always known that someday there would be a price to pay for wanting two plainly contradictory lives, and wanting them with equal fervor.

There was no remedy, not now. All she could do to calm herself after the phone call ended was to go about her tasks methodically, wiping down more hatch seals and performing routine maintenance on the exercise equipment. And then when the mission day was over and she had eaten dinner with Konstantin and Glen and, in the interest of vital fellowship, patiently watched another movie with them, she set herself to the task of composing the most loving birthday e-mail to her son that her maternal imagination could produce. And then, numb, she went to bed.

"Good night, Lucy," Konstantin said from across the module as she floated into her sleep station. She was pretty sure it was the first time he had used her name. Over the last week or so she had become aware that his carefully suppressed resentment of her for being an intruder and a woman had been replaced by a lingering interest. She noticed him watching her, heard the flirtatious gravity in his voice when he spoke to her, and saw in his eyes a weary longing that he would never, of course, actually express. With his heavy face and brutal crew cut, he was not attractive, or at least she had thought he was not; but his voice, in the soft register he sometimes used, had a gravelly allure.

It had not been an advance, just a simple good-night, the one truly human moment the commander of the station had allowed himself since she had come on board. And it was a silly thing for her to have noticed, much less to have dwelled on, except for the fact that it briefly liberated her mind from worry and guilt over her children and led it back to Walt. As she hung in her sleep restraint an hour later, Konstantin's obnoxious snoring obliterated any dawning interest she might have felt for him as a man. But certain sensations had been stirred up just the same, and she wanted Walt. Despite the backaches and fluid shifts, despite the calluses on the tops of her toes and the radiation flashes behind her eyes, weightlessness carried a sensual charge. It was hard to know where it came from, exactly. It was not like being underwater, where a similar freedom of movement was accompanied by the constant awareness of resistant water against your skin. In microgravity, you were caressed by nothing, by nothingness. The *absence* of sensation, once you got used to it, was unnerving. But there was always a lurking possibility of borderless abandon, of a thrilling trespass against the physical rules of human existence.

She and Walt had had only two nights of lovemaking, interludes ruled not just by earthly gravity but by a weight of regret for the damage they were doing. Lucy tried to fall asleep by imagining that that weight had been suddenly lifted, and that they were here in the station together. Instead of the brooding Konstantin and the ever-chipper Glen, she was with Walt. With him, she was floating free of gravity and guilt. With the only man on earth who loved and understood her no longer *on earth*, but with her on orbit, the span of time she faced was no longer unendurable.

With this fantasy in her head, she could not sleep. She unstrapped herself from the restraints and drifted free of her sleep station, pushing off with the heel of her hand until she was out in the corridor of the Service Module. Then she propelled herself aft, toward the Node where the IP phone was located. The lights in the station were dimmed, but the earth's light as the sun rose and fired the solar arrays shone from the nadir window like a spotlight. The sound of Konstantin's snoring grew distant as she traveled toward the Node, and the low-grade industrious thrumming from the Destiny Lab grew in volume. She imagined herself naked in weightlessness, expert and graceful, flying toward Walt.

She needed to talk to him right now, this moment. It would be intolerable if she could not. But when she got to the IP phone she saw the green arrows were not lit. For whatever reason—the weather on earth, the altitude of the station relative to the orbital plane—the KU band that powered the phone was temporarily down. She slipped her foot into a nearby restraint and hovered there in her fetal curl, trying to relieve the pain in her back as she stared at the green arrows, until finally they came on and she typed in his number. He answered on the first ring, and said, "Lucy?" but there was still something wrong with the downlink, and when she spoke he could not hear her. He said her name again and again—"Lucy? Lucy, are you there?" But not a word that she said got through to him in return. There was no point in trying, but she stayed on the line anyway until the comm pass was over, and then she flew back to her station to stare at the pictures of Vassily and his family until she finally fell asleep.

Chapter Thirty-five

November.

Lucy and Glen were working to repair the carbon dioxide removal assembly in the Destiny Lab. The system had been on the blink for weeks, and various software patches had not worked, so the only thing to do was to tear apart the whole assembly and replace the sorbent bed where the faulty valve was located.

It had taken them four hours just to get the bed out of the rack, and before dealing with the intricacies of replacing it—all those hoses to be set precisely in place—they took a break for lunch. The crew still had dinner together at the end of every day. It was crucial for morale and cohesion that they all sit down together—to the degree that one could "sit" in weightlessness—for a meal. But lunch was a different matter. It was a welcome solitary time, during which Lucy could drift away quite literally from Glen's incessant chatter and Konstantin's silent, glowering concentration.

And since an unmanned Russian Progress vessel had rendezvoused on schedule with the station two weeks ago, delivering Lucy a new menu of more-or-less palatable meals to replace Vassily's dreadful left-overs, lunch was something she could at last look forward to. The fresh fruits and vegetables that had come in the Progress had all been eaten within the first few days, as had the pecan pie that had somehow miraculously made the journey, but she was still hoarding cans of spicy black beans and black-eyed peas, and the chocolate pudding for which she had developed a frightening craving.

Glen flew into his sleeping station to put on his earphones and listen to music while he ate. Konstantin was at the other end of the Lab monitoring one of the experiments. Lucy stationed herself at the window and carefully opened a tiny pouch of salsa, aware that an unintended squeeze would turn the contents into a propulsive missile that would be impossible to track down and recover. She layered the salsa over black beans on a flour tortilla, then folded the far end of the tortilla closed to keep the beans inside when she took a bite.

It was night on earth. She had done as Brian had suggested and schooled herself in the features of the planet, so that she was able to recognize at a glance what city she was looking at by the pattern of its sprawling lights, which mountains she was passing over by the way the clouds piled up against the peaks. Now, as she ate her lunch, she gazed down at southern Spain, the glow of the coastal cities forming a vulnerable dam of light against the cresting blackness of the sea. From this altitude, massive lightning storms along the French coast, where no doubt smoldering tree limbs were dropping onto the roofs of houses and dogs were howling in fright, seemed as gentle and silent as fireflies. And further east, as the clouds thinned away, she followed the reflection of the moon as it traveled unendingly across the surface of the Mediterranean.

The view was as intoxicating as ever. If you didn't fall into an enchanted spell when you saw the earth in this way, she reasoned, you would have no soul at all. The beauty of it, the satisfaction in contemplating it, simply did not wear off. But it was a more distant beauty now. She was starting to lose the ability to equate the splendid panorama below her with home. So much of the earth was visible—cities, highways, towering thunderheads, drifting smoke from crop fires—but so much more was not. Even though her perspective was lordly, it was one-dimensional, just a broad, never-ending sweep. If the earth, as she sometimes imagined it to be, was a great carpet, her children were hidden so deep in the fabric there was no microscope powerful enough to allow her to see them. Her life with them—her true, tactile life, not this wrenching flurry of e-mail messages and interrupted phone calls—was becoming an abstraction. It was November for them, a week past Halloween. From her command post in the sky, she had consulted with Davis and Bethie on their costumes and seen photos of them wearing them, but even as she stared at the images the two children pictured there began to seem vaporous and unfamiliar. Davis and Bethie were living in a tangible November now, the wind sharper, the water of Clear Lake steelier, the temperature dropping, even if not by much. Their world was changing. They were revolving within it instead of revolving constantly around it.

The earth was unapproachable to Lucy, not just physically but increasingly in an imaginative way. Her reality was slowly accommodating itself to the seasonless void in which she was trapped, where people flew instead of walked, and where the sun rose and set on such a hurried schedule that the concept of day and night was something she had to actively remind herself to remember.

She did not want to admit that Walt was receding from her memory in that way as well, but perhaps it was true. The beautiful earthly moment in which they had found each other, and to which she had been unable to return, could not stay in suspension forever. Their private phone calls had been dismayingly infrequent. Lucy's priority for the IP phone had to be her children, and when the green arrows were lit and there might be an opportunity to get through to Walt it seemed that either Konstantin or Glen was always in the Lab or in the adjacent Node, easily within earshot of a conversation she did not want overheard. E-mail was far more reliable, and they wrote each other at least once a day. But these exchanges were maddeningly cautious. Knowing that the messages could be accidentally routed or eternally archived in some NASA file, Walt couldn't declare, as he had in his last phone message, that he passed most nights in a fitful half-sleep, tormented by short-lived dreams that she had returned to him. What passed between them now was mostly news. Walt was training a new mission, scheduled to launch six months after the accelerated mission that would be taking off just before Christmas to bring Lucy home. He kept her up on what was going on with the team: Sylvia's new boyfriend, an auditor at the same Big Four accounting firm where her brother worked; the powder burns Gary had received during a reenactment of the Battle of Palo Alto; Kyle's abrupt decision to join one of those suburban churches that catered to young professionals; Mickey's continuing clean bill of health after his latest six-month cancer checkup.

She was glad for this information. Along with Buddy and Surly and all the others who were sending e-mails, Walt was assuring her that her friends back home missed her, needed her, felt it was important to keep her in the gossip loop. But what she needed from Walt was something more, the reassurance that everything that had taken place between them was still alive and not just some dreamy vestige of a past that was being buried under an alien flurry of sunrises and sunsets. What if the wild, warm hope she had allowed herself to feel with Walt no longer existed?

Night was ending on earth as she finished her lunch. She watched another sunrise, another of the meaningless forty-five-minute days that threatened to erase the memory of her own human clock, and then she and Glen resumed work on the sorbent bed. They were puzzling out how to configure the thermal loop hose when they heard the intercom.

"Alpha, Houston," the CapCom said. "For Lucy."

Elise Trube was the CapCom today. Her voice was usually vibrant, but just now its pitch was flat in a way that made Lucy go rigid.

"Go ahead," Glen said when she glanced at him over the mass of hoses they were working on together. "I've got this covered."

She pushed off the deck of the Lab and soared over to grab the handheld mike. She keyed in and said, "Go ahead, Houston."

"Uh, Lucy," Elise said, "we need to set up a PFC with you. We'd like to do it on the next comm pass."

A dreadful calm seized hold of her. A PFC was a Personal Family Conference. Something was wrong.

"Roger, Houston," she said. She marveled at how steady her voice was. "I'll be waiting to hear from you."

"Shouldn't be long," Elise said, a hint of reassuring warmth in her voice now.

The next comm pass would not be for at least another ten minutes. She had to pass the time somehow, so she went back to work with Glen on the carbon dioxide assembly.

"Everything okay?" he asked, looking at her face, which she realized must be pale and slack.

"PFC."

"Probably nothing."

"I know," she said. But as she continued to work with him to route the hoses she helplessly began to run through the checklist of personal calamities she had been carrying in her head ever since the launch. *Stop it!* she commanded herself. Don't think about any of that. It won't do any good.

She clung to the pathetic possibility that Brian, in one of his hallmark moments of insensitivity, had requested a PFC for some non-emergency reason. Maybe Bethie had an ear infection, or Davis needed a medical form signed before he could go on a class trip, and Brian hadn't thought through how deeply he would unnerve her.

But weighing against that hope was the fact that Brian, since that night on the beach when he had given her his wedding ring, had been more considerate and aware than she was accustomed to. And in the long, stagnant crisis that had begun with her disastrous EVA, he had been not just helpful and uncomplaining but close to consoling. He had lived through long-duration spaceflight himself, if with ill grace at times then at least with a store of practical understanding, and these last few months had been almost the only time in their marriage when she had thought they really did have something to share.

After fifteen appalling minutes she was called to the mike again. When she was patched through to Brian on his cell phone, his voice, the moment he said her name, sounded strained and frightened.

"What's going on, Brian?" she said, keeping her own voice calm out of habit, out of protocol, but the mike was trembling in her floating hand.

". . . three treatments, but his peak wouldn't come up . . . school nurse started to get . . ."

"Brian, I can't hear you! You're breaking up!"

". . . called the EMS . . . still having a lot of trouble when I got here. They want to do a—"

Brian's voice disappeared with savage abruptness. She called down on the air-to-ground loop to talk to Elise.

"I just had a sharp cutoff," she said.

"Roger. We've got some atmospherical issues that are interfering with the KU band. Maybe on the next comm pass we can get a better connection."

Lucy knew she had to summon all her self-possession. Something had happened to Davis at school, his breathing had apparently crashed. If she weren't strong right now—if she weren't *nominal*—she would begin whimpering in panic.

"Houston," she said, as slowly and carefully and firmly as she could, so that anyone listening on the open loop would not think to suspect that she was at the door of helpless terror, "I want to request a PMC *as soon as possible.*"

She was on a crisis footing here, she needed Ground to understand that, and a request for a Private Medical Conference was the clearest signal she could send. Elise heard her; she asked Lucy to hold on for a minute. Lucy hovered there, afraid to take a breath, looking down at the daylight earth revolving through the window, until Elise's voice came back.

"Okay, go for PMC on Space to Ground Two."

Then the flight surgeon came on, speaking over an open loop that had been encrypted so that the whole listening world could not hear their conversation.

"What's up, Lucy?" he said.

"There's something wrong with my son down there. I can't get through to my husband."

"All right. Tell me how to help."

"I want you to find Walt Womack," Lucy said.

Chapter Thirty-six

Walt had just finished a four-hour sim with the crew of the new mission he was training. The exhausted crew and team were starting to filter into the conference room for the debrief when Lance Briscoe called him on his cell phone.

"How soon can you get over here?"

"What's up?"

"Something's going on with Lucy. She needs to talk to you."

He handed Sylvia his notes and told her to start the meeting, then left the room as calmly as he could and did not start sprinting until he was out of the building. In five minutes he was in a small conference room on the third floor of Building 30 South, his headset plugged into a control pad on the table. A tech came on the line and told him he should have comm in about a minute and a half, and Walt sat there and stared at the control pad, now and then glancing up through the window at the blank hallway outside, where Lance and the flight surgeon, a young Pakistani doctor named Qamal, stood gravely conversing with their hands in their pockets.

When the tech told him they were coming up to the comm pass, Walt keyed in and said, "*Alpha,* Houston. For Lucy."

"Walt?" came the plaintive voice from space.

"It's me," he said, not bothering to disguise the feeling in his tone. This was a Private Medical Conference and the loop was encrypted. They were only speaking to each other. "What's wrong, Lucy?"

"Something's happened to Davis. I'm pretty sure he's in the emergency room at St. John's. I can't get a connection with Brian. I don't know what's going on, Walt. I don't know if—"

"All right. I'm on my way over there right now. I'll get back here as soon as I can and tell you what I find out."

"It sounded serious, Walt."

"I'm going to get back to you, Lucy," he said. "I'm going to tell you exactly what's going on, okay?"

Her voice dropped into a whisper. "I'm scared."

"I know you are," he said. "But I'm going to help you. It's going to be okay. Now I'm going to put you on with Qamal. You need to tell him to authorize another PMC when I get back."

"Thank you," she said, still whispering.

Walt knocked on the window to get the flight surgeon's attention so he could put him on the loop with Lucy. Then he ran back to the parking lot in front of Building 5 and got into his car and drove to the hospital, which was less than a mile away, on the other side of NASA Road One.

This emergency room would always be familiar to Walt. It was where Rachel had been pronounced dead, where he had seen her body after the ER doctors and nurses had withdrawn and the tumult to save her had subsided. It was where the members of his team had come to stand numbly beside him as he dialed the number of Rachel's parents on his cell phone and tried his best to speak to them and make them understand, in a way he himself could not, what had just happened.

The nurse at the reception desk took him at his word when he said he was there at the urgent request of Davis Kincheloe's mother, and gestured to a door leading to the treatment area. Half a dozen curtained cubicles radiated out from a central nurses' station, but at this calm midday hour only one of the cubicles was occupied. In it, Brian and several nurses were holding Davis down as a young ER doctor struggled to insert a plastic tube in his throat. The boy was pleading to be left alone in a fluttering, wheezing voice that had no strength at all. His fingertips were blue. He called out weakly for his mother as Brian told him, "It's all right, Davis. It's going to be all right, son. I promise."

Brian's voice was breaking as he said this, and Davis didn't believe him. As the tube went in he thrashed about wildly, causing the doctor to curse and remove it and then try again, all the while the boy crying for his mother to deliver him with that painful wheeze that reminded Walt of the air being squeezed out of an air mattress. Finally the tube was in and he lay there wide-eyed, in captive calm. Walt stood uncertainly at the entrance to the cubicle. No one had noticed him. He watched Brian wipe the sweat from his son's forehead and bend down to kiss him.

Finally the doctor, almost as stressed as his patient, turned to speak to one of the nurses and saw Walt.

"Yes?" he said. "Can we help you?"

Walt said nothing to the doctor but met Brian's eyes as he turned to the sound of the doctor's voice. There was a fatherly anguish in his expression that startled Walt with its intensity. Tears of helplessness were making his eyes glisten.

"Walt? What are you doing here?"

"I just need to talk to you a minute."

The boy was still now and he didn't want to confuse or excite him by mentioning his mother in his hearing.

"Now?" Brian asked.

"As soon as you feel you can get to it."

Brian met him out in the lobby a few minutes later, looking more composed, the color back in his face, along with his normal expression of suspicious alertness.

"Lucy asked me to come over," Walt said, before Brian could ask what he was doing there again. "She's going crazy up there not knowing anything."

"What? She called you?"

"She set up a PMC when your call cut off. Is he okay, Brian?"

"I think so." Brian walked over to a complimentary coffeepot and poured the last inch of stale coffee into a Styrofoam cup. "At least that goddamn tube is in. Jesus, that was hard, to watch your son go through that."

Walt grabbed an insurance form off the top of the reception desk and turned it over to the blank side and took his ballpoint pen out of his pocket.

"What are you doing now?" Brian said.

"She wants all the details."

Brian took a sip of the repellent-looking coffee and said "Fuck" and threw it in the trash.

"She's not going to like hearing about the tube," he said. "We've never had to do that before."

Lucy heard Walt say the word "intubation" when, after an agonizing hour, he was able to get back to her on the loop. The word caused a frightened spasm in her chest, as if she had just received a dull electrical shock. She flexed her feet, tightening her hold in the foot restraints. She felt the need to dig in and hold on. Even though she was already as weightless as she could be, some nightmarish force seemed to be pulling at her, pulling her away from her moorings so she would be helpless to act.

"Oh God," she said. She didn't say anything for a moment as she tried to deal with the image of her little boy lying on a hospital bed with a tube down his throat. She had seen a kid being intubated before on one of Davis's previous visits to the emergency room, had prayed that her son's condition would never reach such a desperate level. But now it had, and she had not been with him.

"Lucy?" Walt said.

She keyed the mike. "I'm here."

"Brian wanted you to know that Dr. Trimble was on his way to the emergency room. I thought about waiting until he got there to get back to you, but I knew you'd be going crazy. In the meantime they're admitting him to the hospital. They've got him on some kind of IV—hold on, let me check my notes."

"Prednisone," Lucy said.

"Right. Prednisone."

"They're also doing some blood work and a chest X-ray."

"A chest X-ray? Do they think he has pneumonia?"

"My impression is they're kind of concerned about that. Listen, as soon as he's stable, Brian can come over here and get on the loop and explain all this better than I can."

"What are you saying? He's not *stable*?"

"He's getting there, Lucy. He's going to be all right. Are you listening to me?"

"Yes," she said. She looked around the module. Konstantin was still at the forward end, tracking the progress of some soybean plants that were being grown in weightlessness. The plants had leafed out, and even in her intolerable concern about Davis Lucy could not help regarding this tiny grid of greenery with the predatory eyes of someone starved for vegetables. Glen, meanwhile, was still wrestling with the hoses in the sorbent bed. Neither of them was looking in her direction, neither of them could hear Walt's end of the conversation, but it was plain from their studied concentration on their tasks that they were monitoring what Lucy was saying in response and the emotion visible in her face. In their place, she would have been doing the same. She had learned months ago that, in this confined space, moods were unwelcome, even threatening. You had to keep your fears and grievous homesickness to yourself. In order to be considerate to your crewmates, you had to be courageous.

"I'm going to stay on top of this," Walt was saying through her headset. His voice was strong and even and she could feel it working on her, helping to push back the panic that kept threatening to rise. "I'm thinking about you every minute, I'm thinking about what you need. I've got a call in to this Dr. Trimble. As soon as he looks in on Davis we're going to try to get him in here for a PMC with you. Then maybe we can set up a video conference from Davis's hospital room."

"Oh, yes, please," she said. "Please. I need to see him. I need to talk to him."

She rubbed her eyes, releasing a scatter of tiny tear bubbles.

"You okay?" he asked.

"I think so," she said. "I'm trying to be. By the way, just for the record, you're doing everything right."

"I'm not going to let you down, Lucy."

"I love you," she said. It didn't matter to her at the moment if Glen or Konstantin overheard.

What Walt said in reply she didn't hear, because it was drowned out by a loud bleating alarm. Lucy saw Konstantin look up from his soybeans, his lugubrious slumbering features suddenly keen and alert. He and Glen exchanged the briefest of alarmed looks and then flew off to opposite ends of the module. Lucy could feel her ears popping, and she was aware of a faint whistling sound.

"What is it?" Walt was saying into her headset. "Is that an alarm?"

"I've got to go, Walt," she said. "Don't let anything happen to my children."

She pulled off the headset before he could answer and turned around in time to see Glen floating back to her with a PBA, a portable breathing apparatus.

"Hang on to this in case you need it," he said.

The alarm kept sounding. All the contingency alarms had different tones, and it took her a second to clear her head and run through them in her mind. This one, she realized, was the Depress Alarm. Air was leaking out of the station.

"Leak confirmed," Konstantin said from his workstation, where he was staring at a laptop screen. "Glen, bring the Red Book. Everybody up to Soyuz. Lucy, you first!"

She took off without a word, glad for the idle time she had spent in learning how to propel herself through the adjoining modules of the station. One push-off took her from the Lab through the Node to the Functional Service Block to which the Soyuz was moored. Glen was behind her, carrying a big red binder in addition to his PBA, and behind him was Kosntantin, clumsily bringing along the breathing apparatus and a big portable pressure gauge called a Mano-vacuumeter.

The Soyuz was their lifeboat out of the station. The first order of business was to make sure the leak was not coming from there, so all three of them pushed their way down into the tight space of the capsule and Glen closed the hatch. They all stared nervously at the dial of the gauge. The M-Vac was a curiously antiquarian-looking device, more like some quaint gadget from a Jules Verne novel than a twenty-first-century space instrument. They saw that the needle, which had been spooling down, was now up into the safe zone.

Lucy had been in the Soyuz only once before. She did not like it. It was a grim piece of Soviet-era engineering about the size and shape of a cramped diving bell. The three of them floated around inside it clumsily, like fish trapped in a weir. She could smell her crewmates' long-unshowered bodies and see the sweat beading up on Konstantin's spacious upper lip as he continued to stare at the M-Vac.

"Soyuz is okay," he said. "Leak is somewhere else. We'll have to work our way down the stack till we find it."

Lucy nodded, oddly winded. The hurried flight to the Soyuz from the Lab had required almost no physical exertion, just a few strategic push-offs, but she felt as if she had run a 10K race. Konstantin and Greg had their problem-solving faces on as they looked at the gauge and paged through the Red Book, so it was impossible to tell from their expressions whether the situation was as serious as she feared. Nor could she ask. Her job was to stay out of their way and do what Konstantin told her to do. At least, she thought, if worse came to worst, the Soyuz was not leaking. They could ride this unforgiving craft back down to earth, they could be there in an hour's time, back down to the planet where her child lay on a hospital bed with a tube down his throat as the doctors struggled to restore his breath.

They left the Soyuz and began the process of sealing off each module of the station in sequence and testing the air for leaks. Glen's calculations from the Time Reserve table in the red binder told them they had two hours and forty-five minutes before the pressure in the station reached the level at which they would have to abandon it. Konstantin was methodical and imperturbable. He calmly directed Lucy to disconnect the cables and vent ducts running between the modules so that the hatches could be closed. After twenty minutes they had tested the entire Russian segment of the station: the Soyuz, the Service Module, the Vestibule, and Cargo Block. That meant the leak had to be in the American-built part of the station, in either the Node or the Lab.

They sealed off the Node and floated inside while Konstantin checked the M-Vac again.

"Normal," he said. He turned to Glen, who was still holding the red binder. "What does T-Res say?"

"Two hours twenty-five minutes."

"Okay," Konstantin said. "Leak is in Lab. First we go in and pull out everything necessary to save. Medical kits, extra PBAs, fire extinguishers, computers. Then we find leak."

Lucy did her best to mimic Konstantin's deliberate pace as they ransacked the Lab, removing everything necessary for their survival in case the leak could not be located and fixed. She kept her breathing device close as she shuttled supplies and equipment from the Lab to the Russian storage block. She could still hear the faint sound of escaping air, but none of them had any idea where in the Lab it was coming from.

In twenty minutes, when all the critical gear had been relocated, they began the work of removing one by one the dozens of storage racks that obscured the Lab's hull. The leak, they all knew, had to be behind one of those racks, a puncture in the hull of the station so tiny they might not even be able to see it. Lucy unfastened the racks and pulled them away one by one as Konstantin and Glen scanned each new exposed section with stethoscope-like ultrasound detectors. The racks weighed nothing, of course, though on earth she might not have even been able to lift one on her own. In space, unfortunately, they still retained their unwieldy mass, and she was careful as she manipulated them. They still had crushing force, whether she could feel it or not.

The needle on Konstantin's gauge was steady. After half an hour they had worked their way through half of one side of the module and still had another two hours of good air pressure left. Lucy was starting to feel it was going to work out. They would find the leak, patch it, then take a break before they began the laborious process of moving all the equipment back into the Lab. By that time Walt might have a video conference set up with Davis. She felt that if her boy could only see her face, if he could *know* that she was looking down on him, watching over him, he would fight that much harder to breathe. But what if there was pneumonia? What if there was an infection that the doctors couldn't control?

Don't think about that. She almost said it aloud as she planted her bare feet in the nearest foot restraints and pulled back the next rack in the line. That was when the faint wheezing she had been hearing ever since the alarm went off suddenly sharpened and increased.

Then she saw it.

"Konstantin!" she yelled. She was staring not at a microscopic puncture but at a visible seam in the hull, three or four inches long. Still holding the rack, she maneuvered out of the way so Konstantin and Glen could see it.

"Oh, shit," Konstantin said.

"Is it getting bigger?" Lucy said. Maybe it was the play of light on the hull, but the crack seemed to be traveling, extending itself.

"It is!" Glen said. "It's propagating."

Konstantin shot a glance at the gauge of the M-Vac. Lucy followed his eyes. She saw the needle sinking downward.

"Get the fuck out!" Konstantin yelled. "Everybody! *Now*!"

Their two hours of grace had vanished in an instant as the crack extended, worrying and weakening the hull around it so that it grew even more, the precious air of the station rushing through it into empty space.

"Go! Go! Go!" Konstantin was screaming. He grabbed her by the arm and pulled her away as the accelerating pressure drop caused an agonizing squeeze in her ears. She had to let go of the rack she was holding. As she pushed herself off from the foot restraints, it tumbled wildly in midair and smashed her right hand against one of the lockers on the other side. The pain was breathtaking. In her angry instinct to heave the rack aside, she caused a reaction that sent her body spinning along a wild axis, going nowhere. It took a long time to stop herself, to figure out where she was and which way to go. She saw Konstantin and Glen at the forward end of the Lab, waiting for her with their hands on the hatch. Blood bubbles, rising from her torn skin, floated in front of her eyes. In the emergency, distracted by the surging pain in her hand, her imagination regressed. It yielded to memories of gravity, causing her to try to stroke through the empty space to the safety of the Node. It took only a moment of nightmarish flailing for her to wake up to the understanding that she would never get back to her children this way. She had to think clearly, to move with precise, directed force. She found a surface and pushed off with her feet, and sent herself spiraling like a rifle bullet toward the Node. As Konstantin and Glen pulled her through, she heard the hatch clang as the deadly falling pressure in the Lab sucked it closed.

Chapter Thirty-seven

The November sky over NASA Road One was already a searing blue at six-thirty in the morning as Walt sat in his car in the McDonald's parking lot, eating a sausage-and-egg biscuit. He stared groggily at the fading, almost transparent vestige of last night's full moon. It seemed to be in reach of the giant fiberglass astronaut that hovered at the front of the restaurant.

It had been thirty years since the last human being had set foot on the moon. In the space program in which he had spent his career, the Apollo landings were as distant and storied now as if they belonged to some old Norse saga instead of the national memory. Why had the moon been abandoned? It had, he supposed, been a dead end, a solitary stepping-stone on the bank of an infinitely wide river. Walt had never really bothered to question the space program and the overall wisdom of its objectives, and he was too weary—after a sleepless day and a half—to embark on reflections that should have begun twenty-five years ago. If his career, and his life, had been a waste, there was nothing much to do about it now.

Eating breakfast alone in his car in the parking lot of a fast-food restaurant, under the mocking shadow of an astronaut effigy holding out a bag of French fries to the moon: had he consciously stationed himself here just to showcase the futility he was feeling? Lucy was alive, but no thanks to him. In the end, the contingencies for which he had trained her had barely applied. His expertise had been irrelevant in the accident that had caused her to be stranded on the space station, and even more so in the frightful crisis of the last few days, when she and the crew had barely managed to save themselves by sealing off and effectively abandoning the entire U.S. section of the station. The three of them were squeezed now into the Russian Cargo Block and Service Module, their already meager living space halved. And Lucy was hurt, three fingers on her right hand broken, according to Qamal, the flight surgeon, who had walked Glen and Konstantin through the first-aid procedures over the space-to-ground loop. She had a deep gash in her hand as well, Qamal had told him, and the Vicodin she had taken for the pain had finally stirred up the case of space sickness she had been dodging for more than two months.

Walt had been camping out at Mission Control for a day and a half, scrounging information off whomever he could get to talk to him. Talking to Lucy herself was now all but impossible. The crew had managed to save the station, but in closing off and powering down the U.S. Lab they had lost the entire KU band system, which meant no files or procedures or even e-mail could be uploaded to the station. It also meant the loss for the duration of the mission of the precious IP phone. Now there was no way Walt could communicate directly with Lucy. To talk to him, she would have to publicly request a privatized conversation over the space-to-ground loop. Walt understood she could not do this. If she were to put in such a request, she would be broadcasting an intimacy that needed more than ever to remain secret. Any private conversations that would take place from now on rightfully would be only between her and her family.

A rescue mission was on the way—the training time line of the next scheduled mission had been accelerated—but it would still be at least two long months before a shuttle could be launched to repair the damage to the Lab and replace the shell-shocked Expedition crew with a new one.

He could wait out the time, but he was full of apprehension that some sort of vital ground between him and Lucy would be lost, and of course there was the deeper fear that she might never return at all, that the next emergency to arise on her star-crossed mission would be fatal.

"Don't let anything happen to my children." Those had been her last words to him when the Depress Alarm went off. Walt had clung to those words in the last few days, to the sense of ongoing trust and consequence they suggested. You would not say such a thing to someone you did not count on returning to, whose emotional importance in your life did not continue to loom large.

But it was a command he had neither the experience nor the authority to really act upon. All he had been able to do so far was to gather as much information on Davis's condition as he could and relay it through the flight surgeon to Lucy. There had been no pneumonia, no rampaging infection. The breathing tube had been taken out, and though he was still receiving steroids through an IV, his peak flow readings were improving and he was likely to be out of the hospital in another day.

Walt drank the last of his coffee and wadded up the biscuit wrapper and stuffed it inside the empty cup. He had not been home for thirty-six hours, and had not slept at all except for twenty minutes now and then on the floor of an empty conference room in Building 30. Breakfast had revived him a bit. He knew he needed to go to bed, but he continued to sit there in the parking lot, watching the morning traffic build on NASA Road One. He could not seem to get all this desperate, revving energy out of his system. His body would not discharge. He did not want it to. In some way he couldn't explain, relinquishing his vigilance meant relinquishing Lucy.

He turned on the ignition and eased out into the growing swarm of traffic, then instead of going home he turned off into the parking lot of the hospital. The television in the reception room was tuned to a cable news station, and the crawl below the anchorman's face read "Crew of Imperiled Space Station 'Camping Out' in Russian Module."

The gift shop in the lobby was just opening, and its toy selection was limited to the standard fare found in space souvenir shops all over Clear Lake, cheap models of the shuttle or video games or foil pouches of the freeze-dried "astronaut ice cream" that, as far as Walt knew, no astronaut had ever eaten. Walt went to the sparse book rack instead, and bought a couple of titles from what seemed to be a popular kid's mystery series, and then he threw in a package of Skittles in case Davis had already read them or had no interest in doing so.

Walt had not changed his clothes or shaved, so on the way up to Davis's room he stopped in the men's room to spruce up as best he could. He was not a complete stranger to Davis, but he was afraid he might startle the boy by walking into his room looking like a sleepless wreck. In any case, he was counting on Brian to be there. Walt would give Davis the books and candy he had brought, talk to Brian just long enough to reassure himself that all was well, and then find some way to pass those reassurances on to Lucy and then go home and go to bed.

The room to Davis's room was open a few inches. Walt rapped gently on it and pushed forward until he was standing tentatively inside. The blinds in the room were closed, the lights were still off, but he could make out Brian sleeping on the bed, one outstretched arm beneath Davis and another cradling his four-year-old daughter, who was lying asleep on his chest with her thumb in her mouth and a blanket remnant under her chin. An obscure twinge of conscience began to work on Walt as he intruded upon this peaceful-family tableau. He started to withdraw, but before he could get out the door Bethie opened her eyes and stared at him with placid curiosity and said, "Hi."

"Hi," Walt whispered back, paralyzed. What exactly was he doing here? He realized, in the cold moment of clearheadedness that had just now overtaken him, that he had taken Lucy's plea to watch over her children too much to heart and imagined himself in a role of heroic consolation for which he was not equipped. He had come here this morning believing himself to be not just her lover but the protector of her children, the grown man, the selfless comforting presence that Brian was not. But Brian was apparently handling that job on his own. Certainly his trusting children seemed to think he was.

Walt smiled at Bethie and backed out of the door, stunned by the sudden icy awareness that he was not a protector so much as a transgressor, that he had come to the hospital to reassure himself more than Lucy. If Davis was all right, if at least this crisis had passed, it would help free Lucy's mind. It would help keep alive the possibility that they could return to the reality that had existed before she launched into space.

"Walt?" Brian's puzzled voice called out to him just as he was making his escape. There was nothing to do now but creep back into the room, where Brian was inching up to a sitting position in the crowded bed.

"What are you doing here?" Brian said. "Is anything wrong?"

"No, nothing's wrong. I just dropped by on my way home to see how he was doing."

Walt kept the bag from the gift shop behind his back. He hadn't bought anything for Bethie, and he assumed she would be disappointed if her brother received a present and she didn't. The girl continued to contemplate Walt as she sucked her thumb. Davis remained sound asleep, the medicine in the IV tube trickling into his forearm.

"He's doing a lot better," Brian said.

"He's going home today," Bethie volunteered.

"Maybe, honey," Brian said.

The door to the room opened and a girl in a tank top brushed past Walt, smiling and saying, "Excuse me." She had short, spiky hair, and there was a complicated tattoo of some sort on her lower back.

"Zokie!" Bethie called. She leapt out of bed into the girl's arms and stood there patiently as Zokie got a brush out of her backpack and started smoothing out the tangles in Bethie's hair.

Davis opened his eyes and took in the activity in the room, along with Walt's mysterious presence, and then went back to sleep. Walt stood there helplessly, listening as Brian went over Bethie's school schedule with Zokie, and then swerved out of the way as the door opened yet again and a nurse came in to wake up Davis and monitor his breathing with a device Walt had learned was called a peak flow meter.

"I think I'll take off," Walt said.

"No, hold on a minute," Brian said. "Let me get Bethie off to school and I'll meet you down in the coffee shop."

Walt was reading the *Chronicle* when Brian came down. It was full of news about the accident, of course, along with profiles of Lucy and her two crewmates, and a hometown editorial about the indispensable space program and the heroism of the men and women who put their lives on the line everyday to inspire the world and advance the frontiers of human thought. Walt could see just from scanning the stories that the news was stale, and his mind was too uneasy to contemplate the official NASA photo of Lucy and to read with any focus the testimonials to her uncomplaining and adaptable character from God Doggett, among others. The paper had tried to contact Walt for a quote as well, as had *USA Today* and *People,* but he had not returned the calls. It seemed wrong to talk about her in public. He didn't think she would like him doing that.

"Don't you want some breakfast?" Brian said, as he set his tray down on the table. On it was an abstemious bowl of oatmeal and a single piece of dry toast. Walt said he had already eaten and passed the newspaper across the table to Brian.

"Hmmm," Brian said, eating his oatmeal and seeming to forget about Walt's presence as he read the profile of Lucy and skimmed the news stories. When he was through he pushed the paper back across to Walt without comment.

"Anybody over there have any idea what caused it yet?"

"I talked to a few people on the station side," Walt said. "The favorite theory now is that it happened when the shuttle got hit."

"That was two months ago."

"Yeah, but they think spall from the original strike may have hit the Lab. Made a dent in the shield that caused a hairline crack in the hull so small it was undetectable. But after two months of the hull flexing with every orbit, with the temperature going from two-fifty to minus two-fifty every forty-five minutes, it just kept getting bigger."

"Sounds like the shield wasn't much of a shield after all," Brian said. There was the familiar tone of accusation in his voice. Everything that went wrong had to be somebody's fault.

"So Davis is going home today?" Walt said.

"We're hoping. They'll take some more readings before they let him, but he seems to be out of the woods. Jesus, what an ordeal."

"Pretty hard on Lucy," Walt said.

Brian looked at Walt as he ate the last of his toast. "I know. That's what I meant."

He slid the tray aside and drank a glass of orange juice in one long gulp and then looked across the table again. Walt was aware of how he must look to Brian: disheveled and sleep-deprived and disconcertingly present.

"I've got a question," Brian said. "You mind?"

"I don't mind," Walt said.

"Maybe I'm just slow catching on. Did Lucy send you here or something?"

"I sort of volunteered to look in."

"Oh," Brian said. And then: "Why?"

"I'm not sure what you mean."

"Did she say something about not trusting me? Is she worried I'm not going to keep her informed about what's going on with Davis? Is she worried I'm not going to take care of our *children*?"

Walt sat back in his chair and did his best to silently shrug this question away, but Brian was leaning forward across the table, staring at him. There was a territorial challenge in his expression, but also something bewildered and imploring. Walt was sleepy and worried about his judgment. Had he been more clearheaded he would not have come to the hospital in the first place, and now that Brian was stumbling toward the truth about him and Lucy he could not count on being up to the task of deflecting him.

"Maybe she thinks *you* can do it better," he pressed.

"Brian," Walt said, in the calmest tone he could manage. Meanwhile he was bracing himself for the confrontation that seemed to be brewing, that might very well turn out to be physical. But in another moment Brian went slack, easing back to his side of the table.

"I'm sorry," he said. "It's been kind of tense here."

"I know," Walt said.

"I almost lost my wife and son in the same week."

Brian rattled his spoon around musingly in his empty oatmeal bowl and then set it aside.

"Lucy better make it back here," he said.

"All she has to do is wait it out in the Service Module until they come to get her."

"Yeah, but then there's reentry. Lots of bad things can happen during reentry. A few loose tiles and the whole shuttle could burn up. That's all I can think about these days, you know? Losing her. I don't know how you go about handling something like that."

I could tell you, Walt thought. But that wasn't really the frame of mind he was in. It was clear to him that this time Brian had earned his self-absorption. Forced into the pitiless role of consoling this man whose life he had been actively tearing apart, Walt was more desperate than ever to get away. He muttered something vaguely reassuring and then started to excuse himself, but Brian spoke again with an urgency that held Walt in place.

"I'm a pretty good father, you know," he said.

"Of course you are."

"I'd appreciate it if you'd tell her that, the next time you talk to her."

"I'm not going to be talking to her. Not till she comes home. The KU band's down."

"They've still got the space-to-ground loop. She could request another private conference with you."

"She's not going to do that," Walt said.

"Why not?"

"You know why. With no IP phone, no e-mail, all the communication with Ground has to be over the loop now. She's not going to ask them to tie it up for a private conference unless it's a big deal. Unless she needs to talk to her family about something important."

Brian sat there and said nothing. He was thinking in a way that made Walt nervous.

"I'm not in that category," Walt emphasized.

Brian nodded, not listening. He noticed the paper sack from the gift shop sitting on the table.

"What's that?" he asked.

"Something I picked up for Davis."

Walt watched Brian as he opened the sack and inspected the books.

"*Goosebumps*," Brian said. "He hasn't gotten into those yet. A few of his friends are reading them, though. *Goosebumps* and *Harry Potter*. Thanks."

"You're welcome," Walt said.

Brian put the books back into the bag, pulled out the bag of Skittles and stared at it for so long that Walt thought he might be reading the list of ingredients.

"Just give me a minute here," he said.

"Okay."

"I'm just . . . am I crazy to be thinking that you're having an affair with my wife?"

Walt tried not to let anything show through. He gave himself the incredulous beat he judged would be appropriate if he were innocent.

"We're not having an affair."

Brian stared at him. Walt did his best to stare back, though Brian's angry face seemed to be shifting in his sight, jumping subtly from one plane to the next, the way objects sometimes did in the light of a wavering candle flame. There was another long, unreal silence as Brian marshaled his concentration.

"I know I've got this reputation for having lousy social skills or whatever," he said at last. "I don't know how to read people, I always have the wrong reaction to things. But something's going on, Walt. I can tell when somebody's trying to score points with my wife by bringing a present to my sick son. Tell me I'm wrong."

"You're wrong."

"Tell me with a little bit more conviction."

"This is crazy, Brian. I haven't had any sleep. I'm going home."

"I have to admit I'm a little clueless about what I'm supposed to do about it, though. What do you think? Jump across the table and grab you by the throat?"

"If that's what you want to do, Brian, go ahead."

"How about a little consideration in one little area? How about not lying to me about it anymore?"

Walt said nothing. He made himself keep focusing on Brian's eyes, desperate to give the impression of being unfairly accused, but they both knew the illusion was crumbling.

"You were my team lead, Walt. You were Lucy's team lead. We both trusted you with our lives. What kind of bullshit is this?"

"If you need to talk about this, let's find a better time."

"Yeah, let's get out our appointment books. How about lunch on Tuesday? That good for you, Walt?"

He held Brian's hostile stare for as long as it took. The cafeteria was starting to fill up, health workers in green scrubs and shoe covers taking their seats beneath the inevitable posters of shuttle launches and signed pictures from astronauts thanking the hospital staff for their successful knee surgery or exhorting young patients to "reach for the stars."

Brian backed down in careful stages: he shook his head in disbelief, shot Walt a final angry glance, and then picked up the bag from the gift shop and walked over to a nearby trash can and threw it away.

Walt stood up and started to walk out, but Brian caught up to him and they walked together out into the parking lot as if they were continuing a companionable lunch conversation. Walt reached into his pocket for his keys, bracing himself to receive a punch in the face, but Brian had settled into another register by now, his anger giving way to a kind of wondrous hurt.

"Maybe you better start by apologizing."

"I'm not going to apologize," Walt said.

"What? You feel like you've done the right thing or something?"

"I'm just not going to apologize, Brian."

He left him there and walked to his car, but before he opened the door he turned back.

"Don't tell her about this, okay? The last thing she needs right now is something more to worry about."

"Always thinking of other people," Brian said.

Walt got into his car and started the engine, but before he could pull out of the parking lot Brian jogged over and hovered at the window until Walt rolled it down.

"I just want to make sure we're clear about one thing," Brian said. "When she comes home, she's coming home to me. To me and our children."

Walt rolled up the window and pulled away, too angry and conscience-stricken and brokenhearted to trust himself with a response.

Chapter Thirty-eight

Under the bandages that Konstantin had applied, Lucy's hand had swollen to the size of a baseball glove. The wild surges of pain in her broken fingers had been unendurable, but the side effects of the medication she had taken to control it led her to a new plateau of agony. What had started as a gentle note of nausea had suddenly mutated into a roaring case of the space sickness she had managed to avoid for months. A shot of Phenergan—thank God they had rescued all the medical supplies from the Lab!—finally brought it under control, but for a day and a half she had done little but heave into the emesis bag she held in her good hand, longing in her weightless state for a floor to lie down on, for the settling and soothing press of gravity as she whimpered in despair.

She was of little use to Glen or Konstantin in the days after the accident. All she could do was try not to distract them with her suffering while they attended to the endless emergency decisions that were the result of having had to abandon the U.S. portion of the station. Lucy mostly kept to herself, hovering in her sleep station, doing her part by making an effort to keep her vomit confined to the bag so that it would not float throughout the already-reeking station. Glen played his harmonica to calm his own nerves and, he touchingly thought, to take Lucy's mind off her raging pain and nausea, but the reedy sounds of

"Raindrops Keep Fallin' on My Head" and "Blowin' in the Wind" were a spectacular affliction of their own, and in those brief, harrowing intervals when she managed to fall asleep Glen's harmonica seemed to pursue her through every corridor of consciousness.

Everyday tasks—pulling on clothes, scraping the grime off her body with a washcloth, going to the bathroom—were difficult enough in zero gravity, but with her useless, inflated hand Lucy found them almost impossible. They were also living amid unaccustomed clutter, since all of the gear and supplies they had pulled out of the Lab had to be stored in either the Cargo Block or the Service Module. Glen, whose own sleep station had been in the Lab, had now become a third occupant in the crowded Service Module, sleeping wherever he could find space to hook up a spare sleep restraint. All his personal gear and family photos, everything but the hateful harmonica he had been carrying in one of his utility pockets, were now out of reach in the dark and unpowered Lab, but with his cheerful adaptability he didn't seem to care.

Konstantin was uncomplaining as well. He was steadfast and reliable, but the trace of inwardness that Lucy had noticed when she first met him after *Endeavour* docked with the station was steadily deepening. Waves of solitary reflection washed over him as he contemplated the ruin of his mission and the effects of that, justified or not, on the future course of his career. In her misery, Lucy preferred Konstantin's weighty introspection to Glen's relentless attempts to cheer them all up. Gloom at least tended to be silent and required from her no effort at a response.

In a sense, though, none of this mattered. The fact that Davis was at last out of the hospital, that his peak was back up, that his health had suffered no lasting damage, made her own purgatory almost an abstraction. She had finally been able to talk to him, and to Bethie as well, when Ground had managed to patch her through to her house shortly after Davis came home. His voice had sounded weak, and the second-and-a-half-delay transmission gave the conversation a tone of frustration and aching distance. But even over the space-to-ground loop she had been able to hear his steady breathing, no hint of struggle or wheezing. He had been happy to talk with her. There was none of the punishing silence and hesitations that had marked his demeanor before the launch. And Bethie, when her turn came, had chatted to her with no discernible longing. She seemed happy in her preschool, secure in the keeping of her father. Lucy noticed with only partial regret that the passage of time made the children less resentful toward her, as if she were no more than a beloved relative from whom nothing exceptional was expected. But she knew she could awaken in them the full range and intensity of their feelings toward their mother. All she had to do was to come home.

She might be home by Christmas, she told them, struggling to keep her voice level as her broken hand throbbed with pain and another wave of nausea began to gather force. And if she didn't make it by then, they would have a special Christmas later all on their own. One way or another, she was coming back to them soon.

But when the crippled station next passed over Texas, and she looked down at the familiar nick in the coastline along the Gulf of Mexico that was Galveston Bay, she was momentarily breathless with despair. All the physical laws of the universe seemed united against the possibility of her ever reaching home again. She could not keep her mind away from Challenger Park, from that black monument on which the dead astronauts' names were written. She could not stop thinking about Christa McAuliffe's refrigerator door, where the taunting normalcy of family life had remained on display after her death. What had been on Lucy's own refrigerator door when she left their house on Purple Plum Court that last time? If she could bear to train her thoughts in that direction, she was sure she could remember every magnet, every snapshot, every child's drawing, every test brought home with a smiley-face sticker applied by an encouraging teacher. If she did not come home, if she died there in the emptiness of space, in a few weeks or months all those tokens would come down or be replaced, and in the years to come there would be a forbidding monument somewhere like the one in Challenger Park, a cold black stone upon which her children could trace her name with their fingers.

The space sickness passed, the pain and swelling in her hand went down, and in a few days she was once again a functional member of the crew, able to pitch in where needed even though the splints on her fingers still left her essentially one-handed. Most of the experiments had had to be abandoned. The meticulous itinerary that had been uploaded with the Execute Package on the now-defunct KU band was a thing of the past, so Lucy and Konstantin and Glen had to improvise to keep themselves busy, to create some sort of moving current in the stagnant pool of time in which they were trapped. First they stowed all the rescued equipment from the Lab, then they set about maintaining every system in the station with an obsessive rigor, taking apart the treadmill and the bike until all the glitches were gone and both machines were working smoothly, rigging a vacuum jumper hose to correct a malfunctioning Microconstituents Analyzer, vacuuming every last crumb and water droplet and floating dust bunny out of the racks and crevices of the Cargo Block and Service Module.

Lucy cut the men's hair and asked Konstantin to cut hers. He was terrified. He had never cut a woman's hair and had no idea how to go about it, but it was because of that fear that Lucy trusted him more than Glen to do at least a conscientious job. As he hovered above her, Lucy heard the snap of his scissors and the incessant buzz of the vacuum as it sucked up the clippings. His mouth was shut tight in concentration and he breathed worriedly through his nose. She wondered if she smelled as bad as he did. Probably. None of them had had a shower in months, just a daily wipe-down with a wet washcloth and the application of a rinseless shampoo.

When Konstantin was through, Lucy was relieved to see that her haircut, if artless, was at least symmetrical. She told him she was pleased, which she more or less was. "More or less" was becoming good enough for her. She could more or less move her broken fingers now, more or less trust in not being visited by any further catastrophes, more or less depend on seeing her children not too long after Christmas.

And she could more or less still dream about being with Walt. But something had shifted, she could feel it. She knew that with the loss of the IP phone there would have to be silence between them. She could not risk asking for another private conference when it was hard enough to engineer an opportunity to speak to her family. The intensity that such a request would reveal would be obvious to everyone, Brian especially. Walt would not expect to talk to her until she came home. And yet this unavoidable silence felt deliberate. Surely he could find a way to get a message to her, something the CapCom might pass on, seemingly casual but charged with private significance.

Back on earth, something was not the same, and there was no one to ask what it was, no way to probe without showing her hand. Perhaps it was in Brian's time-delayed voice over the loop that she first noticed the difference. He had been as terrified as she had by Davis's latest health crisis, and it had been Brian who had witnessed the doctors shoving a tube down their son's throat. But the subdued and weary tone in his voice had caught her off guard. She had not known how to react to such a new signal from a husband whose vulnerability had always before taken the form of aggressive carping. He was holding something back, keeping it to himself. For a few troubled days she imagined he might be withholding from her some grim information he had learned about Davis's health, not wanting her to be tormented with it when she could do nothing to help. But she came to the conclusion that Brian would not do that, that he would understand that willfully holding her in ignorance while her little boy was in peril would be an act of omission that she could never forgive. No, it had something to do with Brian himself.

There was some change in him, but with the minimal communications available on the station now she could catch only scattered impressions of what that change might be. Some quality in his voice, barely discernible in the gulf of time-delayed conversation, was different. He seemed attentive in a wounded sort of way, the way he had been on the beach when he had handed her his wedding ring. On the eve of her launch, he had started to sense that he might really be losing her, and in the dangerous weeks and months that followed, that fear must have sunk deep into his mind.

As it should have, Lucy thought. He *was* losing her, and had been for quite some time. What she had avoided working out was exactly how and when it should happen. She and Walt had put off discussing their future until after her mission, but the mission itself had extended so far into the future that she could no longer be sure what reality she would come home to. Sometimes, looking out the window in the Service Module, seeing the earth spread out before her as she endlessly traveled across its surface, going nowhere even as she approached the human record of distance covered, she thought of those two evenings with Walt as beautiful but evanescent incidents, like the play of lightning over the oceans, or the swirling patterns of a gathering tropical storm: something that would have played itself out or shifted form by the time she saw it again on the next orbit.

But he *had* to still be there. Walt was not a passing cloud bank—he was as immutable and solid as a continent, a landmark that remained in place beneath every orbital pass and through every earthly season.

But in her children's lives it was Brian who was the landmark. Brian was constant as a father, as constant in his way as her own father had been to her. Lucy had spent so much thought enumerating Brian's faults—all the traits that went into his agitated, aggrieved, and predictable smallness of spirit—that it sometimes surprised her that Davis and Bethie did not share her critical acuity. They did not see what was missing in their father, they saw only what was there. His children were his duty. Perhaps it was no greater than that, perhaps there was no natural lovingness in his role as a father, perhaps there was no joy as she understood it, but he would stand by them, and they knew this and trusted him.

So the question was, could they trust *her*? She had not yet found the courage to really face where her relationship might be taking her, to imagine the conversation in which she would gather Davis and Bethie in front of her and tell them she and their father were getting a divorce. They would be able to see it in only one way: that the mother who had left them to go to space, and who had promised to be back in eight days, was now telling them in effect that it had been her own happiness, her own ambition, that had counted all along.

She did not have to think about that now, she decided. On her sixty-fifth day on the station she stared down at the earth. If you counted each forty-five-minute orbital day, that made a total of two thousand and eighty days. If *Discovery* launched on schedule to rescue them, there would be sixteen hundred orbital days more.

It did not matter. She could endure it, had already endured it. She was no longer a stray that Konstantin and Glen had taken in but a full member of the crew, even a critical one, working hard to keep her mood up during even the most distressing times and to learn the systems and put herself to use. Proving herself in this way was a deep satisfaction, almost as deep—why not just say it?—*as* deep as mothering her children. And it was around that sixty-fifth day that the fear and isolation she had felt for so long began to ease and the static timelessness in which she was trapped began to dissolve.

She and Konstantin and Glen were a disciplined family now, accustomed to and tolerant of one another's faults, expert at staying out of each other's way in a cramped and foul-smelling space and at finding consequential things with which to occupy themselves. There were daily conversations over the loop with the friendly voices at Mission Control, and from time to time a patched-together talk with her family on earth, the children sounding increasingly healthy and patient, eager for her to come home but not suffering quite so terribly from her absence. And of course Brian with that new note of solicitude in his voice, a wounded awareness that both pleased her and made her afraid, because it meant that back on earth the ground was shifting, time was passing, people were changing in ways she could not judge.

The only voice missing was Walt's. But she continued to think about him at night, every night. She thought about her love for him without allowing herself to truly consider the cruelty that would be required to sustain it. There was plenty of time to think about that, to think about how to make it work: hundreds and hundreds of the miniature days that swept across the broad earth below her but made no mark upon the black space that was so final and consummate.

She was always busy, stowing, maintaining, preparing meals, helping with the experiments that could still be run, but toward the end her mind fell away from planning and anticipating her return to earth and settled instead into a dreamy lethargy. Time no longer seemed to move or not move. It was just a barely detectable stirring that offered the illusion that there was something in the universe besides stillness.

Six days after Christmas she saw *Discovery* at last cruising silently toward them, its commander and pilot waving from the orbiter windows. Even as she heard herself laughing with joy, even as she joined Konstantin and Glen in a tumbling, weightless embrace that knocked them all against one of the storage racks, a part of her still seemed suspended in that stillness. For an instant, the idea of returning to earth was even a little startling to her, as if she were a comfortable dead soul who had been commanded back to life.

Chapter Thirty-nine

Walt and his team were up all night. There had been a long series of ascent and entry sims for the new mission they were working, and afterward they had all gone over to Building 4, where a portion of the hall had been ceded to them by the team that had trained the *Discovery* crew that had just launched. That mission's goal was to ferry up a new space station crew, repair the damage to the Lab and the Unity Node, and bring Lucy and her two weary crewmates home. Walt and the others worked for hours to put up Lucy's welcome-home decorations, not just the usual pictures and quips and banners but laminated copies of the stories that had appeared about her in dozens of magazines, including a cover story in *People*.

At five in the morning they went to the IHOP on NASA Road One for breakfast, the same restaurant from which Walt had called Lucy a year and a half before to tell her that her husband was safe and that the software crisis he had created on the shuttle had been resolved. It was the day after New Year's now and the Christmas decorations were still up. Walt assumed it must have been hard on Lucy to miss Christmas with her children, but she had proved herself so resilient in the last four months that a postponed holiday was just one more thing to be taken in stride.

"Do you think she'll even be able to walk?" Gary asked, attacking a stack of pancakes glued together with some sort of strawberry compote that looked like a pale pink syrup. "After four months in space she's going to feel like a jellyfish."

"Brian was on *Mir* longer than that," Kyle said, "and he walked off the shuttle on his own two feet. So did Jerry Linenger."

"If she's smart she'll just let them go ahead and carry her out," Sylvia said. "I mean, what does she have to prove that she hasn't already?"

Mickey lifted a forkful of pancake in a salute to Sylvia's good sense and said, "Amen."

Walt settled back in the booth, listening to the conversation. If he hadn't been so on edge, he would have been happy. Here he was again before dawn in an overlit restaurant finishing up another all-nighter with his team. The sense of cohesion and sleepy accomplishment he felt on these occasions had always been close enough to real happiness for him. Lucy, of course, had raised the bar on happiness, and the purgatory of self-doubt and suspense he had been in for the last two months was founded upon the knowledge that he might never rise to that level again.

He didn't know if Brian had told Lucy what he had found out that day in the hospital cafeteria. He guessed he had not, since Walt could think of no secure way such volatile information could be delivered, given the bare-bones communications capabilities on the crippled station. Calling Lucy to account for unfaithfulness when she was sequestered away in space would have been a cruel and punitive act, and Walt did not think Brian would go that far. Six months ago, he might have believed him capable of that sort of vindictiveness, but after seeing him asleep in that hospital bed with his trusting children, Walt had had to recalibrate his opinion. As exasperatingly rigid as Brian could be, he had a defining core of personal honor. There were standards of conduct he held to. Walt had always assumed the same about himself, but he was not so sure anymore. He could not have said precisely what his own standards were, or who he thought himself to be. He was just somebody who wanted to believe it was still possible to spend the rest of his life with Lucy.

Without her, that life loomed static and blank. Looking around the table, he felt a seeping awareness that this would be the last mission he and his team worked together. It was time for Sylvia to move up to become a team lead herself, and in a few years so might Mickey, if his health held out, and even Kyle, assuming he kept going to his AA meetings with the patient resolve he had demonstrated so far. Gary would need to make over his carefully cultivated geek persona if he wanted to advance in any meaningful way, but if not he would be content enough in NASA's bureaucratic backwaters for twenty years or so, until it occurred to him to retire.

Walt himself could retire, get a job with a space contractor, or move up the NASA ladder to become a SimSup or make his way into management. It was time for some sort of forward movement. But he understood clearly enough that any career progression he embarked upon would be cosmetic. His life needed the deeper shift, the redemptive surge, that Lucy had promised. But four unexpected months in space meant that Lucy would have necessarily undergone a shift of her own. She could come back so changed and sharpened by everything she had experienced that he might be almost a stranger to her.

Sylvia's cell phone rang.

"Who's calling you at five in the morning?" Kyle asked her as she took the phone out of her purse.

"One guess," Gary said, and Sylvia smirked at him as she turned her back to them in the booth and answered the phone.

"Hi, honey," she said. She stood and walked away from their hearing to sit at another booth on the other side of the empty restaurant. After a few minutes she came back and resumed eating her breakfast without comment.

"They're so in love," Gary said.

"Shut up," she told him. She glanced across the booth at Walt, trying not to smile. Walt was happy for her. He had met her new boyfriend several times by now. He was a nice guy, an auditor for one of the big accounting firms, with a solid, low-key manner. When it came to Sylvia, he looked like he meant business. Walt supposed in another few months they would be engaged. Good for him, and good for her.

Walt made a point of drinking another cup of coffee, calculating that it might carry him through the rest of the morning even though he had not slept for almost twenty-four hours. Then when the breakfast meeting broke up, he drove home, packed a suitcase, and managed to pull into the remote parking lot at Hobby Airport before the traffic had started to build up on I-45.

He was an hour early for his flight. He was sitting by the gate reading the newspaper when Louis walked up and took a seat in the plastic chair next to him.

"So she's finally coming home," Louis said.

He was wearing his Roman collar and toting a trim black carry-on bag. To Walt, he looked thinner. They hadn't seen each other since that night in the rectory, four months before, when Louis had decreed what had amounted to a time-out in their friendship. Walt had not been to Mass in all that time, and they had talked on the phone only once, when Louis had called to express concern about Lucy after the emergency air leak in the station.

"That's right," Walt said, doing his best not to express interest at seeing Louis there. For as long as they had known each other—all their lives—they had placed an odd premium on cool and casual greetings, sometimes carrying the attitude to absurd lengths, as when they had once unexpectedly run into each other in the Zócalo in Mexico City and had each instinctively reacted with a nod and a half wave as if they had been bored office workers passing in the corridor.

"And that's where you're going now, I bet," Louis said. "To Cape Canaveral to welcome her back."

"Only if it's okay with you," Walt said. "Where are you going?"

"Sacramento. A conference on the role of the laity in the twenty-first century. I know it sounds boring to you, but to me of course it's scintillating."

Walt responded with an appreciative smirk. He'd missed Louis, missed their Sunday afternoon canoe trips and their barbecue expeditions, even missed going to Mass and facing him down from the congregation while he gave his sermons. He looked up at the television mounted overhead in the gate area. It was tuned to CNN, but there was nothing on at the moment about Lucy and the Expedition crew and the shuttle mission that had just docked at the station to rescue them.

"Brian knows about it," Walt said, lowering his voice.

" 'It' being you and Lucy?"

Walt nodded. Louis glanced around. Most of the seats around them were empty, though there was a long line at the gate where passengers were still checking in for the flight.

"Did he beat the shit out of you?"

"Would you be disappointed if I said no?"

"It's sort of a funny idea," Louis said. "You in a fistfight. So what's going to happen now?"

"I don't know."

"How much was your plane ticket? Did you get it online?"

"What are you talking about, Louis?"

"How much was your plane ticket?"

"Three hundred and sixty-six dollars."

"I'll write you a check for three hundred and sixty-six dollars. You won't be out any money. Just go home."

"We agreed you weren't going to lecture me about this."

"No," Louis said, "I think the agreement was we weren't ever going to speak to each other again. There she is."

He was looking at the television screen. There was a brief shot of Lucy and Konstantin and Glen welcoming the *Discovery* crew, but they couldn't hear the voice of the commentator over the flight announcements.

"I'm the next gate down," Louis said. "I better get going if I want to get in the first boarding group."

"Have a fun time discussing the role of the laity," Walt told him.

But Louis didn't move. He continued to stare at the television screen, where the report on the space station had been replaced by images of a flood somewhere in the Midwest, a lonely wet dog shivering on top of a house.

"Go home," Louis said.

"You're going to miss your boarding group."

"Have you thought about how her kids are going to—"

"Shut the hell up, Louis."

He said this loud enough that several people turned around and stared at them.

"I know what they're thinking," Louis said, whispering now. "They're thinking, What kind of guy says shut the hell up to a priest?"

Walt just stared straight ahead. He wished he could tell himself he didn't care what those people thought, but he was going to have to share a three-hour flight to Orlando with them.

"So let me try to get this straight," he said to Louis. "I'm too careful about things or I'm not careful enough?"

"What do you mean?"

"Well, you'll recall from a previous lecture that you were complaining about the fact I was always creeping up to the edge of things. So I've gone over the edge, okay? Why doesn't that make you happy?"

"It's not about making me happy, Walt."

"You know what? I think it is. Because the impression I keep getting from you is that you've hit the wall. You've lost your faith, you've lost your faith in *yourself.* You don't want to be a priest anymore, but you still need an excuse to be a pious asshole. You don't have the nerve to make a change in your own life, you're afraid to be a real live three-dimensional fucked-up human being like the rest of us, so you just sit there and take it out on me."

Louis absorbed this with a calm expression on his face. There was a flush of color on his cheeks as he stared at the travelers hurrying down the concourse, walking briskly along trailing their wheeled luggage.

"So you won't take a check for the three hundred and sixty-six dollars," he said after a moment.

"No."

"Well, okay." Louis stood up and hoisted the strap of his carry-on bag over his shoulder. "Fuck you, then."

Walt didn't look up. He kept his eyes on the television screen as Louis walked down to the next gate.

Chapter Forty

The de-orbit burn thrust Lucy back against her seat in the mid-deck of *Discovery*. Except for periodic re-boost burns that had been performed on the station to keep their orbital altitude from decaying, she had not felt anything close to acceleration in months, and this sudden surge of force, relatively gentle though it was, was startling. This first intimation of gravity was thrilling to her: it meant she was going home. The burn, which slowed the shuttle so that it was now falling into an elliptical path toward earth, was irreversible. There was no fuel left to boost them back into orbit. They would land on earth now, or die trying.

There were no windows in the mid-deck, so she and Glen and Konstantin had to listen to the conversation over the loop to know what was happening. They lay on their backs in the recliner seats that had been specially designed for returning long-duration astronauts, upon whose bodies gravity would be a significant assault. Lucy had no idea how much bone mass she had lost in weightlessness, but even the fractional g-force she had just felt had registered with oppressive power.

If they survived reentry, they would be wheels-down in an hour and a half. After so many months away, in a place that had seemed as distant as her imagination could reach, she was astonished that she could be home in less time than it would take to drive across Houston in rush hour traffic, as magically swift as Dorothy returning to Kansas after clicking the heels of her ruby slippers. But first they had to pass through fire. Lucy could feel the craft shudder as it struck the veil of molecules that marked the beginning of the upper atmosphere. The friction of contact caused the thin air around the shuttle to bloom into a fireball. Stowed away in the mid-deck, she could not see the eerie plasma glow visible through the windows to the crew members on the flight deck, but she could hear the furnace-like rumble as the shuttle descended, the flames that were roaring at the black insulation tiles on the underside of *Discovery,* as light as Styrofoam, that were all that stood between her and fiery annihilation. She felt still-weightless bubbles of sweat forming on her forehead. She closed her eyes and held her breath. Let me see my children again, she pleaded, or demanded, or prayed. She might have actually been speaking above the roar of the superheated air.

She could feel gravity settling in now, the suspended sweat on her forehead pooling and draining into her eyes, her body pressed back hard against her seat. Food crumbs and water droplets rained down from the ceiling of the mid-deck, no longer captured there in weightless suspension. The deceleration felt like it was mashing her flat, but she didn't mind, because the more the pressure increased the closer they were to the surface of the planet.

She felt the shuttle begin the series of wide banking turns that served to dissipate its speed as it dropped deeper into the atmosphere. At each turn the gravity increased, forcing her deeper into her seat, pressing on her chest so that drawing breath was an active effort.

Over the loop, the CapCom relayed a nervous inquiry from the flight surgeons, wanting to know how the three station crew members were holding up. They each pressed their comm buttons in turn to report in.

"Feeling good, Houston," Lucy said, in a labored, rattling voice, but the unfamiliar gravity was oppressive and she was ready for this ride to be over, ready to be in a dark, unmoving room. She heard a sonic boom, and then another, and then felt the vessel as it made its final wide turn above the Kennedy Space Center runway. Lucy lifted her arm at the elbow; it felt like using the bicep machine at the gym. If there was an accident on landing, if a tire blew and the shuttle skidded off into a ditch, if there was a fire, she knew she would be helpless. She would need the strength of a competitive weight lifter just to move her own body out of the seat.

But there was no accident. The shuttle reared upward as it pulled out of its severe glide slope, the landing gear descended beneath her, the drag chute deployed, and Lucy felt its restraining hand as the shuttle rolled down the endless runway until the pilot called out, "Wheels stop."

In the seat next to her, Glen let out an uncharacteristic yip of joy. Konstantin was silent, lying on his seat in his pressure suit, staring up at the ceiling of the mid-deck as he listened to the applause and cheers of the rest of the crew. Lucy was silent as well. She let the tears settle into her eyes and laboriously lifted a hand to wipe them away.

Konstantin disconnected his comm cord and took off his helmet. Lucy did the same, very carefully, feeling the gravity weighing down on her as if she were several atmospheres beneath the surface of the ocean. She started to say something to Konstantin, but even her voice felt trapped and unable to rise. As she was laboriously unstrapping herself from her harness, somebody opened the hatch behind her from the outside. Something beautiful and almost forgotten rushed inside: air. Infinite layers of fragrance—ocean salt, beach grass, burning rubber from the shuttle's tires on the runway, even the aftershave of the man who had opened the hatch—flowed and wafted around her, making her feel as if she had just emerged from a tomb.

"Anybody home?" a voice said. It was Qamal, the flight surgeon. Lucy turned her head to welcome him, but that one movement in this suddenly alien world set off a violent whirling she could not control. Everything she looked at swept back and forth across her field of vision with the velocity of a windshield wiper.

"Vertigo?" Qamal said. She couldn't speak, and nodding her head was unthinkable, since the world was already rotating so violently.

"Don't worry," he said. "Your inner ear's not used to gravity yet. It'll pass. We'll get you some meclizine. In the meantime I've got just the thing."

He handed her a barf bag and she grabbed it as if it would save her life and immediately vomited out all the salty chicken broth she had drunk that morning to keep up her fluid levels during reentry. Then she lay back on the seat again and closed her eyes to try to keep the world from spinning.

Konstantin managed to struggle to his feet and shuffle out the hatch under his own steam, but Lucy and Glen both had to be carried out on stretchers to the waiting medical van, where she vomited yet again before giving blood and a urine sample and changing out of her pressure suit into cotton scrubs. On the drive to the O&C medical facilities, the vertigo worsened, a weird centrifugal thrill ride that was so vicious that the simple task of lining up her mouth to the opening of the barf bag had all the complexity of an orbital docking. When they arrived at the medical building, the cheers and applause of the personnel lined up to welcome them were like an assault, and she was glad to get to a bed and lie as still as possible as the world hurtled around her for another hour. At last the meclizine Qamal had given her took effect and the Tilt-A-Whirl sensations subsided, but her body still felt like it was filled with sand and her head felt as full of swirling residue as the inside of a snow globe.

But her family was waiting for her. She could not lie here forever. With two medics supporting her, she stood up and stumbled to a mirror. She was mostly horrified at what she saw. She had shed the extra pounds she had been trying to lose for her entire adult life, but she was pale and slack and ill-looking, and her long-unwashed hair was a lusterless, ragged thatch. In the space of two hours she had changed from a being who glided about like an angel into a staggering and sickly pedestrian.

"I want to take a shower," she said.

"You better not try that just yet," one of the medics said. "You need a few hours at least to get adjusted to gravity, or all that water bombarding you is going to freak you out big time."

Lucy reluctantly acknowledged the reality of this. She did what she could with her hair, flattening it down against her head with a brush, and then washed her face at the sink with real soap.

"Are they out there?" she asked.

"They're waiting," the medic said. "Should I get the wheelchair?"

"No, I want to walk."

And she did walk, though she had to hold her head absolutely still to keep the vertigo from attacking her again, and under the bizarre weight of gravity she felt as if she were pulling a loaded sled. Instinct told her not to lift her feet, because the sudden shift in weight that resulted would, in space, have sent her tumbling out of control. So she shuffled forward in the running shoes they had given her. That was different too. She had not worn shoes in so long the idea of having her feet encased in these strange devices seemed absurd.

The corridor through which she walked was lined with more applauding people, some with tears in their eyes, a few of them reaching out to pat her on the back or arm, gestures that made her flinch, since her upright position in this world of overbearing air was so precarious. She smiled gratefully, exchanged words with some of the Kennedy techs and support people whose faces she had last seen on the way to the Astro Van that took her to the launch site. But her heart was throbbing with anticipation and she could not force herself to linger any more than the polite minimum.

At last someone held open a door to a private conference room. Lucy walked inside. The three of them—Brian, Davis, Bethie—were standing together on the far side of the room. When she saw her mother, Bethie came at her in a dead run, her arms wide, with a joyous smile that Lucy could only nervously return, because the sight of this onrushing child made her body freeze up in startled response. If Bethie leapt into her arms, as she was surely intent on doing, Lucy knew she would fall over backward and shatter one of her weakened bones.

She braced herself as best she could, but at the last moment Brian raced forward and grabbed Bethie just as she was about to launch herself at her mother. Bethie shrugged out of her father's grasp and made do with grabbing Lucy around the knees and squeezing tight as she looked up into her face.

"I can't pick you up, honey," Lucy said, as she stroked Bethie's hair. "I'm sorry. I'm not strong enough."

With Bethie still attached, she sidled over to a nearby chair and looked across the room. Davis was standing there by himself now, heartbreakingly taller, looking lost in his mother's presence, waiting for an invitation. Lucy held out her arm to him, trying not to break into pleading sobs, and Davis slowly advanced with his hands at his side and laid his head against his mother's shoulder. Out of long habit, Lucy listened for the quality of his breath. There was no wheezing, no hesitation. After a moment, she gently urged him off her shoulder so she could look at his face. Tears had started in his eyes and were running down cheeks that she was glad to see were no longer swollen from steroid treatments.

Davis was embarrassed. He looked away as Lucy wiped the tears from his face.

"It's all right," she said. "Everything's all right. I'm here now."

Bethie was still clutching her mother's knees. Lucy turned to Brian. "Can you lift her into my lap?"

Brian bent down and did as she asked. She saw the tears in his own eyes and realized she had not even said hello to her husband.

"Are you glad to see me too?" she asked, taking his hand.

He nodded silently, and held on to her hand, and she was oddly touched by the fact that they had to silently remind each other to kiss.

Lucy was due for more medical tests. She was able to stay with her family for only a half hour, but when the time came for her to be wheeled away she was emotionally and physically depleted enough not to mind so much. Bethie's face tightened in disbelief when Lucy told her she had to go.

"I don't *want* you to go away again!" she whimpered.

"Don't be stupid," Davis said. "She's not going to *space* again."

"Davis, honey," Lucy said, "she's not being stupid. Don't say that. Bethie, I've just got to go see the doctors for a little bit. But Daddy's going to bring the two of you over to crew quarters, and guess what? We're all going to stay there together tonight. Okay?"

Lucy gently pried the girl's clinging arms away and gave the children back into the temporary keeping of their father. Then she endured another hour or so with the flight surgeons before being taken to crew quarters, where she sat down with Konstantin and Glen for a beautiful meal—a vivid green salad, fresh grilled redfish, a steaming baked potato, and chocolate chip cookies—that she stared at in stupefied appreciation but seemed to have no real interest in eating. She walked out of the dining room and to her private room under her own steam, but her mind was still skeptical about lifting her feet and unless she moved her head rigidly in line with her body the world threatened to go skittering off its axis again.

She closed the door behind her and sat down on the bed in her room. Someone, thinking they were being thoughtful, had tuned the clock radio on the bureau to a soothing easy-listening station, but the music had a swarming, infiltrating presence, and in her groggy and slow-moving state she had to inspect it with the same concentration as that torn-apart sorbent bed before she finally found the switch that turned it off.

She wanted to lie down, or thought she did. She wanted the light off, but not enough, apparently, to raise her hand against the crushing weight of air to reach the switch. She just sat there, alone, on the bed, on the earth. She had seen her children again. She would spend the night with them. You are happy, she told herself. But there was something missing, and she knew what it was, and when the phone rang ten minutes later she knew it would be him.

He was waiting for her in a small private conference room just down the hall. He wore a white shirt and pressed khakis and, uncharacteristically for him, a sport coat.

"You dressed up," she said.

He stood with his hands on the back of one of the office chairs at the far end of the table, not answering, just looking at her. She had changed, of course. She was thin and ravaged. In her shapeless scrubs, she moved as cautiously as an old woman. But her eyes were brilliant in her sharpened face. She closed the door behind her.

"I know I look hideous," she said.

"No, you don't. You look glorious. You're exhausted, though."

"I've got a bit of vertigo still. And gravity isn't my friend anymore."

He was still hesitantly stationed on the far side of the room.

"It's all right," she said. "We're alone in here."

He walked over to her and set his palm against the side of her face.

"I was hoping I could wash my hair before I saw you."

"It doesn't matter."

"Be careful if you decide to kiss me. I can't really move my head."

"What do you mean, if I decide to kiss you?"

She held her head still and parted her mouth. As she kissed him, she traced the weave of his sport coat with her fingertips, she smelled the soap he had washed with, tasted the toothpaste he had used. Freed from the sterility and stale air of the space station, her senses were riotously sharp. Everything about the earth, every texture and smell, the feel of her own load-bearing body, was like a distant memory from childhood that had come rushing back to her with thrilling clarity. In Walt's arms, she seemed to feel the embrace of the earth itself.

"I'd better sit down," she said after a moment, when the swirling in her vision threatened to start again. Walt eased her into one of the office chairs and sat down next to her and held her hands on the surface of the conference table.

"You flew all the way out here," she said.

"Did you think I wouldn't?"

"I didn't know. I didn't know what you would do. I was afraid you might have forgotten all about everything."

"You couldn't have really thought that."

"You're right," she said. "I couldn't. I like your jacket. I've never seen you wear anything like that. You look nice in a suit, I bet."

Walt said he didn't wear suits that often. Lucy tightened her grip on his hands and pulled him toward her to kiss him again. Then Walt leaned back in his own chair again and looked at her with an expression of gathering significance.

"You're about to drop some kind of bomb," she said.

"I don't know. It depends on whether or not Brian has told you."

"Told me what?"

"That he knows."

Lucy dropped her eyes in dismay, an instinctive response that was too fast for her confused brain to catch up to. The bright veneer surface of the conference table started to whirl. She closed her eyes and tightened her grip on Walt's hand.

"You all right?" he asked her.

"Give me a minute," she managed to say. "Maybe you could bring that trash can over here."

Walt hurried over to the other side of the room, picked up a small plastic trash can, and set it next to her feet. He put his hand on her forehead while she kept her eyes closed and breathed deeply and evenly. Slowly, the world settled back into a tentative steadiness, and the wave of nausea passed.

"How?" she was finally able to ask.

"He found out while Davis was in the hospital."

"He's known that long?"

"He just guessed," Walt said. "We had sort of a confrontation down in the cafeteria, not violent, mostly just a staring contest. You know, it's a point in his favor that he didn't tell you, that he decided not to take it out on you while you were up in space."

"I wish you wouldn't do that," Lucy said.

"What?"

"List points in his favor. I don't like it when you do that. It scares me."

"Why?"

"Because I love *you*. Because I came back to *you*."

Walt asked, "Did you?" His tone was urgent, but his voice was barely audible to her. She was conscious of the heavy, unstable presence of her own brain. It seemed to be made up of some sort of sound-baffling material.

"Yes," she answered him. "Of course I did. Why wouldn't you think so?"

"I want to think so. It's just that you've been through so much. Maybe things are different. Maybe they *should* be different."

"What are you saying?"

"For your kids, I mean."

All this was happening too fast for her. What Walt had just told her, the life-altering news that Brian was aware of her infidelity, just sat there in her mind. She was too weak, too confused, to even it approach it right now.

"Let me worry about my kids," she said. "I'm already an expert in that. When am I going to see you again?"

"Maybe not until you get back to Houston. Is that all right?"

"Are you backing away from me, Walt?"

"No. I'm just being cautious."

"Don't be cautious. Please. Let's find a way to make it work."

"I want to, Lucy. How?"

"It's not fair to ask me that right now. Everything on earth is so new, so strange. Give me time to adjust. Give me time to find a way to love you."

Walt leaned in and kissed her once more. Then he held her head in his hands for a moment, looking into her eyes, helping to steady her vertiginous perceptions.

"So," he said, "I'll be waiting for you in Houston."

After he left, she walked carefully back to her room. She was determined to get her body as clean as possible before Brian and the children came back, but the showerhead in the crew quarters bathroom looked ferocious. There was a chair thoughtfully placed beneath the shower, but it would be a while, Lucy realized, before she would have the nerve to even sit beneath a percussive stream of water. And the thought of taking a bath was truly frightening. After five months in weightlessness, she could not consider submerging her body in a pool of water. At the moment, water seemed to her as dense a substance as setting cement. Nor was she certain she could even lift herself out of the tub. Her muscles had atrophied, and she had the sensation that the nerve signals from her brain were firing in slow motion, so that she was not even sure she could move her arms in time to prevent a fall. It was even a little scary to stand at the sink, soaking a washcloth in the Niagara of water that roared out of the faucet. When she turned off the tap, though, she felt calmer, and she gave herself an approximation of the spit baths she had been taking on the station, careful not to look in the mirror at the depleted muscle tone of her naked arms and at her slack, pale face.

She wanted to take a nap before Brian and the children came back. She left a request not to be bothered and turned out the light and tried not to think. An awful scene with Brian was coming, but she did not have the mental or physical sharpness to deal with it anytime soon. She needed to understand better where she stood—with Walt, with herself— before she could face her husband. But things were not moving on her timetable, and if she was honest with herself she had to admit that they should not. She was the transgressor, she was the betrayer. It was reasonable and fair that she just steel herself as best she could and wait.

She had been lying on her side in bed for an hour, squeezing her eyes shut, trying to force the guilt and anxiety out of her mind, when there was a soft knock on the door and Brian walked in and took a seat on the edge of the other queen-sized bed in the room.

"You sleeping?" he asked.

"No. I can't."

"I brought you a smoothie. I remember that was the thing that tasted best to me when I came home."

She tried to roll over onto her back, but couldn't seem to remember how to apply pressure against the mattress to perform such a simple maneuver.

"Not easy, is it?" Brian said, smiling. He stood over the bed and took her arms and levered her onto her back, then put some pillows behind her neck and helped her scrunch up so that she was in a sitting position.

"How's the vertigo?"

"Better."

He handed her the smoothie. "Strawberry okay?"

Lucy nodded. She took the lid off the smoothie and took a few sips. Nothing had ever tasted better to her in her life.

"Thank you," she said.

"No problem."

"Where are the kids?"

"Glen Dippie's wife is watching them for a minute. I wanted the two of us to have a chance to talk."

The words were ominous. She could feel the weight of each one. They were bricks in her prison of gravity.

"So is this a poison smoothie?" she said. She may have even smiled, though she hoped not. Brian didn't deserve her grim jocularity, the slightest suggestion that she was taking this lightly.

But he ignored the remark. "With all the bone mass you've lost," he said, "you want to make sure that you don't push yourself. I know the flight surgeons have already been lecturing you about it, but they don't know what it's like from the inside, not like somebody who's been up there. It's hard to really get it into your head how fragile you are. But you can break a bone just trying to do a push-up."

She hitched up higher on the pillows and looked at him. He was holding something back, of course—holding a lot back. Perhaps he was too deeply hurt and angry to trust himself with his own reaction if the subject of Walt was opened. Or perhaps his silence represented something stronger, some new level of maturity and consideration. That was possible. He had shown intermittent signs of change in the past half year: his clumsy declaration of love when he presented his wedding ring to her on the beach, his patient and practical advice about how to survive her tenure on the station, and most of all his steadiness and vigilance when Davis had been ill.

"What else are you feeling besides the vertigo?" he asked her.

"I don't know. Vague things. For instance, I'm having trouble getting my body to obey me," she said. "It's like my brain has to fill out a bunch of paperwork before it has the authority to move my arm or leg."

"I remember that feeling," Brian said. "It'll pass in a few days. What you want to do now is just lie there for a while and let all the weirdness start to wear off. Then when you get back to Houston, start with some low-impact water workouts to build your bones back up. There's a great trainer named Brenda. I'll make sure she's the one you work with."

He remained sitting on the edge of the other bed, pretending to examine a callus on his palm. He'd had a scorched-earth haircut recently, she could tell, but it was growing out a little now, framing his taut, concentrated face.

"Did you hear what I said?" Lucy said. "I know you know about it."

When he lifted his head to look at her, his dark eyes held less anger and suspicion than raw hurt.

"I got that job at U of H," he said.

"The teaching job?"

He nodded. "I start in the fall."

"You didn't tell me."

"You were in space."

"You still could have told me, Brian."

"I wanted to have some news for you when you came home. Turns out you were the one who had news for me."

She raised a hand to wipe the tears that were running down her cheeks, noting again that strange time delay as the muscles in her arm hesitated.

"I suppose you love him," Brian said. "I don't think you'd do this to us with somebody you didn't love."

"Yes, I love him," she answered, coldly excited to be saying the words out loud, aware of their damaging force.

"You've known about it all this time," she went on. "That must have been hard for you."

"Pretty fucking hard, Lucy."

"But you didn't say anything to me."

"You were in trouble up there. I didn't know what it would do to you to have an argument like that long distance. I didn't know what it would do to me."

He stood up from the bed and walked over to the other side of the room and leaned against the wall, his head resting even with a framed photograph of the shuttle taking off from the Cape, soaring into the sky on the tip of a pillar of exhaust that looked as solid as a beanstalk. Brian was wearing a white polo shirt and jeans, his bare feet in sandals. He was even leaner than usual. His face was sharper. She understood that it was worry, not just exercise, that had caused him to lose weight.

"I'm sorry," Lucy said.

"We can't get into it now anyway," Brian said. "The kids'll be here in a few minutes. That's the last thing they need, for us to be dealing with this in front of them. We've already torn each other up. Let's not do it to them."

He slid off his wedding ring and turned it over in his fingers. "You know who brought this back to me? Walt. Pretty ironic."

"Yes," she said, the tears sliding down her cheeks with the downward velocity that was still a novelty to her.

"You've got a pretty serious decision coming up, Lucy. And it's going to be *your* decision. If you think we shouldn't be married anymore, if you think our family shouldn't stay together, you let me know. I trust your judgment. I don't want to be around you if you don't love me. But I want you to know something. I love you and I love our children."

She could imagine these words being delivered with a bitter, sarcastic undertone. She had heard such declarations often enough in their marriage, as Brian had outlined the conspiracies standing in the way of his career or narrated his latest grievance. But there was no edge in his voice now, just the words themselves. His grievance was real this time. He understood the stakes and seemed to respect them, almost to welcome them.

He slid the ring back onto his finger. "Anyway, we can talk about this later. When you've had a chance to get acclimated."

"Yes," she said. "That would be better."

"I'm going to go get the kids. They wanted us all to watch a movie together tonight. I rented *Toy Story*. Okay with you?"

"Okay."

"And we've got a tape of Bethie's dance recital that she wanted you to see. You ready for me to get them?"

"Give me a few minutes, will you? I don't want them to see me upset. I need to pull myself together somehow."

"Yeah, I know," Brian said. "I've been working on that one too."

She thought he was going to walk across the room and kiss her, and she had an anxious moment trying to sort out what her response should be. But instead he made an attempt at a smile and veered tactfully toward the door, on his way to round up the kids so that the whole family could spend the night together as she had promised.

Chapter Forty-one

She saw Walt two days later at the welcome-home party the primary training team held for her in Building 4. They had decorated the hallway in her honor, mostly with photos taken during training and with laminated copies of all the articles published in newspapers and magazines about her adventures as a stranded astronaut. They had also brought in a TV and VCR, into which Gary inserted a greatest hits videotape he had put together of all the television coverage, from sober reports of her predicament on the network news to jokes on the late-night talk shows. She had been aware to a vague degree of her sudden celebrity, but seeing it displayed in such a panoramic way just added to the persistent unreality of life on earth.

She watched and laughed along with the team and the crew as David Letterman made his way through his Top Ten List: "Top Ten Reasons Why a Woman Wouldn't Want to Be Stranded on the International Space Station with Two Lonely Astronaut Dudes." She was drinking a glass of champagne, sitting in a chair with her elbow crooked, and when the routine was over and she wanted to free her hands to join in the ironic applause, she just thoughtlessly let go of the glass, as she was accustomed to doing in space, confident that any object she released would simply hover in place next to her hand. But the glass dropped and shattered on the floor. Lucy and the others stared at it in surprise.

"Busted!" Buddy said, and everyone in the room doubled over in laughter. Including, Lucy was glad to notice, Walt. He had been standing on the periphery during most of the party, doing his best not to let anything show. There had been a round of toasts earlier, and his had been so careful it had come across as almost studiously flat. Not like Walt at all. She hadn't taken it personally, but she had allowed herself to wistfully speculate about the lovely things he might have said if he had been free to express himself. Even though they had to be careful not to give themselves away, they were safe here, more or less. It was a team and crew party, not for family members. There was no chance that Brian would show up.

"Don't listen to us, Lucy," Surly said when the laughter had died down. "You just keep defying gravity all you want. You've earned it. I know that I've already given a toast, but I just want to say . . ." He started to choke up, and gave a scoffing sort of laugh at his own emotional overreaching before he continued. "I just want to say that pulling away from the station and leaving this girl here behind was about the hardest thing I've ever done. But she never complained. She stuck it out. She made the crew look good, she made the team look good, I'm proud to have flown with her. And by God if I get the chance I'm going to fly with her again."

Lucy glanced at Walt as somebody handed her another glass of champagne and noticed that there were tears in his eyes too. He gave her a half nod, lifted his glass incrementally upward, and then through some almost undetectable gesture or look managed to convey that he would see her later, when they could manage a private moment to chart out the rest of their lives. So when the party started to break up he was one of the first to drift out the door. Lucy stayed until the end, of course, still seated in her chair, the blood still sloshing around in her head, and her brittle bones not to be trusted to support the weight of her standing body for more than a few minutes.

By the end it was just her and Sylvia, and they walked out together to their cars in the parking lot, the stars overhead so pale and murky after their enthralling clarity and abundance in space that Lucy wondered when she would be able to look up into the sky again without a sense of disappointment.

"So I hear you might have something serious going on," Lucy said.

"Possibly," Sylvia answered, smiling. "Maybe even probably."

Lucy listened as Sylvia told her about her accountant boyfriend, as

she dared to confide her hopes that the relationship was real and speculate on when they might make it official. While she talked, Lucy leaned
against the hood of Sylvia's Accord, feeling too unsteady to remain
standing.

"You need to get home to bed instead of listening to me drone on,"
Sylvia said, gesturing toward a white van parked a few spaces away.
Astronauts were not allowed to drive for a week or so when they
returned to earth, and the driver who had been assigned to her was
reading a newspaper beneath the dome light. "You're going to wear
yourself out."

"I'm fine," Lucy said.

She saw a familiar car out of the corner of her eye in the dark parking lot, and moved her head—too fast, as it turned out—to see it better.
The world spun a little, but not in the unmoored way it had just after
she had come home, and by holding her head still she made it go away
quickly enough.

Sylvia noticed her glancing at the car.

"That's Walt's car," she said. "I guess he hasn't gone home yet. He's
probably over in Building Five, going over a script or something."

"Maybe so," Lucy said.

"Did Walt tell you about my educated guess?"

"No. What educated guess?"

"About the two of you. Sometimes I think I'm the only one around
here with any radar."

She found him sitting in one of the empty simulator control rooms.
He had not bothered to turn the lights on but just sat there in the glow
of his computer console, looking through his logbook.

"What are you doing?" she asked him as she stood at the door. It
was late and there didn't seem to be any sims scheduled, so the building
was unusually quiet and empty. He was surprised to see her there, but
maybe not that surprised.

"I'm going back through the mission," he said. "Just looking at
stuff. Notes I made. Trying to find where it was exactly I fell in love with
you."

She got a chair from in front of one of the other consoles and rolled
it over beside him.

"Maybe here," he said, holding out the logbook. By the light of the
computer screen she could read the note next to her name: "Uh."

"Uh?" she asked.

"That was what you said before you told Surly you didn't think the MPS/TVC ISOL valve was closed. 'Uh' is a bad word. It's useless, it conveys nothing but a lack of confidence. But I kind of liked the way you said it. Here's something else I wrote: 'Good S.A.' I thought your situational awareness was sexy."

He closed the logbook and turned to her. "That was the first sim."

"I remember."

"I assume you had a talk with Brian."

"Yes," she said.

"Where are we?"

"Where do we want to be?"

"Here," Walt said.

He kissed her. They heard distant voices down at the other end of the hallway—a maintenance crew or a late conference with members of one of the other training teams—but they weren't coming closer. For a moment, Lucy wasn't even sure anymore if she cared if someone found out. But it was only for a moment, because what came into her thoughts as she was kissing Walt was the idea of Davis and Bethie witnessing this moment, witnessing the willful sacrifice of their happiness to hers. And she thought of Brian too, of course, the mask of calm on his face as he struggled to endure the pain she had caused him.

"Even if it had to be over . . ." she began.

"No."

"Even if it had to be over, Walt, we'd still see other, wouldn't we? We'd still both be at JSC."

"I don't want to talk about it being over."

"I don't either. I don't know how to stand this. How are we supposed to stand it? You're the team lead. Tell me what to do. Find a way that it makes sense for us to be together."

Walt's cell phone rang. He ignored it. A moment later it rang again.

"Answer your phone," she said, pulling herself away from him. "I've got to go home anyway."

He started to rise and walk her out, but she put her hand on his shoulder and made her own way, walking stiffly and sluggishly down the hallway as Walt reluctantly answered his phone.

Chapter Forty-two

The Truckee River, as Walt followed it east along Interstate 80, was shallow and braided and bright in the winter sun. The day had a ringing clarity, and Walt kept scanning the rims of the sage-covered foothills, thinking he might see one of the herds of wild horses that the cheerful girl at the rental car counter had told him to keep an eye out for.

It was very cold, maybe twenty degrees, with a slicing wind, and his South Texas winter wardrobe—a windbreaker over a cotton sweater—was ridiculously inadequate. He thought about pulling off in Fernley to see if there was a Wal-Mart or something where he could buy a warmer jacket, but he wouldn't be in Nevada that long, and the little Saturn he had rented had a workhorse heater. If all went well, he'd be back in Reno and on the plane back to Houston by tonight.

He drove another twenty miles and dug a piece of paper out of his pocket on which he had written down the directions the woman who called yesterday afternoon had given him. "You sure you got that, hon?" she'd said. "Just past Fernley you want to take Highway Fifty East—the alternate one—and after about ten miles you'll see a kitty litter factory, and right after that you take the first road to your right."

He found the kitty litter factory and turned off down a semi-improved road leading through a barren spur of some nameless salt flat and then on to a semblance of contoured land where the sage had been hacked away to make room for two separate compounds of portable buildings facing each other from behind high chain-link fences, like the outposts of a demilitarized zone. The sign above the complex on the left identified it as the Horny Toad. The other establishment, Walt's destination, was called Jackrabbit Sue's Gentleman's Club.

He sat in the car with the heater running and stared at the caricature painted on the sign, a fetching female jackrabbit in a cowboy hat. The chain-link fence glistened in the sun, and the drab buildings it guarded were set on cinder-block foundations that rested in turn on plain dirt. No landscaping, no ornamentation except for the sign's cartoon jackrabbit, no promise of anything except a utilitarian turnaround. A sixty-year-old man in a cowboy hat and down jacket walked out the front door, fished his keys out of his Wranglers pocket, and drove away in a chrome-heavy pickup. There were two or three other trucks in the parking lot as well, and a few rental cars like Walt's. Whether or not this represented a good day's business, Walt had no idea. His knowledge about bordellos was limited to what he had learned from a documentary on legal prostitution that he had watched one late night on HBO.

One thing he did know was that this dreary assemblage of graceless buildings looking out over a salt flat was pretty much the last place on earth he wanted to be. After Lucy had left the control room last night, he had called her to tell her he might be gone for a few days, and told her why. She had listened with sympathy but also with a wary attention that made him nervous. The next few days were critical; they both knew it. They had to be in each other's company as much as possible in order to remind themselves of why they had taken such a risk and caused such damage, to convince themselves that it was time to move on to a life together, even though that life would be selfish and unforgivable. He was starting to think he could live an unforgivable life if he had Lucy. What he could not do was sink back into solitary, stagnant propriety.

For now, he had an appointment with Jackrabbit Sue. He stepped out of his car into the freezing wind and hurried through the big gate and up to the front door, trying not to let his extreme self-consciousness show. There was no doorbell, and since it was a place of business and not a residence, he assumed he did not need to knock. As he walked inside, the wind caught the door behind him and held it open for a moment.

"Fuck!" yelled a young woman in a Jackrabbit Sue T-shirt who was standing behind a counter. "Get that door closed before we all freeze in here."

Walt turned and wrestled the door shut. When he turned to face the woman again, all was forgiven.

"Hi, darlin'," she said.

Walt said hi back. She was older than she had seemed at first, maybe thirty. She wore designer jeans and her T-shirt was cropped below her breasts, exposing her toned midriff to the cold air that had come rushing into the room. She was holding a calculator in one hand and seemed to be doing some sort of inventory of the merchandise in what a sign over her head identified as Jackrabbit Sue's Souvenir Boutique.

"Come to see anybody special?" she asked as she put down the calculator. "Anybody from the Web site you want to meet?"

"Lisa called me," Walt said. "She said to ask for her."

"Lisa?" The woman behind the counter looked puzzled for a moment. "Lisa doesn't usually. . . . Wait a minute. Are you that guy from Texas? Are you *Walt*?"

Walt said he was.

"Hold on a second," the woman said. "Let me get her. Make yourself at home. You want something to drink? A beer? A Snapple or something?"

"I'm fine," Walt said.

She disappeared into a back room. Walt glanced past the ATM machine to a small bar and reception area where another middle-aged rancher was enchanting one of the whores with a discussion of how the BLM was threatening to cut his AUM allotment because he happened to run a few extra cows on his lease last year.

"You know what my break-even point is, Charlene?" he said. "Seventy-one goddamn cents! The fuckin' BLM is callin' me a cattle baron. What I am is a hardscrabble rancher. Don't you ever forget that."

"I won't ever forget that," Charlene said. She was smiling sympathetically, but her restless eyes were roaming around the room. They assessed Walt briefly, along with several college-age boys at a table in the corner, before moving wearily back to the rancher. Walt found himself not immune to the flicker of mercantile interest she showed in him. She was clinically pretty, he had never been in a whorehouse before, and the cheerful sexual licentiousness on offer seemed like something a reasonable person could regard as a reasonable commodity. But he was too sick at heart, too conventionally upright, too worried about what he was going to find here to allow these trespassing thoughts to linger.

"I'm Lisa Bonifacio," said the woman who appeared from the back of the establishment. She offered her hand, and Walt had the unnerving sensation she could have been an astronaut. Her focus was that sharp. She was like Patti Halapeska and several other women he had trained, people from whom all traces of distracting humor had long been burned away by ambition. She was his age, still defiantly slender, but her hard face had been made harder by what Walt assumed was a lifetime of desert weather.

"Is he okay?" Walt asked.

"Was he okay when he came here?"

"I don't really know," he said.

"Well, as far as I can tell there's nothing physically the matter with him. But he won't really talk to anybody. He just gave Terri your phone number and asked her to call."

"Who's Terri?"

"Terri's the girl he partied with," she said as she led him briskly down a corridor. "If you could call it a party. It seems like it was about a half of a percent of a fuck and then he melted down. When Terri took his wallet out of his pants to get paid—since he couldn't seem to manage that himself—she saw his driver's license picture with his Roman collar on and freaked out herself. She's Catholic. Today's her day off, so I just sent her home and let him stay in the room. We're not a motel, though, I hope you know."

"Of course not," Walt said.

"And we're not a charity home for wayward priests either."

"I'll pay whatever you think is right."

She stopped in front of a door decorated with a laminated picture of a dolphin surfacing in moonlit water. She sized Walt up for a moment before opening it.

"Fuck it," she said. "Just take your friend home."

Louis didn't even look up when Walt and Lisa entered. He was in a chair staring at a row of pastel-colored teddy bears sitting on a shelf on the opposite wall. Care Bears, Walt remembered. Years ago, Rachel had bought her niece one when they had been in vogue.

"Father Mondragon?" Lisa said to Louis, touching his arm with a kindliness he would not have expected from her. "Your friend Walt is here."

Louis said nothing, and did not acknowledge Walt. Were it not for the obvious fact that Louis had just suffered a nervous breakdown in a Nevada whorehouse, Walt would have written his silence off as the sort of petulant stunt that he was capable of from time to time.

"Louis," he said, crouching in front of the chair and trying to get Louis to focus on him. "Let's go on home, okay?"

Walt could almost see Louis's mind turgidly rising from the profound depths of shame and misery in which it was trapped. He seemed aware of Walt for the first time.

"Let's go home," Walt said again.

"Fine," Louis blankly agreed. "Whatever."

Walt turned to Lisa. "Got his suitcase?"

"It's right there in the corner. His wallet's in it."

Walt thanked her and walked over to grab Louis's black duffel bag, then he went back to his friend and touched him gently above the elbow to guide him out of the chair. Louis obediently stood, but before they could take a step toward the door his body tensed and a bewildered fury came into his eyes. He shook himself out of Walt's grasp.

"Louis," Walt said. He started to take his arm again, but this time after shaking it off Louis went a step further and took a wild swing. Walt dodged the flailing fist easily enough, but then Louis came after him with a slack force that took him by surprise and caused them both to trip over a nightstand and break Terri's ceramic unicorn lamp.

Walt got to his feet and thought that was the end of it, but Louis wasn't through. He attacked Walt again with a series of sideways arm swipes that Walt batted away easily enough with his forearms until Louis finally settled down and sank against his friend's chest and began to wail. Either to give them privacy or to keep Louis's sobs from alarming the other customers, Lisa discreetly withdrew and closed the door.

Walt was able to get them out of Reno on a Southwest flight that same evening. Louis had not said anything on the drive back, or in the airport as they returned the rental car and hurried to board the flight, and Walt had not asked him to. All that seemed to matter at the moment was that he was compliant.

In their rush to catch the last flight out they had not had time to eat dinner, and Walt asked the flight attendant for extra bags of peanuts. Louis ate his ravenously, a good sign maybe, and smoothed and folded the little bags when he was through and then stared out the window at the trackless darkness below.

"I can name almost all the Care Bears," Louis announced. It was strange to hear his familiar voice again after such a long, deadening silence.

"Go ahead," Walt said.

"Bedtime Bear, Share Bear, Tenderheart Bear, Laugh-a-Lot Bear. . . . She was really a pretty nice girl, Walt. You can see how all that Mary Magdalene stuff got started . . ."

"You should have told me you were planning this," Walt said.

"Jesus, Walt, do you think I planned it? It just kind of happened to me. I was eating breakfast in the coffee shop in the hotel in Sacramento. I heard these guys at the next table talking about Nevada, how all you had to do was drive up to one of these places, present yourself at the door, no muss, no fuss. I thought, that's an easy way to finally lay my burden down. It was the last day of the conference and there was a tour of Sutter's Fort. But I just decided to rent a car and take my own tour. Drive into the flames of hell, as it were."

"Shut up about hell," Walt said.

"Assuming you were right, that I'm a pious asshole, do I get any points for this?"

"No, and I just realized we left your rental car there."

But Louis was still too dazed at the enormity of what he had let happen to him to take this logistical detail into proper account.

"It was just too powerful, Walt. When Terri took off her clothes in front of me? It was like a 3-D IMAX movie. You can't stand apart from that kind of thing all your life and think you can just . . . approach it. It's so big it's not even real."

"I know what you mean," Walt said.

"But maybe you have to approach it. It feels right that you have to try. It doesn't really feel like a mortal sin."

Louis looked out the window again for a while. There was nothing to see but the blinking red lights on the forward edge of the plane.

"I guess they're going to ship me off somewhere with all the child molesters," he said. "Should be humbling."

"Nobody has to find out about it," Walt said. "You'll be back at work in the morning."

"No, I'm overdue for some kind of tune-up. Might as well admit it. Thanks for coming out here to get me and everything, by the way."

"You're welcome."

"It was weird there in the bottom of the slough of despond, or wherever I was. I kept hearing all these women hallooing down at me, asking who they should call to come get me and bring me home. It was surreal. Remember all those creepy, wiggly cartoons from the thirties, with dancing skeletons and stuff? I felt like I was trapped in one. Did I hit you?"

"Yes."

"Maybe that's why. Maybe you were one of the dancing skeletons. Don't take it personally."

Walt silently consented. Louis grabbed a shopping catalog out of the seat pocket in front of him and stared for a long time at a picture of an elaborate cats-versus-dogs chess set.

"How was Florida?" he said at last, putting the catalog away and seeming to rejoin the world. "Where'd you leave things with Lucy?"

"I don't know," Walt said.

Louis waited a long time to pick up the subject again, and when he did, he was looking away from Walt, out the window again, and his voice was so low it was almost as if he were talking to himself.

"I'm not just lecturing you this time," he said. "I'm not just busting your chops. I'm speaking from my newfound perspective as a moral grubworm. You should give that woman another chance with her husband. You should do what's right for those two little kids."

Walt pushed the button on the side of his armrest and slid his seat back. He stared down at the rows of lights running along the sides of the corridor in the darkened cabin.

"I'll think about it," he said.

"Of course, if you do, you're back to being a man of constant sorrow."

"Can we drop the bullshit, Louis?"

"I can if you can," Louis said. "Count of three, okay?"

Louis counted to three and then they dropped the bullshit. They flew over the Southwest in comfortable silence. Louis finally fell asleep and Walt looked past him out the window. West Texas passed below, bare and dark, but after only an hour more the clustering lights of cities and interstates told him they were drawing near to Houston.

Chapter Forty-three

So you're saying we missed our chance?"

Lucy's voice was no more than a whisper. They were sitting in the Starbucks on NASA Road One where they had had their first serious conversation, when Lucy had confided to Walt her fears about leaving her children to go into space. It was an absurd place for them to be now. She wanted to be in his bed, in his arms, in his touchingly vacant bedroom.

"Maybe we didn't really have a chance," he said. Walt was groggy from lack of sleep, but he thought he knew his mind. He thought he knew hers as well. It was not in her, not really, to shatter her children's lives. It was not in Walt to demand such a thing. She had flown in space. She had held her children hostage to that dream, but she could not do it again for the sake of mere earthly happiness with a man who was not their father. You could not live a worthwhile life if you did not reach out for something, if you grew too dependent on the solace of caution. But there were also times when caution had nothing to do with it, when both daring and decency demanded that you stay in place.

The problem for Walt was that the possibility of reaching out and the need to stay in place had come at almost the same moment. His love affair with Lucy, his two nights with her, seemed now to have been only a glimpse of something he should have known all along was unreachable. But getting people to unreachable places was the business he was in.

It was the fifth day after her return to earth and she still looked pale. He had noticed her slow step when she walked into the coffee shop, planting one foot securely on the floor before she dared to lift the other. She had washed her hair and had it cut short, and the slight puffiness in her face caused by the fluid shifts in weightlessness was long gone. Her face was thin and sharp and purposeful. It was nine-thirty and the morning rush was over and there wasn't anyone else in Starbucks but them and a man by the window doing a crossword puzzle on his laptop. Walt and Lucy sat with their hands on the tabletop, the tips of their fingers less than an inch apart, not touching. Walt's cell phone rang. He glanced at the display screen but had no intention of answering it. The screen read "Private Caller." It would be Lisa from Jackrabbit Sue's, responding to his offer of five hundred dollars to drive Louis's rental car back to the Sacramento airport. Lucy waited out the ringing of his phone and then the roar of the espresso machine before speaking again.

"I'm not ready," she said. "Not yet."

"What do you want to do?"

"I want to go to your place." She glanced at the man doing his crossword puzzle and whispered even lower. "I want to make love with you one more time."

"If we do that," Walt said, "we'll never be ready."

Lucy took a sip of her neglected latte. She sat there for a long time.

"So if I stand up and leave right now," she said at last, "are you going to be all right?"

"After a while."

"You're not going to quit your job and move away or anything."

"I heard there's a SimSup position opening up. I might apply for that."

"But you'll still be here?"

Walt nodded, touched by the anxiety in her voice. "I'll be here," he said. "One way or the other, I'll be working your next mission."

"I'm not ready to think about going into space again."

"You will be someday. When the kids are older. You won't be able not to think about it. You're an astronaut."

He watched these words register on her sorrowful face. He watched her struggling, as he was, for some resonant and brave remark, something they could console each other with as they closed out the great shining possibility that had kept their lives aloft for the last year. But when nothing of that sort came, and when the conversation threatened to dissolve into regretful small talk, Lucy took the initiative and leaned across the table to kiss him. Then she rose from her chair, still tentative, her confused brain still believing that any force or pressure she brought to bear would send her body tumbling through the coffee shop.

"Okay?" she asked. Walt was not sure what the question was—whether she was asking permission to leave, or pleading for reassurance that they would both be all right. But he nodded anyway and watched her walk carefully out the door, and he then sat there for a long time until he had finished his coffee and recovered the strength to return the call from Jackrabbit Sue, and then to stand and walk to his car and go back to work.

This January night, still less than a week since her return to earth, was tiresomely mild, just cold enough for a sweater. She and Brian and the kids had gone to the Kemah Boardwalk to eat at one of the Mexican restaurants there. Lucy's image had been a fixture of cable news and magazine features for so long that there had been some delighted stares and a few requests for autographs, but Clear Lake was still a company town in which an astronaut, even a suddenly famous one, could subside easily enough into anonymity. Her appetite finally returned when she read the description on the menu of a crabmeat-stuffed redfish, and after dinner she announced to the children that she had a sudden craving for frozen yogurt.

So they went to the familiar yogurt place and drove home down NASA Road One under the clear winter sky. Lucy opened her window a few inches and breathed in the smells of earth, which after five days still remained deliriously present. She smelled tar from a road resurfacing project, the diluted salt water of Clear Lake, fragrant winter honey-suckle from someone's backyard. This suburban landscape that she had once dismissed as bland and overgrown and graceless was unambigu-ously a part of the earth she had looked down upon from space with such longing. How could any part of this world not be her home?

Lucy lingered with the children at bedtime, in no hurry for once to get them to sleep. For the first few days, Bethie had been skeptical that her mother really was home to stay, and had been afraid to leave her presence. She was tired and more secure tonight, but even so Lucy did not leave her side until long after she had put her thumb in her mouth and shuffled around in bed to face the wall and go to sleep. Afterward she lay with Davis in his bed, listening as he read to her out loud from one of the *Goosebumps* books, taking pride in his pronunciations of the difficult words and his theatrical inflections when reciting the characters' dialogue. His breathing was firm and clear as he read, and was still that way after he went to sleep.

Showers were still a problem. She could not quite convince herself that the spray from the showerhead was not a violent force that would send her helplessly bouncing through the stall. Nor was she yet comfortable taking a bath, since the weight of the water in the tub felt like a suffocating, leaden mass. She compromised tonight by setting the showerhead to its lowest pressure and sitting in the bathtub as the water dribbled over her. Even so, each drop felt like a jabbing finger.

She put on a nightgown and brushed her teeth and once again dropped the toothbrush when she forgot to set it down. Then she walked into the bedroom. Brian was rigging a sleep restraint for her out of two rolled-up sheets that he had laid sideways across the bed.

"Get in and try it out," he said.

She wasn't yet used to the wonderful smell and feel of fresh bedding, and as he tightened the sheets across her body she responded to the familiar satisfaction of being locked into place in a limitless world.

As she fell asleep, she of course dreamed of space, as she always would. She dreamed that Walt had been up there with her and that the two of them hung in the center of the module in perfect conformity and balance as the gravitational force of the earth tried to pull them into its power. It was a lucid dream. She knew even as she slept that the fantasy it presented was not true. She had missed her chance with Walt, but there was something fortifying and reassuring in even having glimpsed what love could be like in its full reach. Even if that sort of love was something she doubted she could ever achieve with Brian, at least she now understood what they needed to aim for. And there was so much else that she had not missed: the anxiety-ridden wonder of motherhood that she shared with so many; and the unimaginable privilege of leaving the earth that she still shared with so few.

In her shallow sleep she heard Brian whisper something into her ear, so faintly she could not be sure what he had said or whether indeed he had actually made a sound. Was he talking in his sleep? She didn't even know if she herself was awake. Brian's phantom words had sounded kind and intimate. She knew that he was still absorbing what she had done to him, still reaching out to her so she would not leave him, and that this conciliatory warmth between them could not—should not—last. There would be storms of anger and days of icy resentment, but in these looming conflicts there would be a certain rough justice, real charges and countercharges that they would both have to listen to. She would listen. She was beginning to remember that her husband was worth loving, and so she would find a way to love him.

But as she let herself drift back into sleep she saw herself with Walt, sitting in Starbucks, their hands on the table, not quite touching, the inch or so that separated them as wide as a chasm. The dreamy clarity of that strange little gap between their hands brought her back to her EVA, and the haunted awareness she had had while she was translating along the truss of the station that if her tether came loose or broke she could find herself drifting a foot or so away from the station but unable, in the vacuum of space, to exert the force necessary to close the distance. Two bodies in space could stay that way for a long time, coasting along, almost touching but unable to reach out far enough to connect, until their orbits finally decayed and they burned up in the atmosphere.

Sometime during the night Bethie walked into their room and crawled into bed with them. Lucy gathered her into her arms and fell instantly back to sleep. But when Bethie, an hour or so later, shifted her weight and rolled away from her mother toward the center of the bed, Lucy sat upright in alarm. She thought her child had drifted away in zero gravity. She screamed in her sleep and flailed and groped with her arms through the blackness of space, searching for her little girl, until Brian calmed her down by setting Bethie back against her mother's body. Then, when Lucy had fallen back to sleep, he got out of bed and secured the makeshift sleep restraint around both mother and daughter, so that neither could drift away again.

Acknowledgments

In my efforts to learn about the textural and technical realities of today's space program, I was fortunate to have the following books at hand: *Dragonfly* by Bryan Burrough, *Off the Planet* by Jerry M. Linenger, *Waystation to the Stars* by Colin Foale, *High Calling* by Evelyn Husband with Donna Vanliere, and *Space Shuttle: The First Twenty Years,* which is a compendium of first-person astronaut experiences edited by Tony Reichhardt and the editors of *Air & Space/Smithsonian.* Two wry question-and-answer books by former astronauts that proved extremely informative were R. Mike Mullane's *Do Your Ears Pop Up in Space?* and William R. Pogue's *How Do You Go to the Bathroom in Space?* I would especially like to acknowledge Henry S. F. Cooper Jr.'s wonderfully reported *Before Lift-off: The Making of a Space Shuttle Crew.*

The voluminous NASA Web sites that can be reached through the portal of nasa.gov are filled with rich information about all aspects of space exploration. Particularly useful for my purposes were Web journals from two astronauts during their tenures on the International Space Station: Peggy Whitson's Letters Home and Don Pettit's Space Chronicles.

No amount of reading, however, can substitute for the candid interviews and on-site visits to the Johnson Space Center that gave me what I hope is an authentic glimpse into the lives of astronauts and the people who train them. For this crucial help I am indebted to: Kacy Kossum, Stephen Nesbitt, James Hartsfield, Kelly Humphries, Steven Williams, John Poffinbarger, Sean Collins, Terry Pappas, Tricia Mack, Trisha Sims, Pete Beauregard, Mike Jensen, and Steven Nagel. I'm especially grateful to three women astronauts—Anna Fisher, Linda Godwin, and Peggy Whitson—who helped shape my understanding of who Lucy Kincheloe might be.

Without the help of Lisa Reed, a former team lead who has trained many missions, I could not have put all of my scattered impressions into a coherent context. Her experience, kindness, and intuitive understanding of what I was trying to accomplish were vital to the completion of this book. And I should add that any mistakes or deliberate factual distortions that might have made their way into my story did not originate with any of the experts I consulted.

For advice about other details or for general insight and encouragement, I'm eager to thank Anthony Giardina, William Broyles Jr., Robert Reyna, Daniel Okrent, Tim Lowry, William Moran, Joseph Rainfield Lewis, Mimi Swartz, Jan McInroy, Steve Saunders, James Magnuson, Gregory Curtis, Lawrence Wright, Jeffrey Hallett, Robin Hallett, and Ricardo Ainslie. Elizabeth Crook's writerly counsel was once again crucial, as was the editorial guidance of Ann Close and the unflagging support of my legendary agent, Esther Newberg. My wife, Sue Ellen, and our three children, Marjorie, Dorothy, and Charlotte, provide the real life without which my imaginative meanderings would be pointless.

In some important ways, this book was a family enterprise. It was my mother, Marjorie Berney Harrigan, who first suggested there might be a novel in the daily lives of astronauts. During a canoe trip with my brother Tom Harrigan, which exposed me to the mysterious natural richness of the Clear Lake area, I suspected she might be right. My brother Jim Harrigan fulminated to productive effect on various issues ranging from titles to covers. My late sister Julie Sharp shared her own experiences of raising children threatened by asthma, pointed out the wall honoring "Astronaut Moms and Dads" at her kids' elementary school, and in ways I am still discovering helped fashion the emotional core of this story.

A NOTE ABOUT THE AUTHOR

Stephen Harrigan is the author of seven books, the most recent of which was the national best-seller *The Gates of the Alamo*. His essays and articles have appeared in many magazines, among them *Texas Monthly,* for which he is a contributing editor. He is also a screenwriter who has written numerous award-winning movies for television. He lives in Austin, Texas.

A NOTE ON THE TYPE

The text of this book was set in Sabon, a typeface designed by Jan
Tschichold (1902–1974), the well-known German typographer. Based
loosely on the original designs by Claude Garamond (c. 1480–1561),
Sabon is unique in that it was explicitly designed for hot metal com-
position on both the Monotype and the Linotype machines as well as
for filmsetting. Designed in 1966 in Frankfurt, Sabon was named
after the famous Lyons punch cutter Jacques Sabon, who is thought
to have brought some of Garamond's matrices to Frankfurt.

Composed by Creative Graphics,
Allentown, Pennsylvania

Printed and bound by Berryville Graphics,
Berryville, Virginia

Designed by Soonyoung Kwon